The Eighth Day

VOL. 1

M. M. DOS SANTOS

Edited by Heather Marie Adkins | CyberWitchPress.com

Cover Art by Giovanni Banfi

Interior book design by CyberWitch Press, LLC

For Rafael and Andrea

Warning

This book contains scenes
that some readers may find disturbing.

Content includes violence towards women and children, scenes of extreme gore and violence, profanity throughout, and scenes of a sexual nature. If you have a history of depression, mental illness, or do not wish to be shocked and offended, discretion is advised.

The Eighth Day

Vol. 1

I.

EPHRYIUM

The Eighth Day

ankind has written several books trying to explain what God is, and after 6000 years none of you can agree on even the idea of God. So when I refer to God as 'he,' it is not because God is a man, it is because it is what you can understand. When I say 'day,' it is not the period of a 'day' in which the events took place, but millenniums of yours which are only a moment to me.

I could try to explain what, or why, or even how, but what is most important is what happened afterwards, and what is happening now, because we have not yet begun but are nearly out of time.

On the seventh day, after the creation of mankind, God stepped back to rest, watch.

We all loved them as he did. Despite his warning, with hopes to show him that we could all exist on one plane, that his caution and warnings were not necessary, we all went down to Earth to see the new beings.

We regarded the young mankind as our counterparts, our comrades, our siblings. We had come down with intentions of teaching, enlightening, and elevating them. They quickly understood the new knowledge we provided as something they needed to live. They learned to read the stars and clouds, predict their harvests, they yearned to exist past the primal awareness that he intended for them.

There were legions of Angels on Earth on the Seventh Day. It seems inappropriate now to call me — us — Angels, especially after all that has happened, but that is your understanding, and I need you to understand. I was once an Angel, and God called me Ephryium.

I remember being on Earth in moments, proud and gentle in one, and in another, filled with disdain, rage, and righteousness. I don't know who did it first. Whether we poisoned you, our insight and powers corrupting your innocence, or if you infected our divinity with your basic nature and primal instincts. I know from watching that the ones who don't deny God today blame us, blame one. But it did not happen this way.

The infection of evil began.

Our error became obvious to me. I begged our Father for forgiveness. Even as I pled with him on my knees to take us back, I remember the shadow that was cast, the cold death surrounding me. Something that was never meant for me, something that was never meant for any of us.

God said he would release me of the gas chamber Earth had become, but instead of restoring me to my place in heaven by his side, he imprisoned me in a place in-between Earth and Heaven. Forcing me to watch as the infection took over my brothers, corrupting them, degrading their pure divinity into something wicked and vile. Once they could no longer dwell in their heavenly bodies on Earth's plane, they retreated into the shadows, into the Earth itself, becoming a cancer spreading under mankind's feet.

Every generation that man lived through, evil's roots grew deeper into the Earth, bred deeper into humanity, distorting and destroying man's psyche.

God became disgusted with his creation; his love for man dissipated. He didn't feel hate for the young species; he was indifferent to man's existence. All who were stranded on Earth together were now each other's problems. Not God's. These were not his laws. This was no longer his Earth. And men were no longer his children.

On the Eighth Day, God abandoned us.

He turned his back on mankind, his fallen angels, on Earth, and on me, but I still took my punishment from him hoping for reprieve. I stayed within my prison walls despite being left unguarded.

I was the last, the only being closest to God's original design. I struggled to reason that maybe now my rebellion would be forgiven if I went down to balance the energy, to restore mankind to their former purity. But I knew no matter how pure my intentions were, God's original warning held true. I would only suffer if I descended down again. I would be consumed by the same disease that had eaten away at the benevolence of men.

So instead, I obsessively watched. Overseeing the men desperately re-create God, and the demons who came to answer their prayers. Watching the thousands of religious and spiritual rituals that were performed all over Earth at any given time.

One stood out, a ritual I recognized from my time. A ritual taught by my kind — a desperate ritual, a ritual that should have never been shared — being practiced by a congregation of humans who remembered their ancestors and our teachings. They drew power from the demons they knew walked among them, along with the residual power God left behind. This small group of humans knew that the demons were no greater than man. I saw I was no longer the only one looking to restore balance to Earth.

This was the opportunity I needed to step in. This child that they were creating would transcend every other human on Earth. The child would be the closest thing to the celestial children God had originally conceived: Born out of evil with the ability to wield and concentrate the original gifts we had passed down.

I wouldn't be able to influence the child towards goodness, at least not directly, but I could shield the child, protect it from all the evil that it would be vulnerable to. I hoped I would survive long enough for the child to realize itself as mankind's cure from the wicked.

During a time of the red moon, I set my course for Earth and descended in a flash of light into a deep dark wood.

I, and all of mankind, would either find a redemption in this child or be condemned to total annihilation.

II.

LILI

Thunder Bay, Ontario
June 16th 1996

"*I*'m scared," I whisper to my empty room. The muscles in my shoulders hurt from being tense for so long. "You scare me. Go away." She's here again. They all are. But they're always here.

Even though the blankets are pulled over my head and my eyes are closed, I know she's here. I don't want to see her. She's getting worse. Every time I see her, she appears less and less like herself. I wish I had the courage to run out of my bedroom. The silence becomes cold and heavy.

She's standing over me.

Why can't I scream? I have forgotten how to use every muscle in my body.

"Liiil … liiii," she whispers. The warm blankets slide off my head, down to my shoulders. I am powerless to stop it.

My heartbeat quickens, thumping so hard against my chest I can hear it.

"Don't be scared, Lili." Her whisper seems to come from my walls. I'm surrounded by each word.

I see without looking. She forces me to. My bladder lets go. As the warm, almost comforting urine pools around my waist, I try to force the corpse's image from my mind, and open my eyes. She stands there, beside my bed — not alone — in the darkness of my room.

Her cheek bones jut out; her jaw dangles by her neck, ripped open and holding the few black teeth she has left. Her grey, opaque eyes are sad and scared as mine. And my ghost — the tall beautiful man, that never leaves the shadows — stands behind her, blotting out the street light's light.

I fight back tears, the tip of my nose so cold it hurts. Crystal is my neighbour. *Was* my neighbour. We haven't played together for a while now. Something very bad happened to her. The ball of tears and vomit in my throat grows as she leans down and puts her face next to mine.

"Find me, Lili. I need to show you something."

With a sharp intake of breath, I will myself to sit up. I'm going to run. Past Crystal, past the dark man blocking my window, past all the other whispers. My feet never reach the floor. I'm thrown back onto my pillow.

She's going to show me something.

III.

I beg for it to be fast. To wake up. For morning. For my mom. *Please help me!*

My nostrils fill with the smell of wet earth and death. No matter where my eyes dart, I see him. His face is everywhere. He resembles a man, but I know better. His eyes draw me in; the colour of them is magic. I feel safe and then very small. He burns up in flame and shadow, and I am left in a fog.

I see her face first, her skin whiter than it used to be, her thick black hair reaching her shoulders. We were so similar we could have been sisters. I can't remember her smile. So she stands in front of me exactly how I remember her: Dead.

"Lili. I need to show you. Find me, Lili."

I crumble at her feet, scared and alone. She's brought me to a house at the end of our street. Her house. I'm awake enough to know I'm dreaming, but not strong enough to control what I'm about to see. I sob helplessly into my hands. I *have* seen it. I know what happens to Crystal in my dream.

"I don't want to see it, Crystal. Please. Please let me wake up."

Images force themselves into my mind. Crows swoop down from atop the towering stone house to peck away at me. Crystal's home is a castle compared to the rest of the houses on the block, despite the fact rusted, worn out remnants of life and childhood litter the yard.

Her house is the nicest, the biggest, the most evil.

Thick stone walls exude the despair of the powerless child behind them. The never-ending cruelty seeps out onto the street and wraps itself around me, pulling me in. Crystal steps in front of me. Her naked body covered in cuts and bruises. Washed in shades of pain, they are a reminder of what's to come after I walk through the blackness beyond the door.

Shame. Hatred for myself consumes me.

Crystal's mom made us ham and cheese sandwiches while we played.

She holds Crystal down while they do it. A smile surrounds her cigarette. I don't want to be a witness to this; I don't want to see it again. Laughter and muffled screaming. I'm scared, and my chest hurts. I sense I am being watched from the shadows, as if I am a part of this. Watching this thing is killing me, the way it kills Crystal.

A man with scars all over his face walks through me to the table where Crystal lays. She makes me watch.

He teaches the big kids at my school.

He punches her, whaling down on her like a gorilla until she stops moving.

Please! Please don't make me watch!

The jangle of the belt. The pants on the floor. The table *scrape scrape scrapes* on the floor.

I want my mommy.

The smell of metal. So pungent, until it sours in my nose. Crystal's mom emerges from the shadows of a fog-filled door.

She taught me 'Engine, engine, number nine.' Mama pays her $7.50 *to babysit me for one hour.*

CRYSTAL, PLEASE!

I beg her to stop, for someone to come and save me. I cover my eyes and try to shake out what I've seen, screaming to drown out the sound of the hammer turning Crystal's face into something that has put me off Jell-O. Even with my eyes closed, she makes me see. The blood seems nuclear as it spills off the table onto the floor. It splashes warm onto my feet.

She lets go. The wind is knocked out of me as I'm pulled out of the room, out of the house, back into the street, out of the fog, and into the flames.

Beneath a black sky, the heat is inescapable.

Wake up!

The screaming begins. Screams of pain and anguish fill my head. The plummeting feeling of weightlessness is overwhelming. I think I'm in hell. Through the flames, a dark silhouette approaches. I see green eyes. And horns.

Mom says there are no good spirits. They are all demons. People who talk to spirits will die in Armageddon. Am I going to die?

I wake up hyperventilating, clenching my sweat and urine-soaked sheets. Crystal's gone. The orange light coming from the street light outside provides me with some comfort from the darkness. This is the third time Crystal has come to me this week. This will be the third time this week my mama has to wash my sheets.

Daddy said he would spank me if it happened one more time.

Stripping the bed as quickly and as quietly as I can, I struggle to find the courage to go out, sheets in hand, into the dark hallway ... downstairs ... into the basement.

I have nothing to worry about, right? All the monsters are in my room — not hanging out in the dark, cold basement. How hard could it be to use a washing machine?

IV.

I'm about to open my bedroom door when it flies open. Sprawled on the floor, still holding my wet, stinking sheets, I peer up.

A tall dark form hangs from my doorway.

This is not a dream. I put a hand up to protect myself. I try to scream but my throat closes, and all I am able to let out is a pitiful whimper.

"Hey, what's wrong? What are you doing?"

It's Vinny. I feel dumb for not recognizing his shaggy blonde hair, for scaring myself. He steps through the door and flicks on the light. I shut my eyes and let them properly adjust, as he softly shuts the door behind him. He picks me up off the floor, making sure to stay clear of the sheets.

"You peed again, Lili? Dad's gonna flip. I don't understand. You're ten years old, you shouldn't be doing this anymore." He stops. His shoulders drop along with the tension in his voice. "What happened?"

"I ... I ... " I don't know what to tell him.

"I heard you."

"What did you hear?"

"You, I dunno, sounded like you were freaking out. It almost sounded like you were talking to someone else. Bad dream?"

"Yea." I can't hide the shame on my face.

"Do you remember it?"

"It was Crystal … and the other thing."

He rolls his eyes. "Your closet ghost? Really? If you were a ghost would you hang out in a *closet*? It's not real."

I can't help but giggle. That's absurd!

"Crystal is fine. Well, maybe not 'fine,' but stop telling people she's dead. Services prolly came in and got her. You can't go around telling people Mr. Hawkwood kill — "

"But he did!" I hesitated, too embarrassed to tell him what I actually saw. The words stumbled out. "They … hurt her. Really really bad." Through tears pooling in my own eyes, I studied my older brother's face for some understanding before it was lost in blur. "He hit her again and again, then he, he pulled down his pants and he, he … " I couldn't. "There was blood. She's buried in the trees at the dead end!"

"Jesus Christ, Lili! What the fuck are you watching? You cannot, I repeat — " He places both hands on my shoulders and bends down to my eye level, " — cannot tell mom or dad or *anyone* what you just told me. The mischief and compassion had run out of his now steely blue eyes. "You're gonna get in trouble. It's not gonna be good. True or not, trust me. You miss your friend. You're having bad dreams, that's all."

"And the ghost?"

"I don't know. Maybe mom smoked crack while she was pregnant with you." He cracks a smile, knowing full well I am about to punch him.

"Sleep in my bed. I'll throw this in the wash."

I tiptoe down the hallway to Vinny's bedroom. I'm so

grateful to have an older brother like him. Sometimes — most times — he's the only one who understands me. As I make myself cozy under his blanket, something sharp pricks my legs. I rub the pain away, and then reach down into the sheets to feel for whatever it is. My hand re-emerges with a black feather.

I'm not surprised. I find feathers more than I think most people do. Sometimes in strange places; mostly after something scary happens. A girl in my class once told me that her grandma believes finding feathers means an angel is watching over you. I liked that thought so much, I kept it. It makes me feel safe. Especially after the bad dreams and seeing the shadow people. But everything is happening less and less. I don't see as many shadow people, and only Crystal bugs me now. She comes a lot, but there used to be so many more. And now there's not. I snuggle deeper into the covers when I realize that there used to be more feathers, too.

I fall asleep before Vinny gets back, and when I wake up in the morning, he's not beside me.

Mom and Dad wait for me in the living room. Mom stares at her folded hands. Vinny has been teaching me things about 'body language.' I remember that glancing away from someone might mean not wanting to deal with a problem.

Am I a problem?

Dad has no problem dealing with it, though. The problem. Me.

"What did I say would happen if you wet the bed again?"

What? Vinny told?

My heart sinks at the realization of my brother's betrayal. "But, I didn't mean to — "

He takes a wooden spoon out from behind him and places it in on the table front of him. "Lili, this isn't acceptable. You're too old to be doing this. You think your mom wants to be washing your bed all the time?"

"I don't mean to wet the bed, I promise." I hide my hands behind my back. "I have bad dreams." I plead my case as I eye the wooden spoon.

My mom's gaze darts up to mine, although she says nothing. I know she can hear the desperation in my voice.

"Bad dreams? What bad dreams?" Dad demands.

I bite my lip, determined to keep the secrets in. I hear Vinny's voice inside my head, giving me the advice he'd given me last night. But he lied. He said I could trust him, and I couldn't. He *told.* Maybe if I tell them about the ghost and Crystal, it would help me?

"I see a man in my room sometimes."

My parents exchange concerned glances with each other, and then turn back to me.

"A man? What kind of man?" Dad's face grows redder. My mom's gaze returns to her lap.

"He comes when there are lots of whispers. And sometimes he leaves little feathers for me. I think he told Crystal she could tell me — "

My dad flies to his feet. "What are you talking about? What little girl of mine is talking with a man? Whispers? Are you hearing this, Carmella? Are you hearing what our daughter is saying to us?"

"Dad. Dad, listen! It's not a *real* man. I think he's an angel."

"An angel?" He comes around the table, spoon in hand. "I don't know whether you're a liar or you are talking to demons, but I won't have either in my house!"

He holds me down. Between the stinging cracks of the spoon, I sob through what I saw last night. When he is done, we are both exhausted. My bum is hot and tender, I can barely breathe let alone talk.

I am told to go to my room and pray to God.

V.

IGNACE

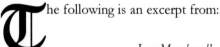

The following is an excerpt from:

Luc Marchand's

Queens of Hell
An Occult Specialist's Search for the Devils in the Background

Published 1997

October 17th 1986
Kenora County — Near Ignace, Ontario.
Night of the Blood Moon

They stayed off the highway. They knew it was there and ignored it on purpose. They didn't want to be seen. They didn't want anyone to know where they had come from. Or even that they'd come. Barefoot, naked, covered in dirt, blood, and semen; no one could come out of that all right.

The ritual had been completed. The girl had given birth. Both men had seen the demon passing through the ceremony. The demon devoured the sacrifices as foretold, but then the air had surged with hate and hunger. The bright light. There came another, who struck down everyone. Their thoughts turned to shame at their own ignorance and weakness. They both had hid under the bodies, listening to the screams of their priestesses. Their blood rained down, hot as tar, soaking past the dead bodies through to the forest floor. They were ignorant. Even in the deepest depths of their imaginations, they could have never visualized what took place on this night. This is why they were the 'lowly,' the tools, the sacrifice, the *creatures*. They had been there to die, and this is why they had ran.

The two men had been together for so long, there was no conversation needed between them as to the decision. Their memories of the last seven years had eclipsed anything good they had ever been a part of. The madness they played servant to was implanted in them. They knew there was no escaping their memories of the blood and the carnage they had witnessed, whether it was ordered or not. They knew that, eventually, they fed off of the evil. They could escape that place, but they'd always be in the seventh circle of hell, in memory and in craving. There would be no escaping what would come next, not even in death. If she was alive, she would find them. But for now? They were free.

A far away light seen through the quiet forest set their route. They didn't vocalize how they both saw the light in the distance, or how they were going to head there. But they both did. Their legs shook with exhaustion. Sweat dripped into their eyes, making the pitch-black forest even harder to navigate. The plan wasn't to kill whomever they found there. The plan wasn't to enjoy it.

VI.

LILI

The skin on my cheek bones is tight. The tip of my nose and lips are burning.

Darkness.

I don't realize my eyes are closed until I open them. A shroud lifts with my eyelids, exposing flames. I inhale through my nose quickly. It burns. I turn my head away from the source and wince in surprised pain. Far in the distance, as if coming from a hole in the ground, deep down in some dark cave, the screams start.

My palms prickle with sweat. My eyes dart frantically to find escape. The flames are everywhere, burning nothing but giving no sign of extinguishing. I plead with my subconscious to dream of something else. I imagine wrenching myself away, but something stronger than me drags me deeper into the vision.

Anything! Anything but this!

A wall of darkness approaches me. In the middle of the

darkness is a ball made of colours, so many colours swirling and swaying.

Pick one.

Deep into the gasoline puddle, I reach and pick a dream.

I gasp as the flooring of the blank dreamscape vanishes beneath me. The ascension is fast, too fast. I fall away from flames, shadows, and night skies down into a well of cold, damp air. Closing my eyes, I brace for impact.

Even though I'm plummeting, I slow to a stop before my feet touch down onto a crumbling, familiar road.

Cracks and potholes litter the asphalt. A thick fog obscures houses lining the street on either side of me. I let out a sob as I recognize my surroundings.

This neighbourhood. The nightmare still haunted my childhood. The terror infected all of my dreams.

I glance over my shoulder, anticipating the corpse's shadowy outline to materialize. My hairs stand on end, one by one, until the pricks reach the bottom of my hairline. They fall into a chill wiggling its way down my spine, emerging as near-painful goose bumps on my arms. My shoulders tense when fingers dig into my biceps and pull me back. I surge forward, but the weight behind me pushes me to the ground. Only one shoulder is still in a painful vice. My knees scrape the pavement again and again as I try to kick myself free, to get out from under what's holding me down.

Over my right shoulder, past the thick, grey fingers gouging into me, his face comes forward, his breath like stagnant shit. My stomach lurches. I'm unable to turn away. Rimmed in raw flesh and fresh blood, his voided eye sockets take in my fear. His cracked, grey skin peels away like old wallpaper, receding its lips to nothing.

I'm about to puke, to vacate my insides right before death

instead of after. The corpse's mouth is empty and black except for jagged, yellow teeth that are nearing my neck. I inhale as much air as I can so I can scream. I'm unable to force any noise out. My ears fill with the sound of my pounding heartbeat.

Panic and adrenaline take over. I jerk my right elbow back using my entire body, and it connects with his nose. I kick his thigh and knock him off balance. With all the strength and will I have in me, I scramble to my feet and turn around to face my demon. He lurches at me, but I react immediately and kick him in the gut. He staggers momentarily before he recovers from my minor assault. I know I can't hurt him but I can put distance between us so he can't hurt me.

I break into a sprint. His feet hit the ground as fast as mine. His screeching hiss makes my head pound. I run through the fog on this never-ending road, sweaty and out of breath. I can't go much further. My mind has put forth doubt, so my body starts to give in.

My childhood home looms behind the fog. On the curb in front of it, a junker car sits rusted and dead. They appear like omens, threatening to deliver forth the ghosts of my childhood. Somewhere in the fog sits a house where a little girl was murdered. Still out of breath, I search the fog for a place to hide. I slide underneath the car with little room to spare, making sure no extremities are hanging out. Gravel crunches nearby. I hold my breath. Another crunch.

Two big, black boots slowly walk past the front tire. They stop. My eyes widen; my jaw clenches. I pray. *Oh, please, God.* The boots slowly walk on, my gaze following until they disappear into the fog. I slide out and make my way to the front of the car hunched over to keep cover. I strain my eyes to make sure no figure lies waiting in the mist, hunting me.

I double back and run to where I started. There is an orange glow hidden deep in the thick clouds of fog. As I get closer, it expands left and right, still giving off the comfort of a nightlight.

Fast steps approach behind me. I feel like a cat struggling to claw its way out of a locked box. I need to get to the light. The hiss whispers in my ears. I am almost there. It's fire; the glowing light is fire.

I no longer know which fate is worse.

I turn to face the demon. An inferno expands, making a circle around me. The demon hits the wall of fire. Its body ignites, hurling flames into the dark sky above. The hollowed out, decomposing face descends on me, dissipating as it gets closer. I was back where I started — in flames.

I give up. I'm done. I can't run any more. I won't face anymore.

I crouch down and sob, burying my face in my arms, just waiting for this shit to be over. A deafening scream of horrific pain drops on me like a bomb. As I scan above, the first crimson raindrop lands dead centre of my forehead. The flames wash away. My breath slows and my anxiety diminishes.

Blood.

Blood is everywhere.

Falling from the sky.

I am drenched in blood.

VIII.

Calgary, Alberta
September 16th 2000
4:06 p.m.

"No way, Lili. You're fucking lying." Justyne's icy blue eyes burned into me. I don't know if they are playful or actually angry.

"I'm not. You're the only person I've told. I trust you." Other than Vinny, she is the only person I've told. Even though she can't understand, she'd never really be able to truly understand, but Justyne is just as broken and lost as me. She found strength in being alone, in the pain of it all. I look up to her. I can be a normal teenager when I'm around her, maybe even a rebellious one, and there is no doubt that I can trust her with my life let alone with my secrets. I don't think she really knows how special she is to me.

"I think you're bullshitting. What does that even mean? Every house you and your family move to is haunted? Really?"

"No," I say before taking a hoot and passing her back the little glass pipe. "I don't think the houses are haunted. I think I am."

As she packs another bowl for us, she squints at me suspiciously.

"Have I ever lied to you? Ever?"

"No, but it's just all so ... fucked up."

I pause, hesitant to tell her more. In the act of trying to convince her, I'd just lied to her.

"Actually, I just lied to you."

"I fucking knew it. Lili, you are such a motherfucker. You had me, too. Fuck you." Justyne playfully punches me in the arm, giving me a relieved smile as she puts the pipe to her mouth.

"You're not the only one that knows. Vinny knows. And my parents know."

She stares at me with wide brown eyes, appearing more confused than before. "Your parents and Vinny know? This is for real?"

"Vinny knows everything: about Crystal, about the man. He's even seen some of the things I have."

"Like what?"

"Not the shadows, or the spiders or anything like that, but the everyday shit."

"The everyday shit?"

"Yea, the things that happen all the time. Like lights turning on and off. Or my room being turned upside down, even if I'd just cleaned it. Coming home and having all the doors in the house shut. Stupid shit like that, things that, if you're not paying attention, you'd miss."

"And your parents? I can't imagine them dealing with all of this well. Do they stand over you and pray?" She laughs. "Oh my God, is this why you aren't allowed to have any friends or hang out with anybody who doesn't go to church?"

"Pretty much. The whole thing with Crystal really freaked

them out. After the cops found her body, it was all over the news. Her uncle was arrested for it, and then they couldn't spank me anymore for saying fucked up things. I think they thought if we all drank more of the Jesus juice, it would go away. We don't talk about it. I think it's easier to pretend it's just not a thing."

"Well, can you blame them? They're living with Carrie!" Laughing, she leans into me, eventually draping her arm on my shoulder.

"I'm glad you find this all so amusing."

"I don't, I don't. I swear. Everything is starting to make sense actually."

"Yea? Like what?"

She hesitates, regards me for a moment longer before she speaks. "Well, maybe you gotta stop numbing yourself, Lili. Have you ever tried to, I dunno, search for answers? Get closer to it? I know you trust your family and that they have good intentions, but your parents are telling you that you're evil, to hide yourself and pray the devil away. And Vinny, although I directly benefit from it, Vinny supplying you with so much weed might not be so good for you. I mean look at you — you have no real friends, I don't even think you want any. You're isolating yourself. Maybe it's time to try something new?"

The image of Crystal's rotting corpse nestled away under the grassy field floats into my thoughts, planting itself there as I remember her sad, dead eyes staring at me. I don't want to get closer to that. And I don't want to make anyone else get close to that either. And 'that' is me. I regret telling Justyne. She already has so many problems in her life. I shouldn't have told her; she'll want to help.

"I dunno. That's not really something I'd like to do, ya know? It all feels really dangerous. I think ghosts, spirits, all of this shit, could really fuck me up."

"But has it?"

I stare at her, dumbfounded. Has she not been listening to me?

"No, I mean really. I know it scares the shit outta you, but has it ever hurt you? Everyone is taught this shit isn't real — only retards believe in angels and demons, and you're being taught that it's pure evil. But it's never hurt you. At least nothing you've told me suggests that it has. Maybe this thing is actually protecting you, or has some sort of message — "

I interrupt her. "Justyne, if I'm not pretending like it's not happening or wishing it away, I'm encouraging it. And there aren't enough drugs in the world for me to go on to handle any more than what I do now." I glance over my shoulders, making sure we are still alone in the thicket behind the school. "I'm fourteen and still piss my bed. I can't hold normal conversations with people. If anyone ever found out … If my parents knew everything … They have a ward at the hospital just waiting for me."

She knows I'm desperate. I can see she's searching for a way to help. I want to tell her she has done more for me than anyone just by listening, by making an effort to understand what I go through. I've finally found someone I can unquestionably trust.

"Lili, I know you have your way of doing things, and I respect that. We smoke here two, three times a day? I'm here no matter what, even if you're anti-social, and I know you keep me a secret from your parents. I'm here, and I think I can help you, but you gotta let me."

"What do you want to do?"

"How much do you know about witchcraft?"

Grabbing the pipe slowly out of her hands, I carefully say, "That's enough smoke for you. Love you, babe. You're the only bitch I could tell 'Hey, I'm crazy!' to, and you didn't judge or laugh … much. But instead responded with 'Hey, I'm crazier!'" I laugh. Even though she's serious about her offer, she can't help but laugh, too.

Maybe she's right, though. My life sucks. I've managed to keep Justyne a secret for two years, and she's the smallest of my secrets. Maybe I do need to start looking at this differently.

"Come over tonight," I say. "Let's do it."

She's stunned. "Do what?"

"I don't know. Whatever you wanna do, your voodoo hoodoo shit or whatever. I need to know why. It's been with me for so long, and I can feel it changing. I feel like maybe if you're right, and I do need to know something, if I wait, it might be too late."

I have a hard time reading her. She stands up and lets out a sigh like she's disappointed. "I can't. Not tonight. My mom is allowed to have visitors at the hospital again, and the doctors said she was back taking her meds. I'm going to go see her."

"Oh." I understand. "That's fine. You need to go. We'll do it some other time. I should go, anyway. If you're not coming, then I don't really have a reason not to be going to church tonight."

"You have church tonight? It's a Wednesday!"

"Yea, 'every day is God's day.'"

Reaching into her bag, Justyne pulls out a couple of books and hands them to me. "Read these. I've been reading and study-ing magic since I was a kid." She glances down at her feet and quietly says, "Mostly just to see Brian again. It was all so fucked up after he died. Everything went to shit, and I thought if I could just find a way to bring him back, to see him again, my mom would feel better and get out of the hospital, and my dad ... Well, he might be a dad again. But the more I read, I learnt it's about much more than just spirits and ghosts and spells. There is a lot of history, and science." She taps the cover of an old faded blue book. "This one has a chapter about universal energy and how to manipulate it. There are some mantras and incantations in it, too, but" — Pausing, she smiles and leans into her hip — "if you're *not* lying, maybe don't read those. Not out loud like you mean it, anyways."

I place both books into my bag. "You don't have to justify yourself to me. Ever. Thanks so much. Go visit your mom, and I'll call you tonight."

𝔙𝔍𝔍𝔍.

SOPHIE

June 10th 1989
Denholm, Saskatchewan
June 7, 1989

Sophie Kinsley
Maymont Central School
1ST E
Maymont, SK S0M 1T0
RE: Honour Roll

Dear Miss Kinsley,

I wanted to extend my most sincere congratulations to you for having achieved Honour Roll for this 1988/89 school year. It is a great academic achievement that you have earned in your 10th year at Maymont Central School. Your parents and teachers are very proud of what you have accomplished.

You are an exemplary student, keep up the good work. We look forward to hearing more from you as you continue your journey through life.

Sincerely,
William Sherlock
Mayor

Principal Ludwig had come down before the bell rang and announced in front of the whole class what he held in his hands. Some of her classmates half-heartedly clapped. The first thought that crossed her mind was, *My dad's going to be so proud of me! I did it!* Her second thought was much sadder.

I wish I could tell Mum.

She brushed her long, blonde hair off her shoulder and got up to take the envelope from Mr. Ludwig. She couldn't hold in her smile if she tried. It wasn't something you saw a lot of, Sophie Kinsley smiling. But it was undeniable the girl had an angelic smile that radiated through her big, blue eyes.

Blonde hair and freckles; a quiet beauty. One of few in the village.

Denholm wasn't big. In the school, the town, everyone knew each other. Everyone knew Sophie. They knew her mom died when she was twelve. They knew she lived in a single trailer on Second Street with her dad, Tom. Everyone knew that if you needed to find Tom, he'd be at the town's only shit-hole bar, drinking until he was barely able to stumble home.

One part of her couldn't wait for Pa to come home. Sophie had read her letter twenty times since she first opened it. "You are an exemplary student." From the mayor! She placed the letter on the TV table beside her dad's recliner. She grabbed a Lucky Strike from the fridge and placed it beside the letter. She studied the presentation with her fingers over her mouth.

It's perfect.

No wait.

She hurried back to kitchen and poured a bag of peanuts into a bowl and placed them beside the beer. No, no, the bowl and the beer were taking up most of the space on the tray now; her letter was lost. It would go unnoticed. She grabbed the letter and propped it up against the bowl.

Perfect.

She clapped her hands. She wanted to get changed into a dress before Pa got home. He'd be so proud.

Another part of her didn't want to show him. She stopped halfway down the hallway. Maybe she should hide the letter in her closet. She bit her lip. What if the letter made him mad?

"You think YOU'RE BETTER THAN ME?"

She grabbed at the bruise on her arm, still so tender.

"YOU'RE JUST LIKE YOUR MOTHER. A nogood-fornuthin' cunt."

She bit her lip. Her chest tightened. A part of her knew that if her dad went to Denholm's after work … If he drank … She wished her mom was here. Tears welled up in her eyes. She went to the phone.

It had been five years since they found the cancer in her mom's lungs. She was weak and tired for the longest time before Tom had finally given in to see what was making his wife hack up gobs of blood. In the doctor's office, after Tom received his wife's diagnosis, the only sound was the hum of the florescent lamps overhead. He retreated into himself and stayed there. Soon after, they would make arrangements for her to stay at the Saskatoon Cancer Centre, and even though it was only an hour away, Tom wouldn't make it up very often.

Within the first weeks of her mother staying there, Sophie's Aunt Renee came from Vancouver. She took Sophie to the hospital every day after school and dropped her back home in the evening. More than once, Renee and Tom had shouting matches. It was unknown to everyone except Tom how he could be so callous to his dying wife.

Sophie lost both parents at the same time, going back and forth between two hells. The pain she felt inside wasn't relatable to her small town. She cried alone in her room. Prayed to God. For her mother. For her father. Confiding only in her aunt the pain she felt for herself.

The cancer was vicious. Sophie's mom stayed at the hospital for only a month before they told Tom he had the option of putting her into a hospice to say goodbye, or they would provide at-home care until it was her time, which would come quickly. Sophie begged at his feet to please bring her mother home.

That was the last she would ever see of the mom she knew. The last time she felt safe.

The hospital bed took up most of the small living room in the trailer.

When Tom would come home at night, one of two things would go down.

He would slowly approach the bed, stand over the near-skeletal body of Sophie's mother, and weep. He would sob loudly into the night. He would hold her hand tightly, and beg her not to leave him. He was so sorry for the fights, for the hard times. If she would just get better, he would move them away, somewhere nice, just like they had always talked about.

Or, he would come home, rip the covers off of his wife in her death-sleep and pound the bed with his fists. He would scream in her face. "Die already! Fuck off! Go already!" He would shake the bed, throwing Sophie's mom to the floor where he would leave her. Then he would stomp to the other side of the trailer to get Sophie. He dragged her from her bed by her hair, telling her to pack her shit, get her fucking mother, and leave.

Sophie was helpless. As soon as Tom turned his back, she would run for the phone and dial her Aunt Renee, pleading for her to come. And she did. The first couple of times. But she wasn't a match for Tom. He was just as violent with her as he was with Sophie and her mother. When she arrived the first time, Tom walked off the porch and started to throw beer bottles at her car. She was too afraid to get out. Until she saw Sophie standing behind him in the doorway, blood running down her face.

Renee got points for trying. She got out of her car and tried to talk to Tom calmly. He put her on the hood of her car and slapped the shit out of her. She was put in her place, unlike her jaw, which had been taken out of it. She had no choice but to retreat. She went to the police. They told her to have a heart. "The man is losing his wife."

Aunt Renee limped away, swearing the whole town was a bunch of "Small town, inbred motherfuckers."

Aunt Renee left after the funeral. Even though Sophie sat in her car and begged to be taken, she was left behind. It wasn't fair. There was no hero. Aunt Renee left. And Sophie continued on, following behind Tom, picking up all the broken pieces.

When things got really bad between Sophie and Tom, her aunt was still there, but only as a sympathetic ear. She urged Sophie to get good grades, stay out of his way, and get a job. Then, as soon as she was eighteen, she could come to Vancouver and live with her. It was what kept Sophie going most days. A dream.

Sophie wanted to tell her aunt about her letter, ask her advice. Is this something Tom should know about? Renee would probably advise against it, say that it wasn't good for Sophie to call attention to herself. Not when her dad could come home and be so volatile. It was impossible to predict.

Stay quiet, but be proud. Sophie wouldn't get stuck in the dump she was raised in. She was too smart to get pregnant with some fool's child. She was too ambitious not to live her dreams. Sophie would go so far. Wherever her beautiful mind would take her. She would have the whole world at her feet.

But just not right now. Right now, she had to be strong, endure, stay focused, and — most importantly — stay out of trouble, take care of her dad, and keep him happy. This was her means to an end.

The phone rang twice before Aunt Renee's voice came through the receiver.

"Hey, Sophie! Is everything OK?"

Sophie smiled at her Aunt's immediate show of concern. "Better than OK. I have good news!"

Sophie and Renee talked for a couple of hours before Sophie realized what time it was; her dad would be home any minute. She was excited and scared all at the same time, and she needed to calm down. She would have a shower and then go start dinner.

She walked into the kitchen, drying her hair. The clock read 6:30 p.m. She pulled back the curtains in the front of the cabin and leaned forward. No sign of Tom. Sun was going down. She knew he was getting drunk. But at least if she made dinner, when he did come home, there would be food, and he'd be happy. Hopefully.

While putting the tomatoes in a sauce pot, Sophie made a mental note to hide her letter. She ate her dinner alone, made a plate for Tom, stuck it in the microwave, cleaned up the kitchen, and then got ready for bed. As she rested her head on her pillow, she glanced at the clock. 9:14 p.m.

IX.

LILI

Calgary, Alberta
June 15th 2003
3:06 a.m.

I mistake the warmth for comfort. There is an air of safety, like I'm where I belong. The woman's scream startles me. I hold my breath as the anxiety builds, knowing I'll have to open my eyes, knowing I have no control here.

I whisper a prayer of encouragement to myself and open my eyes. For the first time in this familiar dreamscape, the flames that surround me provide me with security as I focus past the fire. A version of myself sits poised on a throne of lifeless bodies. She emanates a sadistic power, as pale and blue as the dead beneath her. Her hypnotizing stare draws me in. Shadows seep through the spaces between bruised legs and limp arms; remnants of the souls she has taken, that she keeps. They slither out, across the mossy ground, over the glowing bodies, approaching and blotting out the fire. I am paralyzed, my legs frozen, unable to move or run or scream. I am forced to watch. My body is not my own here.

The fire flicks its embers up. I follow them as they float into the heaviness of the black sky above me. He's here with me, standing between me and the remnants of the souls, holding the heavy darkness above me from falling. Is he always here with me? My memory of him is so different than what stands guarding me. My ghost is changing. He, now more than ever, seems like he belongs in this nightmare. His green eyes have become cold, focused on the other version of me through the flames. His once-angelic features, only minutely marred by the presence of two tiny horns, are lost to an ever-growing crown of bone ripping through the skin of his forehead. Blood runs down the crown and over his face, glimmering as it reflects the flames of the fire. What has happened to him? Why is he here with me?

Through the tormentingly shrill screams, I hear a whisper of someone reciting words I don't understand, over and over, again and again. With each chant, the hostility in the air builds. The flames grow wilder, as does the face of my demonic double. She starts to rise from her throne of corpses; a small movement, so subtle, like the movements of a lioness before it pounces on its prey.

With a sharp gasp of breath, I am plunged into white light.

She comes for me.

I am nose to nose with my own face. Her veins run black; her eyes drain of colour. In an explosion of bitterness and rage, she cries out. Her voice resonates within me.

"Ephryium!"

In this moment, I am plunged back into the clarity of the nightmare. She lays across her throne, mutilated and still. I only catch a glimpse of the scene before the remnants attack.

The sky collapses on me, wrapping me in cold, suffocating darkness.

Struggling for air, I wake. My cramped hands white-knuckle

my bed sheets. Thunder cracks outside. Even though I'm awake in my own room, I am still agitated and scared. The rain is too quiet, the shadows too dark. The air is laced with tension and apprehension.

Booming thunder and a flash of lightning fill my room. An apparition of my demonic double, enshrouded in blood and rage, clutches the sheets at my feet. The silhouettes of taken souls crowd in around me. I clamp my eyes closed, and the awful shriek fills my ears. I wait to be taken, fearing what's next, and suddenly realize the shriek is familiar to me. My blood runs cold.

It's my voice. I'm screaming like death has found me.

"Lili! Lili! Wake up, Lili!" Little hands on my arms.

I open my eyes to my baby brother, Rocco, on top of me, eyes wide and brows scrunched.

My brain starts to random fire. Was I asleep? Am I awake? Is Rocco another monster? I almost punch him in his tiny face.

"Rocco? What are you doin', buddy?"

"Lili, you scared me. You scared me so bad. You was screamin' so scary. Are you hurt?"

"No, buddy. I'm OK. What's going on? Did I wake you?"

He rolls off of me onto the bed, visibly relieved to see me awake, but I can tell he's holding back. He looks down into his lap and starts to fidget with his fingers. He's still nervous.

"It's stormin' outside. The funder woke me. It was scary."

"Why didn't you go get Vinny?"

"He's not in his bed ... and ... his room stinks like fart."

I laugh but am a little concerned as to why our brother isn't in his room. "You wanna sleep in my bed?"

Without answering, he slides under my blanket and pulls my arm over him. I'm just as happy to have him in here with me as I know he is to stay. The rain outside is soothing.

Right before I fall back to sleep, I hear Rocco's little voice ask, "Who's Ephryium?"

I can't bring myself to wake to tell him the answer. He has always been here: before the nightmares, before Crystal and all the others like her, and still here beside my bed after the nightmare is over. I don't know if I am his or he is mine. But he stands on the same side of the flames as me. And for the first time, I know his name.

Ephryium.

Does Rocco see him, too?

X.

"Psst, Lili, wake up."

It's morning. *Oh, God. It's Sunday.*

Rocco is still under my arm, snuggled up beside me. I give him some sound advice. "Shh. If we're really quiet, maybe they'll all forget about us and we won't have to go." I know it's futile. Eventually, Mom or Dad will come in and wake us up with enough time to get ready and go to church, but still, I grab the blankets and pull them over our heads. *Just a couple more minutes.*

"Rocco, last night, what did you … ? Did you see someone in my bedroom?" I hope to God he says no, that he isn't inflicted with this awful sight. I dread the thought of him saying yes; it might be because of me. I could have brought something into this house that would attack my family. Rocco is so small under my arm, so fragile. An image of myself flashes in my mind: pale as death and covered in blood, going after Rocco in the night.

"Come on, lil buddy, talk to me. Did you say you saw something?" There is more urgency in my voice than I intend. I give him a little shake to prompt him.

"No, I didn't see nuffin."

Relief sweeps over me and I can relax.

"You were talkin' in your sleep. Who is it?" Rocco asks, no louder than a mumble.

I try and see if I can get away with giving him the short answer. "I think of him like a friendly ghost. I think — I hope — since he's never done anything bad to me, maybe he's like my guardian angel."

"Mum says that angels don't talk to people anymore."

"Well, he doesn't really talk to me. He's just here."

"Mummy says that demons pretend to be good so they can get close to you so that they can hurt you and your family."

I roll my eyes. Even though I have been raised with all of the same stories Rocco is now being raised with, I have opened myself up to so much more that has taught me things are not black and white.

"Well, Rocco, why doesn't he come into your room at night and nip at your toes then?"

"'Cause Jehovah protects me."

A pang of jealousy runs through me. I wish I had that, even if it was just a false confidence that there was something bigger capable of protecting me.

"Well, I don't believe that." Lowering my voice to a whisper, I continue. "I don't think God is here, Rocco. I think all we have is each other."

"Maybe that's why the demons are after you and not me." Throwing the blankets off us, he runs to the door.

I stop my thought from reaching my mouth. It scares me, and I know it would only scare him more. Maybe the demons are after him, after all of us. Maybe I'm the only one standing in the way of the rest of my family from being terrorized like I am. But I don't say this. I let him go. The door opens; the scent of bacon and coffee wafts in, and my mother's voice telling me to get in the shower.

Wasting time I don't have, I reach underneath my mattress to pull out a book from my secret library. I wonder if there is anything on demonic unions and what the ritual, if there is one, would look like.

Now, more than ever, I hate going to church. It is hard for me to hear what they have to say during a sermon. That I am being affected by demons. I could pray till I cried, asking for God's help, to make the dreams stop, to make me feel safe when I'm alone. But I'm past hope now. By a Christian's standards, just by reading about what I see, what I hear, who I am, I am welcoming it. Going to church now gives me a whole new kind of paranoia and anxiety.

I'm a hypocrite.

I spend at least twenty hours a month declaring the Bible's prophesies as truth, as well as proclaiming my faith in God and having a genuine concern for the fate of your everlasting life as one of Jehovah's witnesses. I also spend at least twenty hours a month smoking pot, doing drugs, drinking, and masturbating.

And another portion of time gobbling up anything that connected what I already knew about religion and the paranormal: Wicca, Satanism, Paganism, and Occultism, angels and demons, gods and demi-gods. Sacred geometry, tarot, dream interpretations, I read it all.

I am part of a religion that has isolated me from childhood, not only from all the other 'worldly' children that I couldn't play with, but into a secret isolation — my religion deemed me not just a very, very bad Christian, but possessed, demonic. Every time I go near a church, it only solidifies a thought that I am not ready to admit to.

I am not one of God's children.

I am someone else's.

XI.

1 Corinthians 10:21

You cannot be drinking the cup of Jehovah and the cup of demons;
you cannot be partaking of the table of Jehovah and the table of demons.

As we make our way across the parking lot, Mom licks her fingers and cleans milk off Rocco's face, and Dad straightens Vinny's tie. At the end of the lot, our church blots out the sun.

A burning sensation rises in my chest. I lag behind my family. Hoping for relief, I close my eyes, take a deep breath, and pause. A faint whisper just within earshot seems to be coming from the church. I walk slowly and carefully; something is waiting for me. I watch my family ahead of me, approaching the doors, and I know I can't go in with them.

A whisper in my ear, in my head. Then, as if there are a hundred whispers flying around my head like little black bats, they hiss:

FaLsE hOpE

He hAs   aBanDoNed   yoU
ORPhaN

FutILe WoRShiP

EveRLaSTiNg   FIRE

GeT On YoUr   kNEessS

coMe   woRsHIp YouR FaTHeR   tHe

Like a thunder bolt:

DEVIL!

Then silence.

The burning inside of me sends a flare of pain to my throat. *I'm going to puke.*

I open my mouth to yell for help. Red and yellow chunks spew out, hitting the concrete, splashing my shoes and legs. My family stops and turns around. I look to them helplessly. My mom takes a step forward, but I projectile vomit again. My brothers don't move. I drop to my hands and knees and start to heave out acid that burns my throat. Tears blur my vision. I can faintly make out my mother, an expression of concern on her face as she stands over me.

"I'll take her home. Go in with the boys?" she says to my dad.

"Let's go, boys. I don't want this to make us late." His short reply comes out quick and at the same time as Rocco's and Vinny's sighs of disappointment.

As I continue to wretch onto the asphalt, I can't even lift my head to give the boys an inconspicuous celebratory wink that I'll be going home without them. In fact, I think I'm going to pass out …

I am in the land of sleep, just at consciousness's gate. A rough growl brings me to open my eyes. My heart's pounding, hair stuck to my cold, damp forehead. I quickly survey my room. I know I heard something.

It's twilight. The sun's orange light leaks in through the

cracks of my curtains. I hear whispers outside my door. My mom and dad.

"We can't send her away," my mom argues.

"I don't want her here anymore. She's affecting Rocco," my dad whispers.

"I think we need to tell her. She's starting to dream again. Saul, it's going to be even worse if she doesn't understand."

"No, no. I don't want her to know. It will just make more problems."

"If we push her away, who's going to protect her?"

"Who's going to protect us? Rocco? Hm, Carmella? It's not just her. I have to think about the whole family."

"We need to tell her."

"I said no."

I understand the significance of the conversation, but have no energy to get up and have a big confrontation. I drop my head onto my pillow and fall back to sleep.

XII.

SOPHIE

June 11th 1989
Denholm, Saskatchewan
3:46 a.m.

She thought she was being shaken awake. At first, the pain didn't register. Something knocked on her head again and again. When she opened her eyes, she saw bursts of little white dots floating in the darkness. She gave a low moan, placed her arms underneath her, and tried to get up. She couldn't. Something weighed down on top of her, shoving her face in her pillow. She let out a muffled scream as she tried to wriggle free.

"You're both the same. Gonna leave me now, too?"

It was Tom's voice. Sophie didn't know what hurt more, her thighs as her panties were being ripped off of her, or the realization of what was happening and who was doing it.

"Please!" she begged. He hit her again, hard, in the back of her head. His big hand wrapped around her neck, tightening his grip as he tried to place himself between her kicking legs. She coughed as she struggled for air. She smelled the liquor fuming off him, out of his mouth. She cried into her pillow, her pleas lost in a muffle of whimpers.

He smacked her ass. She screamed and tried to move out of the way, but again and again, his hand came down hard, sending pain splintering up her backside. She writhed and twisted, fighting to avoid the barrage of smacks her ass and thighs were receiving. She felt hot, as if her skin would crack open and bleed.

Tom muttered to himself angrily, shouting at Sophie to "Shut the fuck up! Stop moving!"

She wiggled an arm free and started to search. She felt her nightstand. Grabbing at the foreign objects, she tried her best to propel them at him. She felt something land on the small of her back. A picture frame? It was a picture of Sophie when she was six years old, with her mom and dad.

She squeezed her eyes shut. She felt something warm and blunt at the entrance of her vagina. She breathed in sharply and let adrenaline take over. Ripping the pillow from underneath her face, she let her screams of terror ring through the trailer. She bucked wildly, kicking Tom away from her. Fighting to save her life. His hand let go of her neck to hold onto her thrashing legs. She twisted herself onto her back and peered into his eyes.

"Daddy! What are you doing? Please stop, please stop, please don't do this." Tears streamed down her cheeks.

The rage in Tom's eyes glazed over. His grip loosened around Sophie's ankles. She watched in disgust as his boner slowly fell limp against his zipper. There was silence in the room. Tears welled in his eyes. He let out a sob and fell on top of her.

"I'm so, so sorry. What have I done? What have I done? So sorry. You were gonna leave. Just like your mother." He whispered incoherently into Sophie's ear until, finally, his body sagged on top of hers.

She heaved his heavy arm up so she could shimmy herself out from under Tom's deadweight. Gazing down on him, she stood catching her breath. She winced as her searching fingers touched a large, tender bump growing on the back of her head.

He wasn't moving. He was passed out. Probably would be until tomorrow evening. She needed to use her time wisely. She surveyed the trailer. A bomb had gone off in it: Tom.

Her letter. Her letter lay on the floor in the middle of the living room, sopping wet with beer, in amongst the peanuts strewn all over the floor. Shoulders back, chin up, she fought the urge to crumple into a ball on the floor and cry.

She ran to the front closet and pulled down a seafoam-green suitcase that had been her mother's, throwing it down on the floor beside her bed. She quickly chose jeans, a tee, and a hoodie to wear, then started to throw handfuls of clothes into the bag.

She tiptoed over to her nightstand and pulled it forward. As she crouched down to reach behind it, her eyes stayed on the rise and fall of Tom's back. Aunt Renee had been sending her money for the past five years, just on her birthday and Christmas, and Sophie hadn't spent a dollar of it. It went into her savings jar which she hid from Tom, knowing he would drink it away.

Tom grunted and lifted his head, Sophie froze. She held her breath.

He turned his face away from her, dropping back onto the bed heavily. She waited a couple more long seconds before she grabbed the jar and put it into her bag. She watched him as she zipped it closed. One part of her, staring down at Tom, needed to say so much. So much to this man that raised her, loved her, then died along with her mother. The man who tore her down. The man who was nothing to her from this moment on. Another part of her appreciated leaving in silence. This part of her had no words left for the creature that lay in front of her.

A wounded warrior who would still conquer. Shoulders back, chin up. She let go of her breath and headed for the door.

XIIII.

SOPHIE & ARNOLD

Denholm, Saskatchewan
June 11th 1989

As the door hit the frame with a loud bang behind her, Sophie felt panicked and began to run down the dirt road leading to the highway. She ran away from that tiny trailer. She ran away from all the pain and suffering that lingered in the air like a noxious fume, waiting to be ignited. She ran and never looked back, her cowboy boots clicking as soon as she got off the dirt and onto the asphalt. She bit her lower lip and started to make plans. She would have to walk for at least forty-five minutes before she got to the truck stop at the edge of town. She could get cleaned up there. Her face was sore. She hadn't the slightest clue what she looked like — no time for mirrors in her escape — but if it was anything close to what she felt like, it was rough.

She would call Aunt Renee. She would need to count her money, see how far she could get with what she had. Did she have enough for a bus ticket? She felt her back pocket, reassuring herself that her ID was still there.

She stayed lost in her thoughts as she walked carefully alongside the painted white line on the road. She felt the transports approaching behind her and drifted off to the grassy ditch as they passed, returning to the road when they were gone. She could make out neon lights in the darkness ahead of her. Like a warning, the ground underneath her began to rumble again. The vibration ran up her legs. She would need to veer off to the side of the road soon. Didn't want to get hit. *That would be tragic.* Sophie laughed at the dark humour and shook her head.

She peered over her shoulder. The headlights illuminated her whole body as the transport slowed. For her? She kept on glancing over her shoulder, making out the dark silhouette of the truck behind the lights. It slowly crept beside her. The window was much too high to see the driver. What were they trying to do? She turned forward and walked faster. The transport picked up speed and passed her, the rush of wind made her involuntarily cross one leg over the other. She fell down the grassy embankment, landing sprawled out in the gravel and sand at the bottom of the ditch.

"Fucking asshole!"

She got to her knees to watch him drive further down the highway and turn into the gas station. Tired and exasperated, she rubbed her hands on her jeans until the little grains of sand embedded in her skin had rolled off. She tugged her sleeve over her hand and rubbed her eyes.

Almost there.

As she walked past the buzzing neon signs towering over the store, she took in her surroundings. All was quiet. Only a couple of trucks parked for the night. One at the pump. No one seemed interested in her.

The smell of stale hotdog and cigarette smoke came in a wave of hot air as she entered the store. The only person in the store stood behind the counter, staring at her.

"Your bathroom open?"

"Naw, you needs da key." The skinny, drowned rat of a man stretched his yellow-and-black plaid covered arm, pointing to the far wall where the key did, in fact, hang.

"You got a phone?"

"Yup." He nodded, pulling his long, greasy hair out of his face.

"One that I can use?"

"Out back. Beside the bathroom."

Sophie walked past him to retrieve the key from the wall. Her skin crawled. Buddy looked like he smoked a bucket of meth. Everyday. His whole life. She gave a reflexive shudder.

She shoved through the glass door and walked along the white cinderblock building, staying under the sick, green light of the lamps buzzing above. The phone was bolted to the wall beside the bathroom.

She sighed with relief. She'd wash up and call her aunt. Everything would be OK. She pushed through the door with the scratched out woman symbol on it.

Someone had taken a shit in the corner. And then, like a cherry on top, was a bloody tampon. She gagged, turned to face outside, and heaved. *Fuck this.* Going back into the room, she saw who whoever had laid the tampon there was also probably the owner of the blood clots strewn around the floor. She put her nose into her elbow and closed the door behind her.

When she saw the toilet her bladder recognized the potential relief and flinched inside of her. *Nope. No.* A used, shit-covered condom lay on the side of a bowl filled with something that might have been alive at one point. She leaned in. *Was that fur?* She heaved again.

Taking a deep breath into her sleeve, Sophie ran over to the mirror. She felt worse than she looked. Combing her hair down hurt her poor, aching skull. Using paper towels to turn on the hot water, she quickly gave her face a couple of splashes before she had to go back into her elbow for more air. The rank smell of the place was going to make her puke. She looked at herself in the mirror. One. Last. Time.

She threw the door open and gasped for the fresh air. A tall, round man in a blue, trucker cap stood with his thumbs locked into a golden, oversized belt buckle.

"Well, hello there, pretty lady." The space between them closed fast.

Her eyes widened. His fist hammered into her face. She smelled cologne. Cheap cologne. *Huh. Same as Tom's.* The sick, green lights above faded to black.

𝔛𝔦𝔙.

IGNACE

𝕿he following is an excerpt from:

Luc Marchand's

Queens of Hell
An Occult Specialist's Search for the Devils in the Background

Published 1997

October 17th 1986
Ignace, Ontario.
Night of the Blood Moon

The man inside had heard them coming; a man of the woods, like them. He was defeated quickly by the strength of their numbers. With a half empty bottle of Jack on the table, his gun hadn't been fast enough.

The cabin was small. There were only three rooms: Nowhere to run. The man's name was Matthew. He lived alone. He didn't expect anyone to come. He knew he was going to die. And he was the type of man that the reason *why* didn't matter; it wouldn't change the facts.

The two men hadn't seemed like men when they had come crashing through the door. Matthew saw they were wild, covered in dirt and blood with scars down the lengths of their bodies. He wasn't a man to shake or scare. Even faced with death, he had his pride, but Matthew, and later whomever else came into contact with these two men, these two creatures, would believe that the two of them appeared undeniably bigger than they were. There was a force, a coldness, which came before them, that would fill the air until it was thick with it, then linger after the two had left.

The two men stripped Matthew naked and hung him by his ankles with his own chains. He hung from the cabin's beam, silently watching the men search the cabin. When one of the men came out of his kitchen holding his hunting saw, he knew he was done for. He wouldn't plead, he was never that kind of man, and even in what he knew to be his last horrible moments, he would die the way he lived: wishing he had drank more.

Matthew might not have begged, but he screamed for his life as the man brought the saw down to his jaw and began to cut through the bottom half of his face. As the blood rushed from his face onto the floor, the other man panted heavily. Tingles pulsed through the man's body. Grunting quietly, he pulled and stroked his dick, pausing so he could build up a need for more, then start again. Dizzy and euphoric, the man, the *creature*, held onto Matthew's chains for support, while his cohort had retired from mutilating Matthew's body and had begun mutilating himself.

Breaking the bottle of whiskey that was at arm's reach, he began to stab his legs again and again with the shattered pieces. He felt every shard enter, the skin splitting open, the sting of the exit. He came into the blood dripping down his leg. Panting, nostrils flared, his eyelids drooped. He stood there, high on the adrenaline, breathing in the smell of the blood and feeling the emulsified liquid make its way down his legs, catching one single hair at a time.

Both *creatures* knew that if their master was still alive, she would smell the pain and fear of Matthew's death. It would call her to come feed off it. If she was alive, this is how she would find them.

Both men stood at the cabin door to throw the severed jaw out into the forest. The symbiotic energy of their evil expanded out of the cabin into the darkness of the forest, searching for the one from whence it came.

The *creatures* turned back into the cabin to finish the ritual. To finish dismembering the first of many. Matthew Linton.

XV.

ARNOLD & SOPHIE

Unknown Location, Highway 376, Saskatchewan
June 11th 1989

He set himself down on one knee beside the crumpled little blonde.

FuCk heR, ArNoLd!

FuCk hEr.

So SweeT. So, sO swEEt.

KILL   HER.

JuSt A litTLe GiRl.

FucK hEr!

BaSH hEr hEaD IN!

Such a pretty little thing, he thought to himself.

Licking his dry, cracked lips, he admired the stitching on her cowboy boots. He traced the swirl on the leather, running his finger gently up the side of her leg to her inner thigh.

ToUCh iT, ArNoLd.   ToUcH hEr

PuSsy.

STIck   yOur fIngERs …   InSidE.

She didn't stir at his touch; she was out cold. An image shot across his imagination of himself fucking the pretty, little thing in the back of his truck's cab — her eyes closed, body limp. Biting his bottom lip, he got tingles and smiled at the thought. He might even fuck her corpse. He chuckled to himself as his hard-on reached the button of his jeans.

Oh, the fun he would have.

He'd been driving rigs for years, seen and done just about everything, was even indulgent in the most disgusting things the world had to offer. But even he couldn't stand to be in this truck stop bathroom for one more moment. He took off his red-and-blue checkered over-shirt and threw it over the girl's face.

MOvE hEr   quICkly, YOu fAt fuCk!

                                    DoN't wAnt No

                                        tROubLe

It could go either way. Small village? May or may not miss one of their kin. Pulling his hat down, he hocked a loogie onto the wall, scooped her off the floor, and ducked out the door. He slipped to the back of the building, keeping his face down. There was a railway yard about fifty meters behind the stop. He walked with confidence across the dark field to where he had parked his rig along the fence of the yard.

He pushed her into the back of his cab, dropping her onto the worn, stained mattress.

Do iT hErE!

                STiCk it   INnnnn

FuCK AND DuMP!

                        HeR   moUTh

                                pUt iT in HEr moUth

✳ ——————————————————————————————————— 57

sHe'S

GARBAGE!

Reaching onto a shelf and grabbing his duct tape, he got to work. He bound her ankles and wrists, then wrapped the tape around her head twice, covering her mouth. Her eye had already begun to change colour.

He shook his head and tsked.

ShE's wEak.

WeAK

WOn't lAst loNg

He dropped into his seat, tapped the wheel a couple of times with his fingertips, reached down, and grabbed the container of Skol on his dash. First things first.

A thought crossed his mind to drive her all the way back to home to Debbie; they could have fun with her together. The thought excited him, but not as much as having her all to himself. He shrugged. Debbie wouldn't mind. Shit, Debbie didn't even have to know 'bout this one, did she? He'd double back to Maymont, get off the Yellow to 376.

A smile crept over his face as his eyes darkened with the memories of last time he'd taken that route: that perfect red barn behind the brush, the sheds with all the … tools. The little, dark girl he'd spent so much time with there. Not in his top five, but one of the most fun 'cause he got to take his time. That's where he wanted to go — even if he drove slow, which he wouldn't, it'd only take him twenty? Thirty minutes? The perverse smile stayed on his face as he pulled out onto the highway.

There was no traffic on 376. No headlights. No houses. Nobody around for miles. If you didn't know the narrow drive-way was there, you'd pass it without a thought. He had found it by pure chance. It was perfect, positioned about a kilometre off the road, overgrown with brush, like God himself had placed it there for Arnold. A sanctuary in which to fuck, kill, torture, talk, play Monopoly, or whatever else Arnold wanted or needed to do. He could do it there.

The whole barn was painted red. Yup, the red you're imagining, but it was a little bit more worn by the elements. It was more solid than it seemed, the doors heavy. They creaked as he pushed them open wide enough for him and the girl in his arms to shimmy through, then closed with a heavy bang. They were left in the pitch-black room. But if all was how he had left it, no problem.

He put her on the dirt floor in the middle of the barn. Shuffling along the wall, he found his lanterns in their place and lit all four. Shadows were cast of all the things he'd left behind. They swayed to and fro at the candle's whim. Old cobwebs kept sturdy in each corner. Two stables in the back of the room waited empty with hay-covered floors, whereas the rest of the area was pretty sparse. Scanning the room, he placed his tools, table, bloodstains, an' all.

Home sweet Home

Arnold slowly walked up to his pretty, little captive and gave her a light kick to the shins. There was no movement.

SsSsshHhhE waNTs iT

He bent down to slowly remove the tape around her ankles. He slid one boot off, then the other and tossed them to the side of the room.

Pretty, young thing.

SHe'S a   ViRGin!

FUCK HER!

TIGHT   PUSSY!

He reached up to the button of her jeans and pulled it open.

ThE tABlE!

FUcK hEr oN   the TabLE

MOVE IT, YOU FAT FUCK!

He glanced up at the large worktable on the other side of the room. There. He picked her up by her waist; she couldn't have weighed much, 110 pounds wet. He gently placed her onto her stomach atop the table, leaving her legs to dangle. He didn't need to encourage himself — he was ready to begin.

Hooking his thumbs into her jeans, catching her panties as well, he tugged them down to her knees, unzipped his own pants, and pulled his already hard dick out for the show. He slid it along her asshole, in-between her lips, leaning in finally to touch the tip of her clit. It was dry. She moaned and wriggled. She was waking up. Perfect.

He hacked back a wad of phlegm and spat it at her upturned ass. Using his dick, he spread the mixture of spit and snot down to her slit. She squirmed again, this time letting out a confused and distressed yelp. He stabbed forward, driving into her. He closed his eyes. She screamed under the tape, her hips coming off the table as she violently tried to kick her attacker away. Arnold leaned into her, heavy on her, she was no longer able to move. Burying himself in her, he smiled and relished this moment.

"Well, isn't that nice. A pretty little thing like you, still a virgin, huh?"

He kneaded the soft skin on her butt and thighs before placing both of his hands on either side of her hips. Using them as handles, he jackhammered into her, slowing down every couple of seconds to let her squirm and try to wiggle away. She had no idea she was adding to his gratification. Every time she would try to scream, her pussy would tighten around him.

"Me an' you are gunna have some fun tonight." He let out a deep moan.

Tingles shot through his body. He began to drool onto her back. He was close. Reaching up, he grabbed a handful of the girl's long, golden hair and pulled back, pushing the full length of himself so deep into her his balls rested on the swollen lips of her vagina. Her head was pulled so far back that when she tried to let out her screams, they were lodged in her throat with no escape. He leaned over her, expending the last drips of come.

"Oh, little girl ... oh, fuck me," he whispered into her ear as he let go of her hair and ran his hand down her back, through his spittle, spreading it down her hip. She rested her forehead on the table and began to sob underneath the tape.

"Oh, little girl, don't cry. Don't cry, baby, not yet. This? This is just the beginning."

His hand cupped her ass. He placed his thumb over her asshole and began to slowly push into her. It was tight.

"Well, I reckon you never been touched before, is that right?" He took his thumb out and stuck three, then four fingers up her, scooping out his gunk and cupping it into his hand.

He reached over and slapped his come-filled hand into her face. She tried to turn away, letting out an angry growl that stopped before it got to her mouth. Her legs jolt backwards, futilely.

"If you move, little girl, I'm going to have to chop you up into little, tiny, fuckin' pieces right here on this here dirt floor. I'll walk away like it neva happened. Stay still. Maybe you'll get to do the same."

KiLL hEr.

LiTTle   PIEceS ...

She cried out in pain. It was like music; he was soothed as he plunged her with his fist, blood trickling down her thighs, off the tips of her toes, and into the dirt. He could go deeper. The line of blood wasn't past his wrist. Leering down at her, he was overcome with pride. She didn't move. Well, not enough to make a bother over.

ShE'S reAdY fOr mOrE

FuCK Her LikE a PIG

WEEEE

Weeeeeee

His eyes darkened. He was hard again.

Turning her over, the two got their first real look at each other.

Her — a beautiful, tanned girl with freckles, blue eyes, and blonde hair. An angel. All he wanted to do was make a mess in her mouth.

And him — a greying, overweight man, with small, black eyes and severely yellow, crooked teeth. A wife beater with age-old pit stains covered a body that had never had a good day.

Reaching down with his sticky gunk and blood covered hand, he pet her face gently.

What a pretty, little thing.

Scooping away a small amount of the blood and semen that had emulsified at the opening of her vagina, he lubed her tiny pink asshole into a slick opening. Ready or not, here he comes. She shook her head back and forth wildly as it dawned on her what he wanted to do. While staring into her eyes, he forced his way in. As her face flushed purple with strain, she let out a long and loud grunt. She was forcing him out! He smiled down at her. It made him excited; she wasn't kicking or squirming. It was her last line of defence.

She was giving up. Which meant he was almost done.

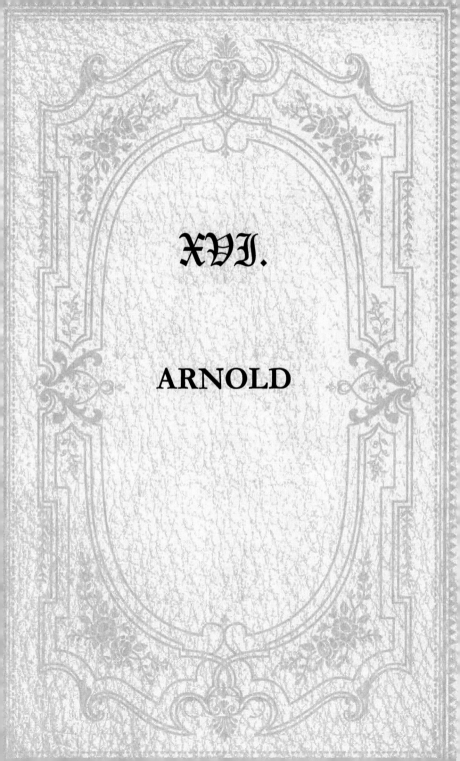

XVI.

ARNOLD

Unknown Location, Highway 376, Saskatchewan
June 11th 1989
5:42 a.m.

ot quite as feisty as he hoped for, but he would make the most of it. Exhausting himself, his fingers dug into her thighs as he pounded into her. Her glazed eyes stared off into nothingness, arms lying motionless by her sides, no longer taking part in her demise.

YoU'rE nOT gOOd   enOUgH,

ARnold!

YoU're UseLESs,   ArNOld!

ShE dOEsn'T gIVe a FuCk   aBoUT YOu.

WeaK

YOu DOn'T SCarE   hEr

"Wake tha fuck up," he said, smashing his knuckles into her chin. "You fucking look at me!"

Rolling her head, her glassy eyes fixed on him in an un-readable and vacant expression.

"I wish my Debbie was here. She'd fix you right up."

KILL HER

Gripping each of his fat fingers around her twig-like neck, he began to squeeze, driving into the tight opening again and again, squeezing tighter and tighter. He enjoyed watching her face turn from pink to a deep shade of plum, tears streaming down her face. Finally, her arms came off the table to scratch and push at his arm.

"Life in you yet, lil lady! Wooooohhooooo!"

He let go of her throat to slap the side of her face. It was rapidly changing colours with each breathe of air she took.

"I'ma ride you like a fuckin' cowboy! All the way into the fuckin' sunset, lil girl!" Smacking both of her breasts to the left and then to the right, he slammed into her with such force that if he didn't hang on to her, he'd have fucked her right over the other side of the table. Even though he was close to coming again, his mind had already moved on.

Salivating and hungry, he was ready to kill her now.

He needed to kill her now.

He glared at her for an instant before leaning over her and enclosing her head in both of his hands, coming in her as he crushed her face. In his power hungry frenzy, he felt a snap — her nose giving way under his palm. It sent her into a conniption, wildly bucking, throwing her body up and down. Underneath his weight, her muffled screams barely escaped. This sent him over a euphoric edge. His entire body vibrated. His eyes rolled into his head, jaw slacking, dribble sliding out from his lips. He squeezed her tighter. There was silence. Her struggles became sporadic and feeble.

NoW

Do iT

NOW

Opening his eyes, he scanned the room through the dim, orange lighting and made a checklist. The hatchet was by the far wall in the shadow of tall, dead weeds. Pliers, baseball bat, shears, rope, all lay in a pile by the door. Although everything lying around in the open with easy and quick accessibility was convenient, Arnold was forced to consider the possibility of his quiet haven being discovered. How hard would it be to trace any of this back to him?

Shaking off the thought, he pulled out of her. Along with

his dick, the contents of her bowels were also expelled. Bits of runny shit, blood, and semen splattered onto his boots and jeans. The smell wafted up to his nostrils, making him turn away in momentary revulsion.

"Now look what you gone an' done. My sweet Debbie aint gonna wanna clean yer shit an' blood outta her husband's Levi's!" Red slowly coloured his scornful, gawking face.

She didn't move. She didn't make a sound.

"You're fucking inconsiderate, is what you are." Impulsive violence brewed in the silence.

"You fucking, little bitch!" He balled her hair into his fist. "Did you hear me? Where am I gonna clean up? You see a fucking bathroom 'round here?" He motioned around the dark room and then plummeted a fist into her face.

Dropping her into the dirt, he kicked her sides, smearing some of the shit off of his boot and back onto her.

The listless and exhausted body lay motionless. He let a deep breath out, and his anger subsided. Listening carefully, he could hear the rapid breaths coming from her nose.. She wasn't going anywhere. He drifted to the far wall to retrieve the hatchet. He paused a moment to reminisce and study the bits of skull and hairs that still clung to its blade. It took all he had in him not to throw it at the wretched body on the ground. No. No.

Calm down, Arnold.

You're better than that.

What would Debbie think? Wastin' opportunities an' what not?

She'd be mad, though, if she saw the mess I had left.

Surrounded in shadows, the girl lay beneath the light of the lantern. Waiting for him.

Us. WaITinG fOr   uS.

The point of the scissors got caught on her chin as he

wedged them underneath the duct tape covering her lips, splitting the skin open, revealing her lower teeth in a bloody show.

LeT's HeAr HeR ScrEAm.

The screaming that filled the barn was as beautiful and serene as a choir singing the church's Sunday morning prayer. As much as it soothed him to hear it bouncing off the walls of the barn, to be lost in its inky shadows, he was compelled to mute her. He shoved his dick in her bloody, swollen face. His jaw clenched as her teeth sank in at the base of his member like a mutt and its ball …

A smile inched onto his face. With fluidity in his actions, he stabbed the pair of scissors into her back, grabbed the back of her head to keep her from pulling away, then pushed himself further into her mouth, making her choke and gag on him. Letting out a laugh, he continued to pump into her mouth. Tears streamed from her face as she gagged and heaved, finally throwing up. Pulling out of her mouth, he expended what come he had left onto her swollen face.

It wasn't as satisfying as he hoped. He had fantasized so much more.

KiLL HeR

TiE   heR uP

     liGHt hEr oN   FIRE!

      LEt hEr BURN   BURN burnnnnn

Securing the last knot on her ankle, he placed his hands on his hips and admired his job well done. She was secured to the table and ready for surgery. What exactly would he be taking today?

hEr sOuL

As the girl forced out pathetic cries, Arnold walked around

the table and leaned down to her face.

"Play time's over, liddle lady. Daddy's got to get home to the missus."

How hard would he need to crack her with the bat for her to lose consciousness?

WhO CarEs?

NO MERCY

MAkE her FeeL iT!

Inspecting the bat in his hands, he took a firm grip of its handle and swung it down onto her head with a crack.

Her head lagged to the side and then back again.

Walking around the table, never taking his eyes off her, he watched her eyes flutter as he positioned the head of the bat at the raw opening between her thighs. It slid up inside her with ease. Her moan filled the chapel.

GoOD

YeS

DeEPer

He pushed it in a little deeper, releasing a soft whimper. Stepping up to stand beside her face, he sheared off the hanging skin of what was left of her lip, peeling it back down her chin, following the line of her jaw. Her eyes widened as if they themselves were screaming in terror, then rolled back into her head, revealing just the whites.

CoMe bACk

We'Re not doNe.

BuRn hEr

SHE

CAN LEAVE WHEN WE

SAY SHe CAN LEAVE

ThEEeee haTChet

Fixating on the hatchet, memories rushed forth. He brought the blade, bits of skull an' all, up to his nose, closed his eyes, and inhaled the metallic aroma. His focus shifted back to the demolished body waiting for him on the table. Sniffing the blade again, he closed his eyes and brought the hatchet down violently. It hacked and cut, sometimes cracking the wood of the table and sometimes cracking her bones. He continued his hack an' slash until his arms started to shake with exhaustion.

He opened his eyes. Raised the curtain. Started the show. Ladies and Gentlemen, for your viewing entertainment, imagined in the deepest bowels of hell, the recesses of a corrupted mind, we give you: The Virgin!

Admiring what he had done, surprised at his ability, he studied the exposed meat. It looked like she might have been too big for her skin, causing it to rip open. Her hands and feet were unrecognizable as such, so deformed by the brutality they didn't resemble anything that once could have been whole — let alone attached to something living. Bones, muscles, and organs, all out of hiding beneath the once flawless complexion of a young woman. The only thought that floated across his mind as he stood there, like a man in a museum admiring a piece of art with no explanation, was: I need to show Debbie this; if I could only take a piece of this with me …

With that, he snipped a ponytail's worth of hair from the girl's scalp and stuck it deep down into the pocket of his jeans.

At the back of the barn, the sky had started to show signs of dawn. He might have forty-five minutes until the sun rose. He used the time to dig a shallow grave. After filling it with her remains, her clothes, and the cowboy boots he had liked so much, he ran to his truck cab and came back with a gas can. Hocking a loogie over his shoulder, he dropped the can at the foot of her grave, dug out a cigarette from his breast pocket, and had a moment of calm before he took out his dick to empty his bladder into the grave.

"That'll do it," he said to himself, zipping his fly.

He emptied about half of the can onto the girl before he put it down again and flicked the butt of his cigarette into the hole. He took off his plaid button-up and threw it into the hole with the body. Shaking his head, he scoffed at himself. He really liked that shirt; why'd she go an' ruin it?

During the cremation, he returned to his cab with a four litre milk jug filled with water, and scrubbed down his arms and face, giving his boots the last splash. Debbie, he was sure, would take care of the rest of it, but he sure as shit didn't want to go into his cabbie smelling of shit for another two to four hours. Fuck me, what time was it? He'd stop and get a 'chug' full of coffee before heading out.

Before he left, he made sure the girl was at least mostly gone. She was still pretty juicy, some parts crispier than others. It would definitely give the decomp a head start … wouldn't it? Whatever. The sand and loose gravel smothered out the bones that were still burning. Didn't want a fire. Nope. Not out here. Who knew what kind of attention it could attract? Or, Lord forbid, the barn to catch? That shit would wreck everything; this place was perfect.

XVII.

LILI

Calgary, Alberta
June 20th 2003
3:46 a.m.

I am only seconds away from being grabbed from behind, but stuck in that moment, right before I run, escaping narrowly. I'm standing in front of the church again, surrounded by remnants. My stomach lurches as the ground falls out from under me. I land in a pit surrounded by fire. It's all happening too fast; the places, the dream, it's all familiar, but it's different. My own shallow breaths fill my ears. I expect the woman to start screaming. Instead, those hoarse whispers that are so clear in my memory call out. They say my name. They're close. No.

They are everywhere! *I need to wake up.*

No sooner has my subconscious-self thought it, my eyes open. I'm not startled or tired. I just simply open my eyes and am awake, as if I had been all along. I think it is a wonderful thing; *alright then, I will get an early start on my day.* I swing my legs off the bed and drag my feet to my bathroom. Everything is fine. After sleepless nights and haunted dreams, I am so happy the air felt light, easy to be in.

As I step out into the hallway, I realize I have fallen into a trap. It is hanging from the corner as if hanging from the shadow itself. Rising and falling, pulsating. I am petrified as I watch it fill and expel. The wall behind is drenched with blood, which is slowly making its way down the wall, soaking the carpet. I need to turn back, run. I stand frozen as spiders, so many spiders, surround it, bloating its presence from the corner.

The spiders scurry across the walls, ceiling, and floor. I can't breathe any more. The ringing in my ears is deafening. My heart pounds in my chest. On the brink of succumbing to my cowardice and collapsing, I watch as arms, legs, and a long torso emerge from this shadow of arachnids. I moan a barely audible whimper, but it's cancelled out by what I can only describe as blaring white noise. I fall onto my butt and scramble for my bedroom — hopefully, my sanctuary.

I am reduced to a child: alone, scared of the dark, desperate for her mommy. My eyes, wide and peeled, never leave the door. I have no plan should that thing walk through my door. I will die. My mind is made. I can't handle it. I crab-walk backwards until I reach the side of my bed. I let out a yelp as my vibrating phone falls off of my nightstand. The plastic lands on the floor and breaks the overwhelming silence.

It's … Vinny? Why is he calling me from his room? I answer. "Lili?"

"Vinny, come and get me."

"You're making a fuck ton of noise. Shut up. You can come to my room if you need — just be … quieter."

I can't. There is no way I'll make it alive down the hallway. I stay silent.

"God, Lili. Seriously? Gimmie a sec."

I listen to the sound of his footsteps in the hallway.

XVIII.

You shouldn't be reading all that demon and magic bullshit, Lili. It was bad before, but you're definitely losing it now."

Vinny sits on his bed, counting little red pills stamped with a bull. "Red Bulls," five hundred of them. I sit on the bed beside him and grab a small baggie. With my eyebrows raised, I wait for his direction.

"Twenties, then tens, then fives. Keep them separated."

I get to work.

"I know, but I'm kinda damned if I do and damned if I don't. I'm just reading. I'm not practicing, or doing voodoo or anything. I know it's not happening to you, but aren't you in the least a bit curious as to why the fuck I'm like this? I just want answers."

"About a year ago, there was some Asian kid who got dismembered. It was on the news. Morning commuters found his body parts strewn around downtown. A leg on Sixth, his torso in a dumpster somewhere in Chinatown, a hand on the sidewalk in front of the court house, blah blah, blah. News said he was a good kid, good family. All the bullshit. But he didn't get chopped up for nothing ... "

I continue to listen even though he's stopped talking, and wait for him to fall onto the point of his little story.

"My point is, if you're messing with bad shit, there's gonna be bad shit. You should — "

"Just pray the evil away? Or pretend like it's not happening?" I don't wait for a response. "You know what's really fucked up? I think Mom and Dad know about me. I think it's too late. I'm not gonna get help from them. I think they're gonna kick me out."

"That sucks, Lili ... " His eyes are full of guilt. He can live comfortably in his own double life of drugs, sex, and violence on Fridays, and church on Sundays, while I can't get away with anything. One way or another, I will be punished.

"Thanks, Vinny. You wanna get me? You should throw a couple of these my way." I wink at my brother and hold up a baggie I've filled up with five pills already.

"You want all five? You're going to do five? Christ, Lili! I don't think — " I can tell he is choosing his words carefully now. "A person like you shouldn't do drugs. If reading books opens you up to scary-as-shit hallucinations, I don't even want to think of what you'll see on this stuff. No, no drugs for you."

"Boo." Even though I know he might be right, I still slip the baggy into the waist band of my shorts first chance I get, tell him thanks and go back to my room. I am sure I can put myself to bed. "I have some stuff I can read." I give him a playful smile before closing the door behind me.

My nightmares are more frequent; the shadows are more invasive. My hallucinations are no longer confined to the darkness. My dreams are becoming more lucid, and I have started to see more. I know now that beyond the fire and the darkness, there is a forest, thick and dense. There are others with me, others around me, all playing a role in my nightmare. When I wake up, there is a dark shadow at the end of my bed, unmistakably grim.

On those happy thoughts, somehow, I am able to sleep. When I wake, I glimpse down at my phone. It's only 4:30 p.m. My mom and dad will be home soon. *How did I sleep all day?* We haven't talked since after what happened at church, after what I heard them say. If I want to get out of here without having to see them, I should start getting ready to go out with Justyne. Thoroughly convinced I am not as bad as I feel, I get up. I need to put away the books that litter my bed. I would rather my parents' find the stash of shrooms in my desk than my secret library.

Since she gave me the two books nearly four years ago, I have ritualistically copied down pages of notes on anything resonating with me, searching for a way to understand without putting myself in a vulnerable position. Justyne helped; she had rewritten ceremonial practices, spells, and chants, all to help me figure out the what and the why of the dreams, the shadows, Ephryium, and the bumps in the night.

Last night, I finished reading a book published in the late 1700s by a renowned Italian demonologist, occultist, and scientist. The whole philosophy of the book grabbed me and gave me the clarity I needed. I had written down a couple of paragraphs from the book that stated:

" ... *many early occultists would disagree, spiritual ritual was relatively unnecessary to fulfil the everyday workings of genuine magick and dark art practices. That one has no need to denounce God or put together elaborate ceremonies to invite spirits of another realm into a practitioner's presence. The balance between creation and destruction, and the romanticism of religion and spiritualism has long since been contrived for human emotional and spiritual stability ...*

"*The veil between the spiritual realms is relatively thin. A practitioner only has to open themselves to demonic presence and influence for the invitation to be accepted. The exception being made in the cases of demonic unions and forced spiritual progression and regression … "*

I figure if I am going to invite a spirit in, maybe it would be too intense to invite all of my craziness to the door. But Justyne has a brother that I'm sure she wouldn't mind seeing. It gives me the opportunity to start small, and show my appreciation to her for all the help and support she's given me.

As I pack up my notebook, I hear a noise from my closet. While turning to find the source, I hear it again. Someone, *something* is in my closet. The white noise fills my ears.

"I'm getting in the shower."

Yup, fuck this. I can't stay here.

I exit quickly.

I run the hot water, drop my clothes on the floor, and step into the steaming shower. Every time I lean my head backwards to wet my hair, it's as if something is just at the edge of the shower curtain, peering in at me. Startled by the intrusion, the *feeling* of intrusion, I quickly pull the shower curtain back and inspect the bathroom thoroughly for goblins hiding under the sink or behind the toilet. No one is there.

I work a lather onto my body. The anxiety — yes, of being in the shower — subsides. I start taking deep breaths, calming myself. It's no use; I imagine something … Someone? Is stepping closer, coming for me, intentionally not making a noise, to catch me off guard. I'm being watched. I can feel it. A part of me can see myself through someone else's eyes.

I jerk the curtain back once more. Again, no one is there. But the feeling doesn't go away. My slow, deep breaths — to ward off the fear my imagination is creating — become hard and fast, and encourage my mind to spiral out of control. As the water cascades off my face and streams down my body, I see a shadow.

The shadow plunges the room in darkness. The only illumination left is myself, alone, under the water.

I am about to be swallowed.

The shadow pulls back for an instant before it rushes forward, consuming me. I scream and reach out to grab the curtain for support. I lose my balance and fall. One ring at a time gives out under my weight. As I fall backwards out of the tub, I try to spot where I'm going to land.

I slam down onto the cold floor. Pain shoots up my arm as I slide across the slick tile. My head connects with the wall, sending starbursts into my vision.

You can die like this, you know.

I gawk in horror. The demon stands over me, dripping with blood, every muscle bulging, every vein exposed, as if it had been skinned. It is no victim. It stands strong, with broad shoulders, and hands hanging by its sides, each long, pointed fingertip three times the length of a man's. Its hollowed eyes are portals into an abyss. Its skull does not end at the top of its forehead; it has grown into a crown of bone, from its raw and burnt flesh. The mouth opens in a painful gape, as if the skin is being torn apart, one vein, one fibre at a time.

Time slows as the blood drains out of my face. My body goes cold. I choke, and my breath fogs in the air. I search for anything, a sign, a message, in the deep socketed. It starts to scream, this high-pitched scream that curdles my blood. It bends down to face me. I close my eyes tightly and tuck my head in, surrendering to the screaming that pierces my body, my soul.

The door to the bathroom slams open. The steam dissipates, cool air rushing in to replace it.

"Lili? LILI?" My mom's thin hands firmly wrap around my arms and shake me.

I don't want to open my eyes. I'm petrified of what I might see. But when I do, I see my mom on her knees beside me, still dressed in a suit. She continues to scream my name, asking, "What happened? What's wrong? Lili! Talk to me!"

The shrill scream rings in my ears, louder than ever. I lay my head down onto my mom's lap and bring my knees to my chest.

"What's wrong wif her?" Rocco holds onto the door frame, genuinely concerned.

"Rocky, go get your Daddy. Right now." Mom is crying when she turns back to me. "Baby, what's wrong? Lili, you need to tell me what happened."

It's me. It's my voice. It's my scream. I stop and lunge onto my mom, holding her tightly. I cry and bury my face into her shoulder.

"Shut the door." My voice is hoarse. My throat hurts. The adrenaline is subsiding, and I feel pain in my legs.

Mom reaches behind her and swings the door shut, leaving us alone.

I whisper, "I'm going crazy! What is happening to me, Mom? I'm seeing things. I think I'm going to lose myself to this. Do I need to go on drugs? Mom, I'm so scared." I lose my breath. My eyes sting as another wave of sobs forces me to retreat back onto her shoulder.

She says nothing. She rocks me back and forth, staring at the wall. I'm suddenly hit with an epiphany: *she knows*.

I pause, to control the anger welling up inside of me before I snap. "You know what this is."

"What? What do you mean?"

Pushing away from her, I point accusingly at her. "I know you know! I heard you talking to Dad! You know it's getting worse! You have to tell me!"

Waiting. Waiting for anything. Tears fill her eyes, but she

says nothing.

"You know what's happening to me. You knew before, too. How could you? How could you pretend to not know? To punish me?" I can't control my voice; it wavers between a whisper and scream. Finally, as I break emotionally, it cracks. I am so hurt. So betrayed. Tears overflow from my eyes despite me desperately needing to hold them back. Straightening my shoulders, I shake my head at her in disbelief, in disdain.

She lowers her gaze to her lap and wrings her hands. Tears drop, leaving little, dark stains on the thighs of her pants. This is her chance. This her chance to be with me, to save me, to say something! The silence is heart-breaking, for the both of us.

I get up, grab a towel, and wrap it around my body. "Move. I'm leaving."

She slides off her knees and onto her butt, her head bobbing up and down, crying without a sound. There is enough room for me to open the door and leave.

I bend down behind her before leaving her in the bathroom, and whisper in her ear, "Oh, poor you."

My dad is coming down the hallway with Vinny and Rocco hurrying right behind him. "Lili? Was that you screaming? What's the matter with you? Where's your mom?"

I walk past him, not saying a word.

He makes room for me to pass, but stares at me, expecting an explanation. "Where's your mother?" When I don't respond, Rocco and my dad open the bathroom door. "Carmella? What happened? What's wrong with Lili?"

Vinny leans on the wall next to my door. "Bad trip?" he asks with a smirk.

Not in the mood, bro. "No, she's a bitch. I'm getting out of here."

"Hm, sounds like a period problem to me."

I give him the stare of death. He raises his hands to surrender and walks back down the hallway.

I should have stayed. Made her tell me. I should go back, dig deeper. I want to scream at her. I want her to tell me everything I know she knows. I want her to say sorry for abandoning me. I want to leave. I never want to come back. I take a deep breath. I can't do my make up while I'm this mad; I'll end up looking like a whore. *Ha!* Maybe I want to. Maybe tonight's the night I just don't give a fuck. Tonight's the night I give in. Or do I mean give up?

I already know me leaving is going to be met with opposition. I literally have never left my front door without opposition. No one trusts me here. I guess I have never given them a reason to.

With who? With what? Why? How long? I never have any truths for them, and after a while, I just get so sick of lying.

I stop short of swinging my closet doors open to pick out some clothes for the night. My hands hover over the knobs, becoming sweaty and twitchy. I stare at the doors intensely. This is what I am reduced to: I am scared of the boogie man in my closet?

No!

I need to empower myself.

My home. This house.

This place, my room, my family.

This is — *was* — my sanctuary. My place to hide. To be alone. To be protected when I feel vulnerable. No matter what angsty teen problem I have with my parents, or how hypocritical I am as a Jehovah's Witness, I am loved in this house.

I *was* loved in this house.

This place scares me now. It's dark and violent.

It hides betrayals and secrets from me.

I can't take a goddamn shower without shitting my pants. I

have seen enough scary movies, read enough scary books to know I need to get the fuck out, or burn it all down.

But something tells me it wouldn't make a difference. In the back of my mind, in a thought not yet properly formed or articulated, I know. I know when I leave, it will leave with me. But right now? I want to believe I am setting myself free. I want to feel free.

I finally place my hands on the knobs. Whatever is in my closet or in this house, there is nothing scarier than me. I pull the doors wide open to reveal …

My clothes. I roll my eyes and shake my head, mocking my stupidity. I pull on a pair of black leggings, a black wife beater, and my knee-high stiletto boots and a hoodie. My time is running out. I rub off the pink lipstick I previously applied and put on red lipstick in its place.

I want to eat before I leave. Maybe Justyne can bring me something. I call her. It rings a couple of times before she picks up. There's a lot of noise in the background. I can hear the rev of a bus engine. She is either on the bus or one just passed by.

"Hello?"

"Hey!"

"Oh, hey. What's up? You're not bailing, are you?"

"Nope, on my way. Where are you?"

"On my way home. Just went to visit my mom. I have so much to tell you! She totally freaked out. I think she had something — "

"Hey!" I interrupt.

"What?"

"If I don't leave now, I'm not gonna be able to go. I just need to know if I should pick up something to eat or do you wanna have dinner with me?"

"Awww, Lili, are you askin' me out?"

0

"I am, you sexy bitch. So? What'll it be?"

"Yea, come over to my dad's. I am sure he has … something. If he doesn't, we can pick something up."

"'K. See you soon. Bye."

I'd have to literally run out of the house. Peeking down at my boots, I think twice about them. *No.* No fucking way I could stay on my feet in these running down the stairs. The image of me falling down, hitting the bottom, then dragging my body out the door, determined to leave, makes me laugh.

I chuck my phone into the bottom of my bag, pull off one boot at a time, and tuck them under my arm. *Ok, here it goes.* I open my door as slowly as possible, saying a little prayer to the door gods for it to open without creaking. It does. But only a little bit.

Stealthing it down the hallway, I take one stair at a time, plotting where I'm going to put my foot before it actually touches down. If there is even just a tick of a noise, I lift my foot and place it down in another spot. Although my initial thought had been to run, this was a job that needed finesse. I check out the sitting room and the front foyer from the top of the stairs. The lights in both rooms are on, but as each room is revealed one footstep at a time, I see they are both empty. I hold my breath until I'm able to let out a huge sigh of relief. I'm in the clear.

Bolting out the door, boots still under my arm, I don't look back until I'm several street lights away from my house. The house stays put and doesn't chase me.

XIX.

Leaning against a street light, I put my boots back on, and then walk to the park path a block down. I stick in my ear buds. I'd stay in the land of Marilyn Manson till I got to Justyne's.

The park is unlit. Not pitch dark, but dark enough to hide in. I hesitate, rethinking my path. Fuck it. I live in a pretty good neighbourhood. If I run into anyone, it's most likely not going to be Tommy-the-pecker-puller, but low-income-housing kids from the bottom of the street, hiding in the bushes and drinking forties.

In that case, I'll demand a squatter's tax and make them share. Those kids are rough, but only in ways of upbringing and environment; the guys I have actually gotten to know are loyal, goodhearted, and probably wouldn't try to fuck me if I passed out drunk. Obviously, the boys I've been exposed to haven't been the highest quality if they are rated on a "Will Not Fuck Me If I Pass Out" scale.

I pull my hood up and stick my hands deep in my pockets.

The music blares in my ears. I should have taken the street. There would have been lights, traffic, things to see, people to see me, people I could disappear from. There was no one here to witness me not being here. Suddenly so alone, I pick up my pace. My chest tightens.

I feel like at this very moment, behind me, someone is coming for me at full speed. With my ear buds in, the bass going, I strain to hear over the music. But it isn't about hearing something coming. It's about *knowing* something is coming.

What the fuck?

My ankles buckle as I break into a run. I try to scream, but my throat is cold and burning from the night air. I am too panicked to function properly. THIS is why girls are always falling over themselves in horror movies! Even though the killer is barely at a brisk walk, they are able to keep up with this fumbling, blubbering piece of meat that's about to be slaughtered. Oh God! That's me. Fuck my brain! I did myself in.

I trip, landing on my knees. I know immediately that I have ripped my pants. My knee is bleeding. Fuck! I give two more fucks for having such shallow thoughts about wrecking my outfit before I die.

My arms shoot up from under me, ripping out my ear buds. I hear the slapping of heavy feet, coming impossibly fast. It's got me.

I flip over to face it. My whole body is shaking, tears streaming from my eyes, my breath laboured and forced. I don't feel as if I am getting any air into my lungs. Blinking to clear my eyes, I see the canopy of the trees, the blackout of the sky. My fists ball into a white-knuckled clench.

I see nothing. My heart pounds in my ears. I clench my jaw and scan the park, squinting into the shadows beyond the trees. I relax my face. I want to scream again, out of embarrassment and frustration, but I reconsider. I have already screamed a couple of times in an unlit park; it's questionable what kind of attention I am drawing out here. Raising my knee up to my chest, I cuss as my leggings split a little bit more. My knee is bleeding and raw. I let out a hiss.

Rough night. Fuck it. I am going to sit right here and turn this shit around. I am not walking another step until I do. I reach into my bag and pull out a tin of Altoids. I open it and grab a joint and a Bic out. I was saving it — but this is an emergency situation. I just narrowly escaped my own imagination.

Flicking the Bic, joint between my lips, sitting in the middle of a park in the dark, I smoke. By the time I toss the roach into the grass, I am level-headed and relaxed enough to push myself up and wobble out of the park to my bus stop.

Just as I emerge from the path onto the sidewalk, my bus pulls up. That's more like it. The doors slide open. An unimpressed overweight man sits in the driver's chair. The fluorescent-lit and buzzing aisle of the bus is empty. I turn my attention back to the driver, swinging my bag in front of me to start digging for fare.

"Don't worry about it. I won't tell if you don't."

I don't think twice. "I won't. Thanks."

I walk to the back of the bus, going up two steps to sit in the last row. I scoot over to sit beside the window so I can prop my legs on the bench in front of me. Putting my ear buds back in, I close my eyes and plan to hide out for the duration of the trip.

I'm woken with a jolt. My legs have slipped, and I am lurching forward. Quickly throwing my hands up, I catch the seat in front of me before my face does. I take in my surroundings and remember where I am. I'm so cozy. The heater is blowing on me. The bus is filled now. No one glances in my direction. No one makes eye contact. I catch my reflection as I turn to stare out the window. My mascara and eyeliner are little black rivers caked onto my face. The red lipstick that I applied so perfectly is smeared. I look like shit.

Shifting my focus outside, I search for landmarks. I'm close to Justyne's. I won't have time to fix it before I have to get off. I roll my eyes. I can't even handle it. Didn't I just say that this night was turning around? And now I'm the weird, wrecked girl sleeping in the corner of the bus. Surveying the passengers, I try to determine who has seen me in my current state.

They all have. Haven't they?

Turning back to the window, I duck my head low to reduce the glare from the lights overhead and use the window as a mirror, tracing my finger along my bottom lip, wiping off the smeared, red stain. I use both hands to give my face a dry-hand wash, trying to take off as much of the black streaks as I can. Leaning forward, I get as close to underneath my eyes as possible. My focus goes in and out, like an adjusting camera.

Pulling my head back, I see a speck on the outside of the window at eye level. As I lean in to examine it more closely, it drops in a fluid motion, staying with the reflection of my right eye. I'm not able to make it out. I lean closer still, nose nearly touching the glass. I realize it's not on the outside of the glass. It's on the rim of my eye.

Slowly bringing my hand up to my eye, I am finally able to make out what it is through the blurriness of my reflection in the window. My finger hovers over a tiny spider. Two legs emerge from underneath my skin. Eight little eyes stare at me. My mouth opens just enough to let out a helpless whimper. My eyes lose focus on the spider wriggling its body out of my eye socket to focus on the other side of the moving bus's window.

Empty, black eyes are fixed on me. The same raw and bloody face that hovered over me in my bathroom hangs in the air in front of me. My mouth trembles as its jaw unhinges, tearing its flesh apart. The long pieces of meat are finally stretched as far as they can go. They snap. The jaw falls loosely, releasing a horde of demonic spiders at me. They hit the window with such force that it cracks, shooting everyone's glance my way at the exact moment I lose my fucking mind.

My entire body flies to the other side of the bus, hitting one person with my flailing legs and landing on another. In my fit of hysteria, I punch at my face, trying to kill Satan's spider who has made a home in my eyeball.

The passengers watch in stunned silence. Eventually, the person I'm having a fit on pushes me off their lap. I land on the floor, a mess of screams and random words like,

"SPIDERS!"

"FUCKING SHIT!"

"HELP!"

"HES GONNA GET ME!"

"Uhh, ma'am? Ma'am? I'm going to have to ask you to calm down, or you're going to have to get off at the next stop."

Bringing my head up, I survey the bus. Everyone avoids my eyes. It seems as though I have made them uncomfortable.

"What's wrong with you? Don't you see?" I motion to the cracked and bloody window I was sitting next to only a few moments ago.

Using the benches on either side of me, I carefully bring myself to stand. The bus screeches to a halt, sending me toppling down the stairs again. I belly-flop to the floor, winded and sniffling. I put my arms underneath me and push myself up, craning my head to see out the bus's windshield. It's standing in the road. The headlights illuminate every black vein running through the tall, lean, muscular body. It turns its broad shoulders to face the bus — me — head on.

"FUUUUUCK!" I am lost inside my screams as I scramble underneath a bench to hide. The steps sound faster. I close my eyes tightly, burrowing my head into my arms. The footsteps come closer, then stop.

"Ma'am? You'll need to get off the bus now. Ma'am, if you don't get up from underneath there, I am going to have to remove you forcefully."

Fuck that.

"Fuck you!"

"Sorry, ma'am."

He grabs my ankles, drags me from under the seat, and lays me out in the aisle. I'm yanked to my feet and shoved to the open door of the bus.

"No, please! Please! NO!"

I prop my feet on either side of the door frame and push back. I struggle in amongst these indifferent strangers, pleading for my life. It's for nothing. My legs give out, and I am pushed out the door, onto the grass. The doors close behind me. The engine blows hot air out from underneath the bus, spraying my back with warm road dust. I sputter, cough, and fall into the fetal position. I stay like this. I feel safe. Face down in the dirt, I cry.

Turning my head slightly, I let the amber street light into my cave of darkness. It shines down on me, brightly reminding me that I have places to run. I'm not alone. *Justyne.* I'm so close.

The demon looms over me, eclipsing the street light with an amber halo around its head. Kicking my legs, I try to get up and run, to not be so helpless. But I am. I don't even muster a cry before its sharp hand comes down on me, throwing me into a vision of flames.

The way that the fire swirls and sways, a blur in front of me, I grow lightheaded and disoriented. I'm lying on my back. I shut my eyes to find peace, but now it feels as if I am spinning out of control. I force my eyes open again. When I do, everything has taken on a new life. The cracks and pops of the fire echo into the chill of the night, releasing embers that glitter on the dark backdrop. Tall trees tower over me, sheltering me, giving me a sense of being inside, somewhere secure.

I'm deep in the woods.

I search past the fire surrounding me, down to the forest floor.

There are bodies everywhere: shining, reflecting the warm light of the fire. Lying in amongst the trees on a bed of moss, they line the ring that confines me. Their bodies are writhing, entwined like snakes, moving back in forth in carnality. Animalistic moaning fills my ears. A congregation of every sexual appetite is alive in front of me. Hungry mouths, gaping assholes, juices flowing steadily from every orifice. Man, woman, beast, and child, all in a rapture of Earth's darkest delights. I, in the centre of it all, exposed and naked.

The whole scene gives off such an intoxicating energy, I am woozy again. It's hard to stay focused, to keep my head up. On the brink of vomiting, I try to regulate my breathing, try to make sense of what I'm seeing. A savage wail severs all thought, startling me back to attention. I look over the orgy in front of me and watch as a beautiful porcelain woman emerges from the mist beyond them, out of the trees that envelope us.

Us? Am I with these people? Am I part of all of this? Why am I naked? I sincerely hope the vision doesn't have me wandering the street naked, as well. That this only going on in my head, just demon orgies in my head.

As she glides across the garden of people, her black eyes never leave me. I realize I am watching myself. She gently raises the bloody scythe in her hand, bringing it down violently on a man's neck, washing the lustful crowd in blood. He slumps down onto the earth, the woman on top of him still rocking her hips back and forth, hungry for more.

Another crowd of women, covered in blood, crawl toward the body on hands and knees, hungry and savage. They stab the body with knives and daggers, bathing in the blood, chanting and moaning words I don't know in a language I do not recognize. The sexually charged scene is being taken over by something even more heinous.

Screams, moans, the sounds only carnage can make. The sound of a massacre, and of those enjoying themselves, all of these things pound inside my head.

The woman stands unmoving in front of the fire, her glare boring into me. I'm transfixed by her. I watch as her face mutates from intensely tranquil to black and demonic. Her skin chars as she steps into the fire, emerging as the red beast.

With outstretched arms, it charges me. Crawling in-between my legs, forcing its weight on top of me, pinning both of my arms above my head. It gives off a rotten stench and warmth that I am both repulsed and comforted by. Its face lowers closer to mine. Bits of flesh hang down from it, just brushing my skin, leaving me wet with blood. Its deep black eyes, level with mine, are void and dark. They give off a sadness so profound, I cringe in sympathy for this creature that is readying itself for me. I am readying myself for it.

Breaking our focus on each other, I study its body, its crown. Through the thick layer of dried blood, I catch glimpses of the clean, white bone beneath. Then on to its long, muscular arms, holding me down. When I come back to its face, I am overcome with a craving, an all-consuming desire to be fucked. I inhale sharply at the epiphany of my new infatuation and devotion. Something warm and enticing pushes up in between my legs.

I use the grips it has on my wrists as leverage to push myself down, forcing myself open on just the tip of what is a hard and massive beast unto itself. I whimper in pain as the grip on my wrists tightens. I'm suddenly impaled, spread open to my absolute limit. Then a little bit more. Every pore, follicle, and fibre of my being is injected with ecstasy and then washed over in cold tingles, starting at the point of penetration that pulsed within, lubricating itself, readying for something more, some-thing harder. My body shakes with excitement. My arms lose all strength as this cold shiver makes its way up to my shoulders, then my face. I open my mouth and let out a deep moan, closing my eyes. I hunger for more.

But when I open them again, the vision is lost. I'm lying on my back, in the grass on the side of the road with the street light casting its amber light down on me. Propping myself onto my knees, I look around. The street is quiet; most house lights are on. Justyne's house is only twenty meters away.

I'm so close.

I'm not going to make it.

Ephryium's face eclipses the light. My head falls back. I welcome the dark.

XX.

JUSTYNE

Calgary, Alberta
June 20th 2003
7:16 p.m.

*J*ustyne yanked the covers up past her knees. She couldn't get comfortable, but there was no comfortable way of doing this. This was strange.

"Brian? Can you hear me? Are you here with me?"

What did she expect? An answer? The ghost of her dead brother to appear in front of her just like she remembered him? She sat in awkward silence, but tried again.

"I went and saw Mom today. I brought you up. I said you were my guardian angel. She freaked the fuck out on me. The orderlies had to come in and strap her to her seat again. It really scared me. Why would she be so upset? Brian?"

Pulling the blanket up, she tucked it under her chin, as if to protect herself from the embarrassment of being alone and feeling abandoned.

"God, I miss you. I wish — "

The sound of a loud bang at the front door cut her off. She waited to hear what came next, hoping it wasn't her dad or a drunk version of him. The thought flitted through her mind that it could be Brian. It made her even more scared, which confused her. She thought she'd be happy, excited even, to find him at her front door — hadn't she just asked him to come? She changed her mind. It wouldn't be good. Would it?

There was another bang, this time with more force behind it. The wall at her back shook. Her shoulders rose to her ears, but she was no coward. She got off her bed. Just bad timing was all: attempting to contact the dead followed by someone knocking like an asshole while she was alone.

The sound of glass breaking, making tinkling sounds as it hit the floor, made her take a sharp breath and hold it.

"Oh, fuck," she whispered as she let her breath out.

She tiptoed out into the dim hallway to see the light spilling from the stairway to the front door downstairs. She moved slowly, not sure if she wanted to see who was down there. Were they already inside? It couldn't have been the window on the door that broke; it was big, would have made more noise.

Maybe the side window? They could have unlocked the door.

"Hello? Who's there? Dad? You OK?"

Nothing. Terrifying silence.

She took another deep breath. The floor moaned beneath her feet, ripping into the silence as she peered down the stairs at the doorway. A silhouette stood at the door. Surprised, she immediately pulled her head back into the shadows. The thought entered her mind that even though the glance had been brief, it had only been a silhouette she had seen. If the person was outside, they would have been standing underneath the porch light ... the light was behind them ...

There was a creak in the floorboards downstairs. Justyne crouched down. She needed to peek again. In her head, she repeated a mantra of being strong, handling everything head on, not being scared. Adrenaline pumped through her veins one heart beat at a time. She peered down the stairs.

Yes. Yes, there was definitely a person inside. And they had not moved from that same stance they'd been in when first she'd seen them. The dark figure stood stiffly with its arms down by its sides. It was tall ... was it wearing boots? It was! Long wavy hair surrounded its head, coming down past its shoulders.

"Lili?"

With a huge, booming stride that shook the entire house,

the dark figure sprinted up the stairs, like a tarantula leaving its den. The figure crept off the stairs and began to scale the wall. It was above Justyne when it pounced off the wall at her. Pushing her down to the floor, it straddled her, first grabbing one wrist and then the other, placing them just above her head. Lili's face was clearly visible now. She lowered herself closer to Justyne. Her eyes were vacant, while the rest of her face was covered in dirt and blood, makeup running down her cheeks.

"Lili! What the fuck happened to you? Lili! Get off of me."

Lili held strong on top of her, breathing raspy breaths onto her face.

Justyne's eyes widened in fear as a line of blood cleaved Lili's face. The skin began to part in two, another visage emerging from beneath. Driving her hands into the floor in an attempt to get away, she found herself powerless to keep from choking on the blood that was spilling out of Lili. Justyne screamed in fear and panic as Lili's green eyes bubbled and popped, sliding down her face in a milky ooze. Left in her sockets were two black voids Justyne couldn't look away from.

Horns, or at least what Justyne thought were horns, crunched through Lili's skull, protruding upwards. She couldn't handle anymore. She closed her eyes tightly, wailing and screaming, still struggling to pull her arms free from the long, sharp fingers gripping her, holding her down to the floor.

Closing her mouth to swallow, only for an instant, she felt soft lips on hers. Her eyes flew open. She stared into black eyes, alive and enticing, even gentle. Lili was on top of her. The grip on her wrists had loosened.

She gawked at Lili's face, pale, but alive. She was beautiful. She was terrifying. Justyne's cautious eyes never blinked. Neither did Lili's.

Slowly, Lili let go of Justyne's wrists. They examined each

other, Justyne searching for the friend she had trusted for so many years, and Lili staring right into her soul. She got to her feet to stand. This was not Lili anymore; she was in danger, grave danger. She needed to get away.

Calmly rolling onto her stomach, Justyne began to creep towards the stairs. She would throw herself down them if she had to.

"Justyne?"

The voice was unexpected, instantly making her nostalgic for her childhood. She had asked for this. Turning to confirm her thoughts, to see a dark profile that was unmistakably Brian's standing in her bedroom.

"Justyne? What am I doing here?"

Pushing herself to her feet, Justyne let her fear die away to her curiosity. "Brian? I didn't — what's happening?"

The figure stayed away, back in the darkness of Justyne's room. Her eyes darted around the hallway, where had Lili gone? Moving deeper into the shadows, Justyne took an unsure step closer to her lost brother.

"You don't want to see me. Keep your memories and stay back. You shouldn't have called me. This is wrong."

"Brian! Let me see you! I miss you so much. I have so many — " She reached out to touch him. His cold dead hand shot forward abruptly and seized hers tightly, too tightly.

He squeezed her hand as he stepped out from his cover to reveal himself. His face dangled in shreds around his mouth. The wounds of his accident revealed the parts of his face, head, and body that were eroded away by the concrete he had slid over. The trauma, the gushing blood, were fresh.

With one hand, he held his jaw up to be able to properly speak. She jerked against his grip, but found herself without strength. Her legs buckled. She abandoned all reason and wrapped her arms around her brother's legs.

"You need to stop. Stop! You need to listen! I'm here because of Lili."

Petrified and sobbing, she whimpered, "Lili? Where's Lili?"

"She's here, Justyne. She's able to openly call out to us. She shouldn't, though. She was here when you called me — that's the only reason why I heard you, why you're able to see me. She wanted to give this to you, but this is bad, not just for you and me, but for her." He put a hand gently on her face.

She closed her eyes tightly and remembered Brian. Piggybacks and underdogs; big brother Brian. Energy surrounded her, a protective and loving energy that seemed panicked.

"Something happened to Lili, Brian. She's, I dunno, I think something got her."

"Something is definitely with her, Justyne. When you called to me, I wasn't the only one that heard. They're all around, waiting for him to let his guard down and sneak in through a side window, and she's here opening the front door for them."

She had no idea what he was talking about. She thought hard. "Ephryium? Are you talking about Ephryium? The ghost in Lili's closet? Is he her angel?"

Brian furrowed his brow and shook his head. "Is that his name, Ephryium? No. He's not an angel."

"Are you my angel?" She looked at him with tears of hope in her eyes.

"Just, you have to let me go." He sighed with strained patience, but he couldn't hide his worry. "I don't know how long I have before they get here. They'll use me to kill you."

Her grip tightened around his legs. She was still the lost, hurting child she was when he died, and she needed an answer. She needed to know.

"No. I'm not your angel."

The room grew colder; the corners, the shadows, deeper.

His time was up.

"You need to help her. She needs to — "

Whispers circulated the room. Brian's eyes widened. "They're here."

"Who?" Justyne had seen the brief look of dread on his face.

"It doesn't matter. It's Lili's problem now. You're the only one I care about." He bent down to her level, and their eyes met. "Justyne, I'm not your angel. I'm your dead brother, and I have never left your side, and I never will. No matter how shitty life is, you are *never* alone. OK, kid? I love you."

The shadows closed in, and he was gone. The air remained heavy and cold, filled with a lingering panic. Justyne's adrenaline subsided, but left her shaking and struggling with every sense of reality.

"Lili?" she whispered, a tremble in her voice.

The bedroom was frighteningly dark. A part of her wasn't ready to admit to what just happened. The image that would be the opening and closing of every nightmare for the rest of her life already seemed like an impossible memory. The other part of her was anticipating no longer being alone or safe with Lili, who was lying face down on her bed.

"Lili? Are you … " *Still possessed seemed insensitive.* " … OK?" she asked. She stared, fearfully, waiting for an answer, worried why Lili wasn't answering or moving, worried that something in the corner of the room had moved, worried that she had actually seen and spoken to Brian and that he came with a warning. A warning about Lili.

Getting onto the bed with her friend, Justyne gently rolled her over. Lili was still pale, but her body radiated heat. She was luminous in the darkness of the room.

"Lili? Can you hear me? Wake up." She gently shook her friend to rouse her. When there was no response, Justyne's heartbeat sped back up. With the ever-present fear of ghosts in the dark and far away whispers, the fear of Lili dying took over. Fumbling through the sheets, Justyne found her phone and began to dial the number her intuition steered her to.

"Hello?"

"It's Justyne. I need help. It's Lili."

XXI.

IGNACE

The following is an excerpt from:

Luc Marchand's

Queens of Hell
An Occult Specialist's Search for the Devils in the Background

Published 1997
All rights reserved.

Ignace, Ontario.
October 25th 1986

They wished they hadn't killed the man so soon. One couldn't kill something again and again, no matter how much they wanted to. Killing the man had been the only unrestrained demonstration of power and freedom that they had experienced in a decade.

The *creatures* walked by the still-hanging, now-stiff corpse and began to hack at one of its arms, the knuckles of which were browned and blackened from scraping through the puddle of blood that had collected on the floor.

Once they had successfully hacked through the shoulder bone, one ripped the rest of the arm off and brought it up to his nose. Mr. Linton had already begun to decay. Blowflies had laid their eggs, but nothing had yet hatched and burrowed into the meat. The creature's eyes met his accomplice's just as he bit into the bicep of the arm, digging his teeth into the grey skin, ripping off a mouthful and swallowing it. He watched him, studying to see if the meat was satisfactory. He tossed him the arm and gave the nod of approval. It tasted like sour pennies and was tough to chew but, for the starved men who had been eating squirrel and bugs for the past seven years, it was mana from heaven.

Had the blood moon been read correctly? Would they be part of the coming? Had everybody been savagely ripped apart, or had there been more survivors that might be searching for them? Had the girl survived? The more they thought about it, the more it settled into their minds they had been cowards to run. It was why they didn't deserve to be treated as humans. An animal would have shown more loyalty to the coven, and to the ritual. That's why they were just pathetic, useless, disgusting *creatures*. These thoughts went unspoken between the two.

They had been sleeping in the cabin for just over a week. They weren't accustomed to the bed or blankets the cabin had provided, so they slept on the floor, taking advantage of the wooden stove at night to provide heat to their naked, dirty bodies.

It was the morning of the eighth day in the cabin, feasting on the scraps of Mr. Linton's body, when they heard the engines approaching.

They crouched behind a rotting log, just to the side of Mr. Linton's cabin. Waiting and watching for the aftermath. They knew — it was packed deep in their memories — they knew in this society, there would be consequences for their bloodlust. People, the law, would come around and need to know *Why?*

No words were exchanged, just glances. They were calm and knew exactly what both of them wanted to do. They went to hide out of sight, to survey the visitors, to see if they could overcome them and once again quench their blood lust. It was hard for the two men — *creatures* — to contain their excitement as they slathered thick, cold muck onto their chests, arms, and face.

Camouflaging into the dense Northern woods, they waited and watched.

XXII.

LILI

Black Diamond Outskirts, Alberta
June 21st 2003

This morning, I woke up in a stranger's bed. My mouth tasted like shit, my head pounded, and my body felt like it had been thrown down a flight of stairs. As I tried to focus on the floral wallpaper, I felt little legs crawling all over my body, covering me in pins and needles. My eyes stung with vague memories of spiders, a demon illuminated in headlights, faces covered in blood, and Justyne.

Justyne. Did I make it to her?

Before the panic set in, a woman came into my room to introduce herself as 'Clairey.' She 'is a friend of my parents,' and this is 'her and her family's home.' I had been dropped off by my father late last night. She told me I am safe, and I should take my time. "By the looks of it, you had a rough go of it."

What am I to do but take her word for it? She had just confirmed I looked as shitty as I feel, she knows my parents' names, and if the roses on the wallpaper weren't screaming 'God-fearing Christian folk,' they might have only been whispering 'this is a new special hell.' Just for me.

A bag lays at the foot of the bed. Mine, I suppose. A ball of frustration and confusion wells up inside my chest. I need to know what happened; it might ease the pain of feeling abandoned.

"Why would you just leave me here?" I cry in my room until I summon enough courage to leave it and ask a stranger to use their phone. I call home.

It's not home.

I can tell through the handset there is just as much stress there. Dad tries to remain cool and calm. "Lili, I didn't leave you there. I think, we think — "

"You did leave me here! Where the fuck am I? Where is Justyne? Is she OK?" I shouldn't have interrupted him. No matter the situation, with my father at least, I should have known respect is paramount. The conversation probably would have gone another way had I remembered that.

He snaps. "What were you doing out with her? You both smelled of drugs! We won't allow you to see Justyne again, Lili. Did she give you the demonic books under your bed?"

"You don't know what you're talking about. If they're demonic, what does that make me? You can't just toss me aside! You can't just dump me here!"

"You bring demons into this house. You bring drugs. We owe you nothing, Lili. We don't know you or what you're doing! You won't be in this house, around Vinny or Rocco, while you are doing these things. You are hanging out with that worldly girl, Justyne. She has been nothing but a bad influence. You need to be away … from everything."

"Let me talk to her, Saul." I hear mom's voice in the background, sounding emotionally worn and short, as if she has been fighting all night. That makes two of us.

"No, she needs to know this. Lili, we won't have you back here. The Rutherfords are good people. *We* have obviously failed you. Maybe you need to hear it from someone else. Jack and Clairey have two daughters around your age — "

"Dad! Come get me! I need to be home. This … these people are not what I need!"

"Daddy, is that Lili? Can she come home if she promises not to be bad? Daddy? Please?" Rocco is hearing all of this. Maybe they are right; maybe it is better if I'm away. My heart breaks a little hearing Rocco's voice asking for me.

"No, Lili is where she needs to be. Lili? Stay there, be respectful, and let them help you. If you put as much effort into bringing yourself closer to God as you have been hiding this double life, your drugs, and your gateways to the demons, you would be happier. You will see you have no need for these awful friends. We love you."

"Yea." The tears pool and stream down my face. Abandoned. I hear a soft click. I wait on the line. If I put the phone down, I have to face the family that has been charged with 'saving me,' who have no idea. I'm not ready for that yet.

"Lili? You still there?" Vinny whispers.

"Mm."

"I told you not to read that shit. You did this to yourself."

"Thanks, Vinny."

"I got your phone. I'm sorry I didn't get to your room before they did. It's been insane here. Mom and Dad are losing their minds."

In my current situation, none of this information is good, or means anything at all to me.

"Justyne texted you. She said she's sorry, she didn't know what to do. I guess she was with you. She called Dad."

Bitch!

"She says she put something in your bag, said it might help you see without ... opening any doors? If it's bud, you need to get rid of it, Lili. It's gonna get you into trouble."

"Anything else?"

"Yea. This sucks. Play it straight, don't fuck up, and get home."

I can't take anymore. My chest hurts. I let out a sob.

"Ok, 'bye."

"Love you."

XXIII.

THE RUTHERFORDS

Black Diamond Outskirts, Alberta
June 22nd 2003

"Now, we don't know how worldly Lili has become, but it is clear that she needs help."

Jack and Clairey Rutherford joined hands over the table while addressing their daughters about their new houseguest. The two girls sitting across the table from them nodded in understanding. They were used to having houseguests like Lili. People who had strayed from God, from the church, who had been tempted into the world by Satan with drugs, sex. From what they had been told, Lili had been reading demonic books and hanging out with worldly girls. Nothing they and their parents couldn't fix with some 'good association' and 'spiritual food.' They would make Lili's relationship with God strong again.

"She smells like cigarettes," Hannah, the younger of the two daughters, complained.

"And she swears a lot. She seems very sad."

"Well, Brooke, she is. We thought you girls could maybe go upstairs, take her some lunch, and do today's Bible reading with her?"

Taking a long sip of her lemonade, Brooke tried to put off what she wanted to say.

"What is it, Brooke? We have certain duties we have to up-hold in the church, and helping Lili is a part of those responsibilities. She's no different than anyone we've helped."

"But she is! Ever since she came here." Brooke looked around the small, yellow farm kitchen. "The house feels … smaller … darker. I don't like going into her room. Actually? I don't even like going near her door! It seems ... it feels ... I don't know ... "

Jack and Clairey exchanged worried glances but said nothing.

"Let's try to stay positive?" Hannah said, breaking the thoughtful silence.

"Good idea, Hannah. On to other news then? Which one of you girls was up first this morning? Your mom said one of you left quite the mess down here. Not a cabinet that hadn't been overturned. You girls know better."

Interrupting her dad, Brooke stood from the table and said, "It was probably Lili looking for something ... "

XXIV.

LILI

Black Diamond Outskirts, Alberta
June 24th 2003

I am terrified as to whether this tumour that has attached itself to me is malignant. What does it want from me? How can I make it all stop? Do I want it to?

Jesus Christ! Is that another spider? My thoughts are interrupted by the tiny invader.

It was only one; a small one, hanging from the ceiling. I squint suspiciously at it. The hairs stand up on my arms, making me itchy at the thought of spiders in my bed, in the covers, crawling on me! This can't be real. I close my eyes and try to will the spider away.

Taking a deep breath, still clutching the tarot cards Justyne gave me, I open my eyes. The tiny little guy hanging from the ceiling is now hanging in front of a horde of long legged spiders. They flood out of a non-existent hole in the wall, spreading along the walls and ceiling, engulfing the room in a shadow, isolating me in fear and panic. I close my eyes, and beg for them to be gone; from the wall and my mind.

I'm a crazy person. I need to tell someone. This is not good.

Clear my mind.

There are no spiders. There are no spiders.

I open my eyes. The room is bright and sunny. The deluge of spiders is gone, and my racing heart slows. Letting out a long sigh and looking down to my cards, I focus my energy.

Please be good news ... let's have a happy reading.

I pull the ten of wands. Mental and physical burdens, hopelessness, and depression. Being attracted to negativity.

Or is it attracted to me?

Choosing to walk the hard road.

Choosing? Really?

Taking in a deep breath, I exhale and draw the eight of cups. Start anew; there is nothing good left for you here. I can't help but roll my eyes.

I'm so glad I wanted to read cards today.

I reach back into the deck of cards, determined to see a better fortune unfold in front of me.

The knight of wands. A new adventure? Or a guy? A handsome and charming guy! *Least likely, kind of a bitch over here.* Trust my instincts. *Well, duh* ... Perfection is an illusion.

Ok, not bad, let's wrap it up. I place the final card over the three cards in front of me.

The Wheel of Fortune. A card of destiny. Something is heading my way, something big. *I think it's already here.*

Whatever is coming for me, I'm not going to see it coming. It will change my course, bringing me closer to what I'm supposed to be doing.

Grabbing the dealt cards, I shuffle them all back into the deck, shrug, and nod. OK.

Who knows? Maybe it's a doctor coming my way, and I'm

off to the loony bin. Maybe my purpose is to live out the rest of this miserable life hearing whispers, scared of shadows, pulling the wings off flies, and lining them up on my windowsill. Or maybe, I'll meet a really fucking hot guy. We'll run away together. A whirlwind romance. Fucking and doing E all day and all night.

Yea, right.

"What are you doing?" I hadn't heard my door open. Brooke and Hannah had already let themselves in and are leaning over me.

"What are those?" It sounds as if Brooke is accusing me instead of asking me a question.

"These?" I say, looking down at the cards in my hands. I'm busted. "These are just cards."

Avoid eye contact.

"Those are not just cards, Lili. You know better than to play with these. The devil speaks to you through these things." Hannah looks deeply concerned for my salvation.

I want to ask her if the cards are still a tool to speak with the devil if I don't believe in the devil, but refrain. So far, my stay at the Rutherfords' country penitentiary has been a relatively smooth one. I took Vinny's advice. I shut the fuck up as much as possible, do what I'm told, and keep my dreams to myself. It's been hard though. I miss Justyne, and with Clairey and the girls everywhere all the time, I haven't had many moments of privacy to call her. I want to call her to tell her I forgive her, and I understand why she needed to call my parents. I can't imagine what happened to her that night. She must have been so scared. Really, I'm the one who should be sorry.

It's hard not to talk about the house, the acreage, how it all seems so big. But at the same time, since I first woke up in my bare, rose-covered bedroom, it feels small, dark, and cold. Like somehow it's on top of me, weighing me down, crushing me. If I can make it, if I can keep things together, I can go back home sooner. I need to convince the girls not to take the cards to their parents.

Getting off my bed to get out from under the girls' judgmental stares, I go to the window and look out.

"My friend gave them to me. I miss her. You know? I just wanted to feel closer to her." Glancing over my shoulder, I'm pleased to see Brooke and Hannah's expressions soften with sympathy.

"Lili." Brooke takes a step forward, holding her hand out. "I know it might be hard to see, but your friend isn't really your friend. She's Satan's temptation. If she was really your friend, she would be a friend to God, too. I think we should take your friend's cards to Mom and Dad. I think they'd want to know about them."

Looking back out the window, I hide my cringe. If Hannah and Brooke achieve a personal victory with me, they could justify keeping this between us. Knowing what I'll have to lose in order to try and keep peace for myself makes me feel sick to my stomach.

"You're right." I say, turning to face the two girls. "I'm trying to make changes here. I need to let this go. I need to let old friends go."

Brooke and Hannah exchange a quick smile. Too quick — I anticipated satisfaction, but it isn't that.

"Let's burn them!" Hannah's eyes are wide with mischief.

"In The Ferns! Oh what a good idea. Lili," Brooke continues, "we could bring all of your Satan worship stuff to The Ferns and burn it. We could have a ritual to say goodbye to your old life and really denounce Satan from your heart. Then we can pray to Jehovah to fill your heart with goodness again."

Jesus Christ! Is this what this family really thinks of me? I'm evil? I have evil … in my heart?

For a second, I wonder who is playing who. The two girls

move quickly, asking me questions like, do I have anything else I would like to burn? Cigarettes? The weed? Books or pictures? Before I can properly answer, Hannah is elbow-deep in my bag.

Her hand comes out holding the notebook I had forgotten about. I rush across the room, fuelled by desperation to save the book, but I realize it will have to go. Maybe it is better I don't have it. If I really do want to follow Vinny's advice, I will need to be convincing.

Brooke is still inside the house finding matches and 'grandma's old Bible,' as Hannah leads me, cards and book in hand, into the forest. To The Ferns.

"This is our spot," explained Hannah. "A place where we can be alone."

"And your mom and dad are OK with that? You being alone?"

Hannah raises her brows. Her tone is contemptuous as she says, "Yes, Lili. They trust us. Brooke and I love to explore this forest. There's a well down that path." She points to a small, worn path through the congested birch trees. "We found the field of ferns when we were really young. We used to play Home Free there."

Behind us, the sound of Brooke fast approaching grabs our attention. If we weren't about to burn all of my shit, I would say the day was beautiful, the forest was magical, and the girls? Mean well.

"Come on, let's go," Brooke says, pushing through us. "I thought you two would be there by now."

We follow her through a thicket. After climbing over the tangle of moss-covered branches, we are in a clearing filled with five-foot ferns.

So this is it.

"We used to play games in here," Brooke starts to explain.

"Crawling around on our hands and knees. There's a spot in the middle we cleared out. We're gonna go there."

Brooke and Hannah place my book and cards in a small pile on the ground.

Clenching my jaw, I try my hardest not to show my resentment for the girls and the situation we are in. Now more than ever do I miss Justyne. I can't hear what Hannah reads; her muffled voice sounds far away from me. The sun, still high in the sky burns brighter, hotter. The breeze dies to nothing; the buzzing of insects fills my ears. Brooke sets the match in amongst the pages. It all happens slowly, like this moment is meant to last forever.

I hear my name being called. The voice is soft, far away. The flames grow, licking at the pages. Another whisper of my name. This time, it's like it is coming from the ferns themselves. The buzzing in my ears grows louder; the sun comes closer, making me sweat.

The pages, my notes, the closest understanding I have ever had of what is happening to me, is on fire. But isn't burning.

"Run, Lili!" Brooke screams.

I can't bring myself to come back down to earth. My eyes stay fixated on the pages that don't burn. The buzzing makes my head pound.

The ferns whisper.

"We fOunD yOu, LiLi."

There is a hard tugging on my arm. Screaming, panic, wasps everywhere.

"Lili! What's happening? Run!"

The sun is no longer in the sky. The ferns, once vibrant green and standing tall to touch the sky, are brown and rotted to the ground. Hannah is gone. Brooke waves her arms madly, protecting herself from the swarm of wasps attacking her.

The book and cards are still aflame, still intact.

I run.

The unmistakable feeling of being chased by something close behind.

Clairey and Jack come running across the yard. I can't stop, can't catch my breath enough to yell they need to run the other way.

Brooke screams from behind me. "Where's Hannah? Is Hannah here?"

Her parents, just as panicked, respond with their own questions. "What happened? What's wrong?"

I keep running to the house. I don't want to know what happened, or how long has passed since Brooke lit the match. There is nothing good for me in that conversation, or here. Or anywhere.

Now far away, I can hear Brooke frantically say, "It's because of her! She needs to leave! Hannah is still there! Hannah is still there!"

XXV.

ARNOLD

Highway 16, Saskatchewan
June 11th 1989
7:26 a.m.

Arnold drove back, past the gas station just outside of Denholm. He saw, laying there under the florescent-lit canopy outside the women's bathroom, his girl's seafoam-green suitcase.

It would probably be a better idea if Arnold passed this stop and drove to the next for his coffee. He would be driving another couple of hours to Battleford and probably wouldn't get home till later in the morning.

He stopped at the next fluorescents, filled his big gulp with gas station coffee, and headed around the building to get to the payphone.

Digging into his pocket, he grabbed a couple of quarters. He pounded in the number. After one full ring and a half, the receiver picked up.

"Hello, lovey."

"What you gone done, Arnold? Hmm, where's the sweet talk comin' from?"

"Oh, no reason. Can't wait to be back home is all."

"Well, where you at?"

"Oh, I found myself a nice quiet spot, Deb. You'd like it here … "

"Arnold Arlington! What are you up to? You sound like a boy who just got his nuts off … Are you fuckin'? Arnold Arlington Tenner, are you fuckin' around with some piece of truck stop pussy?"

"Now, now. Don't get upset. I don't want you to give yourself a headache. It ain't nuthin' like that. I — "

A wail came out of the earpiece.

"Come on, now."

"I swear to god, if you bring home diseases, Arnold. I won't have you!"

"Aww no, no. Nuthin' like that. She was a virgin … "

There was a long draw of silence before Debbie said anything. "What she look like?"

"Awww, Deb, you'd like her. She had shiny blonde hair, and a purdy lil mouth … " He giggled. "Aww, Deb. I made a mess of it!"

"Oh, Arnold. You're such a boy. Finish there an' come home to give me some of what you been givin' your little girl?"

"You betcha. I'll be seein' you soon, love."

"Mmhmm, 'bye you."

Arnold loved Debbie so much. For so long, he had thought he'd be by himself, die alone. It was never even a possibility for Arnold to love. Growing up, he never felt anything — not unless he was killing things. Right away, he knew he found something special in Debbie. The same darkness that hovered over his life like a warm, cozy blanket was a comfort to her as well. They had courted through Junior High in a small town in Saskatchewan. Debbie lived in a single-room cabin down in a valley with her ma, pa, and six older brothers. They were all in the room when he had lost his virginity to Deb. Cheerin' him on. He knew he had found his family. Instead of going to prom, they drove down to the city landfill and lit a dog on fire.

Debbie understood him better than he understood himself. Except for the voice. Debbie was driven forward in her taste for blood and carnage by sadistic curiosity. Bloodlust. He was driven. Just that, driven, as if he were a vessel. But the car can enjoy the ride, too, right? Even this little girl he had burned and buried. If he just wanted to get his dick wet, he had Deb. He could have even fucked a hooker and been done with it. But no, something … something had compelled him to stalk that highway instead of going home from his run. Something had whispered for him to —

Hunt.

That same something. That cozy blanket of darkness. The thing that had consumed him right out of his mother's festering vagina, would chaperone him while he took this life. But taking it wouldn't be enough; he would need to ritualistically humiliate and degrade it as well. As if that were the only way it could be done. There was no sense in it for him. He found it amusing, at the most; an enjoyable pastime. The motivation lay elsewhere.

Arnold drove all the way home with fond thoughts of his night and of Debbie, periodically reaching down into his pocket to thumb the handful of soft golden hair. He would grow erect and excited to tell his wife, to show off his creativity.

XXVI.

North Battleford Outskirts, Saskatchewan
June 11th 1989
8:02 a.m.

He pulled off the highway and drove down the long gravel road leading to the bottom of the valley. He and Debbie lived in the same valley she had grown up in. Her family had long since moved away, but Debbie and Arnold liked it there. Close enough to town if that's where they needed to be, but so far out of the way they could get on with themselves with no bother from anybody.

The fog hadn't lifted from the road yet, but soon his house came out of the mist. Through the window, he could already see Debbie at the stove. Makin' him bacon and eggs, no doubt.

He walked through the door as quietly as possible, meaning to surprise her.

"Go take a shower, then come and eat. You can tell me all about your little girl, too."

He was foiled!

He hugged her from behind, brushed her wiry, greying hair

out of the way, and gave her a kiss on the cheek.

"Eeew, Arnold, you smell like you stepped in shit." She turned to face him then pushed him to arm's length.

"Sorry, hunny. Had me a lil ax-see-dant is all. I want to show you sumfin', doe." He giggled as he presented the lock of hair to her. She reached out and took the hair from Arnold's hand, eyes wide with astonishment.

"Arnold! She wad'nt no bottom feeder! This is white girl hair! Now, where'd you find yourself a lil white girl in the dead of night?" She sniffed the hair. "This hair smells like apples. Green apples, Arnold! No white girl is hanging around in these here parts after dark. She was tidy, taken care of. Did you kidnap this girl? Are we lookin' at trouble?"

Arnold's gaze falls to his feet.

"No, no, it wudn't like dat at all, Deb. She wuz wonderin' out at the truck stop last night all by her lonesome ... Nobody was lookin' after her, I swear it, Debbie. There gonna be no one lookin' for my sweet, young thing."

A moment of silence passed between the two. Arnold waited for the verdict while Debbie made sense of it, accepted it, and finally, as Arnold had hoped, praised him for it.

"Well, well, you little rascal, you." She patted his butt. "I can just imagine what kind of fun an' what-not you got up to," she said, winking at her partner.

He replied with a sheepish giggle.

"Now, go on, go shower. I can only assume that smell is her on you. Although, I wish I had seen it — maybe even have been there witcha — I don't want that smell in my kitchen."

Arnold turned on his heels and called over his shoulder.

"Yes, boss lady."

Debbie had already filled their bathtub with hot water. She loved him. And she was right; he did smell like he had stepped in shit. He piled his clothes on the floor by the door, grabbed a cigarette, lit it, and got into the tub. Laying back and closing his eyes, he inhaled his cigarette deeply, and relived his night once more. The warm blood splashing on his face, the sound of bones breaking. With some, like the skull, it was a crunch, but most others just a *click, click, click*.

Debbie was right; it was apples. He knew she had smelled good, but couldn't place the smell. He just appreciated it was there in place of what he was used to, which would never smell as sweet as her.

After he had taken a leak on her for a second time, he had fantasized about what kind of — he had made up his mind — well-to-do family she came from. She had a ma and pa, and maybe a little brother, too. He imagined fucking and killing them all in one manner or another. It ended with him walking away from a pretty little house, with a small, green, grass yard, lined with a white picket fence. Lighting it all on fire and walking away.

Satisfying what was on the inside.

After Arnold washed and got out of the bath, it warmed his heart to see his clothes were laid out for him on the bed. He went into the kitchen to sit down and eat, and tell Deb about his trip. This haul was a longer one: two weeks. He'd be back now for about two weeks. He would be able to help with the yard, go to the property in town, and do what was needed to be done there; he was sure Debbie would have a whole list of things for him to do. And she did.

She came around him and hugged him, reaching down to give his dick a squeeze.

"I missed you, both of you. You were gone a long time this one. I got bored. We had guests."

On long stints, when Arnold was away for a while or sometimes just outta sheer boredom whether Arnold was there or not, Debbie would take the car into town, pick up a hooker or vagrant, and offer them a meal and a place to sleep for the night.

They would use their 'guest bedroom' as just that: for their 'guests,' who would stay chained to the bed and were fed a cocktail of heroin and methamphetamine, depending on what Debbie or Arnold wanted to do with them. Sometimes, they would host their guests for weeks before they dumped them back where they had found them. Dead, alive, mostly dead … almost always dead.

A couple of times, they had taken up residency in Debbie's garden. The thought had crossed their minds to use their inherited house for guests. It was a central location, convenient. But North Battleford boasted a population of around 13,000 — all at your doorstep and up your ass.

He pulled out from the table and walked the short distance to the door of the guest bedroom, opened it, peered in. There was a huge, rusty, red stain on the bed; dark red spray marks were splashed across the walls and closet doors. A thick trail of blood led from the bed to the doorway in which he was standing. Hand and arm marks came sporadically out of the trail which stained the wooden floorboards.

He turned and sat himself back in front of his plate.

"Have that cleaned up in an hour or two. You helpin'?"

She scoffed at him. "No. Don't go away for so long next time." She rolled her eyes and glanced away, then beamed back at him and smiled flirtatiously, flashing her yellow, snaggle-toothed grin at him. It was reciprocated, so she moved down the list.

"We need to fertilize the garden. Should'a been done months ago."

"I have some shit on my pants you can use … "

"Not funny. While you were gone, the shitter filled up. Needs to be cleaned out. Also, rent's due. Only the Kings paid.

The Stines and the Corbetts aren't answerin' ma calls, so I want you to go collect. Sound good?"

"Sounds good, lovey."

XXVII.

IGNACE

The following is an excerpt from:

Luc Marchand's

Queens of Hell
An Occult Specialist's Search for the Devils in the Background

Published 1997

In 1986, Ignace, Ontario had a population just shy of two thousand people. Even if it fluctuated up and down throughout the next two decades, two thousand people was a peak. But even in its boom, two thousand people were all accounted for: two hundred mill workers; one hundred and fifty students; three RCMP officers; bar workers; gas station workers; the folks who ran the fishing resort at the start of town and the tourists who stayed with them in hunting season; the teenagers and young women who worked at The Burger Scoop; even the small clan of people who collected unemployment. Everyone had their place.

Even Matthew Wilfred Linton, a seventy-four-year old man who had arrived one night in the summer of 1956, purchased land right off the highway, and built himself a cabin between Raven and Sandal Lake. You'd miss it if you didn't know it was there. Matthew had been accounted for.

The horrific events that took place in the cabin thirty kilometres outside of Ignace were only the tip of the iceberg. Ignace's RCMP would spend the next several years quietly uncovering the horrors hidden in their small town, unbeknownst to anyone. They would work even harder to make sure what was lurking in the woods never made it past Ignace borders of Highway 599 and West St.

The *Ignace Courier* would report:

Apparent Homicide in Rural Ontario
Matthew Wilfred Linton. Age 74. Found Dead in Home

Sgt. MacDonald and Sgt. Olson discovered Mr. Linton's body in -his home in an apparent homicide on October 25th at 9 a.m. when the officers performed a welfare check after locals reported him missing.

When asked about the grisly affair, a clerk at TEMPO gas station had this to say: "Old man Linton came in 'ere like clockwork, eh? I knew sumpin was up day two. He dint show up for his steak 'n' eggs an' pack'a Golds. He set the time here. Six a.m., e'ry fu**** morning, eh? Day two! I knew it!"

The Local RCMP has remained silent on the details of Linton's death. Sergeant Olson released the following statement: "Right now, we are doing everything we can to follow up on the investigation. We are asking the local residents of Ignace, and of Kenora County, to please come forward if they think they may have seen something out of the ordinary, or if they have any information pertaining to Mr. Linton's death. It could result in more leads."

When asked about any current leads, the officer responded, "No comment."

XXVIII.

THE RUTHERFORDS

Black Diamond Outskirts, Alberta
June 26th 2003

The past week had been a test of faith for the family. Both Jack and Clairey were nervous to watch their household change. It happened so slowly, so clandestinely, the entire family couldn't put a finger on what had made them all so uneasy. It was a surprise to them that both Hannah and Brooke had seen it first — felt it first. Doors opening. Every single one. Small and odd, but easily forgettable. The morning they woke up to the lights being on, and then the next, and the next ... dismissed.

They hadn't discussed it, but from the very first night Lili slept in their quiet farm house, they all had dreamt of her. Of flames and blood, of a pale, naked Lili walking the dark hallways, entering their room, and standing over them. Waking up to a room that was unnaturally dark, the silence unnaturally loud.

The cold house overflowed with fear. They found it hard to admit that Lili was the cause: polite and quiet, beautiful and seemingly eager to fit in with them. Why were they so scared to go into her room? Behind her bright green eyes was something secret, so full of sadness.

Brooke still hadn't been able to tell Jack and Clairey what had happened to them at the ferns. She only said she and Hannah had wanted to help Lili, then "It wouldn't burn, it wouldn't burn," and "There was no more light, there was no more goodness." She was convinced the swarm of wasps had come because of Lili. Both Brooke and Lili had stayed confined to their rooms. Hannah, stung more times than the doctors could count, had gone into anaphylactic shock and lay in a coma at the hospital.

Although their daughter was hysterical, and adamant about not being left alone in the house with Lili, Jack and Clairey were emotionally drained and knew in their hearts there was just no possible way Lili was responsible for wasps. Knowing Lili heard Brooke's accusations, they went to Lili's room to tell her they didn't hold her responsible.

"We don't think you did anything bad here, Lili. Brooke is upset. We all are. But we think you are an amazing girl. You're like a ball of fire. You have huge potential. But you need to choose sides. It's so important you choose the right side of things."

It was undeniable: a darkness had descended upon the house. As Jack and Clairey drove down the driveway, they saw the darkness seemed to envelope the acreage, as if the moon's light could no longer reach it. But the shadows were not what made them question their decision to leave the girls at the house to go see Hannah; it was the panic they felt. The dread of something coming for them out of the darkness, like there was life in the darkness itself.

XXIX.

LILI.

Black Diamond Outskirts, Alberta

*T*his house makes so many fucking noises.

I sit in my rose-covered room alone. It's almost alright to be in here with just the bedside lamp on. I wish there was more in it, though. More to do, more to look at. Anything to keep me from having to be alone with myself and my thoughts.

I carefully brush the dirt off my notebook and tarot cards, still relieved that I had the courage to go back and get them. No matter how brave I try to force myself to be, I still can't help but find comfort under the covers of my bed. Going back to the place amongst the ferns came with an image of Hannah lying lifeless in Jack's arms. It's not just the image I can't shake from my head; it's the guilt. No matter what Clairey and Jack said, it had been my fault.

Whatever is here, is here for me. The Rutherfords will be collateral damage.

𝕏𝕏𝕏.

BROOKE

Black Diamond Outskirts, Alberta
June 27th 2003
2:56 a.m.

"Brooke."
It wasn't the unknown voice that set her heart racing; it was that she had felt its breath in her ear. It was that when she opened her eyes and sat up, she saw her bedroom door gently close. The corners of her room grew in depth, becoming blacker than black. A small scratching noise came from somewhere underneath her bed. Fear took hold in her throat, and she choked on the words she was only able to whisper out.

"Mom? Dad?"

The dark corners whispered back. She sat in her bed, hearing the disgusting things being said around her. She cowered like a child, praying to her God.

BrOOokE …

MoM And   DaD   Left you
TheY HavE GoNe To SeE HannaAh

You LeFt HeR tO dIe

WhY DiD You LeaVe HannAh?

GoD HatES CowaRds

KiLL yourself.

She clutched the blankets to her chest, fighting to keep them there. Something she could not see pulled them from her hands, leaving her uncovered and vulnerable. The horror of seeing the blanket mid-air, transform into a gaping demonic mouth, the long beast-like teeth within coming together as it spoke shook her to the core.

"BrOooke … GO GET LILI," the words boomed. The room vibrated. With the scratches still coming from under her, she was petrified to leave the bed. But to stay was no longer an option either. The monster had come for her.

Brooke swung her legs off the bed as she tried to escape her blanket's new teeth. The floor was wet with something warm and thick, and she tumbled to the hardwood. Forced to look into the black abyss under her bed, Brooke could feel eyes on her before she saw them. They appeared one at a time, emitting a white light. Enough light for Brooke to see the sheen on the small pointed teeth, to see the pale rotting face of Hannah under her bed.

"Mom! Dad!" Brooke's hands slipped underneath her as she tried to push herself away from the face that hung in the shadows. She screamed for help.

"Lili!"

Brooke watched as two grey, rigor-mortised hands inched through the blood on the floor. She stumbled for the door and lost her footing, slamming into the wood. She struggled with her doorknob, panicking when it wouldn't budge. A cold sweat soaked her nightgown as she began to claw at the door.

"GeT uS LiLi." Hannah's raspy voice came from under the bed.

The walls vibrated; whispers and faint cries of sorrow and pain came from every shadow. Two withered corpse arms splayed in the blood beside her bed, and Hannah's face was now emerging from the darkness, her eyes locked on Brooke.

With the same suddenness by which she had been awoken, with a sharp intake of breath, there was silence. The handle turned in Brooke's hand, and the door swung open. She fell out into the empty hallway.

The silhouette of a horned man stood in front of her window. Brooke's feet shuffling backwards broke into the now overwhelming silence. Two doors down from her room, Lili's door hung open. This was because of her. Brooke knew it. The demons attacked Hannah, and now they were coming for her because of Lili. Well, if they wanted her, they should have her.

As the thought of dragging Lili out of bed and pulling her down the hallway back to her room had crossed Brooke's mind, the hulking silhouette leaped forward and sped across the room. In the moment before it reached her, the doors slammed shut. The sound of doors slamming echoed throughout the house. Brooke fell into a heap of sobs on the floor. Scared and knowing she was alone was becoming too much to bear.

"Lili! Lili! Wake up! Please wake up!"

"YeSsss, open The DooR, BrooKe. BrinG hEr To US."

Brooke looked down the hallway at Lili's bedroom door. It was gone, lost behind shadow. A shadow Brooke knew was alive. Every instinct told her to stay away, while the whispers told her otherwise.

BrInG HeR OuT.

He wOn't   HuRt YoU

As MuCh As We WiLL.

LeT Us   iNNnnNn.

YoU and HannaH   wiLl StAy With   US   tHen.

A draft came up past Brooke carrying with it the stench of rot, and a creaking sound that was familiar. Footsteps on the stairs.

"What are you waiting for, Brooke? She's right through that door. Go get her, and we'll leave you alone." The voice was Hannah's.

Brooke closed her eyes and began to rock back and forth. "I can't. Please. Please stop."

She felt Hannah's warm breath on her cheek. Her breath was so sour Brooke tried to control each sob so as not to breathe it in. If she closed her eyes long enough, it would stop. If she didn't move, it would all go away.

You STuPID LiTTle   SluT!

We ArE GoIng To Make You watch Us

RapE YouR   FathER,

FuCk Hannah's PrEtTy LiTTle   mouth

We waNT LiLi,

NoT YoU.

A barrage of loud bangs came up the stairs, startling Brooke into opening her eyes. Hannah's demonic eyes burned into her. She ran.

"Lili!" She begged and pleaded at the bedroom door, screaming, frantically digging through the swarming spiders, scratching at the wood underneath. Two icy hands wrapped themselves around her ankles and jerked her backwards. Gasping for air, try to get her breath back, Brooke clawed at the floor as Hannah dragged her down the hallway.

"Lili!! Help me!"

She was dragged back into her bedroom, where an unseen hand slammed the door shut. Through the blood on the floor, into the shadows where her screaming stopped and the whispers told her, *"They're all going to die because of you."*

XXXI.

LILI

Black Diamond Outskirts, Alberta
June 27th 2003

"Lili! Wake up, Lili!"

My shoulders hurt. They are being clutched tightly. A rough hand clutches my face.

I'm up. Grabbing the wrist of whoever thinks this is OK, I shout, "What the fuck? Don't touch me!"

"Lili, where's Brooke? Brooke, Lili! Where is she?"

My eyes shoot open to see a red-faced Clairey at my door and a pale Jack sitting on my bed.

Sitting up, I shake my head. "Isn't she in her room? When did you guys get back?"

Clairey's eyes are red and swollen. She's been crying. Looking at Jack's weathered face, I assume so has he. He avoids my eye and quietly asks me to get out of bed and get dressed.

My room is colder than usual after they leave, closing the door behind them. I wrap the blankets around me and get up to peek out the bedroom window. Police cars line the driveway, officers standing beside them talking. One man, standing away from the crowd of uniformed officers, stares at a note pad. He can sense me peering down on him; he stares up at my window for a moment longer than I am comfortable with. I should get dressed.

Voices come from downstairs. Multiple conversations at once. But when I open my door and follow the dark red stain on the carpet leading to Brooke's door, only one conversation stands out. I hear Clairey's voice, shaky and emotional.

"They don't know where she could have gone. We got the call from the hospital this morning, right after we got home and saw that Brooke ... that Brooke — " She cuts off into small sobs, unable to finish the sentence.

A dark stain smears the wood floor in Brooke's room. Under the drying smear are distinct scratches spanning the room to her bed, where I can see they disappear somewhere in the dark.

"What the fuck?"

A round-faced man pops from behind Brooke's door. "You must be Lili."

He steps out into the hallway as I nod, still listening to Clairey's voice downstairs.

"This is just too much. We want to help, but this is too much. Please come get her."

"Do you mind if I ask you a couple of questions?" He digs into his pockets, assuming my answer will be yes.

"I guess." I have questions of my own though. "What happened?"

Glancing up at me from the phone in his hand, he looks surprised. "Well, actually, I was hoping you knew. Where were you last night?"

"In my room."

"All night?"

"Mmhmm."

"What were you doing?"

I lit a bunch of tea lights and read a spell out of a notebook I keep that documents occult, demonic, and spiritual beliefs as they pertain to me. I drew what's called a 'sigil' on the floor for protection and then asked aloud for the spirits haunting me to show themselves.

"Nothing. Read a little bit, then went to bed."

"Read and went to sleep?" He motions with his arm for me to walk back down the hallway to my room. As I walk, I lean over the banister to see if I can see Clairey, but I can't.

"Did you hear anything?"

"Like what?" I ask, turning my attention back to the man.

Reaching past me, the man pulls my bedroom door closed. With his pen, he points out the short, frantic scratch marks embedded in the wood.

"You didn't hear this happening to your door?" he asks.

I can only reflect the flabbergasted look on his face. "I didn't."

"You were in your room, the whole night, and you didn't hear anyone at your door?"

There is nothing I can say here that will help me. The truth was, after I had gone to sleep, I battled my own demons, trapped inside of a nightmare. Hannah was outside my door, whispering, asking me to come out. I could see her, out in the hallway. Her eyes grey, she was decomposing; a living dead girl. Only a glimpse before the walls began to gush blood and bugs filled the room. Ephryium stood at the door. A deep voice had told me explicitly to "keep the door shut."

"I was really tired. I didn't hear anything. After what happened with Hannah ... I just haven't felt well. I know Brooke was really upset about Hannah, too ... " I explain, while keeping my thoughts to myself. "Where are Jack and Clairey?"

He puts down his phone. "They're both downstairs. Thanks for your time."

I can't tell by the way he says 'thanks for your time' if he believes me or not. But from the sound of it downstairs, I'm on my way out anyways.

Police officers fill the kitchen. At the table, Jack and Clairey sit staring at their interlaced fingers.

Without bringing herself to look at me, Clairey can barely speak. "Go ... pack your things. Your ... your mother is on her way."

As the police cars dwindle in numbers in the drive, clouds roll in to cast away the sun and cover the house in its own personal storm. When Jack comes out of the house to see off another handful of officers, I didn't expect him to turn and sit next to me on the stoop.

"I have to tell you something, Lili."

The situation is so fragile. He wears all of his worry and grief on his face. It is a good time to just listen.

"Hannah and Brooke." Tucking his chin in, he turns away from me to hold back a sob. "They really cared — care. They really care for you. My girls are so innocent. But they're strong." He rests his hand on my shoulder. I think he needed to tell me this, to say these words out loud, to reassure himself rather than me. "I don't want you to worry. They'll come back. They will, you'll see."

His eyes give it away that he knows he's lying.

We both know the girls are gone, and they won't be coming back. If the truth is in my eyes, I don't intend for it to be, but he reads me clear as day. We will never know why. We will never know how.

But neither one of us can bring ourselves to say I had something to do with it.

It's a good thing my mom chooses this moment to pull up. A thought like that could drive a man to rage; it could drive a father to kill. It is time for me to go now.

It rains the entire way back into the city. I stay in my head, having conversations with myself. There will be no convincing myself I haven't left that family in shambles. But what about my mom? Would she know? Can I convince her? Or Dad? I silently try to talk myself out of my shame. I empathize for both Hannah and Brooke. I'm scared for them, and I'm sad for their parents to have to go through this, but I'm more scared for me. What did I do?

I have an imaginary conversation with my mom about reading books on magic and bringing things into the house that are spiritualistic or 'demonic.' She tells me I have invited them in. And once they're in, there is no turning them away. A part of me sits, watching the rain hit our windshield, entranced, scared her words might be true. Folding my arms, I shake my head. I push her out of my conversation and tell myself she is superstitious. My whole family is ignorant in a way only religious people are.

Sneaking a quick glance over at my mom, I catch a flash of concern. The way her head tilts back and forth, like she's debating, like she's having her own imaginary conversation. What could she be afraid to talk to me about?

In the dark of night, under the steady thrum of rain hitting the car, I am trapped. Speeding away from one demolition and heading towards another. Simultaneously, the deep voice from inside my nightmare and my mother's voice tell me to 'shut the door.' It's me, though. My mind. That's where all of this lives. There is no escaping this. For anyone around me, there will be no escaping me.

XXXII.

THE BOY

June 12th 1989
North Battleford, SK — 1362 98th Street

"Mum. Mum! Wake up," the little, black-haired girl whimpered, pleading to the woman lying face down on a dark, soiled mattress. "Mum? Did you get food? MUM?" She grabbed her mum by the shoulders and shook her.

She would wish she hadn't.

"Mmfuckingbish, whatthefuck, fuckingpieceofshiii … " The mass of dirty, tangled hair shook back and forth with angry mumbles.

Regretting the decision to bug her mom, the little girl fell off the mattress onto her bum. She quickly scuffled across the floor in a crab-walk to the wall.

She was neglected to the level that, when needing protection, she went to the wall. As if the wall could shelter her from her mother's words, from the violence. It was as innocent as putting her hands over her eyes so she couldn't be seen anymore. And so, her hands came up to her face.

"What THA FACK you want, girl?" Bones loosely wrapped in dark flesh stood over the little girl, who was trying her hardest not to be seen behind her hands.

Neither she nor her brother had eaten for three days. Last night, their mom had finally come home. Peeking out from behind her fingers, she clenched her body, readying herself for the foot aimed at her face.

It's OK; it doesn't hurt anymore. A couple more, and Mum would be tired. Sometimes, she even said sorry. Then she would make them dinner. Sometimes.

Downstairs, the neighbors below lifted their eyes to the

ceiling. The not-so-muffled yelling and the 'moving of furniture' had started. They heard the girl's pathetic little cries. They thought to call for help but stayed silent. Not for fear of 'getting involved' but for fear of exposure. They were no saints ... they had their own set of problems ...

"Always YOU, selfish fucking brat! Me me ME! Do you care what I want?" Mum pounded her skeletal hands into her own face. "I hate you! I hate you! I hate you!"

The little girl reached for her mother. "Mum, I- I-I'm sorry."

"Fuck you!"

From her place on the floor, the girl watched her mother slump back down onto the mattress. She reached into her sack purse and drew out a transparent, browned glass pipe and a lighter. Her mother mumbled to herself incoherently. " ... leave this place ... this stinking apartment ... these bastard, good-for-nothing children .... Welfare! Oh yea, yea, that's right .... That's why I don't kill them ... they could go into garbage bags and into the river ... I get two checks every month ... Every month ...."

The starved little girl dare not move, not make a sound. She wanted to blend into the crusted floorboards as her mom put the pipe to her lips, as she flicked her Bic underneath it, sucking back. She had spied this scene so many times before, she knew her mother was inhaling nothing. Her pipe wouldn't get her there, away from here.

She stiffened as she saw her mother's face grow red with rage, turning to her, lying on the floor. Staring at the little girl with her black eyes. The line of blood streaking her chin, not a deep cut, but the fact it would bruise was enough to make her mom want to kick her in the face again.

"Fuck! I should have taken my shoe off! You can't go to fucking school like that. Those dumb motherfuckers will come give me trouble again." The little girl was used to her mom's garbled snarls.

Their mom glanced over at the sickly thin boy in the corner. He watched her, always wanting something from her. The boiling blood reached her face.

"What's that fucking SMELL? Why does it smell like shit? Fucking animals, what the fuck is wrong with you two?"

With her arms out, she balanced herself as she stood and staggered to the bathroom.

"It smells rotten! What is that?"

The little boy scurried across the apartment to sit with his sister. They stayed silent. Sometimes, it made things better. Sometimes.

"YOU FUCKING ANIMALS!! This is fucking disgusting!" Barreling back into the room, she stumbled straight for the kids, but overshot and reached the wall behind them with a *slap*! Whirling around, she bent down and grabbed both boy and girl by the backs of their necks. She dragged them to the bathroom, where the toilet had overflowed two days ago.

"You want SOMETHING TO EAT? Here you fucking go!!"

XXXIII.

LILI

July 8th 2003
Calgary, Alberta

*W*hat did I do? Why is this happening? I still don't know *exactly what I have done.*

Everything is different.

No, nothing's different. It can't be.

It's not real. The dreams are not real.

The stain? The scratches in my door? Ephryium caught in the headlights of the bus.

It is real. I'm scared. I have to shut it off. I have to shut me off.

I have only spoken once since I've been home. I choose every word coming out of my mouth carefully.

"I need help. There's something wrong with me."

The guilt and fear have taken their toll. There is no more emotion left to beg for it. I only have the facts left.

"There's nothing — " Mom tries, but Dad won't let her say it. There *is* something wrong with me, and he knows it.

"We will talk to the elders in the morning." He speaks in a

way any father would have: like he knows what to do. He has the answer, the solution.

I am not going to get help from the church.

"I want to go to a doctor. I want that kind of help."

Both of my parents seem uncomfortable.

How could I ask to go see a doctor? There is nothing a doctor could fix that the church couldn't. It is an unspoken rule in our house that mental problems don't exist.

If they don't let me have mental problems, they'll have to admit I'm haunted. There hadn't been enough God in their house to keep the devil out. They weigh in on what is more shameful to their reputation, to their family. And here I sit, in the waiting room, wedged in-between the cushions of the couch, staring at the flickering halogen bulb above me, waiting for the psychiatrist to give me the means to turn it all off. To shut the door.

"Hello, Lili. I'm Doctor Taylor." He extends his hand to me.

My hands are clasped together, so I let it hang there awkwardly.

"I understand you have some concerns you'd like to talk about?" His tone changes. His welcome has been taken back and replaced with cold professionalism.

I know I respond. I can feel my tongue against the back of my teeth. But my voice is muffled. Far away.

There's fire everywhere.

"Lili, I would like to ask you some questions. Your answers will better help me to understand you. Are you comfortable with this?"

The flames grow higher.

I'm not comfortable talking with this man. I can't bring myself to say the words, to tell anyone what I'm scared of. There is a piece of paper in front me.

A high pitched scream fills my ears.

"It's OK, Lili. Take your time. No rush."

A bead of sweat drips down my forehead. It's so hot in the room. I need this. I need to answer the questions on the page. As my eyes distort the words on the paper, the whispers read them aloud to me.

"Do you hear voices? Do you have bouts of extreme rage or paranoia? Do you think about hurting yourself or others around you? Why won't the dreams stop? What is Ephryium? Why are you like this? WhY Won't You Let US In?"

Darkness falls on me.

With a hand that can barely grasp the paper, I hand the doctor my scribbled answers. Exhaustion sweeps over my body. I want to crawl up on the examination table and sleep. But that's what they want. That's where they wait. I spring back to attention to see the doctor standing in front of me, speaking.

"I don't want you to stop coming to talk to me, Lili. In the interim, however, I think we can help you get control of this … By the sound of things, it seems like you're suffering from a borderline personality disorder … anxiety … depression … more tests are needed … mild schizophrenia … "

Screams of rage, of torment.

"There is medication to help you with this."

Small, sporadic sizzles as the rain, dark and thick, falls.

"We can start you on a cycle of anti-psychotics … "

An image of me: drenched in blood, standing alone in charred darkness. What the fuck is happening to me?

On my sleeve, a spider crawls through the folds of my hoodie. I jerk my arm back and start to smooth the fabric, frantically searching for the spider. When I can't find it, I start freaking out.

"It's in my hair! I can feel it!" I flip my head over and run my hands though my hair.

"What is it? Lili? You need to calm down!"

Is it happening again? Is Ephryium coming? Am I going to black out and hurt someone? I don't trust myself anymore.

The doctor approaches me with his hands up, speaking in soothing tones. Hitting the floor, I scream and kick. He needs to stay away from me.

"Nurse!"

A heavy knee pins me to the floor. A sting in my ass, followed by coldness, then sleep.

XXXIV.

IGNACE

The following is an excerpt from:

Luc Marchand's

Queens of Hell
An Occult Specialist's Search for the Devils in the Background

Published 1997
All rights reserved.

Ignace, Ontario.
October 25th 1986

For three years, the two men sat beside one another in the same patrol car. They trusted each other. They shared their hard times and their histories. They knew each other's favourite hockey team, and had beers on Sundays. Two vastly different men who had both deliberately put themselves in Ignace for the same purpose: to find some peace.

The morning of the 25th, both men started their shift at 4:30

a.m. They met at the station at 4:10 a.m. and clocked in, badges on, guns at the hip.

"Mornin'," Mike greeted Bruce gruffly, his throat still untouched by coffee.

"Mornin'," he said, tipping his forehead down in a nod.

"Any word on Matt yet?" Several days earlier, one of the locals came to the office and let Mike know that Matthew hadn't been in to eat breakfast for a day or two. It had been roughly a week since anyone saw him, but Matt was his own man; it was like him to leave with no word. He had no family in town, no one he felt would care what he was up to. The boys at the station knew it. When the town was too quite it wasn't unusual for some of the locals to periodically stir up a story or some gossip for entertainment.

Last winter, he disappeared for three days. The staff working at Tempo Diner got it in their heads he was up in his cabin, rotting, so Bruce and Mike drove up there. They trekked down the snow-covered path through the woods to catch Matt cutting wood in front of his cabin with nuthin' on but a cigarette hanging out of his mouth. As soon as Matt heard the twig snap under Mike's boots, he bent over (both men wished he hadn't) and came up holding a shotgun aimed at them.

"Fack aff."

Both men turned on their heels, not saying a word. He was alive. Job done.

Mike and Bruce admired Matt; that kind of man, a 'man's man.' He knew what he wanted and said it in such a way two officers of the law, both brandishing their own weapons, respected every word that came out of his mouth. Neither one of them was eager to intrude on Matt's privacy again.

"Wanna go get some breakfast, then head up?"

"Yep."

With all their years of experience as police officers, you'd have thought they would have been a little bit more intuitive to what boiled beneath the façade of their tranquil town. Monsters don't always appear to be monsters. Sometimes, they are just 'normal citizens.' The Ignace Police Department was unaware they were hostages. Only pigs in a pen. And from this day on, the creatures that hid in the forests surrounding Ignace would now be lurking in the dark corners of their homes.

XXXV.

LILI

"Lili, what the fuck happened to you? Seriously? What the fuck? I miss you."

The emotion in Justyne's voice is enough to make me cry. But I don't. I can't.

The medication paralyzes me. I want to say just emotionally, but it's more than that. I don't think about anything anymore. My mind is blank. I feel nothing; I do nothing. I am numb. I hope tomorrow will be different, that the shadow leaves my side, that the medication starts doing what I need it to do. But it doesn't.

I haven't left my house since Mom and Dad brought me home from the hospital. After they sedated me, I was taken to the psych ward. Flashes of a cold blue floor and dingy yellow walls sometimes float into my mind. I came home over-medicated. It helps. My parents hadn't allowed me to talk to Justyne, or leave the house. Although they are still scared to have me in the house, it scares them even more to have me leave it.

I want to die.

"I miss you, too."

Vinny had smuggled my phone into my room. "Call her, Lili. She misses you. If you're not gonna talk to us, well, you need to talk to someone."

"You sound ... different."

Rolling over, I pull my blankets over my head. I have to keep my voice down. "I'm in bed."

"It's two in the afternoon ... " She let out a soft laugh. "Where did you go? Why haven't you called?"

"I dunno ... I wish you were here." I wish the tears would come. That they would pour out with the words I want to say to her. But they don't. They remain just below the surface, trapped.

"I'm worried about you. You don't sound good. I really need to see you. What happened after you left my house? I can't stop thinking about that night — that was the most fucked up thing I have ever experienced."

"Justyne, stop. I can't. I can't talk about it. Any of it ... it didn't stop." I whispered what I could force out from the now-reluctant memories. "The book didn't burn. People got hurt. The girls are gone ... Justyne? I can't shut the door. They're still here."

"Get dressed. I'm coming to get you."

XXXVI.

IGNACE

The following is an excerpt from:

Luc Marchand's

Queens of Hell
An Occult Specialist's Search for the Devils in the Background

Published 1997

November 3rd 1986

The *Ignace Courier* would report the following story:

> **Kenora County. Ignace, ON; 4 Dead, 3 missing,**
> **1 injured and in custody.**

The grizzly quadruple homicide was discovered on October 31 by Ignace residents trick-or-treating with their children. A parent heard a man's moaning coming from somewhere inside the house. When it was determined not to be part of the house's Halloween décor, the complainant used a neighbour's phone to call local authorities.

The murder took place on Rand St. North and is being investigated by local RCMP. Two of the victims have been identified as Maria Merlo, 17, and Merlo's boyfriend Daniel Tumicelli, 19. The two other victims are one unidentified man, who is a suspect in a homicide committed earlier in October, and an unidentified woman. All were dead upon police arrival.

Another unidentified man was found inside the house, badly injured but alive. Also a suspect in the murder of Matthew Linton, 74, discovered October 25th. He was taken to McKeller Hospital in Thunder Bay where he remains in custody of the RCMP.

It was established Maria Merlo had a 2-year-old son who was not found at the scene. He has not yet been located, but police have opened a missing persons investigation to locate him.

Police are also investigating the residents and owner of the house, Merlo's mother: Antoinette Merlo, 54, and her other daughter, Daniella Merlo, 18. Both were not at the house when police arrived to investigate the call. They have also been declared missing.

RCMP have not released details into the investigation, the relation of the victims, or a possible motive but have reached out to the residents of Ignace for any tips and/or information pertaining to the Merlo's or the other victims. Please call: 807-445-8989

XXXVIII.

LILI

Calgary, Alberta
August 9th 2003
9:45 p.m.

"You look like shit, babe."

She stands in my room like an apparition. I genuinely believe if I look away, she'd be gone.

"Let's get you cleaned up." As she takes the blankets off me, my bottle of pills rolls onto the floor. "What do they have you on?"

She is real.

She's here.

"How are you here?"

Looking up from the bottle in her hand, Justyne smiles and says, "Vinny's got you. He let me in, and he'll cover for us. Your mom and dad are out for the night, and he is going to be a bad babysitter and not see you leave. I told him I'd have you back by morning though. You an' me are gonna go out tonight."

I have to give Justyne and Vinny credit. Between the two of

them, they successfully smuggled me out of the house, unseen and unheard.

The downtown street is illuminated in an amber wash of streetlights. A ghost town. The only sounds are the muffled and far away thumps of bass and two sets of clicking heels.

"We're not going to talk about anything you don't wanna talk about, babe. And you're not going to be taking any more pills. Well, not the ones you've been taking anyways." With her arm draped over my shoulders, Justyne chuckles.

I can't bring myself to say much. I hadn't wanted to get into the shower, let alone go to a club to dance and pretend to have fun. The pants she chose for me are too tight, the heels are too high, fucking uncomfortable. I want to tell her to take me back home, when she stops and holds out her hand.

Two little red pills. Gifts from Vinny, no doubt.

"Take one, not both. We want to get fucking retarded but not die, OK?" She laughs again. It forces a smile out of me.

So this is the game plan. I take a pill from her hand and look to her for more reassurance.

"Let's just let it all go for one night? Forget about it? I just wanna see you happy. And if you need pills to get you there, I can tell you these ones will help way more than the ones you were on. One night. Like old times."

I grin and appreciate the effort my best friend is putting in. "OK. Let's do it."

You could pass by the door of the club a hundred times without a second thought. An inconspicuous steel rectangle in an inconspicuous wall in the middle of downtown nowhere. Located in between two alleys, it could be mistaken for a service entry, except for the unmistakable thumps coming from behind the door: Music, the kind of music that inspires dancing, drugs, sex, and late nights that bleed into the morning.

With a squeal, the door opens, revealing a rather large punk on the other side. We step into a small lobby. Before he has a chance to ask for ID, Justyne sets him straight.

"I know Dimitri and Alex. They know we're coming."

The back wall opens to a narrow, red-lit staircase leading upstairs. Whispering into my ear as we go up, Justyne tells me about the two Russian drug dealers who own the club we have just entered. I need to 'be nice,' and they will give me more drugs.

We are escorted to a booth overlooking the dance floor, DJ, and bar. Rails of coke, ecstasy, and meth cover a table in the centre of the space. I stand at the doorway, watching Justyne waste no time moving in on the coke. Leaning over the table, she sucks a little white line of powder into her nose with the rolled up bill left there by who I assume is either Alex or Dimitri.

"This is Alex!" Justyne yells into my ear, pointing to a fat ginger man in the corner. "And that's Dimitri!" She points to a tall, stoic looking guy leaning over the rail, watching the people below. "I don't know who the fuck that is though." She nods in the direction of a brown guy dressed in black partying on a couch beside us.

I say nothing, a woozy smile creeping over my face. I start to sway on the spot.

"Has it hit you yet? Yea! You're high!" She puts her arms around me and starts to laugh.

I'm high.

Pulling me by the hand, she brings me further into the booth. I don't want to sit by the dark guy or the ginger. If I wasn't so close in proximity to them, I would tell Justyne they look like a bunch of douchebags, or at least the type of guys that would molest a girl who passed out. She could take all of their drugs if it came with them. I shake my head 'no' and motion I'm going to watch the people dance. Before we turn away from each other, I mouth 'be careful.' She's not going to be careful about anything, though, and I know it.

Dimitri, who started on the other side of the booth, is inching closer and closer to me. I try not to pay any attention to the impending conversation coming nearer, and I'm making sure at least one of my feet is still out the door, when he leans in and speaks directly into my ear.

"How's it going?"

"Fine, pretty high though. You know Justyne?" Not thinking, I rest my hand on his arm laying on the rail beside me. I see immediately it's taken as a sign to get closer to me. *Great.*

"Yea, for a while. I never meet you before. You seem like good girl. How long you know Justyne?" His thick accent, mixed with whatever is making him clench his jaw, makes it hard for me to understand him. This conversation is not made to last.

"Forever. We've known each other forever." I'm tempted to ask him if she does this many drugs on the regular. Glancing over my shoulder, I see her wedged between the ginger and the brown guy with a bill sticking out of her nose. Even high, I hate the brown guy and the way he leers at Justyne.

Turning back to Dimitri, I ask, "So, if Alex is your brother, who's the other guy?"

"Him?" He motions behind us. "He wants to be resident dealer. Guy's a fucking *oyobuk*. Why the fuck we want one dealer only? Fucking stupid leb."

"What's his name?"

"Krish. Fucking bad guy. Nice girl like you should stay away from him."

I nod and stare down at the people, watching them dance, some to the beat, others to something else. Dimitri leans out over the ledge, sending out a distinct vibe he isn't done talking to me. I'm done talking to him though.

I am mad that Justyne is behind me and not beside me. I border on resentful that's she not here right now to distract me from myself. I'm losing myself in my thoughts. For the first time in months, they're clear. I know what questions are the most important to me.

The memories and the dreams unravel. Somewhere in my childhood, I remember kind eyes and waking up feeling safe. As my life has grown darker, so have my memories of Ephryium. A beautiful memory has slowly turned into the star of every nightmare. Is he responsible for me seeing the remnants, the demons, the ghosts? Or is he here because of it? In all of this, if I'm not a mental case or possessed, am I being watched?

I spiral into depression and loneliness when the thumping of the music becomes quieter, muffled. The lights dim. It happens so swiftly, so smoothly, I almost don't notice. Gazing over the ledge, I see the dancing people are all expanding into fuzzy, moving figures. One person overlapping into the next, all surrounded by auras of bright, beautiful colours. The once fast-paced music lags into a song, so slow and so melancholic, as if everyone were dancing at their own funeral.

Is it just me, or is the whole room getting smaller, colder, darker? It seems as though the room is gradually being covered by a cloak. My mind is sharp. I readily adapt to the strange shit happening around me. I'm at full attention, anticipating everything and anything.

Except for what comes in the wake of the shadow.

The only person in the room who is in focus, the only thing in the room that makes sense. A dark figure — black hair, dark skin — steps onto the dance floor with an air of the utmost confidence. He is superbly intriguing.

As he walks through the fuzzy orbs of colour, some of the people's beautiful energy leaks out, stolen into his dark aura. He leeches their energy, just by walking by. I've never seen anything like it. Everything behind him is changed slightly, left depleted and smaller, greyer, weaker. It's fascinating to watch. In a blink, the music rushes back into my ears, the lights blinding; the people, still high, bounce around the dance floor. Frantically, I search the floor. I lost sight of him.

XXXVIII.

ARNOLD

North Battleford Outskirts, Saskatchewan
June 12th 1989

First on the 'Ta Do' list today was visit the Doctor. Arnold felt a small twinge of guilt for not mentioning his little appointment to Debbie when he left the house this morning. It wasn't that he needed to tell her, but the fact he went out of his way not to tell her didn't sit well with him. He didn't want to worry her. It was his problem, no need to get her upset.

Doctor Gregor was about Arnold's age but looked half it. With a thick head of black hair and a tidy, black moustache, he was overweight but he held every pound with confidence. Arnold knew he thought Arnold and Debbie were a bit strange, but probably no stranger than any of the other backwoods folks he'd met. He was sure the doc was just happy all his clients were white, farm folk, and not the inbred, meth head, neech garbage the other clinics got, the kind of people renting Arnold's and Deb's house.

The doc stared up at Arnold as he hoisted his ass up onto his desk. "How goes it, Arnold?"

"Oh, you know, Doc, it goes."

"And Debbie? Haven't seen her in a while."

"Oh, you know Debbie. She's a tough bird."

"Just as well. Have her make an appointment with me, too, OK?"

"Will do, Doc." Arnold gave a 'yea, got it, let's get down to business' kind of nod. Didn't have time for the jibber jabber.

"Well, then, Arnold. Let's get to it." The Doctor shoved his hands deep into the pockets of his white coat.

"Uh, you see, I got them headaches again, Doc. They're comin' with the sweats. And fuck if I can see straight."

"Headaches again, eh?" The Doctor pulled the ophthalmoscope off the wall and brought it up to Arnold's eyes, shining the light in his right and then his left. "Worse than before?"

"Mmhmm … "

Doctor Gregor put the scope back onto the wall and grabbed the blood pressure cuff to wrap it around Arnold's arm. "Have you cut back on the caffeine like I told you to, Arnold?"

The reply was written all over Arnold's face. He glanced off to the side with a sheepish grin on his thin lips, showing crooked, browning teeth.

"You're not helping yourself here. A Big Gulp of coffee — " Stopping mid-sentence, he made sure he had Arnold's attention. " — and I know you don't just have one — isn't good for anybody." He sat down behind his desk. "Anything else, besides the headaches?"

Arnold peered down at his shoes. His knuckles turned white as he clutched the side of the table.

"I'm open here, Arnold. What's going on?"

"I don' know, Doc." He glimpsed up for a moment of eye contact, then away. "I feel like I lose control. Not all the time, just sometimes. Oh, I don't — " He cut off, still staring at his shoes, shaking his head back and forth slowly.

"Do you get angry?"

"Oh no, no, nothing like that."

The doctor sat back in his chair, studying Arnold.

Arnold hated it. He knew what he was thinkin; *Oh the poor man. He doesn't have the intea-llectual ca-paci-TEE to art-ic-ulate his problems. Stay quiet, don't want the old boy to clam up, let 'em try again. Fuckin' asshole.* But he didn't have a choice; he would need to try again, he needed what the doc could give him. Help.

"Well, sometimes' I feel like I'm not all me, but there's more … of me. I can hear myself thinking an' what not, not in my voice though … I don't always want to do what I'm thinking, but most of the time I do … So it's OK … right, Doc?"

"Hmm." The doctor stroked his chin methodically. "Well, now, I don't know if that's OK Arnold. Do you mind if I ask you a couple of questions?"

"Naw, sure, Doc. Shoot."

"How long have your thoughts been, hmm, in a different voice?"

"Long as I can remember."

"Would you say they — your thoughts — do they come at you at a pace in which you understand, or are they racing, overlapping each other?"

"Uhh, I understand purdy gewd."

"OK. Are your thoughts distracting you? Say from, driving your rig, or holding a conversation?"

"Naw." He shook his head and began to swing his feet. "They just add to what I'm already thinking."

Doctor Gregor grabbed a small pad and a pen from his desk drawer and asked, "Are they negative thoughts, Arnold?"

"Naw, they are usually purdy encouraging … Naw, sometimes they can be pretty darn negative too, I suppose."

"Do you suffer from delusions or paranoia?"

"Hmm?"

"Do you think something is there when it isn't, or believe people are talking about you behind your back, negatively?"

"Who? Who said what?"

"Never mind, Arnold. I think, firstly, you need to cut back on the caffeine."

Arnold nodded with his whole body.

"Secondly, here is a prescription for T3's, to help with the headaches. And if you want, it wouldn't hurt … " He leaned forward and handed Arnold two pieces of paper from the notepad. "I have given you a colleague's name. His name is Doctor Tasier, Wayne Tasier. He is a psychologist at the hospital. I think it might be a good idea for you to go and have a chat with him."

Arnold read the piece of paper in his hands. "A head doctor, huh?"

"A psychologist, Arnold, and a very good friend. If you trust me, you can trust him, I assure you."

"Hmm, OK." He stuffed the paper into his overall pocket, slid off the table, and put out his hand.

With that, Doctor Gregor took Arnold's hand. Both men nodded. "Remember to tell Debbie to make an appointment?"

"Will do, will do. Thanks for seein' me, Doc."

"Anytime. 'Bye now."

Arnold walked back to his truck with his shoulders slumped forward, his steps heavy. He was mad and embarrassed. He shouldn't have said a god damn thing to Doctor Gregor.

Great. Now the Doctor thinks I'm a fuckin' looney toon.

He sat inside his pickup truck in the parking lot, hands gripping the wheel, eyes focused on the door of the doctor's office. Enough time had passed for him to convince himself Doctor Gregor and that cunt bitch receptionist, PAM, were sitting inside laughing at him, laughing at crazy fucking Arnold with the ugly wife.

"Debbie is fucking BEAUTIFUL! DON'T YOU SAY A FUCKING WORD ABOUT MY DEBBIE!" Spit flew from his mouth, clinging to his chin as he slammed his fists down onto the steering wheel. He burrowed himself deeper into his seat and imagined Doctor Gregor fingering Pam on top of his desk. *As he worked his fingers in and out of the dry, mummified cunt, he pointed over to the table where Arnold had sat.*

"He just sat there, Pam, like a BUFOON! I swear —" he laughed haughtily, "— he started to drool when I asked him about —"He turned hard to his right, then to his left and whispered, "— the voices in his head."

Doctor Gregor then cupped his hand, brought it to his mouth, and spat into it, bringing it down to the dusty cave and rubbing the mucus up into her. They both — the bastards! — threw their heads back and laughed and laughed and laughed!

Arnold stared down into his lap. He was fully erect and threatening to tear through his own zipper.

"Fack!"

BuRn iT doWn,   ARnoLd

TheY aRe lauGhiNg aT yOu

KilL tHEm BoTh,   ArNolD

A twisted grin unraveled on Arnold's face.
Yes. Yes. Kill them both.

Debbie's voice rang through his head, drowning out the encouraging thoughts.

"Collect the rent, Arnold!"

He nodded at the imaginary Debbie and started his truck.

XXXIX.

IGNACE

The following is an excerpt from:

Luc Marchand's

Queens of Hell
An Occult Specialist's Search for the Devils in the Background

Published 1997

Ignace Courier Archive
November 5th 1986

In the wake of a quadruple homicide and a man hunt for the Merlo family, the local Ignace RCMP have declared three more people missing.

32-year-old Sara Olson, and her two daughters Rebecca Olson, 4, and Elizabeth Olson, 7, have been missing since October 20th. Sergeant Mike Olsen, father and husband to the missing persons, reported his wife and daughters' disappearance this weekend, but also reported that he had thought Sara had taken the girls to her parents.

Sergeant Olson has been actively investigating the string of homicides that has devastated this Northern Ontarian town and has not released any comment as to whether he believes that these murders have anything to do with his family's disappearance.

Sergeant MacDonald, Olsen's partner, has been reached for comment and stated, "We are going to try our best to bring the girls back home. If anyone knows where those girls are, they need to come forward."

The suspect for the murders of Matthew Linton, Maria Merlo, Daniel Tumicelli, and two other victims that remain unidentified was discharged from McKeller Hospital on November 3rd. He was to be put into custody for questioning, but has now been admitted back into the hospital for a psychological assessment.

The suspect remains yet to be identified.

Maria Merlo, Daniel Tumicelli, and the unidentified man and woman are the 125th, 126th, 127th, and 128th homicides in Ontario this year.

𝔛𝔏.

LILI

Calgary, Alberta
10:45 p.m.

                        COWARD!
            sO

                                    PaTHEtiC
It'sS
        SsO
                NiCe
                To SeE

    You HaVe CoMe BaCk HeRe   TO DIE.

"What's wrong, babe? Are you too fucked up? What are you looking at?"

Everything is wrong. I need to get out of this place. I heard the words as clearly as I had heard Justyne's question. I'm already moving for the door as I tell her we should go. Looking annoyed, Justyne puts her hand on my shoulder. I am fairly confident that, even though all the guys wait behind Justyne, the music is so loud we aren't being overheard. We can have a totally private conversation surrounded by people. She pulls away from me and furrows her brow.

"Really, you wanna go?"

I nod.

"OK, so Alex's friend's name is Krish. He's really nice. He can give us a ride. Are you sure though? We just got here. I don't want to leave yet."

I know she can see my disdain, but she pretends not to. She can have her cake and eat it, too. She will get to keep doing Krish's drugs and partying, and eventually, I'll make it home. What choice do I have? Do I leave her alone? If we're both left alone, we will both be in trouble's way.

"'K, let's go soon then?"

Seeing her grow frustrated with me, I lean in to tell her what Dimitri had told me about her new friend.

"This guy chops people up and leaves body parts in the streets as casually as sprinkling confetti on a cake … " I may have improvised a little bit.

But that is the vibe I truthfully had gotten from the guy. Shrugging, I wait for some sort of understanding from her. It crosses my mind to tell her of the voice, but my instinct is to keep it to myself. I mean, she's only had a taste of what I have been living with for my entire life, and it's like she's an absolutely different person. How was she so easily affected? Maybe I should talk about this with her. I am overwhelmed with my current to-do list; it's too much to handle. I reach into my bag and pop another little red pill.

ShE is WEaK.

WhY dO yOu aTTacH youRseLveS To thEsE

iNfEriOr piGs?

YOU

      ArE

                        As weAk As sHe iS

             KiLL hEr

MaKe HER   bleeeeeeeD

      TakE

         THEM

            BOTH

                 yOu doN't bElonG heRe

"Fuck, Lili!" She's mad, but is she going to leave this up to me? I weigh in quickly; did I really need her?

"Justyne! I'm kinda freakin' out here … I thought I had all this figured out, and I don't. I don't know what to do. If you want me to stay I'll stay, just don't leave me, 'k?"

"Lili, I won't! I promise. I just thought we were gonna have some fun tonight. Stay a little bit longer — we haven't even got to dance."

"Stay put. I have to get away from the music for a sec. I'll be right back, and stop doing all the drugs!"

I walk past her to leave the room. No matter what I'm going to do, I need to accept this night is going to be a disaster, and I'm the queen of it. Krish and Alex are both waving at me like a couple of retards. I ignore them and keep walking down the stairs.

     ThE   otHer One BeloNgs   WITH US

                          So eAsiLy broKeN doWn

DOn'T YoU See?

                        YOu'RE NeVeR GoInG BaCk

So

     So

          sHe woN't bRiNg yOu rePrieVe

FoOliSh

BRinG HER to Us

CoMe wIth USssss

Let's   PLAy

No matter how fast I put one foot in front of the other, I can't escape the hissing in my ears. A hand lands on my shoulder and pulls me to face back up the stairs. It's Krish. Everything about him is a dangerous trap, even the way his jet black eyes twinkle at me, hiding the violence and cruelty I know he's capable of. He smells good. For a second, he even seems soft and playful. He is an axe just waiting to come down on me.

"What's wrong? Are you going? We haven't met, and I don't want you to go. Your friend is having fun. You should, too."

I roll my eyes and try to remain calm. I need to be alone. The voices won't stop. Something is different; they're no longer talking to me.

"I don't have fun like that." I turn to leave again.

!!ShE WANTS to FUCK HIM!!

SsssssSUck hisSSS

THEN RiP iT oFF

As if from a distance, Krish asks, "What do you mean? You don't fuck?" He grabs my arm, and closes the gap between us.

"No, listen, I'm just trying to have to have a good time. You need to calm down."

She thinKSSssss you're   SSSSsssSTupid

SHE LIkES IT In ThE ASS!

FuCK Her

Kill hEr

RiP heR   insiDes oUt

His eyes fixate on mine. As he leans away from me he looks taller, imposing.

He reaches out and grabs my throat, pushing my back to wall. He squeezes my wind pipe, making it hard to breathe. The blood rushes to my face. As I am deprived of air, I gasp and cough. He lifts me onto my toes, and shakes me like a ragdoll, my back hitting the wall with each thrust.

ThiS oNe IS SpeCIal

I cAn Slide IntO HeR
feELS

So EaSiLY

ssssooo GooD

Let Us deLiver Her ToGeTher

Ephryiummmm
We wiLL rewARd yOu FoR BriNgiNg HeR

"No one tells me what to do, fucking bitch! You know who I am? If I say you fuck, you fuck!"

I claw at his hand with my nails fruitlessly. The pain of my head smacking the wall behind me doesn't register. Through the tears in my own eyes, I focus on Krish's eyes, still black and flirtatious. *Oh my god, someone needs to save me.* I look up the stairs to mentally summon somebody to my rescue, but no one comes.

Just as quickly as the attack had started, it suddenly stops. His grip loosens enough for me to gulp and gasp for air.

It hits me — the voice I'm hearing is taunting whatever is with me. This seething, malefic, and viable being hangs over me and Krish. Whispering its words into my head, hovering there, making the air somehow feel heavier, it surges forward, with the means to infect us both. Leaching energy will never be enough; it needs pain. It needs chaos.

It needs me.

KiLL HiM

Fire rages behind my eyes. Hate for him consumes me.

Something that can only be explained as pure rage fills my veins.

I Will heLP YoU

FALlEN   OnE

yOu Are too weAK And Pathetic   FoR thiS ONe

USeLEsssss

SHE Will ComE wiTh Us   NOW

He comes forward again, this time with a slink in his walk. The twinkle in his eye and a half smile says it all.

"You're a pretty girl. I think we could have some fun together. What's your name?"

"Lili." My voice is mine, but it's not. There's an edge, a confidence; my name came out sounding like a threat.

"C'mon, I'm sorry I was so mad. I don't know what happened. You make me nervous. Forgive me?"

Justyne clomps down the stairs before I have a chance to answer. I see she's assessing the tension between myself and Krish. She zeroes in on me and comes close enough to talk into my ear.

"What happened?"

"Something bad."

"Are you OK?"

"No."

"What's gonna happen?"

"Something worse."

!YeS!

"You should get away from me." I shout over Justyne's head at Krish. "Don't ever touch me again."

Justyne frowns. "You touched her? You fucking piece of shit! I'll fucking kill, you leb piece of garbage!"

Gently guiding her away from Krish, I tell her to stop. I lean into Krish, and find myself apologizing as I direct the piece of shit down the stairs to his eventual death and tell Justyne to come with me to the bathroom.

Shaken, I hold onto the walls and falter down the stairs. My knees are weak. They wobble as I navigate through the tight crowd. I glance over my shoulder to make sure Justyne is close behind me. She is, but I see more than her. It's as if the club is being devoured by darkness.

I need to get out now! I need to hide.

The shadow looms over the dancing souls behind me, becoming thick like sludge. As it encompasses the crowd, it releases a cloud of spores that rot everyone's insides. No one sees what's happening to them but me.

I have begun to peak. My jaw mashes and grinds together. My skin tingles as if there are hands all over my body. I can't keep my eyes open. I just want to fall into this feeling forever. Overwhelmed with panic and sensuality, I bump into the people dancing in my path, sending me into a downwards spin to the floor. *I just need to get to the bathroom.*

Reaching in front of me, I grab onto someone. Grasping onto their clothes, hoping I can hold on just long enough to regain stability, to pull myself back up and make my way to a corner. *This is such a bad time to peak.*

Forcing my head up, my eyes open and refocus. My jaw unclenches. I stare into a set of dark and absolutely wild eyes. The music is booming from inside of me, sending vibrations throughout my body. The lights spin out of control. My feet are no longer on the floor.

If I let go of this guy, I'll be lost in a tornado of people, E, and demons out to get me.

He is the only thing, the only person who is standing calm, peaceful, and still. I try to ignore the pandemonium raging all around us to just focus on him. Such strong, dark features. He seems to stand over me, making me believe that I am small and vulnerable underneath him. I quickly make up my mind he is the most beautiful man I have ever seen, anyone has ever seen, actually. I am sure of it. He is universally beautiful. It would be a shame if he went to prison … unless he was into that kind of thing, of course … *Fuck me.*

Putting his hands underneath my elbows, he slowly brings me to eye level. The longer we stare into each other's eyes, the more everything else slips away. The lights that are like high beams no longer blind me, but are like flickering candles far off in the darkness. The music goes from a deafening 200 BPM to a sleepy gentle beat. My feet are still unable to find the ground, but it's OK, because he's holding me close, keeping me safe.

If I can't learn to enjoy this feeling, I am going to puke. I am going to puke all over this guy. The thought gets stuck in my head on repeat.

I'm going to puke. I'm going to puke. Fuck! I'm sure my eyes are about to roll into the back of my skull, and I'm going to die. As much as I want to push this guy the fuck away from me, I don't. How bad will it be? Maybe it will be a cute 'how we met story.' No. No, it won't be. *Hands! I demand you unhand the man! God damn!*

HANDS: "NEVER!"

"Are you OK? Are you peakin'? Aww, you're peaking. It's OK. You'll be OK." He strokes my face gently, regarding me with nothing more than genuine concern and the ability to make it better.

I can't control myself; I wrap my arms around him, and he does the same. We hug each other tightly. I tremble as if I am in the moment right after a severe trauma. He whispers into my ear, "Shh, it's OK, it's OK. Where are your friends?"

Being in close proximity to him is paralyzing. No matter

what I want to do, I am being kept right in place, right where I was meant to be. The flutter in my stomach calms. I start to breathe deeper. So does he. Our chests rise and fall together. There are no more lights. There is no more music. It's only us.

AnD   mE.

I want to tear his clothes off, throw him down on the dirty floor, and fuck him until my brain is mush. The muscles in-between my legs tighten, become warm, readying itself to mount him. I know, I don't know how I know, but I know he wants to fuck me as badly as I want to fuck him. My breaths come out ragged and fast. *Jesus Christ!*

I am going to puke.

Pushing myself out of the most intense hug that ever happened in the history of the universe, I focus on the bathroom door and book'er like a hooker. Slamming through the door like a brick, I immediately explode, spewing red and brown chunks onto the floor and up the wall. My initial thought is to get my head into a sink.

But I have overlooked what has actually happened: I have just covered the floor in front of me with vomit. I take a step forward and slip in it. If it isn't bad enough I just ate shit in my own puke in an already disgusting bathroom, the fumes coming off the barf are so disgusting it makes me throw up even more. I'm on my hands and knees, crawling through my mess as I puke even more, trying to make it to the mother-fucking sink that seems to have been relocated to fucking China. My hands keep sliding out from underneath me. What did I eat that was so slimy? I fall again and again onto my shoulder before finally climbing up the plumbing and throwing my head into the sink. I have nothing. My stomach is empty.

Mother Fucker!

Justyne comes running through the door. She slides across the floor, her arms flailing around her head, to keep herself from also eating shit in my puke.

"Aww, what the fuck, Lili?" She goes to put a hand on my back, but the fumes hit her before she lands it, and she wretches. She gets it together. And then loses it again and runs into a stall.

"Aww, fuck! This is fucking disgus — " She doesn't finish her sentence before heaving into the toilet again. She comes out of the stall while I'm still rinsing whatever putridness is left in my mouth and nostrils down the drain. I raise my head to see her reflection in the mirror. The walls and ceiling around her are alive. For every step she takes forward, a throb of veiny blackness surges forward with her.

Her eyes are black. Through the open slit of her mouth, I can see her teeth are tiny and jagged. I whip around, fingers still in my nose, to look at her. At first glance, all seems normal. Upon further inspection, there is something perverse in the way she walks; the sway in her hips. Has she always looked so deviant? The way she is walking, it's a predator hunting ... No, not hunting ... I wonder what is scarier than a predator killing for fun, because it can? I look back into the mirror, back at Justyne's face. Justyne. Justyne is scarier than a predator that kills for fun.

To the right, just above her head, there is something, something seemingly nothing more than a shadow. So black, so dark, it has depth, a chasm that is gone within a blink. The mirror mimics a TV with bad reception. One moment there's something behind her, beside her, in her, like a puppeteer with its hand deep within a puppet, then nothing.

I squint like an old woman with failing vision. No matter how I strain to see it, it won't stay in the mirror long enough for me to make it out. All I can tell is it towers over Justyne. It is bent over. Its back reaches the ceiling. Its arms, two for sure, are long.

With every apparition, the arms extend and stretch, coming nearer and nearer to me. For an instant, I can see the crown, the red, exposed muscles standing tall beside ... *fuck me!* Something else. Something that doesn't want me to see it.

But I do. Just for a moment.

It is like the hug; I need more. It isn't enough to be close.

YoU'LL neVEr gEt youR foRGivNessssss

BROTHER!

WhY Do you INSisT   On BEINg AloNE?

WeAreMany

LeT US tAKE tHEm

"How do you know Delano?" Justyne is behind me, stroking my back. I'm thankful that one: she's not the demon I saw in the mirror, and two: she immediately drowns out the crazy going on in the background of my mind. Her touch is not comforting; she's burping me. I'm going to puke again.

"Don't touch me ... please."

She steps back, hurt, and asks again. "On the floor, I saw you two hugging — looked pretty hot."

"I don't know him. No, it was fucking intense, it was too much."

"That was Delano. He's a really cool guy. I like him a lot. Fucking hot, hey?"

"Hot doesn't even begin to describe what is going on with that guy's face." I laugh.

"We have hung out a couple times. He's kind of a slut. He has a girlfriend, cheats on her with everyone. I heard she's like twelve or something."

I gawk at her in disbelief.

"He has some pretty crazy stories, and people have told me some pretty crazy stories about him, too."

"Oh, yea? Like what?"

"He has done some pretty crazy stuff ... I dunno, I just thought you two knew each other. Wanted to warn you, you know, 'bout him being a giant slut ... and him possibly having gone to jail for beating the shit out of his twelve-year-old girlfriend."

"Well, thanks. Did you fuck him?"

"No!"

"Sounds like a lot of fucking gossip, Justyne. To be honest, look at him. I don't think he could help being a slut. As for the girlfriend being twelve — that's really fucked up." I wonder if it's true with an indiscernible amount of disappointment.

"Just?"

"Yea?"

"I need new clothes, and I think we need to get me back home or something."

"'Cause of Krish? Don't worry about him. He left. I saw."

"I just think it's better if no one is around me right now."

"What? Do you mean me, too?"

"Justyne, let's get real for a second here. Look at you!"

She put her hands out as if she is ready for inspection, but her face is defensive, her eyes wild. The cocaine is making it hard for her to understand.

"You have been popping pills and doing rails like you're getting fucking paid to! I know what you're doing! There aren't enough drugs in the world to make you forget. Trust me, I know."

Her face falls. It's easy for her to conjure up the memory.

"I said I didn't what to talk about it, 'cause this is like a never-ending nightmare." I have to scream over the bass that seems to be leaking in through the paper-thin walls "People got hurt, Justyne. People who tried to help me! I feel so guilty and lost. I want to just melt my brain and make it go away. But it won't. It's here right now with us. It's here right now with you. It's because of me, and I'm sorry."

"I know. He said so," she said soberly.

"Who said so?"

"Brian. He was there that night. He was so terrifying. I can't get his face out of my head." On the verge of crying, her eyes fill with fear as she tried to shake off the image. "But after he left, after he told me to stop encouraging you to dig for answers … " Coming closer, what's left of her demeanour breaks down, her body shudders. "There's something in the dark, Lili. I can hear it … " Her hands shake as she brings them to her face.

"Oh fuck, Justyne." Wave after wave of guilt hits me. She saw her brother because of me. The trauma of that was something I couldn't comprehend. He died in a motorcycle accident. Another image I wouldn't wish on anyone.

"I'm so sorry." I wrap my arms around her and hug her until the sobs slow.

"They want you, you know. They whisper your name constantly."

Swallowing the lump of fear lodged in my throat, I tell her, "I know."

"They tell me to do things … "

Welcome to the mad house, Justyne.

"But I won't," she says, wiping the tears and mascara stains from under her eyes. "I love you, Lili. We are in this together."

"'K. Let's get me some clothes."

As if by divine intervention —

DiViNe?

SurE

— a girl walks through the door, more or less my size. We exchange a glance of understanding.

XLI.

THE BOY

North Battleford, Saskatchewan
1362 98th Street
June 12th 1989

The cherry of the cigarette seared into the boy's flesh as his mother crushed the burning filter into his arm. New and old circular scars riddled his entire body, a testament to what he was good for.

This hadn't been the worst of it. She would smoke the glass and become angry and vicious, putting the kids at the centre of it. The little boy appreciated his sister; she served as a shield, taking the harshest blows doled out by their mother.

After his mother calmed down, they couldn't predict whether she would stay or leave again. This time? She stayed. It confused both brother and sister when she stayed. On one hand, they weren't alone anymore; she served as their sense of direction, their 'mother.' On the other hand, she brought a level of chaos with her. The kids paid the price for the delusion of company and a false sense of security. When she stayed, she induced a constant source of pain and instability. Her warmest moments with her children occurred face down in her own vomit, lying on a mattress on the floor, when they would come and hold her, to make sure she was still breathing.

They had been systematically whittled down to something inhuman. His sister, older than himself, took responsibility for him and for their mother, too. She accepted whatever would come at them. Whether it was their mom returning home, having food again, or the heating bill being paid so the nights spent sleeping on the floor would be a little warmer. She might get slapped instead of kicked, spat on instead of scalded. It could have been hope she held onto, but her brother thought it was foolishness, looking forward to a future that was so obviously not theirs to have.

That's what made him different than his sister: while she hoped for things to get better, he thrived on what he had. The depravity fed the empty shell he lived in. The dark corners in his mind, where no amount of abuse could affect him, was where he flourished. The burns and the beatings by his mother — and the men that fed her need to destroy herself — nurtured his rage. The constant neglect and loneliness became a warm blanket he could throw over himself and just be.

If some bleeding heart happened upon the apartment, basic human instinct would take over. They would be disgusted and horrified at the conditions in which these children lived and would immediately save them from this corner of hell they had been born into. It would never cross their mind they might just be releasing what was meant to stay locked up.

His mother put him and his sister in the bath for them to wash the shit, urine, and toilet water off of them. They sat in hot bath water, scrubbing a mixture of solid waste and stink off while their mother was in the other room. A bitter smell wafted through the door, adding to the thick layer they perpetually lived in. Cigarette smoke would follow.

She came in and told them to unplug the drain and get out of the bathtub. Not that she cared, but the kids still smelled of shit. She weeble-wobbled back out the door leaving the two kids to get out of the tub and find a towel. A lone towel lay on the floor, stinking, drenched in gross.

"Here, feed him. DON'T COME OUT!" She threw in a spoon and a can of beans that landed on the floor beside them, then turned and slammed the door shut.

A faint knock came from the front door.

Standing naked in the bathroom, the scrawny children perked their ears to hear who had come in.

"Arnold! I uh, um, I uh, the rent … um, we can work something out. Right?"

They heard their mother's stoned laugh.

His sister moved quickly to feed him. She hated Arnold. She knew she might not have a lot of time to get some food in their bellies if he decided her mother just wasn't doing it for him today.

She remembered the first time he had come for her, he laid her out on the mattress beside her mother, who had smoked herself into a coma. He hadn't wanted to hurt her, it seemed. He had gently put his finger over her mouth and whispered in the most comforting voice she would ever hear, "Shh. Just a little, just a little. Shh, its OK baby, don't cry."

She hated herself for liking his rough, warm hands on her. As her shoulder rubbed against her mother's, she had gone rigid, praying for her mother to wake up and save her, praying her body would expel this man. Instead of focusing on the pain being inflicted inside of her, she had turned her head and tried her hardest to focus on the sensation of her burning eyes, the two pools forming in them, and how they slowly fell across her face.

There had been a crack of light in the darkness. Her eyes met her brother's, who watched from across the room, emotionless.

"C'mon, c'mon, eat, eat, eat!" She shook the memory aside and shoveled a spoonful of beans into his mouth. He ate quickly and silently. Eventually, he pushed the can away and gave her a nod that said it was her turn to eat.

After she ate, she needed to hunt down a way to warm, or at least cover, their naked bodies. Only time would tell how long they would be in the bathroom. She looked in the tub: bits of shit and black hair speckled the bottom. A chill overcame her. She knew her brother must be cold, too. The floor had been cleaned with the one dingy towel that remained on the tiles. She thought they just might have to bite the bullet. She picked it up and it swung near her, so she stood on her tiptoes and sucked in her distended belly to get away from it without actually dropping it. It smelled so bad, so rancid. Her face turned red as she tried to hold the heaves in.

She threw the towel into the corner, away from them. She could hear muffled moans and Arnold's deep voice. She stared at the door, transfixed, hoping if she didn't move, Arnold wouldn't come in. They needed to be quiet. So, so quiet. They would be OK in here. It wasn't too cold.

Grabbing her brother by the arm, she pulled him over to the vent blowing warm air. If someone came in, they would be behind the door. She wrapped her arms around her brother. Somewhat comforted, she accepted this was as good as it was going to get.

The hum of the air vent provided enough white noise to lull both children to sleep. At least one of them was defeated for the day, emotionally drained. The girl leaned her head back onto the wall and drifted away.

When she woke up, she felt frighteningly light. Before she opened her eyes, she sensed the absence of her brother's weight. Her eyes jolted open, knowing something was terribly wrong.

XLII.

ARNOLD

North Battleford, Saskatchewan
1362 98th Street
June 12th 1989

He rolled up his window and tucked the baggie full of murky glass shards into his pocket. The Steins needed to pay their fuckin' rent. The Corbett woman, though? Mm, not so much. Right after the squaw and her two children rented the place, she offered to pay rent through "other means." She suited his needs perfectly, had even offered her kids to him. But he liked to play with her especially. He exploited her bad habits, then took advantage of "the corpse" he could keep coming back to.

The woman could get so fucked up on the methamphetamines — Arnold had no idea
How
The fack
Were those kids still alive?
Scrawny fucking things, those kids. For a couple of months there, the dirty bitch had the crabs, so she gave her daughter for rent.

She had insisted Arnold still bring a bag for her to smoke … what a bitch! The passing thought made Arnold mad, like she had gotten one on him. Well, now, he guessed she'd owe him one. He let out a goofy giggle to himself.

He thought hard; did she have two girls? No. He would have remembered. There was a boy, no more than six. Quiet, dirty little thing, never made a peep. The thought of the pint size ragamuffin made Arnold regret not makin' the babies with Debbie.

He nervously bit at his knuckle, thinking about how mad Debbie got when he came home from fucking "that got damned neech! Your dick smells like burnt chemicals and stale cigarettes."

"DON'T TOUCH ME! Go wash your balls!"

The thought pained her to know this woman wasn't another "unknown" in a ditch, like all the others. She was only a rent collection away. He had never told her about the girl … maybe then she would understand?

No, no! She got up to her own thing when he was gone. It was alright — fuck — it was good she kept busy! He had his own thing, too. She would just have to learn to accept this.

The truck came to a squeaky stop in front of the white two-storey house. He leaned over and gave the glove compartment a punch. It bounced open, dropping a cluster of keys out onto the seat. Slamming it shut, he grabbed the keys and walked up to the front door.

The house stood in the older part of town on 98th St. Arnold and Debbie had split the place into three apartments with a common foyer. Quickly thumbing through the keys, he found the main and unlocked the door. He stepped in and immediately glanced up the staircase — save the best for last. He banged on the door to his right — the Steins: a couple of punk kids that smoked dope. Probably had a baby or two, Arnold didn't fucking care.

"Open up. Rent's due."

There was a commotion. Whispers — no, not in his head — from behind the door. Arnold slapped it again, harder.

"Open up, ya hear? Don't got all day. Let's get on with it."

The door opened, just enough to put a foot in, so Arnold did. A freckled ginger boy — girl … ? — squished its face into the crack. Arnold squinted, straining to make sense of this kid's face. The pasty, straggly haired, androgynous stoner fit right in with his tenants.

"Uh — erm — yuh?" The voice wasn't going to tell Arnold whether this was a boy or a girl either.

He leaned in. "Where's Wade an' his lil girly? What's her name? Lisa? Rent's due."

The kid looked at Arnold like he had snakes coming outta his head. "I uhh, umm, I'll — " It twisted its head back into the apartment.

Arnold had better shit to do today. He pushed the door open, sending the ugly girl (he had made up his mind) flying back into a wall and onto her ass.

"Wade! Where the fack is rent?" Passing through the door into their living room, he found both of the little twerps sitting on the couch, visually stunned at what was happening but physically not able to do anything about it. They were on some good shit, for sure.

Arnold reached over a glass table littered with pills, dust, and cigarettes. He grabbed Wade by the scruff of his shirt and yanked him over it. He held him in the air at eye-level.

"Same shit, Wade, every fuckin' month. C'mon, let's not have a problem. Where's the fucking rent?"

Wade's red, swollen eyes couldn't stay locked onto Arnold's if he wanted them to. They kept flicking over Arnold's shoulder to Lisa. Arnold turned his attention to her.

"Lisa, c'mon on, Lisa. Where's the money? You're a smart girl, arncha?"

The girl didn't move from her spot on the couch.

"OK." Dropping Wade to the floor, Arnold turned on his heel and started for the bedroom. They had a lil fuckin' baby, he knew it.

Lisa put the pieces together and scrambled off the couch, racing to beat Arnold to the bedroom, and she did. Bracing herself against the doorframe, she took her stand as Arnold saw the infant asleep on the mattress inside.

"Oh, look at that, a baby ... So sweet when they're small, aren't they?" His gaze slowly drifted from the baby to Lisa.

"I have the money! I have the money! Please don't, we're sorry!" She turned into the bedroom and picked a purse up off the floor, still standing in between Arnold and the baby. She handed Arnold a wad of cash.

As he counted it, he shook his head. "Every fuckin' month. What's wrong with you people? It's just nonsense ... " He fixed his eyes on her as he flipped through every bill. Reaching over, he ran his hand gently down her cheek to her chin. Leaning in, he softly said, "And I hate nonsense, Lisa."

She winced at the sight of the crooked black and yellow teeth that were only inches away from her mouth. Releasing his grip, he turned to walk out.

"I'ma be back next month. Let's not have any trouble, OK?" He didn't wait for a response. He closed the door behind him, three hundred and fifty dollars heavier, and made his way up the stairs. He could hear a woman's voice. It was muffled, but he could still make out what she was screaming through the walls.

" — DON'T COME OUT!" A door slammed to punctuate the sentence.

Good, she was home. Not that it mattered; if she wasn't

there, he knew the girl would be. Arnold never left with nothing.

He knocked on the door, gently thumbing the baggie in his pocket. The door slammed open. A mess of tangled, black hair, an acid-wash miniskirt and a neon pink, fishnet tube-top came out of the pillows of smoke. Stuffed into the outfit was decades of meth and alcohol abuse — a dark-skinned woman whose gut pushed the limits of the skirt she had sausaged herself into. A fuck for a toke, and today, Arnold had lots to toke!

Her eyes darted from him to the door to her hand; she was fucked out of her mind.

Perfect.

"Arnold, I uh, um, I uh, the rent ... um, we can work something out. Right?"

He smiled with his whole face. His eyes became fixed and dark.

Moving to the side to let him in, she laughed, turned, and beelined to a bag on the floor. She came up holding condoms, a lighter, and a browned glass pipe. Arnold recognized the $4.99 glass vase they sold at gas stations.

PaCK It!

Pack IT AGAIN!

And aGaiN

Do IT This TimE   DoN'T PuSs OuT

!PUSSY!

ThhissS

TiMe

We

KiLL

HeR.

Sticking his tongue into his cheek, he grabbed the pipe from the worn out Native. He grabbed the baggy out of his pocket, filled the chamber, and then gave it a fire bath before handing it back to her. He surveyed the small apartment; it was trashed. She stood there sucking on the pipe and muttering something about 'good and evil' and 'disgusting.' She was watching the smoke come out of her mouth when she abruptly looked up at Arnold and smiled.

"This is good shit, who'd you get it from?" She didn't wait for him to answer. "The boys by the tracks? Those guys are motherfuckers! Best friends I ever had … " She would go in circles for a bit, talking and twitching.

Arnold knew as soon as he walked in she had already been smoking. She was no longer aware of herself; her pelvis jutted out and her eyes were as busy as her mouth. He'd keep filling her bowl. She'd lose track of how much she was smoking. Fucking tweekers — they won't say no to another hoot, even if it's the one that puts them on the floor. If she kept talking though, he might have to punch her right in the fucking face.

Under the steely chemical smell in the air, the apartment smelt like stale vomit, shit, and mold. It was no mystery as to why; the evidence was everywhere.

She held out the pipe. Arnold prepared another bubble for her, his beady eyes never leaving his prey.

FUCKING DO IT ARNOLD! fucKthElittlEgirL PuSSy!

KillHEr

" … I don't know where they were coming from, oh yea, the highway, and they were just speeding through! Not knowing where they was going, that's why I don't eat peanut butter … "

Arnold smiled and nodded, continuing his assessment of the apartment. There was a vodka bottle spout deep in the wall. Garbage littered the floor, hiding the bugs underneath. Pieces of the wall had gone missing since he'd last been in here.

" … she gonna be bald now, fucking bitch, didn't know who she was messing with. Nope. Nope. Nope. I can't wait, I cannot wait! That's what you get when you're messin' with an angel … "

Do iT

NOW

Arnold reeled around on his heel, cocked back his fist, and smashed the pock-faced woman in the jaw. Every inch of her body made contact with the shredded drywall, sending dust into the air. Blood spurted from her nose and mouth. She opened her mouth to scream, but nothing came out. She was stunned. As she peeled herself off the wall, Arnold's eyes blackened. His pupils pinpoints, he charged for her.

The plan was to smoke the woman into an OD, put her into a coma, but other parts of Arnold had different plans. Why let the meth have all the fun?

Running his fingers along her scalp, he grabbed the back of her head and brought it down, crushing it into the floor. Each blow was sickeningly loud. Yanking her neck back, he lifted her bloodied face off the floor to examine the damage. He let a gurgled whisper pass her lips before slamming her head back down again, putting the strength of his shoulders into each blow. The pool of blood grew. Bit by bit, he demolished her face. Wrenching her neck back, he studied the state of her face again. Her eyes were swollen shut. Her mouth hung open. The blood seeping out of her gums was pooling underneath her tongue. Her teeth lay on the floor.

DontStoPArnold

YoUWanTThis

splitheropen

GraB tHe boTTlE

Making a path through the garbage, he dragged her body to the mattress on the floor and threw her down on it.

The bottle, hey? His spotted the *Smirnoff* bottle in the wall. The bloody fantasy of shoving it in her pussy and then ripping it out was placed on the mental 'Ta Do' list.

But now?

There was sweat gathering on his brow. His breath laboured in his chest. An uncontrollable rage was building within him, coming out through every single one of his pores.

KiLL TheM All

Arnold lunged across the room, pulled the bottle out of the wall and walked around the mattress to stand over the limp body. 'Miss Corbett.' He held the bottle like a club over his head. Like clouds passing in front of the sun, the room was slowly consumed in shade. He hammered the bottle into her skull. With every blow, her skull gave way, concaving. The skin didn't tear or rip. It was like pounding a ball of dough.

ShE'sss at Death's DooR

SenD HeR ThrouGH

Fuck   Fuck   FUCK   HER

makethekidswatch

He clenched his jaw tightly, out of breath and sweating. His heaving chest forced his breaths out of his nose. Tossing the bottle aside, it shattered against the wall. His breath slowed, but the rage didn't. The glass crunched under his feet as he walked around the mattress.

Studying the woman's bloodied and puffy face, he undid his overalls and let them drop around his ankles. His eyes moved up to the sunken-in, bowl-like depression in the top of her head. Her blood was still flowing. A slow but steady pulse thumped from her forehead. *Tough bitch.*

PuT ThE GlasS in Her AsS

SheS A rAT

VeRmIn

PiG

SeND hER To Hell

ruSHing

PutRiD CunT

Licking his lips with delight and anticipation, the chubby in his hand went rock hard. It would be difficult not to jump the gun and come into his palm. He leaned over her; her legs parted, making room — just barely — for his fat, hairy ass. He pulled her pink tube top down off her tits. They fell out of the fabric and immediately sagged to the sides of her body. Scooping her left breast into his hand, he pulled and kneaded it roughly before taking it into his mouth.

His dick rubbed against the coarse, wet hairs of her vagina. As he sucked harder, his dick came to the precipice of penetrating her. Instinctively checking the room, he found himself looking into the eyes of the small, dirty boy standing in the doorway of the bathroom, watching. Emotionless and vacant, the boy didn't move when Arnold snarled at him.

With her breast still in his mouth, he jolted his hips forward, impaling the living dead addict. The boy triggered a new sense of excitement in Arnold; he had never had a third person admire him before. Not unless it was Debbie. This was an un-expected intrusion. He hadn't even thought about the fate of the two kids yet. He bit down over the areola until he felt the little punctures of the skin giving. The warm taste of copper flooded his mouth. The boy's eyes never left his own. He scraped his teeth through the fatty flesh until he held a soft rubbery chunk of the breast in his mouth.

YesSssss

LeT HiM WatcH

Arnold got to his knees, grabbed onto the woman's thighs and rammed into her as fast and hard as he could. He spat the bloody nipple onto the floor. It landed with a smack in front of the child's bare toes.

Sweat began rolling down Arnold's back, through his ass crack, down his thighs. B.O. and waste filled every crevice of the room. It was hard to know if there was an exact source of the smell, or if it was just what evil and death smelled like when they met. As Arnold continued to fuck the near-corpse in a manner that could only be described as 'convulsively,' the boy took his first steps out of the doorway.

ThiSsssss   BeaUtiFul CreaTure

wiLl Be witH   uSsssssssss

WaTCh   Let Him COmE IntO Ussssss

A cold sweat came over Arnold. A shiver ran through his entire body. His vision blurred as his balls emptied into the rotten cavern that was this woman's cunt. As his eyes uncrossed and his sight came back into focus, he saw the boy standing over him. In his hand, he was gripping a large piece of the shattered vodka bottle.

XLIII.

IGNACE

The following is an excerpt from:

Luc Marchand's

Queens of Hell
An Occult Specialist's Search for the Devils in the Background

Published 1997
All rights reserved.

Ignace Courier Archive
November 10th 1986

Three out of the six missing persons cases coming out of Ignace, ON, have come to a tragic close today. Sergeant Mike Olson's wife Sara, 32, and their two daughters, Rebecca, 4, and Elizabeth, 7, were found late in the day on November 8th approx. 40 kilometres east of Ignace, nearing Bonheur River, Kame Provincial Reserve.

All three bodies were discovered together and no foul play is suspected.

The team that discovered the bodies consisted of local volunteers, RCMP, and law enforcement from Thunder Bay, Kakabeka Falls, Murillo, Dryden, and Sioux Lookout. They have been canvassing the area since November 1st looking for Antoinette, Daniella, and Marco Merlo, who still remain missing.

If you have any information as to the whereabouts of Daniella, Antoinette, or Marco please call: 807-445-8989

XLIV.

LILI

Calgary, Alberta
August 10th 2003
12:35 a.m.

The remnants line the streets, shadows stepping out of amber light. The road, glistening with early morning dew, moves. Spiders, myriads of them, on the road. My skin crawls. Sudden urgency overwhelms me as a car rolls up to the curb in front of us.

"Justyne, run!"

It's too late. Krish gets out of the back of the car and rushes to grab us. We don't have a chance. Justyne is slammed up against the car as I'm stuffed in the front seat.

"Get in the fucking car, or I kill you both on the street."

Justyne kicks and screams, holding onto the frame of the car. I hear the kick before I turn to see Justyne being shoved into the back, holding her stomach and gasping. Krish reaches up front to the driver and says something in Arabic. The driver's response is short and also in Arabic. They both laugh. I don't want to know what about this they find funny.

We drive out of the core, destination: Unknown. Krish whispers things into Justyne's ear, bringing her closer to his side. His hand rests on the back of her head, gently guiding it to his lap. Every once in a while, Krish says something in Arabic to the guy driving. The quiet in the car is actually calming.

The quiet in my head is making me worry.

After a while, we exit onto the highway. The houses and the streetlamps have disappeared. It isn't until we make a turn off the highway and onto a dirt road that Justyne speaks up from the backseat.

"Where are we?"

Krish holds her tightly. "Oh, my friend. He lives out here. We're close, shh."

I check out the pair through the rear-view mirror. I see uncertainty in Justyne's eyes and mischief in Krish's. We drive through the darkness, leaving a cloud of dust behind us, for another half an hour before pulling over into a field.

I smile. It's a perfect place to die. There are no lights for days. It is just a tiny part of a huge field; who knows how often it is tended.

It will be weeks before their torched car is found.

"I thought you said your friend lived out here?" There's strain in Justyne's voice. Is she just beginning to understand they brought us out here to kill us?

"You ask so many questions, little bird. Don't worry."

The car comes to a slow stop. The headlights illuminate a couple of feet of tall grass in front of us, and that's all.

"Lili, me and your friend are going to take a little walk. I want to show her something. You and him stay here and play nice until I — I mean, *we* get back. OK?"

I turned around to face Justyne. Her eyes are wide, pleading for me to tell her what to do, but I have nothing. Before I can scream for her to run, the door slams shut.

I sit in the dark car, leaving the silence between us alone, watching Justyne walk into the field. She disappears, and I am forced to confront my own clear and ever-present danger.

The driver seems like he is having an inner battle with his conscience. Biting his lip, furrowing his brow, probably wishing it to 'go away.' I can tell he's losing — he is not weak, he's just not like Krish. He can't whimsically murder me. He is using the time to prepare himself.

So, I prepare, too.

I'm not nervous. I know what has to be done. I need to figure out how to execute it. Casually as I can, I peer down into the side door pocket. A pen and some napkins. The pen could be used if nothing else comes to mind.

"You are a very pretty girl." He was ready.

"Oh gee, you think so?" My sarcastic tone surprises me. I'm antagonizing him; I'm coaxing him into a trap.

"Yes. I think so. Very much. I think it would be a good idea if you didn't fight. Maybe I can tell Krish, you shouldn't die tonight, like your friend."

Opening the glove compartment slowly, I meet his eyes. "I don't think that's such a good idea." I turn my attention back to the glove compartment, but the light comes on, drawing his attention as well.

"What are you looking for? Get out of the car! GET OUT OF THE FUCKING CAR! GET IN THE BACK!"

He rears back and punches me in the side of the head. My body, still strapped into the seat, stays in place. With a loud crack, my head smacks against the glass. My whole head throbs; there's orbs of light everywhere.

When my eyes find him again I see he is getting ready to hit me again: one hand balled up into a fist, cocking back. The other fist, white-knuckled around the handle of a matte black hunting knife. The corners of my mouth curve upwards at the thought of my search being over.

My attention is stolen by the rear-view mirror. Still regaining my breath, saving myself from being knuckle-slapped again, I point to the mirror. "Can't go to the back seat."

His face twists with outrage at my defiance. I hear the click of his seatbelt coming off seconds before I am punched in the face again, my head hits the window with a quick, hard, smack.

It's unmistakable, the thing that sits in the back seat. Its dark outline is clear. It sits upright behind the driver. Watching. Waiting. Pointing once more into the mirror, I shake my head.

This time, he gets up out of his seat, leans forward, and looks into the mirror. *This is my chance.* His eyes go wide. I watch as the blood so clearly drains from his face, leaving his dark complexion sickly and pale.

"It's already occupied," I say.

Thank God you're here, where the fuck have you been?

Quickly unbuckling myself, I throw my back against the door to use it as leverage and boot him in the jaw as hard as I can. I have a second to pull my knee back to kick him in the face again. I land another shoe in his mouth. As I grab at the knife, the dark mass in the back seat lunges at the driver as well.

With the knife now in my hand, we both to turn to face the back seat. Black, sinuous chaos expands outwardly. Its veins shoot forth, puncturing us. Two monstrous, red eyes spring open simultaneously above row after row of rotten, jagged teeth, protruding out of a black, faceless void.

It is upon us. A new and unfamiliar strength courses through my body. Inhaling sharply, my eyes meet with the driver's. His pupils dilate, but his stare never leaves mine, not even as I crawl on top of his thighs, raise my arm above my head and drive the knife down, in between his eyes, through his skull.

I hope to pull it out as fast as it sunk in, but it catches. His head jerks forward once, twice, as I tug on the knife. Third time's a charm; the skull lets go of the blade, my hand snaps back. The blade leaves a slit in his forehead that quickly swells into a crimson line, and then slowly releases a spring of blood that flows down the bridge of his nose. His eyes stare into mine, betrayed, confused. How has he gotten to this place? His pores open to discharge a mixture of blood and sweat. His body shakes underneath me.

I am filled with an ancient rage, a rage that has roots in my very creation, an evil my brain doesn't need to understand. I drive the knife into his chest, shoulders, and face, again and again in a violent frenzy. Blood splashes onto the windows, enveloping us in a red cave of death.

I pause to assess what my wrath has done to this pile of skin and bones. It's no longer recognizable as a human. I'm hit with the realization I'm not done. I might never be.

A smile creeps across my face as he sputters the last signs of life out of his throat. Sliding the knife along the base of his neck, I put an end to his choking. I throw my head back and scream, letting the power flow through my veins, letting the atrocity take over. So much energy floods my body. I lose control.

Still screaming, I flail my arms. My head shakes back and forth. In the window, I see him. The raw skin and muscles glisten in the fresh blood. His skin rips apart as his mouth tears itself open, letting out a deep and deafening roar. It's him, *Ephryium*. He is reaching out to me. I realize he is mine, and I, his, and it is not him I have just invited in.

He's sad, if it's possible. My heart breaks for the pain he experiences for me, for us. He calls to me, to run away, to fight!

I'm drowning in tar. The energy still floods in. My groin pulses, engorging with blood. My nipples are hard. Every muscle is so tense it hurts.

Everything is fading away, going black. I am being pulled into a part of myself that is dark and cold. I am being buried alive within myself, and there is nothing I can do to stop it. As my vision grows cloudy, I take my last breath and plunge the knife into the driver's head as deep as it will go. I watch as his jaw goes slack and his tongue falls out of his mouth to dangle loosely from his maimed face.

Locked inside, I know what's to come.

It knows what's in the trunk. *It* will go find Krish now. And Justyne.

Oh dear god! Justyne, RUN! Please RUN! This is no longer my body!
My voice laughs back at me, echoing into the nothing.

𝔛𝔏𝔙.

ARNOLD & THE BOY

North Battleford, Saskatchewan
1362 98th Street
June 12th 1989

There was absolutely no hesitation. Not in the boy's eyes or in the quick, fluid moment he reached across Arnold to stab the thick shard of glass into his mother's neck.

Dragging it through the meat, he bit into his bottom lip as he summoned the strength to go deeper. Bright red blood jetted from her arteries, spraying Arnold's face. The boy pushed deeper, sawing through veins and tendons. The glass scraped bone first, and then deeper to the mattress underneath the butchery.

The boy was in a frenzy. The glass had begun to cut into his fragile hand. Under Arnold's knees, in the depressions of the mattress, the blood began to pool.

Arnold's jaw sagged as he watched, trying to pinpoint exactly what this overwhelming feeling was. It welled in his chest. It flowed through his veins. It brought his jaw back up to close his mouth, where a smile immediately formed; a smile of pride.

It took all of him not to scoop the boy up into his arms.

ViCiOus LiTTle Creature

So YouNg

ViOlEnt

Ssssssooo RipE WiTh   HatE

LeT uS   FiLL HiM

The little, black-haired boy glanced up at Arnold, not for approval but just to acknowledge his presence, his audience. He ran his fingers through his mom's hair and began to twist her head until she faced the floor.

The boy's voice was a hoarse whisper. "Burn it all down, Arnold. Kill them all."

Lissssten   To ThE BOY   ArnOLd

LiSSsssten To   OuR SsssssoN

Arnold watched the blood slowly ooze out of Ms. Corbett's neck, inching its way closer and closer to him. He pulled his dick out and spat into his palm, giving the ol' cock a spit-shine before spidermaning the back of the woman's head.

"OK, all done."

Getting to his feet, he pulled up his overalls, turned to the door and called over his shoulder. "Boy, stop playin' witch'er mama and git in the bath. Wash that nonsense off you."

Whether or not the boy complied, Arnold didn't know. He was just so fucking pleased with everything. He skipped down the stairs, giggling deeply. Debbie was going to love him. Oh yes, Arnold knew, a little ragamuffin boy would be a sparkle in their eyes. He could've never wished for a child like this one.

With the boy came his sister. *Debbie dunt know I diddled the girl. But she won't know. The girl will come along, too. We'll be a ...* Arnold's thoughts grew deliciously dark as he thought of the little girl underneath him, and the erection growing in his pants, fitting snuggly between her thighs. All the while Debbie would be in the next room waiting for him — NO! Watching!

… *Family.*

WhiLe The

CaT'sss AwAy

Arnold got the message. He needed to be quick and get back upstairs before the boy got into something he shouldn't or had an accident with a piece of glass. Concern quickly turned to curiosity with the thought of the boy still busy upstairs; he was more curious about what the boy had gotten up to than if he needed to stop him.

With the bang of the truck's tailgate coming down, he imagined the boy going at his sister the same way Arnold had seen him go at his mother. The blood boiled past his collar; the boy would need to know the girl was Arnold's. Moving with more purpose than before, he grabbed the gas can out of the bed of the truck and rushed back to the apartment.

Opening the door as little as possible, Arnold slipped back into the pungent smell of blood, sweat, and death. Handfuls of brown, doughy skin were littered in with garbage on the floor. The boy had been busy. The sound of running water came from the bathroom.

Good boy.

The door to the bathroom fell open gently before Arnold got to it. In the doorway stood the little boy and his older sister. They held hands, washed up, and in Arnold's mind, ready to go "home." He got to it.

Burnitburnit

BurNiTaLL

After Ms. Corbett had been given a thorough dose of gasoline, Arnold felt a tug on his sleeve. The boy brought his attention to the little girl slouching in the bathroom doorway. In a fit of tears, unnerved — knowing what happened here and knowing there was nothing she could do to stop what was going to happen next. The tug on Arnold's sleeve persisted and gradually lured his eyes back to the little boy at his side. He held a Zippo up to Arnold's belly, smiling that mischievous smile all little boys do. The Zippo felt warm and heavy in his palm. Full and ready to go.

As much as he loved his place of loneliness — a place that had been just for him — he was elated to have company, to be elbow-deep in entrails, to not only have an inheritor of this beast inside of him but a worthy successor. Yea, he had Debbie. He would always have Debbie, and Debbie him. But having a wife isn't like having a son.

Arnold watched in awe as the boy ran over to his mother's pulverized body and zealously twisted at the partially decapitated head until finally, with a crack, it gave. The boy stuck his foot onto his mother's shoulders and heaved backwards, tearing the rest of the skin that had attached her head to her neck. Landing hard on his butt, he hugged the head to his chest, triumph painting his face. The boy had removed the skin on her face and one of his mother's eyes. The head was now near skeletal, teeth jutting out, with no lips to hide them. Arnold let out an involuntary chuckle. *That's where all that skin was from! What a rascal.*

Springing to his feet, the boy took the head with him to the corner of the room and began to explore its anatomy as casually as if it were a new toy. Arnold could relate, but this wasn't the time. He wanted to get the kids out of the house and bring them home to Debbie. He was excited and a little scared to see her reaction.

SssssssSSet It On FiRe

GiVe   ThEM   All   TO

ME

From the corner, Arnold could hear the boy stop what he was doing. Their eyes met in understanding. It was time. Flicking the Zippo open, he ran it down the leg of his pants and lit it. Like the fire that sparked out of the Zippo, the boy's interest also lit up. Watching the boy's eyes widen, he knew the boy would want to watch, study his mother's skin as it bubbled and blistered, popped and tore, the water oozing out, the edges of each wound charring to an iridescent black. The flames would eat the apartment up in only a moment — with disappointment in his heart, he knew he and the boy would have to move quickly. As if Arnold had whispered his thoughts aloud, the boy slowly took his eyes off his mother and met Arnold's stare. Eagerly, the boy ran around his mother's body and put his tiny hand into Arnold's, pulling him to the door.

"Take me home, Daddy."

As they rushed passed the girl, who still cried quietly in the doorway to the bathroom, the little boy scooped her hand into his own, looked up at Arnold, and gave him a wink.

With the boy's hand in his, Arnold turned back to fling the still burning Zippo onto the fresh corpse, leading the boy and his sister out of the house and across the street.

Loud and panicked screams spilled from the house. The screams of the women being burned alive were so shrill they drowned out the wails of their male counterparts, whose frustrated yells were filled with the confusion of how they could be locked inside the burning house. As the smoke billowed out of the up-stairs windows, the screams waned. They had failed to save them-selves and their families.

Arnold and the boy watched from inside the pickup truck. It was awesome. Front row tickets to the big show. He had never killed so many people at once before, or caused so much damage, and in broad daylight! This was going to be hard to top.

THE RIDE HOME'S only soundtrack was of the little girl's soft whimpers, caught up in the bleakness of her immediate future. The boy could almost hear her mind spinning in rewind, back to the inferno of the ignited apartment. He watched her from Arnold's side, eyes lit up with the excitement of his new surroundings. He dragged his gaze from the window to his sister at his side. The boy watched her face twist and contort; he was entertained by the inner turmoil she was obviously going through.

A boyish grin spread across his face, as he imagined what she must have been thinking. Throwing herself into the flames again and again, tearing her hand out of her brother's screaming, "But I fed you! I took care of you! All we have is each other! How could you do this? How could you do this to me?"

Different variations of these one-sided conversations running through her head, rewind, repeat, rewind rewind rewind. She would be her saviour in her head; she would be a martyr. Dying a thousand times in her head was ultimately better to brood on than the reality she hurled towards. Just as the boy had fed on neglect, cruelty, and chaos, he now fed on his sister's despair. He held her hand, content, fantasizing the horrors still being envisioned by his poor, poor sister while he looked on to the road in front.

The boy's curiosity grew as the truck travelled further down the dirt road. Although it had been a clear day in Battleford, a fog collected in between the walls of the valley. He watched, inquisitively for his sister's reaction, he saw her taking it in, adding to her fantasy. This was exactly what the descent into hell looked like. Her mind would now be the only escape she could hope for. Yes, it pleased him to think she still hoped.

𝕏𝕃𝕍𝕀.

ARNOLD

North Battleford Outskirts, Saskatchewan

The brakes squeaked under the truck's chassis as it rolled to a slow stop. Hands still clenching the steering wheel, Arnold stared out the windshield to the weather-worn grey house. White paint peeled off the wood siding. The windows, still in place, were cloudy and dull. Debbie was somewhere in there, waiting for him to get home. He came to the sudden realization he would have some 'splainin to do.

"Now, you're gonna keep your mouths shut. If you don't, if you think now is the time to act up or cause trouble, you're gonna have another thing comin'."

The boy gazed up at him, smiling from ear to ear. His sister sat slumped over, staring at her feet. He wasn't gonna get any trouble from the boy, he knew it, but the girl was gonna have trouble whether she stayed quiet or not.

"I'm gonna take you inside now," Arnold calmly explained.

His thought process careened. He deliberately moved slowly, taking shorter strides around the truck and pausing before pulling the door open. He was buying himself more time to hash out the impending argument. He wasn't going to try to sneak in now, no surprises.

As soon as his boots hit the linoleum in the kitchen, he saw Debbie come out of their bedroom. Turning over his shoulder, he motioned to the kids to stay put.

"Well, hello there, ma darlin'." The goofy smile, the outstretched arms — he wasn't foolin' anyone, sure as shit not Debbie.

She stopped dead in her tracks, crossed her arms across her chest, and saw him for what he was — full of shit. "What'd you do, Arnie? Dontchu look at me with love in yer eyes and no money in your pocket."

Oh yea!

Reaching his sweaty palm into his overalls pocket, he clutched the wad of rent money that was waiting there to alleviate the tension he was about to create. "Got the rent money right here."

Her face softened. "Oh, so it's just love in those big, dumb eyes then?"

"Naw, I got everything done, but … somethin' happened down at the house today … " Keeping his eyes on Debbie's, he nervously dropped the sweat-soaked money onto the table.

Debbie moseyed around, casually sat down behind the money, and began to straighten the bills out in order to count it. She glanced up from her task and asked, "Have any trouble?"

"No, no. Nuthin' like that. I think it could be a good thing actually … " He was gonna need to spit it out; these kinds of games made Debbie mad. Like clockwork, no sooner had Arnold thought it, Debbie had had enough of the bullshit.

"What are you talking about?" she cut in, raising the conversation another octave.

Arnold should have just said it from the get go — he deserved this.

"We're short two hundred and fifty bucks, Arnie. Does this have to do with that dirty squaw? She overdose? She dead? You better not have fucked her again, Arnie, alive or dead."

Impulsively, Arnold bit his lower lip and let his gaze fall to the floor.

Putting her hand to her forehead, she let out a wail. "You know how I feel about the meth-riddled neech spreadin' her legs for you. You have pussy, Arnie. Make that bitch pay rent!" She wailed again, shaking her head, closing her eyes tightly. "Arnie, I understand you're a man, a man has his needs. I would be a rotten wife if I denied you of those needs, but you keepin' the fucking sack of shit and her two crackhead kids alive is gonna be trouble for us. Don't you like what we have here?"

Now or never. Pulling a chair out, he sat himself across from her, reached across the table and took her hands in his.

"I don't want you to think on those things. Its nuthin' like that, nuthin' like that at all. You're right; we do live a quiet life out here. I don't want no trouble. Its nuthin' like that. I think we could add to our lives, make it better than what it is. I wanted to talk to you about the thought of being parents, Deb."

There was silence, and Debbie's expressionless face, just staring at him. After a thousand years of this, she finally threw his hands away from her own. She asked, "So, is that what you spent the two hundred and fifty on? You smokin' crack, Arnie?"

Before Arnold could get more than a snicker out, the phone rang.

Neither of them turned to the phone hanging on the wall.

The staring contest was on.

Arnold knew Debbie would never put anything past him; he was unpredictable and curious, and those were things she loved about him but one thing Arnold was not, was a bull-shitter, so why the fuck was she sitting there dragging nothing but stutters and babbles from him?

Arnold sat, not knowing what part to tell her first. There was just so much. Usually what he did outside the house, unless he wanted it to, didn't come back to the house. It didn't affect Debbie or their lives at all. Every element of what had taken place today would affect her, and he hadn't even bothered to see how she would feel about it first.

Should he open with — fucking god damn it, he couldn't fucking think a full thought through without the phone going off. Guess Debbie was having an equally hard time focusing on Arnold; she was pretty aggressive about shoving herself away from the table to go snatch the phone off the wall.

"Whatya want? Yes it is … this is she. It what? How? … Oh, I see … Oh, that's terrible news. Oh dear, so sorry to hear that … "

Arnold watched Debbie's knuckles go whiter and whiter around the phone, her jaw clenching more and more with each pause. He hadn't noticed the fire in her eyes burning into him. When he did, she silently mouthed, "What the fuck did you do?" It was terrifying.

"Oh no, they were all locked inside? Oh no! That's just awful. Unfortunately, Officer, I do know all of our tenants were druggies, but what can ya do, right? Rent came in on time, so we turned the cheek. I wouldn't be surprised, though, if it was some drug dealer lookin' to get paid what was owed to him. The woman upstairs — Sorry, the late Ms. Corbett was late on rent more often than not … all I'm saying, Officer, is I wouldn't be surprised if we weren't the only ones she owed money to is all … No … Yes, yes, that's all I meant, not trying to speak ill of the dead … Yes me an' my husband … We will … the baby too, huh? Terrible."

While Debbie was doing her civic duty on the phone, Arnold got up from the table. Still listening to her go on with the officer, he walked to the porch. The kids stood in the exact same place he had left them. He grabbed them by their shoulders, guided them into the kitchen, and stood behind them as he watched Debbie's jaw hit the floor.

"Ye- hhhhaaa!" With a shocked gasp, she let the phone slip from her hand. It smacked the wall a couple of times before it just dangled there, the officer's tiny voice still coming from the ear piece.

And there they all stood, in a tableau that was the definition of a nuclear family. The Killer, the Possessed, and their Nameless Children.

XLVII.

JUSTYNE

Unknown Location Outside Calgary, Alberta
August 10th 2003
1:25 a.m.

K rish led Justyne by the hand. She glanced back to where they had walked from, and could no longer see the car. "Stop."

"Why?" *This was it.* "Please. Please don't."

"Take off your clothes, now."

Krish didn't wait for her response. She didn't realize a conversation about it was not where this was going quick enough. Grabbing her wrist, he jerked her towards him, knocked her off balance, and threw her into the grass. She rolled onto her stomach and tried to get onto her knees. *It's now or never!* It was as if he knew she was going to try to run; like he wanted her to. Before she found her footing, he was behind her, pulling off her shoes. One, then the other.

She let out a scream knowing full well no one heard but Krish and herself. He laughed at her and shook his head. The look on his face told her everything; he was going to kill her, and he was going to enjoy it. Wasting her strength, she tightly held onto the grass, pulling herself away from him. He jerked her legs toward him and ripped her pants off.

Justyne screamed into the night again; the wind took it, and it was lost. As soon as her legs hit the ground, she tried to tuck her knee underneath her to gain some traction so she could run. She wouldn't go out without fighting for her life. At least she would have that.

Instead, he pulled her legs out from under her again and flipped her over onto her back. He quickly mounted her, pinning her beneath his heavy weight, and pounded into her face. He hit her again and again, working her over with both fists. She put her hands up to stop the avalanche, but it was as if they weren't even there.

It came to a stop like a heart attack. She couldn't open her eyes; they were already swelling shut. She lay quietly in the grass, dazed and hurt, shaking her head, pleading internally for Krish to stop, pleading for Lili to somehow come and save her. Wishing for a do-over, to go back and make better decisions so maybe it would have never have come to this. None of this reached her swollen lips.

He ripped her shirt off her body, and then begun searching for something. "Where the fuck is my knife?"

She let out another sob. "You don't have to do this. You don't have to do this."

She could barely make out Krish's blurry face, but she could see that his search had stopped and his attention was back on her. "Fuck. You lucky cunt, I left it back in the car. Hopefully, it will be put to good use on the retarded bitch who thought it was a good idea to get lippy with me." He paused as if in thought and then put his hand around her neck. "I should have brought both of you out here. I could have made you watch as I shoved a knife up your friend's pussy."

"Please." It came out as a painful and faint whisper. "Please, let me go. Please. Don't do this."

He slapped her mouth. "No talking."

He laughed at her. She wasn't going anywhere; he hadn't held back. He meant to put her down for the count, and she was. His grip on her neck loosened, and he sat up straight, looking off into the field around them. The hairs on the back of her neck prickled. She got the sense of someone approaching.

Footsteps?

She hoped it was someone coming to save her. It could be Lili, but what if it was the other guy? What if he killed Lili and now he was coming to help Krish? They both sat in silence. No one was there. She'd sworn she had heard footsteps. She saw Krish had, too. Undoing his buckle, he pulled the half-woody out of his pants, spit into the palm of his hand, and gave it a couple of loving strokes.

"Be useful. Put it in your mouth, come here." He grabbed the hair behind her head and scooped her up towards his dick. She forced her eyes open and her mouth shut. He slapped her face with the tip of his dick.

"Put it in your fucking mouth before I break your skinny fucking neck, chop you up, and leave you on your doorstep with your cunt inside out. Fucking whore, you wanted it so bad before. Put it in." He pressed it against her mouth until her lips finally gave in and parted.

As he slowly pumped into her, tears streamed down her cheeks into her mouth, causing her to cough and sputter on the inches-thick dick moving in and out her face.

With her hands on Krish's belly, she weakly pushed him away. Hoping to find a morsel of strength hiding within herself, she escaped into her mind. She was struck with the realization Lili wasn't coming. No one was coming to save her. Lili was probably already dead, too. She wanted to cry. She was tired and no longer wanted to fight under the idea Lili was gone. Justyne settled into her pain and regret and then resigned herself to death. Nothing more was meant for her.

She loved that they died together. Her sister, her love.

XLVIII.

THE BOY

September 4th 1990
North Battleford, Saskatchewan

The sun was just cresting over the highest peak in the valley. Dawn brought in dewy purple skies and crisp air. The pale sun revealed inky green hills, casting the shadows out. It was all so promising for the first day of school. In the distance, the faint echo of wood being chopped could be heard. Hidden away from the world, away from the evil, from the ungodly and immoral things, sat a perfect, white farm house with a matching wooden shed off to the side.

Inside the charming shed, a boy daydreamed about a visitor who would come walking down the gravel road, hear the chopping from inside the shed, and think, "Wonderful. Probably the owner." They might put together the portrait of a kindly old man, or a strong, beautiful woman, or a sweet, doe-eyed boy, all chopping wood for a warm hearth. The comforting smells of homemade soup or bacon and eggs would come to mind. This place would lure them closer with the promise of safety.

So they would come around to the door of the shed, and it would slowly open in front of them. The knotted wood door would swing off to the side and before they could get a real look of their imaginary woodcutter, they would flinch, blinking rapidly at whatever had just landed in their eye? Perhaps a sliver, a chip? Something innocent? Anything but what it was. The fantasy person's security would dissipate into a nightmare. This was the boy's favourite part of his daydreams, when hope was lost.

The boy, one year older, one year wiser, in a brand new home, meat cleaver in hand, and a box full of kittens still wet with birth beside him on the work bench. And then the hacking noise. The handfuls of sticky fur falling to pieces, tossed into a wastebasket on the floor. As he continued mutilating and killing the helpless little creatures in a robotic fashion, he went back to his reverie. If the lost, wandering soul was human, with just an ounce of compassion, it would be appalling, it would be offensive, it would be terrifying — the mews from the tiny mouths being abruptly silenced, the bang of the cleaver meeting with the wood. This depraved boy would move them to speak out and ask, "What the fuck are you doing? Stop!"

The boy would turn. His once sweet and kind and playful eyes would, if it was possible, go darker, a shade away from black. They would be cold and empty. He liked to see himself this way, powerful on the verge of ultra-violence while in ultimate control. But it was imperative his make-believe victim saw he was healthy and handsome, the hero of this fantasy land, it might seem, and not the villain of a twisted purgatory. He would gently wipe his pink-stained hands on a scrap of cloth and say, as if it were the only answer there was:

"I'm getting ready for school."

The lost person would see this beautiful boy had, with inhuman speed, whipped something towards them. They would even hear the crack of their own skull being split open. The euphoria and adrenaline now being pumped through their body would make it impossible for the thoughts to connect with a conclusion as to why.

The blood would slowly stream down their face, and they would look at the boy, convinced he was playing with them, the way you tease a dog with a ball. With the sound of the lost soul's knees hitting the ground, he woke from this fantasy, faintly hearing the screams of desperation of a lost person being dragged into the mouth of an even darker reality.

Or was that just Mom calling for breakfast?

XLIX.

ARNOLD & DEBBIE

North Battleford, Saskatchewan

Where's the boy at?" Debbie took her station at the stove. Today, she was going to play a spectacular parent.

"Outside, playing witda cats."

"Well, it's time to come in now. It's the first day of school. Let's get some food into this boy's belly and ship him off with the bus. Ya wanna go holler for 'im?"

Arnold was already pushing through the squeaky porch door, heading to the front yard.

The boy had gotten up early. He had been an early riser since he'd come home with Arnold last year. Sometimes he'd be down in the basement with his sister, other times in the shed or the front yard. Arnold had caught him a couple times in the middle of ritualistically killing cats or rabbits, one time a fox, another time a dog. He'd seen all different stages of the boy's rituals: the torture leading up to the killing, and then the killing itself — which reminded Arnold so much of his own methods. It was endearing.

Arnold and Debbie had talked to the boy about keeping his dick in his pants when playing with the animals, not gettin' diseases an' such. Their boy was receptive, smart, and analytical. Other times, playful and mischievous. He made them laugh and loved them like he was their own, providing Debbie and Arnold real insight into what it was to be parents. "Normal" parents.

Then there were times when he would withdraw into himself, become quieter, take up company with darker things, things which led him into the forest to hunt for a victim or down to the basement where his sister slept. It was these times Arnold knew no other parents would do what they did for this boy; Arnold and Debbie knew how to nurture that side of him like no other parent could.

The wet smack of the blade hitting the wood caught Arnold's ear. He changed his course, turning towards the shed.

Brush your teeth.

    Grab the knife

Wash your face.

     Go outside

Comb your hair.

      Collect the kittens

Get dressed.

       Go to the shed

Get your lunch packed.

        See how their hearts beat

        Chop chop

"Mornin'. You ready for school? Let's get in. Mum's got pancakes an' bacon ferya."

Winding his fingers around a long thread of pink flesh, the boy turned to face Arnold. Disappointment pulled his gaze down to the floor. He wasn't ready to come in. He wasn't done.

"You follow it out here?"

Flicking his eyes up at Arnold, the boy whispered, "Yep."

If Debbie hadn't pushed so hard to turn the "savage into a scholar," he would have left the boy to it, but the bus would be comin' around soon …

As the boy slunk past Arnold and out of the shed, he called back, "Don't touch 'em, Pa. Leave 'em be alwight? We wanna save em fer later. See 'em rot!"

What a scamp!

As the bus pulled away, leaving a cloud of dark exhaust fumes, Arnold began to walk down the hill and back to the house. If he didn't hurry, Debbie would have already started in on the girl. It had been a bitch of a year keeping the girl alive. She had only lasted a couple of months sleeping in the guest room beside her brother. Then, it had been easy to crawl into the bed with her, Debbie sound asleep in their room. Sometimes he'd wake the boy with a squeak of the door. He would remind himself every night to WD40 that sonofabitch. Not that it mattered if he was awake or not; in a matter of minutes, the gentle rocking of the bed would lull him back to sleep.

Debbie caught on pretty quick. It didn't sit well with her; she was jealous of the girl. She would go on and on about how the girl was nothing but a useless tit, looked just like her meth-head mother, should have been left at the house to burn.

Arnold stepped in as much as possible, but he still had to go to work. He'd come back from a run to discover the girl scrawnier than he had left her. Debbie refused to feed her. She had left the girl with bald patches on her head; it didn't take much for the hair to be pulled right outta her scalp 'cause she was so malnourished. This last run he'd come back to discover Debbie had started making the girl sleep downstairs. Not that he minded, but it wasn't as comfortable as the bed had been. It wouldn't be much longer for the girl.

He couldn't explain it: he felt a connection, a bond, a love for the boy. But the girl? He'd miss fuckin' her, but at least Debbie wouldn't be screamin' as much. And besides, fucking a healthy body, stiff and dead, or alive and screaming, would always be more attractive than fucking a tight pussy so emaciated she couldn't keep her bowels in.

L.

ONE OF MANY
& LILI

Everywhere, Nowhere — Lili's Body

!We will KiLL Them BoTH!

"NO! PLEASE STOP! Just HIM! Please leave her alone! I
LOVE HER! KILL HIM! TAKE HIM!"
ShES Not NeedEd

OnLY   You

We Will   KeeP You
OuR BeAUtifUl

Creature

She   FEeLs SO
    gOOD!

            We Will StAy With thiS OnE   FOREVER
!OURSssss!

After so many years spent in the shadows, hovering over the
chaos it had caused, it was wonderful to find someone who didn't
break underneath of it, someone who had experience taking the
back seat. Why didn't she want this? Didn't she know she was
made for this? For it.

It used its new capable hands to push the bloody corpse out
of the car. Sitting on the edge of the seat, it bent down and dipped
the tips of its fingers into the man's blood. The fluid felt so warm,
and smooth rubbed in-between its small feminine hands. Taking
a moment to savor Lili's body, to feel every one of her pores,
every strand of hair that fell onto her back. The excitement it felt
bordered on arousal. The sensations the humans took for granted.
It walked to the back of the car to pop the trunk. Grabbed the
gas can and Krish's machete out and slammed it shut. It was time
to do this properly.

As it passed where the leb's body lay in the grass, it stepped onto his head. The skull had been stabbed so many times it concaved under the pressure of its foot easily, and it was able to bend over and slide the protruding knife out with ease. Wiping the blood off onto their pants, it tucked the knife into the back of their jeans. It knew exactly where it was going to go next.

Lili's far away voice echoed within. *"Kill him. Rip him to fucking pieces. You keep your fucking hands off Justyne. She's mine. If you touch her, I will fucking destroy you."*

Rolling its eyes at the presumptuous request, it bent down and reached into the boy's pocket. It pulled out a pack of cigarettes. There wasn't a more perfect time to have a smoke. Smiling at the unexpected treat, it lit the cigarette and sucked in the delicious chemicals. More human sensations it had missed.

The stick itself was death. *Let's see how many people we can kill with one cigarette.* It laughed out loud, at its own joke. With the machete in one hand and the gas can in the other, it smoked its cigarette, striding through the grass towards the couple that lay in the not too far off darkness.

It stood behind them, out of view. The night air kissed its cheek, threw its hair, and embraced it in these moments. It pushed Lili further down into the darkness, keeping her just close enough to see what was about to happen. It was tantalizing to know she was watching helplessly from inside.

The fallen angel was close. Ephryium still had his laughable faith, his hope in the Father and in this *creature*. Somewhere, he was watching. Waiting for the moment he thought the demon was going to release her, but that time wasn't going to come. It wanted to use her until she had to bleed them out. It was going to destroy everything and everyone around her.

Poor Ephryium. No matter how strong his love, he was corrupted, worthy of heaven no more. Their father would make sure he would suffer a millennium down here with his brothers, before locking him back up to rot away into the nothing. How naïve to think he was ever going to gain absolution.

There was a tinge of pity for its fallen brother. Ephryium thought it wouldn't do everything in its power to desecrate and ravage Lili before reuniting her with her creator. He under-estimated them.

Walking closer, taking a drag of the cigarette, it watched intently as Justyne's lips finally opened to take the dick in her mouth. A part of it wanted to stay a voyeur, make Lili watch her friend be taken, but the need to have fun and kill them both was stronger.

Quietly, it unscrewed the gas can cap. It took the knife from the back of their pants and stepped forward just as the man bent over Justyne, was readying to penetrate her. His thighs were spread apart, the mass of black, wiry hair just below the small of his back was doing its best to cover his asshole. Both Justyne and Krish let out loud, stiff gasps as Krish rammed his cock into Justyne's less than encouraged pussy.

It chose this moment to ram the knife past Krish's hairy, brown butt cheeks, up into his asshole, it snarled like a dog as it twisted the knife counter-clockwise, taking a moment to watch the path of the small trickle of blood as it weaved itself down Krish's hairy thigh.

Moving with the grace of a ballerina, or perhaps, an angel, it picked up the can and began splashing his back with the contents. The gasoline dripped off him onto Justyne's stomach and face. Her eyes were open now. She screamed in horror.

"LILI! NO!"

And from the belly of the beast where Lili lay, she screamed back for her friend.

"NOOOO PLEASE, OH MY GOD! PLEASE! STOP!

STOP! No no no no no!"

The demon laughed at her.

It stepped back from the naked animals in the grass. Lips still pulled back, baring its teeth, its green eyes glittering red, it punted the knife and its handle the rest of the way up into Krish's asshole and took one last hard drag on the cigarette. It winked at Justyne, who fought helplessly to get out from under the gasoline-soaked Krish, then flicked the butt. Krish's breath caught in his throat. He tried to force it out with a series of small choked grunts as his body jerked back and forth in a state of shock.

The cigarette bounced on Krish's glistening back twice before it rolled off and landed in the pool of gasoline which had formed on Justyne's belly. They ignited into a beautiful, bright sun of flames, screeching into the night air. The blaze devoured them, as the embers and the tortured screams of pain and death floated up to the stars. An absolutely beautiful song.

The demon stood there, fixated on the two. Swaying in place with a smile on its face, but in Lili's mind, her soul burned along with Justyne. It was blackening like coal, becoming hard. She had never felt such agony before.

She sat defeated in the dark corner of her mind that the demon had expelled her to, staring out through eyes that she no longer directed. She watched the driver who had brought her to this place be dragged across the field to Krish and Justyne.

The discarded pile of bodies gave off a comforting glow as they burned. The blade of the machete caught the light and twinkled, catching Lili's gaze. She watched the machete slice through the air and rip at the crunchy, but still juicy corpses. Fueling her pain, loss, and hatred for the demon, she made herself watch the excruciating scene. The blade came down with reckless abandonment and obvious enjoyment. Justyne's features were all but destroyed, a charred inhuman remnant of Lili's love for her.

Lili called out for help. To make this stop. To put this thing out of her. To go back in time and save herself and Justyne.

She remembered a time when she was young and had woken in the night from a bad dream; her mother was there to comfort her from the fear that still lingered in the dark little bedroom. She held the frightened Lili in her arms and whispered into her ear.

"When you're afraid, and you don't know why, but you know there is reason, call his name, Lili, call his name out loud. Anything that is here that shouldn't be will be scared and will run away. Call his name and pray for protection."

You' Re ALONe

RoT InSide

noNOno

KiLL thEm All

KiLL yOUR mother

FuCk YoUr FaTher

BURN tHEM ALL

BuRn IT ALL!

LI.

LILI

Everywhere, Nowhere — Lili's Mind

I WISH I didn't feel so alone. I wish Justyne could be here with me. I wish she could come here, in the dark with me, and maybe bring me a cigarette? My last one. Our last one. Our goodbye? My heart shatters. I just want to smoke one last cigarette with Justyne. My face is hot with despair. My eyes pool with tears that will scar me forever. And forever is doomed.

From the moment the demon took over, I lost sensation of my body. I am numb. First seeing everything, backing away from a movie screen into darkness. I can see my body, but I can't feel it. I wonder for a second if I am dead. No matter where I run, I am nowhere. I watch what's happening outside through my eyes, from far away. Mixed in with my emotions of panic are the demon's intentions. I experienced his burning desire to massacre Krish, but he was able to hide what he was planning for Justyne. It made it so much worse. I feel so pathetic, like a small animal at the whim of a predator — my master.

Crumpling into the nothingness, I bring my knees to my

chest and hug myself, because no one else will. I'm a slave, the demon has forced itself into my mind, violating every thought and emotion. Forcing me to be a voyeur to its unrestrained evil. The screen before my eyes, an empty night sky, seems to go on and on forever, into the horizon. It forces me to peer into the tangle of arms and legs, I see the detached and dangling blue eyes that once looked at me with love, and the black ones that tempted me into this fate just hours ago. My past, my strength, my friend, entwined with my hatred, my enemy, my fault.

Underneath the web of death sat a spider.

I get to my feet. He's still with me. *Ephryium!*

Excitement and relief wash over me, as if someone has given me a hand of hope to pull me out of the pool of grief I am drowning in. This is a time to be strong; this is the time to pay attention. I had not been paying attention to the whispers; I don't even know if the voices were always there. I'm a bit out of my mind right now.

The whispers coming out of the unseen dark corners of my mind hiss just behind my ears. I crane my neck to listen to what they are saying. There are so many things being said all at once, too quietly but with conviction. I can hear all or nothing. Goosebumps quickly crawl up my arms making me shudder. I become acutely aware I am not alone. Keeping my eyes peeled, I watch for any movement.

This hole, this grave in my mind, isn't a cozy place. It isn't warm. It isn't a place where I am meant to feel safe. I'm sure it's the place you go to before your demons eat you alive. I am not a fucking idiot; I know that if something were to come out of the shadows, it isn't going be something fluffy. It is going to be beyond any nightmarish thing I could ever possibly imagine. Not to put the challenge out there or anything … There was no telling if it would close the gates of hell behind itself.

How do I run away from myself? How do I fight something in my mind?

I can't help it, I roll my eyes and shake my head. I mock myself. Seconds ago, I would have given anything not to be alone, and now? Petrified of company. Listening to the whispers again, I hear a faraway conversation. I carefully pay attention to each word, hoping to pull a clue to help me escape, to help me be prepared.

"Enjoying yourself? I see nothing has changed. Still so consumed in chaos. So blinded in your own volatility, you don't see she's growing stronger. She's getting ready to cast you out. Back into oblivion. Into nothing."

SHE lIkEs It IN HERE

YOU ArE A pAthETiC FOOl

You have fallen far from your state of creation, Ephryium.

I see the Earth has taken its toll on

you.

ShE'S WasTed On You.

We will kill   you   both

Hearing Ephryium throws me back into memories of being a kid. The nightmares, the ghosts and shadows, the steady calming voice in the background that always knew my own strength better than I did. It was Ephryium. His voice is exactly as I remember it. He's as sure of me as he is protective. I had forgotten it somewhere back in the shambles of my childhood. Listening to him now fills me with endearment … and then fear. He's closer to me now than he's ever been, and we're here. I'm lost and out of control with Justyne's blood on my hands.

The demons hoarse and sporadic whispers are everywhere, but then something else forces out. Something solid that doesn't sound insane, something that sounds … human.

"*Oh how far we all have fallen.* You're weak. You feed off them. It's pathetic. You need them. You need her."

So DO YoU …   The battle has been WoN. He iS   GoNE.

"You're right, it has. You taunt me, thinking what? I have come here to right the wrong? To hold onto to something that no longer cares? Before she kills you, I want you to know without me, without you, she is still stronger, closer to creation than either one of us. I have come here to enjoy watching you die."

But you have kept her so blinded.

This is OUR ReaLm, BE with us She WilL Never Win.

You Have not told her.

We Inherit This EArTH

The monster is not I, Ephryium

But Ussssss

Rapeitburnitfuckitkillit

COME GET HER

Killitkillit

the cReaTurE wiLL buRn liKe tHE rEst Of thEm

I'm startled out of my intense eavesdropping by a shuffling noise in the distance.

"Hello?" I yell into the black chasm in front of me.

Click.

Each "click" is immediately followed by the rough noise of something being dragged on the floor behind it. *Here it comes.*

Click … Click.

My heart thump-thump-thumps, threatening to break through my chest cavity, keeping each breath I take shallow. I lower my head and stare through my worst fears. I am ready. *Come get me.*

Click

"Lil- Lili? Lili, are you here?" The sound of her voice breaks my overworked heart.

Tears spring to my eyes as I let out a loud sob. "Just? Is that you, babe?"

Squinting, I try to make her out. What little light there was seemed to be coming from me. With each *click*, *slide*, the closer she comes, I see more of her.

"Lili, what did you do?" she whimpers "What did you do to me?"

Click.

My hands come up to my face to mask the horror of what I see. She steps out in front of me. She? No, she's no more. *My heart can't take anymore*. The friendship, the love, the adventures, rip through me.

"Lili, why? Why did you kill me? I thought you loved me. I thought you were going to protect me. Lili! Lili, I'm scared! I can't feel my face."

"Oh God! Justyne! Justyne! I'm so sorry! Justyne, it wasn't me. I never meant for any of this to happen!"

Justyne's butchered corpse just stands there, wavering back and forth towards me. Her blue eyes burn into me. Her scalp is raw and charred. Her long, gorgeous hair exists in patches, singed and knotted. Layers of her flesh hang off her body, exposing the yellow and red fatty tissue underneath. Her full, beautiful lips are gone, leaving her teeth exposed; drool dangles from the unhinged jaw. I reach out to touch her, to comfort her, to comfort myself. To put her back together. As my hand nears her, her gaze falls to our feet, and I jerk my hand back.

Fuck me, I don't deserve to leave this place. *Do I?* This is me, a part of me I can't control, but a part of me just the same. I deserve to rot. I deserve worse. *Right?* This is my fate. This is what I have invited in. It won't be enough to kill. I'll kill the ones I love right along with the ones I don't. It won't be enough to just take their lives.

I see Justyne and understand what is expected. I'll need to tear the skin off their bones, rip their souls out, and mock their weakness. I'll enjoy it. I'll need to be curious to see just how much one person, one body, can withstand before breaking, and then go ahead and break them anyways. I won't need things like motive or explanation. I will never be able to satiate its blood lust. A tangible form of pure evil walking the earth as human. This is why Ephryium is with me! Holy fuck, he's here to stop me from being some sort of Anti-Christ superstar? What the fuck?

No no no no no. I shake my head. *I'm sorry.* That in itself would make me unworthy for this cause. I need to say goodbye. This girl standing in front of me, she needs to know I am sorry; she died with someone who absolutely loved her. She needs to be set free. And so do I.

"Justyne, I am so sorry for what happened to you. It was my fault. All of this, it's my — " Her eyes suddenly dart upwards to meet mine.

"YOU ThInK I GiVE A FuCk? YoU CUNT!" Pushing my arms away, she lunges at me. "You BItCh! LOOK AT ME!" She shoves me to the ground with an unexpected strength, knocking the wind out of me. Her massacred corpse crawls up my torso until she is straddling me. She's faster than I am; I can't defend myself.

Her face hovers over mine as she screams, "LOOK WHAT YOU DID! YOU PIECE OF SHIT, YOU'RE A FUCKING MONSTER." She holds both of my arms down, laying me out underneath her to take in her rage. "YoU diRty FuckINg Bitch! YoU LeFt me — " Her voice goes down five octaves to a rumble, " — defenseless."

The word came out slower, every syllable enunciated. It shakes the foundation we lay on. She glares down on me with big, black eyes. She is the image I saw in the bathroom mirror at the club. Teeth filed to a point, fucking menacing and dangerous. She is beautiful again, but in the most terrifying of ways. No longer dead, charred remains of a fleshy corpse, she is a demon. *She's going to kill me now.*

YOu Can StAY HERe with

US   LiLi

It's my turn to beg. It's unfortunate I just do not have it in me.

"Fuck you!" I spit in Justyne's pale face. I'm defiant, but truly curious about what will happen next.

Her lips pull back slowly to a sinister smile. She laughs. It starts out low and small, coming from her stomach and eventually up to her throat. "Oh, You CReAtures NEvER fAIL To ENteRtain."

Out of the shadows comes a disfigured half-face. The dangling jaw, the road rash. *Brian.* Limping towards us. *Are you fucking kidding me? Brother and sister reunited.* He came to stand beside Justyne and over me. It's playing on my compassion, my guilt.

There is no doubt in my mind, they are here to kill me, one way or another. The viciousness and cruelty that radiates off them is palpable. They regard each other before staring down on me, speaking both at once:

DoN't You GEt IT?

StuPID CrEAtuRE

YOU KILLEd JuStynE

she's HeRe wiTh Us

WatcHInG You Kill Her   Again and AgAIn And Again

SHE FUCkinG hATEs YOU

You LeT US HavE Her.

I summon all the strength I can and get my hands free to attack her throat, grabbing at her esophagus and digging my fingers into the skin. My fingers puncture through the pale, rotting skin around her throat. Blood gushes onto my hand and down my arm. The bones pop in my hand as they are dislocated from the bone above it, each vein and tendon giving away with a brisk snap. This isn't Justyne, and that isn't Brian. It was right; Justyne is dead, and I did have a part in that. But that only fuels the need to exterminate whatever it is sitting on top of me. It is this thing, or me.

It laughs as the blood spills from its mouth. I jerk my hand back and pull the bones free of its throat. Blood sprays out of its neck onto me, drenching me in hot sticky fluid. With its vertebrae hanging out onto its chest, it jumps to its feet.

Its eyes, along with mine, dart to 'Brian' who is enjoying the show, taunting me and cheering it on. He is oblivious to his innards glowing a deep orange with a fire burning from within. It shifts its attention back to me to confirm I have nothing to do with this. Before I can shrug to say, "I don't know what the fuck," a massive hand pushes out through his stomach. Immediately, Brian turns to it for some sort of reassurance. None is given. It takes a step away from him as he is torn in two from stomach to neck. His last moment, last resort: he looks to me. I blow him a kiss.

Bye bye, Brian. The embers trickle out, floating into the shadows. The claw retreats back into Brian's body just at the base of his head. On either side of Brian's head, two enormous hands emerge out of the darkness. Brian knows they are there, and I can see it in his blackened eyes; he knows he's finished. The claws come together in a huge clap to crush his head; the grey feta cheese of what was left of his brain curdles out of the interwoven fingers. The body crumbles into itself, igniting into a full flame that eats away at the torso. Only ashes and bits of bones are left by the time the knees have buckled, bringing the body down to hit the ground in a puff of smoke.

I hold my breath, as something emerges from the darkness. We are both ready to fight.

EpHrYiuM!

FinALly

The colossal being steps towards us. Forgetting to blink, I watch as the light illuminates Ephryiums raw muscular body. The black claws hang close to the ground. The near-featureless face connects to the spikes of alabaster bone protruding from the top of its head. I swallow my fear.

"Really? You welcome me?" He laughs. "You should be ashamed. She has you; you've lost. You've lost his daughter. I'm surprised you don't just kill yourself."

Feeling the tension in the air, I dare not move. I want desperately not to be noticed in this moment. My positioning in the scenario is horrible. I am situated exactly in the middle of the demon and Ephryium. The longer the silence goes on, the more it becomes apparent I need to move.

To where? I'm in my own head! The demon still has my body!

As I scoot out of the monster's way, Ephryium takes another step closer to it. Time slows as I watch the demon emerge from Justyne's body. Her face rips apart; the fragile human body explodes. I expect blood and body parts to go flying, but they don't. The façade melts away like a yoke from an egg, and the demon slides out of the shell that was Justyne.

The demon seems impenetrable but not solid, like a black charcoal etching. Gaping orifices are scattered throughout its being. In the gaps: blood, faces of the damned, tortured souls of the lost and of the consumed. The orifices, like portals, opening and closing in its form with each movement. Stepping away from the two mammoth entities, I am for the first time able to see just how puny I am compared to them.

It's odd, in all their dissimilarities they still seem ... related: the way they speak, the way they move, it is like watching brothers who have lived contrasting lives. Ephryium stands confident, composed, is strategic in every movement, while the demon is just the opposite. His movements are sporadic, impossible to predict. He seems to be only driven by one purpose: murder. His voice is everywhere. Every syllable is terrifying, filled with contempt, scorn, and hate.

HavE You Come To Take The   *creature*   BacK?

don'T You See SHE LiKes iT HeRE WiTH uS?

Go AWAy!

Do You WaNt tO shAre?

We cAn both HavE a LittLe biT of heR.

"Is there no rank among the wicked? She is above you. You are a pest at most."

YoU WanT Her

ThEn Take HeRrrr

"Wanting her for myself is not my intent, but I'll have her before I let you."

Um, what?

ToO WeaK?

"Don't you see what human possession has done to you? This place is so polluted with our kind, the humans and you dwell on equal planes — you are each other's viruses. But Lili isn't our equal."

ThE OnEs WhO Bring Us

KeEp Us

WiLl Make IT so.

WiTh Or WiTHOUT YOU.

JoiN US.

"I'll die before you or the many use her to bring your presence out into the open. This millennium will forget about you. You are but a whisper, a shadow, a superstition."

I'm lost and confused. After all that has happened, it doesn't seem like the time for a conversation, but what the fuck do I know? I'm just a mere mortal. When the piece of shit that killed Justyne lunges towards me, Ephryium is quick to step in front of me and stop it.

At first, I think it's backing away into the darkness but I'm wrong. It starts in my stomach and then in my knees: a sensation of being lifted. I immediately turn to Ephryium for help, but I can only make out his silhouette.

If I CAN'T HavE Her TheN NO ONE Will!

She burnS with the rEsT of theM

The feeling becomes more intense, as if I am being lifted faster and faster. My knees buckle under me; a blinding light fills the once-dark places in my mind. I close my eyes and brace for impact.

A blurred vision of my blood-stained boots. My eyes dart in all directions. I have no control of them. It's not out yet. But I have a chance to fight back now.

It's hunting for something faster than is humanly possible for me. *The car, the bodies, the blood the blood the blood the flesh.* I am forced to run through the tall grass of the field, *the gas can.* Bingo! If I don't push it out of me, it's going to kill me. It makes me bend down to reach for the handle.

"Fuck you!" I yell, gathering all the strength I can to kick the gas can away.

It flies into the grass, landing on its side, and starts emptying into the ground with a faint *glug, glug, glug*. I have control of my body, at least a little bit. It's hard to see out of my own eyes; the light inside burns so bright. It is like my skull is being split open while my insides are on fire.

Fighting through the pain to make sure I am able to keep it away from the gas can, I realize I'm losing the fight. I know it sees the red rectangle in the grass. It takes a step towards it. I scream for the strength to regain control. I throw myself down to the ground and frantically grasp for something to hold on to. Ripping out handfuls of grass, I am forced forward. I claw through the dirt. It wedges under my fingernails, and they detach from their beds. This is the least of my pain. I muster all the willpower capable to hold my body still. Wrapping my arms around my body, I breathe hard. *I am out of my mind. In so many god damn ways.*

Ephryium, I need your help. This is too much.

LaY doWn and leT the deAth cOme.

You IgnoraNt PiG

It iS InEvItAblE

You ALL EEnnnd Up HERe   ANywAYSsssssssssss

My limbs are no longer twisted around themselves. I smell the gasoline before the coldness washes over me. Peeking out from the dark, I crack my eyes open.

It BURNS!!!!!

When I bring my arms down to press my stinging eyes, something bonks me on the top of my head. I hear it hit the ground. My nostrils burn. The fumes are so strong, it's nauseating; *it* has doused me in gasoline. With every breath I suck in, my nose fills with the overwhelmingly pungent smell of gas and death. It knows if I go deep enough into myself, I can push it out, kill it even. It wants me just below the surface to be here when it lights me on fire!

Panic sweeps my mind. I have no idea what my hands are doing. Deranged laughter and screams bleed into my ears. The shrill screams drown my own out. My mind is in hell, and my hands are about to make sure my body will join it there.

It all comes to a halting stop. The pain, the noise, even the air stands still with the flick of a lighter.

Forcing my tear-filled eyes open, I see the wisp of orange coming towards my face … this is it. I must seem so pathetic to it. I lean into the flame of the lighter.

And blow it out.

"Is this all you have? Let's go! Come on! I'm just starting! I'll fight every moment you have me." Even though I say the words with conviction, the exhaustion drains me. I am emotional. I could cry for days, scream my heart out, but I'm done. My body just can't take anymore. The fist I'm being crushed with inside unclenches. I am released. A whisper is breathed into my ear.

I WiN

No longer able to hold myself up, I fall into the dirt. Broken and defeated, I wait to die, or be taken. Whatever is going to happen to me, I can't stop it. I give up.

QueEn Of ThE AbanDoned,

LearNs HuMiliTY BeFore She ComeS HomE.

The words are strangely intimate.

I stare up into the face of the demon, and catch a glimpse of Ephryium's face behind it before he rips into the demon's neck. Screams of the demon and all of the souls it holds within cry out into the night sky. Instinctively, I close my eyes and cover my head. Fire and the smell of sulphur fill my nostrils; the screech of the demon echoes in my head. I can't prevent myself from passing out. It's a terrifying feeling, welcoming in the darkness; if I could help it, which at this point I can't, I would never close my eyes again. I'm surrounded by warmth, and I know Ephryium has me. I hear his soft-spoken words from above.

"It's OK. You're alright. You just weren't ready. It's OK."

LII.

ARNOLD & DEBBIE

North Battleford, Saskatchewan
March 6th 1991

ow, Mrs. Tenner, let's try an' keep our voices down. I didn't mean to offend you, or your husband here. There is just no other way to put it. Your son has violent tendencies, paired with anti-social behaviour. It makes him, well, a target for the other children."

The principal, in his tweed pants and button down shirt, readjusted his tie as he got up from behind his desk. "Now this isn't the first incident you have been called in on, Mrs. Tenner … I think we both want what's best for — " He placed himself at the front corner of his desk and sat when Debbie cut him off.

"I think you're fulla shit, Principal Willis, and I also think your school is fulla asshole cretin kids, who deserve a good kick in the ass. Ma boy is smart and sweet, and would never hurt no one. He was provoked. And I think we should leave it at that. Street justice has been served."

She made Willis regret closing the gap between them and

watched with disdain while he retreated back to his chair as casually as possible. The conversation with her was obviously over, he turned to try and sort it out with Arnold.

PlUck It OuT LikE A GraPE

Grab THE PeNCil, ArNolD

Arnold was staring at the block full of pencils sitting on the corner of the desk in front of him. He imagined grabbing one of the pencils and sinking the sharpened tip into Mr. Willis' eyeball. Popping it like a boil.

"Mr. Tenner?" Mr. Willis cleared his throat to repeat himself once more. "Mr. Tenner?"

"Heh?" Arnold was snapped out of his fixation. "Whaja say?"

"I was saying, Mr. Tenner, that the student your son attacked had to be rushed to the hospital. They had to stitch his face. I have heard rumours of the child needing to have his jaw reset. This is not the conversation we should be having about children who are eight and nine years old, Mr. Tenner. Wouldn't you agree?"

Arnold slumped in his chair with his jaw slack. Even though there was no comprehension in his eyes, the principal went on.

"Now, despite what Mrs. Tenner might think, this isn't a personal attack; it's just the opposite. I am just as concerned about your son as I am about the boy he, erm, fought with. Your son is an excellent student. His academic record is impeccable, outperforming his class in essentially every way, but — "

"Well, that's all that matters then? Isn't this an insta-two-SHUN of book LEARNIN'? Ma boy is smart, you said it yerself. Now, he said the little Mikey boy was pickin' on 'im. I'm the first to admit, Mr. Willis, I done told him to stand up for himself. I'm not raisin' no pussy for the other kids to pick on." Arnold pulled on the straps of his overalls, arching his back in his chair as if to show he had won this part of the conversation. How could this man not be reasonable?

Debbie sat in her chair, squirming and pulling at the straps of her purse. She pressed her lips together, not daring to say what was going through her mind, at least not here, not to Mr. Willis. She was aware their son's moral compass didn't exactly point in the same direction as everyone else's.

At this very moment, she thought the boy deserved it. Mikey and his mother were a bunch of assholes. But despite that, despite her son's grades, and the trouble she and Arnold had gone through to make this work, their boy had gotten himself into some real trouble here. The small animals on the property, no matter the quantity, didn't cut it anymore. The boy, no matter how young, worked his way up the rungs quickly, and wanted a bigger and more satisfying victim. Mikey was almost it; and if he had been, that would be the end of the boy.

Debbie had encouraged the boy to take his fascinations and blood-lust out on his sister, as she did. For nearly two years, she'd pushed the girl towards death's door. At first, she had been incredibly violent and cruel, acting no different than she did with the drug-addicted prostitutes and vagrants she used to bring home. She was torn, pricked by jealousy. The relationship between the squaw woman and Arnold had been the only one of its kind — the only one he had repeatedly went back to. The girl was this woman's; she couldn't stand that Arnold went to her.

Debbie hated having the girl in her house, around, alive. But Arnold being happy made her happy, so she pulled back and stopped trying to kill the girl (so quickly). They could both get something outta her. But the boy would not take part. Sometimes he watched, more than once he had held her arms down, but he had never whole-heartedly participated. Not like she knew he had it in him to do.

If Debbie and Arnold didn't help the boy find a suitable

outlet, he was going to find one himself.

The men were still talking. She glanced towards her husband; he was bent over, spitting a wad into the trashcan. Mr. Willis was going on about that little prick Mikey. His parents, knowing it took "two to tango" as it were, were thinking of charging the boy.

She cut in. "He's just a child! That's never gonna hold!"

Mr. Willis raised his hands as if to interject, which prompted Debbie to hold both her own hands up, as if to say 'save it, I surrender.' She went on. "I understand apologies are in order. We are not complete savages here. I will have little Mikey over with his mother for tea, and we can start to put this behind us." The words slid out of her mouth like honey.

Mr. Willis wouldn't be appeased so easily. "Well, that's good to hear, Debbie. I'm happy you're wanting a resolution. Unfortunately, I don't think apologies and tea will be quite what we are looking for in this situation."

Debbie rolled her eyes. Letting out an exasperated sigh, she slapped her purse. She turned to Arnold for a response, but he sat there, staring intently at a pencil holder on the desk. A little bit of drool had amassed in the corner of his mouth. Debbie rolled her eyes again — she was surrounded by idiots.

"Well then, what? You want me to kiss'er ass too? Is that it? What more can we do?" She couldn't contain the spittle flying out of her mouth every time she enunciated. Willis remained complacent, which outraged Debbie even more.

The whole thing was bullshit!

Debbie was going to spit in their tea.

"Well, we — Mr. and Mrs. Port and I — were thinking something more along the lines of maybe seeking outside help … ?"

He left the sentence hanging in the air, waiting for a response, like Debbie and Arnold would come to the obvious conclusion and take over. That didn't happen.

"Maybe utilizing a professional? There is a doctor here in town. He is — "

"A doctor? You want our boy to go see a fucking head shrink? Didja hear that, Arnold?" She gave him a sharp jab to the ribs, knocking him back into the room.

"Eh?"

"Mr. Willis here wants us to take the boy to a shrinker. Might as well call in a witch doctor, too! You people, thinkin' you always know what's best, raisin' a generation of fragile little pussy farts. A squabble turns into a whole hoopla of bullshit." She got up, pushing the chair back as she did.

Arnold followed suit.

"Well, Mr. Willis, I think we have had enough of your bullshit!" Whipping the door open, she walked out and got halfway through the office before she realized she couldn't leave on that — not 'cause she didn't want to, but it wasn't what was best for the boy. She charged past Arnold and back to the principal's door, which still hung open, framing a stunned Mr. Willis.

Leaning in, she shouted through the doorway, "I'll call the fucking cunt for tea! Good DAY!"

There. It was all settled.

𝕷𝕴𝕴𝕴.

THE BOY

Just outside North Battleford, Saskatchewan
March 6th 1991

The stairs that led down to the root cellar were narrow, lined with cold cement. The wooden slats creaked and bent under each step. They would need to be replaced soon. The dirt floor gave off a smell of freshly turned earth. The beams that held the house together ran overhead, exposed and covered in century-old cobwebs. Thick shadows covered everything as if they were velvet sheets.

It was the most comforting place in the world.

From the top of the stairs he could hear the whispers, the giggles, and the soft crying.

It was down there, waiting for the boy.

He could only see down to the sixth step. The rest were lost in darkness. He knew they attached themselves to the earth floor, and he knew the floor wasn't a black abyss with malicious intent, wanting him to fall in so it could swallow him up. No, those were a child's thoughts. A normal child's thoughts.

He was no child. He knew down in that pit, somewhere behind boxes of stored vegetables, past the smell of old and must, in amongst the suspicious and sometimes frightening noises of a sump pump and water heater, was a thin mattress. It was stained with the signs of torture and involuntary let-go of a person not able to die ... And on the mattress, chained to the floor like a dog, was his ever loyal, nurturing, and loving sister.

But that's not what held him there at the top of those stairs. There was no guilt nesting in his heart for standing by while his sister became a skeletal version of herself. There was no inkling of some sort of massive betrayal taking place between the two of them. The truth was, once he and Arnold had lit his mother on fire, there wasn't enough time to stick around and watch the skin split and tear off of his sister's bones without being engulfed in flames himself ...

So he'd grabbed her hand and saved her for later.

Somewhere down there, with his sister and the veggies, was a special spot. A spot where the whisper in his head became a manifestation of itself, something he could see, touch, and feel. The voice that had slithered into his ear, snaking through his head before finding that dark, lonely corner of his mind that, up until that moment, he had been alone in.

TeLL Me YouR SecreTsssssss

He hadn't said a word. Instead, he had thought of every despicable thing he had ever thought to do but was unable. And then, suddenly, he was overwhelmed by the feeling of being capable and powerful.

The demon had taken hold of the boy, feeding off his dark thoughts and fantasies. And the boy had welcomed it in with all of his being. He wrapped himself in it, holding on tightly, looking to it for guidance and security.

The boy knew whatever this being was, it had brought him joy and potentiality, and Arnold was the tangible form of it. Arnold *was* the tangible form of it. This wasn't true anymore.

After Debbie had stopped letting his sister sleep in the bed with him, Debbie and Arnold would routinely go down to the basement. It seemed instead of killing his sister as he had hoped, they drew a great satisfaction in keeping her alive, just barely.

In his new home, he was surrounded by a malefic influence. During the days, Arnold would be gone. Debbie would lead him by his hand down the basement stairs. She would smoke cigarettes, always lighting one for him as well. She had taught him to flick the cigarette using his thumb and middle finger. To take aim at his sister. When his sister would whimper or yelp at the cigarette embers rolling off her skin, Debbie would cackle delightedly and encourage him to light another.

He had watched Arnold rape his sister, roll off, and let Debbie have a go with a beer bottle. His headspace was no longer his own.

"Like this boy! Weeeeee-ooooo! Deep as you can!" It could have come from either Arnold or Debbie.

His sister's rusted, brown eyes always stayed locked on his own, wide in pain, terror, and confusion. They screamed to help her. Reminding him of her gentle, caring touch, the way she had tried to never let him starve.

Behind his ears was the hissing.

SsssSHEeee   WAntssss IT
FUCKHER!
SticK iT iN boY
SShhhheee WaNtS You ToOoo
KiLLheR KiLLeR

He had been looking to commit an injustice. That's what his soul had yearned for, to cause something sublimely tragic and undeserved. Shredding his mother's throat and snapping her trachea were all things she knew she had coming. She was a cunt.

An evil, evil cunt.

Who got exactly what she put out; the evil she spawned came back to kill her. It wasn't unjust or unforgivable; it was the circle of life.

When he sat with his sister on her thin, stained mattress, enveloped in the demon's warmth, he fought against its taunts and urges to kill his sister in her decrepit state. He felt the ancient camaraderie of its power melding together with his own inherent atrociousness. It was tempting. But it wouldn't even begin to satiate his appetite. There wouldn't be enough to it. A body was an easy thing to break — he was more interested in devastating a mind, destroying the soul. There was no real victory in preying on something vulnerable and weak — no matter how moment-arily entertaining it was.

The demon had explained this trait separated what he was and what Arnold was. This thing had a plan for him; it was more than anybody else had ever given him. He was meant to be exactly where he was, with Debbie and Arnold. He would develop into something unstoppable in their care. His new parents had mastered existing in this world — binging and purging, prime evil, and all the while barely existing to anyone.

Today at school, he had failed miserably at doing just that. He thought he had been listening so carefully to the instructions going on in the background. Mikey Port was in grade five. He was a cocky, mean son of a bitch, and had presented himself as the perfect opportunity.

But the boy had misjudged his surroundings. He thought when Mikey had slipped behind the school to go into the bushes; they would surely be alone. It wasn't the case.

Mikey's face was covered in blood. The boy was still hitting him with a fist-sized rock in his hand when he felt strong arms come around him, quickly pulling him off of Mikey and tossing him onto the leaf-covered ground. The voice had left him at that moment.

But the echo in his head had made him ruminate over every step he had taken up to the moment he had been caught.

EyeS WatchINg

We ARe NoT So ReCKleSSSsss

StuPid Boy

Chewing on the skin of his knuckle, he stood at the bottom of the stairs encompassed in the gloom. The demon waited somewhere deep inside the basement, emanating its energy. The unseen energy filled the room with a low-pitched hum that made it impossible to hear anything else. Like a sorry puppy, he walked further into the basement. He had messed up. He hadn't listened. And although he was still confident in his own abilities, he felt as if some retribution would be owed from him. He had an inclination of what it would be, what the demon would take from him — yes, take from him. All relationships, the good and the wicked, are give and take.

The boy's ears tingled. His throat tightened. Over the deafening white noise, there was an acoustic spotlight on his sister's laboured breaths. In motive, evil wasn't always so direct, but in communication, there would never be a misunderstanding.

He walked around the towers of crated vegetables, each one taking on an ominous shadow as he approached. Feeling his way with his hands, he walked towards the raspy breaths.

The air took on the smell of bile and rotting meat. His foot hit the edge of the mattress. Straining his eyes to see through the darkness, the boy made out a figure standing opposite of him. The figure disembodied into something darker than pitch that seemed to bleed into the air, making it a part of the entire room. It was it. *Him*. The whispers. The boy lifted his head to look into what would have been its eyes.

The white noise boomed in his ears. His heart raced. His sister's breaths below him. His thoughts careened into distress and desperation.

CAreLessssneSSSsss

Do NOT   Ignore US   CHILd

StupiDyounGchilDWORTHLESSCausE

NOT WORTHY OF US

"No! I am worthy!" The boy pleaded into the darkness.

wE ShAll Have Her   NOW Boy

A hoarse voice broke the barriers of his reality. A sixty-watt hung between him and the demon flickering dimly, illuminating its pulsing, ink-filled veins. Its gaze rested on the starved girl, whose eyes stared forward, blank and still.

ShE WilL BE WitH Us NOwww

CuT Her OpeN

from Her AsSHoLE   to her TITS

HAnG Her FroM ThE ceiling

WiTH heR IntestiNeS

Tellheryouloveherwhileyoufuckhermouth

Do ThiS FoR Us   Boy

Getting down onto his knees, the boy hovered over his sister, taking in her pain, her silent resolve. As he combed his fingers through her long, black hair, each stroke pulled clumps out of her scalp. The demon extended one of its tentacles, slowly and smoothly running it along the girl's body, slipping underneath her, and finally disappearing into the crack of her buttocks. The boy watched as the arm pushed into her, making her body tense in his hands. She forced out a pained moan. Her stomach swelled as she began to slowly turn her head to face the boy.

Her lips parted, as if only a moment from speech. He watched as her eyes pooled and disappeared under black sand. It began to spill from her eyes, dissolving into dust as it fell onto her face. Her mouth opened wider and wider, expanding until it could no more. Her arms and legs were rigid as they pressed down onto the mattress. Every muscle tightened as the sand poured from her mouth. Dispersing back out of her.

The demon continued to flow and push and penetrate her until the black sand came to a trickle, leaving her gaping mouth, dry and empty. The girl's body went limp. She expelled her bowels onto the mattress beside the boy. Her eyes, now voided, rolled around slowly in her head, finally coming to a rest on her brother's face.

She exhaled a weak whisper. "Help me."

With every heavy exhale, the demon's warm breath comforted the boy like a blanket as it covered his back. The boy was still. With his sister in his arms, he slowly lifted his eyes to the demon.

The demon's face, eyes, and body were twisted shapes of black. The rims of its eyes burned red. Its face never stayed the same. Sometimes, the boy was sure he heard his mother's voice, deep in the demon's bowels, and then in those precise moments, its visage had reflected his mother's scorched, meth-riddled face. In the next, the reminder of his mother was gone, replaced with a demonic mask.

In this moment, this stare down, the demon's face was impossible to read. The eyes gave off no emotion. They were cold and void of any emotional intent. The boy bit his bottom lip and reluctantly sealed all of their destinies.

"OK."

BegiNNNnnnnnnnnnnnn

𝕷𝕴𝖁.

IGNACE

The following is an excerpt from:

Luc Marchand's

Queens of Hell
An Occult Specialist's Search for the Devils in the Background

Published 1997
All rights reserved.

Ignace Courier Archive
November 13th 1986

Sergeant Mike Olson, 34, committed suicide in his home November 9th, not a day after the bodies of his late wife and daughters were found.

Authorities say the off-duty officer was discovered at around 6:00 a.m. on the 9th by Sergeant Olson's partner, Sergeant Bruce MacDonald. Mike Olson had fatally shot himself using his

service weapon but further details were not
disclosed.

"Mike never turned away from hard work. He was
liked and respected by all of us. The town knew him
as a caring and loving father and husband. We
respected him as a dedicated police officer, who
will surely be missed," said Captain Gavin Shwap of
his lost comrade.

The 10-year veteran of the police force will be
remembered in a memorial service held in Ignace on
November 15th.

Besides the articles found in the basement of the town library,
there is no physical evidence of these events happening. Nothing
to corroborate any of the aforementioned events, deaths, and
investigations took place in Ignace.

On record, no autopsy reports, death certificates, or any
other media pertaining to the still-missing Merlo family.

In 1986, Ignace, Ontario was rocked to its core. As if a snake
had slipped in between the sheets of this town and stolen the
lives of at least ten people without anyone taking notice. It
happened so quietly that when the snake slipped back out into
the night, it hadn't been a matter of what questions were left
unanswered, but of there being no answers at all.

FOIPPA Canada (Freedom of Information and Protection
of Privacy Act) was contacted as to request the name and
whereabouts of both the journalist who had originally covered
the stories and Sergeant MacDonald, if he was still alive. It was
more probable he would be retired at this time, but having been
so closely involved with the investigation, he would surely have
a wealth of information pertaining to the subject.

The FIOPPA response came promptly. Five pages of

redacted black lines, although, it was noted, it seems to have been one person who wrote all stories.

No information was given as to Sergeant Bruce MacDonald's previous or current station, or if he had, in fact, retired.

While you have curiously read on, we have dug ourselves into a pit of questions. I stand here beside you in this grave of information, waiting to see who or what will cast down the first bits of gravel that will eventually fill this hole.

LV.

LILI

Calgary, Alberta
August 10th 2003
3:09 a.m.

I come down with a jolt. My arms and legs hit the ground hard.

Green glitter nail polish.

My toes. My boots are gone. My toes sparkle amongst the dew-covered grass. They are so normal, mundane. It is a treat to notice them, and nothing else, at least in this moment. I am so scared to leave this moment. I hold onto it, clasping the wet grass between my fingers, swallowing the ball of tears inching its way up my throat.

A fog descends past the top of the streetlamps. The concrete is painted in a fresh coat of glossy black. Everything is still and silent. It is beautiful. And spooky. I am home.

Please, please, stay in this moment for just a second longer. If it slips away, I'll have to admit to this night. I'll have to accept this life. I don't know if I am strong enough for it. Any of it. I could get to my feet, walk home, and stay in blissful denial. Couldn't I?

It's not the first time I have woken up in a neighbor's yard after a rager. I am still a teenager. And somehow, I reason my more-than-recreational drug use is excused, because I have more than just 'girl problems' and 'teen angst.' No, no, there is no rebellion here. Just escape attempts.

I wonder if Justyne got home OK.

My body lurches forward. I brace on my hands and knees as I spew gasoline-flavored blood, marring Mr. Henderson's perfectly manicured Kentucky blue. I pull up fistfuls of sod as my gut twists in pain. I retch out cigarette butts, chunks of bone and teeth, long ringlets of black hair. My eyes pool with tears. The blood forces its way to my face as I choke on something stuck in my esophagus. My belly and chest heave repeatedly, working to dislodge the morsel. Snot, blood, and gasoline jet out of my nose, but I still can't breathe.

A vision of my own death flashes before my mind's eye. My eyes bulging out of my head, having no more breaths to take and landing face-first in the regurgitated memories of last night. The color leaves my face, my neck, and my arms, turning a soft purple blue.

I imagine the fog lifting with the rising sun; the new day, in which Mr. Henderson, who lives a couple streets down from my parents, eventually comes out of his front door to retrieve the paper. And then, he sees me. Steps forward, and gets a closer look at the filthy, rigor-mortised body polluting his lawn, his view, his morning. Fuck, all he wanted to do was eat his toast and drink his coffee. Was this some kind of joke? When he walks across his lawn, getting closer to the punch line with each step, he recognizes the long, black hair, that beautiful face covered in the rusty blood of the night before. It's Carmella and Saul's Daughter. Oh shit! That's Lili.

In my vision, his beautiful cup of coffee slips from his fingers, and he screams. He is screaming for someone. To save him from this. To make this go away. Where was the someone that was supposed to save this girl? He screams so loudly he draws out the neighbors. My mom and dad, maybe even Vinny and Rocco, too, all in their pyjamas, smelling of bacon. They wonder "What the hell is Mr. Henderson's problem?" So they make their way down.

I have to get it together. That can't happen.

The grass is slick under my feet. I struggle to get them moving underneath me, sliding backwards with every attempt to get up. I need to get air into my lungs. Standing on weak knees, I ram my fingers down my throat; it's do or die. My fingers wriggle through the slimy bile still coating the inside of my mouth. Something protrudes from my throat just below my uvula. I hook my finger into a loop and pull. My stomach clenches and lurches, helping me push out whatever it is I am pulling.

The pressure in my face builds as all the blood is forced into it. Tears stream down my face as I pull the barely visible turquoise cords out. I continue to choke and retch. The cords are at arm's length now. I still can't breathe. If it doesn't end soon I'm going to die, I am going to choke to death on — something suddenly plugs my airway completely, sending me into frenzied surprise. I pull down hard. It dislodges from my throat with a *snap* and hits my hand.

I fall back and land on my ass. Gulping down the thick, damp air, I spit into the grass. My saliva is so thick I have to grab the dribble clinging to my lips and wipe it off my fingertips. I clear my nose and finally rub the tears from my face and out of my eyes. I look down into the grass where a turquoise piece of cloth lays covered in thick bile. I pick it up and quickly fling it away from myself when I realize what it is.

It is a G-string. Justyne's fucking underwear. The thought sends a whole new wave of nausea over me. Staggering to my feet, I can hear my bed calling my name from a block down.

Lili … Lili, come lay in me, Lili. I'm cozy and warm. Lili …

I need to get home. Thoughts race through my mind a mile a minute. I want to just sit, cry, and mourn Justyne, but I know sooner than later, I will be responsible for coming up with an explanation as to where she is. I will have to hide my mourning and pretend I don't know where she is like everybody else … I will need an alibi. *Did anyone see us leave with Krish? When did I eat hair and underwear? Should I go see a doctor? Do I have the AIDS? How did I get home?*

The questions flip through my mind as fast as you can flick through the pages in a book. I want to sleep for a hundred years and dream about rainbows.

Summoning all the strength I have left in me, I shakily put one foot in front of the other. Cutting through my neighbor's yard, I fast-track it to my house. I want to stay off the road, even though it's late and dead silent. I don't want to risk anyone seeing me. As far as everyone else is concerned, I never snuck out. I was at home drinking coffee in my room with my big, wool socks on, cozy and tucked in, happily medicated, reading … I don't know … the Bible?

None of this happened. None of this happened. None of this happened.

I walk over the lawn, closer to my neighbour's windows than I probably should be. My reflection takes a peek at me every once in a while. I peer in past the image of myself, into the dark, stillness of the houses. I meet my own eyes in the pane and turn away in disgust. I shake my head, defeated, I stare at my feet and walk on. I watch each step being placed as quietly as possible, until it's time to pass another window, another tableau of myself, standing in another living room of black furniture and shadowy walls. Out of place in each of them.

As I walk by the next house, I can see through the front window, straight through to the other side of the house, into the backyard. I swear someone is there. Against my better judgment, I stop.

That's funny.

Better judgment?

I know by now my judgment is horrible. I don't know why I pretend to be better than that.

Pressing my forehead to the glass, I cup my hands around my eyes to block out the light. It helps a little, but it's too dark to really make anything out at the back end of the house. I wait a tense moment more, holding my breath for ... nothing?

Really? Why are you doing this to me?

Just as I take my head off the glass a big, black dog jumps up into the windowsill right in front of me and unleashes hell. Its nose hits the other side of the window as it lets out a loud, intimidating bark. My heart lurches in my chest, taking my breath with it. The dog is relentless. I need to make myself gone before this asshole wakes everybody up.

After aggressively whispering at the dog to "shut the fuck up," I stare at the tall shadow standing behind it. My first reaction is to run.

I don't.

Bad. Judgment!

I momentarily tune out the dog, I can't tell whether someone is actually standing in the living room. The reflection of the streetlamp hangs right above the shadow's head. He could be standing behind me, to the right. Fully convinced of *nothing*s and *maybe*s, I turn to see the street. It's empty. Behind it, the park. Spooky. Normally, not so much, but with the fog? Bad news. Just as fast, I turn back to face the house, wondering if there has been a man watching me this whole time from inside his living room, and it's just me who is creepy as fuck.

The dog stopped barking. When did that happen?

A yelp slips out of me with a huge hollow *BANG* against the window. A mess of matted fur and blood slams up against the glass. I cover my mouth, trapping the scream just inside my lips. In the reflection of the glass, I see a shadow emerge from the park.

Ephryium?

I book 'er like a hooker. Running as fast as my bare, aching feet will carry me, I rubber-neck the park. There is no one there, but I run like there is. It's the only way to run: like zombies are chasing me.

My feet slap on the pavement, breaking the silence of the neighbourhood but still barely audible over my laboured breath-ing.

No decision is made. I can't even say its instinct; I don't know what grabs my attention back into those big bay windows, but that's where he is. Running through each living room alongside me. When he reaches the walls he doesn't hit them, but he never stops either. Between the houses he comes out, running in stride with me still, then disappearing until he is right beside me again. He is inside the reflection of my neighbours' windowpanes, running behind me alongside the park. I am not outrunning anybody; I am racing.

In between another two houses, I come to such an abrupt halt I stumble a few unintentional steps. We stand facing each other. I don't move and neither does he. Down the row of houses, I see my mom's yellow roses. I'm close, probably three houses away, but I have no more run in me. My heartbeat is pumping in my ears. Each breath might be killing me.

Glimmers of Brian's juicy, rotted face, Justyne's awful

words, and the attractive dark guy go through my mind. *Is it another demon?*

"What the fuck do you want, buddy?" I ask with as much bravado as I can muster knowing I have nothing left. I can't run anymore. I'm scared for my family, but my reality is I can do nothing for them. I am dragging myself back home with wounds that will never heal. The pain stemming from my heart, my fear, my exhaustion feeds a new hate for Ephryium, and everything that comes with him.

With the thought, images of my parents' bloody corpses strewn about the house come to mind. Rocco's small, mutilated body lying in the bottom of the bathtub. And Vinny, no. No. I push the thoughts out.

I lower my head, but not my gaze. Keeping my eyes on my stalker, I walk towards my home. In front of the first house, I know what to expect when I reach the window. He stands in the middle of the room, facing forward. His arm slowly rises to point in the direction I'm walking. His head slowly turns to face me. A small sliver cracks through at the top of the window and ... *bleeds*?

I walk on. He stands at the end of the alleyway, facing me, still pointing in the direction of my house. My breath catches up and finally slows down to normal. The next window brings a message.

Hairline cracks run throughout the glass. Etching their way across the pane, each slowly releasing a thick flow of dark red blood. I watch long enough to see the window be completely washed in the near-opaque liquid. Letters appear, as though someone is writing in the blood with several hands at once. Words take shape. I slowly walk away, but glance back towards the unveiling message before I am completely past the house. It looks something like:

The BOOK

hers

                                                                    secret

                              your mother

The booK

                        answers

                                                      HERS

look in the chest

                        read the book

                                          hidden from you

"Why the games, Ephryium? Why are you doing this?" I say exasperatedly to my reflection in the glass.

Shivers run down my arms. My head sinks into my shoulders, I know I just need to get to my house. I know he's there, down the alley way, walking step for step with me. I walk on and know as I pass the next house, he'll be in there, too. I can't help myself; I take a quick peek. I see him in the reflection. He's across the street, running straight for me with inhuman speed. My stomach drops. I tense, readying myself for the oncoming collision. Instead, I'm left standing in the shadow of the house, fog pooling around my feet. Shivers run down my arms and legs again, worming back up my spine. My entire body gives an in-voluntary wiggle.

One more house to go.

Mom and Dad left the front light on. It makes me wonder if it is a welcoming 'we know you went out and we left the lights on for you' or a 'we left the light on because we know you snuck out. You can't hide anything from us and you're in big trouble. You probably shouldn't even come in. Just sleep in the backyard.' I hope they just forgot it was on …

Heading towards the front door, I say a small prayer inside my head hoping they're asleep and won't hear me.

Through the side window, I can see the thick, black mass standing in the hallway, waiting for me. So much for 'sanctuary.' I bend down to watch it walk down the hallway towards the back of the house, eventually disappearing into the shadows. I walk around to the side of the house and unhitch the lock on the gate, letting the big, wooden door swing open.

I smile, not really knowing if I'm looking at a friend or an enemy. Either way, there he is, standing at the opening to the backyard.

You motherfucker. What choice do I have? Challenge accepted.

He walks further into the yard, leaving my sight. I follow. The yard seems so much bigger; the fences are barely visible through the fog. It could go on forever. My shadow … my angel? My demon, *hmm, yes mine.* He is nowhere to be seen. Fucking typical. A constant, terrifying game of hide-and-go-seek. One I am never going to win.

In the far off world of the corner of the yard, I hear the old hinges of the shed door squeak open. I put my hands out in front of me as I embark on the journey; this is Rocco's domain. God knows what I'm going to trip over or walk into. It takes a couple of steps before the dark entryway to the shed is visible. My imagination takes over; it's an 'abandoned' cabin deep in a wood-ed marsh. 'Beware' skull-and-crossbones emerge out of the fog, above the dark, ominous door.

I am a product of Disney visuals.

Standing in the entrance to our shed, I realize I'm standing on the edge of a rabbit hole. Before I step in, I peer back at my house. The windows are filled with the same dark profile, maybe the ghosts from my past, all of them looking down on me. There is the sound of creaking old wood behind me and a muffled thump.

I turn to the rabbit hole and jump in.

LVI.

THE BOY

North Battleford Outskirts, Saskatchewan
March 6th 1991

Releasing his sister, the boy raced back up the basement stairs. He returned a few moments later with a large bowl filled with soapy water. As he hustled across the basement, the water sloshed over the rim, leaving trails of stained earth behind him. He slowly lowered himself onto one knee on the mattress beside his sister.

The demon could no longer hide its puzzlement; the boy had shut it out of his thoughts, another trait he possessed that Arnold did not. It made the boy vastly more complicated to influence than Arnold.

GiVE HER To USsss

              YoU HAvE FOrfeited   TimE By DEfYiNg US

                             ONCe   Boy

The boy plunged his hands into the bowl, pulling out a washcloth. He leaned back onto his heel as he rung out the water.

"I told you I didn't want this. Not like this. Don't you care?" Lowering his eyes, he leaned forward and lifted his sister's arm. He wiped away the pus and dirt that had accumulated in the folds, being careful not to scrub too hard as the skin was raw underneath. He waited for his answer as he gently washed his sister with hot, soapy water.

"I'm not like my dad. I don't think you're the boss of me." The light overhead flickered on and off again. The heat was being sucked out of the room, and once again, the loud noise of nothing filled the boy's ears.

In front of him, the demon grew more and more grotesque. He writhed from side to side, snarling, as the thick skin of his torso ripped open, exposing a hellish bloodbath inside. Souls that had been locked away in the depths of this evil being begged in pain and torment to be set free, for salvation. They wept hysterically into the madness, only to be muffled and finally drowned out completely as the torso closed up.

The boy took it as a warning of what could be. He could be in there with the stitched up and bruised infants or the battered little girls or the woman who stood in the background of it all, eternally burning.

"I think you play with Arnold. But I think you love me … " As the words came out of the boy's mouth, his breath became visible puffs of clouds. His wet hands chilled to the bones. The demon grew bigger. The house began to groan. As the beams overhead shifted, dust fell onto the boy's head and his sister's body. He continued to wash her, sometimes leaning down, close to her ear, and whispering, "I love you. It's almost over."

YoU MoCK USSSsss?

IGnORAnT LiTTLE BoY

thinks HE CAN

DiCtaTE Thissssss

WE WerE So FoND Of YOu   ArraNgeMent?

Like an exasperated parent, the millennia old demon shook with anger. The ground he hovered above began to quake.

The boy had been born with a dark seed in his heart. For him to exercise compassion, after all the demon had taught him was truly a disappointment. It was just a reminder of how much he loathed man in the first place. Weak creatures, with no conviction of their own. He would crush the boy's very soul out of him, and then take the sister anyway. The boy was arrogant. He was in the providence of demons — any will he thought he had was an illusion. He was just as worthless as the people the demon would have him kill. He wouldn't have needed to think twice before disposing of the boy, if it hadn't been for the stark contrast of his Arnold. It might be a long time before the demon would come upon another with a seed as dark as the boy's.

How dare this boy — this *child*! — refuse him? How dare this child deny the evil that flowed through his heart, and rebuff his guidance? What a waste. From the moment the demon had truly felt the little boy's presence — the moment he had opened himself up to the horror that Arnold was subjecting his mother to — he knew. He relished in what this boy would be. He was a vessel, already filled with an evil as alpha as the original.

The demon outstretched his poisonous grasp. The boy, ignoring the building tension in the air, calmly tended to his sister, which infuriated the demon even more. He gazed up at him with his big, deceptively innocent eyes. He looked past the terrifying face of the demon, past eyes provoking the most evil fantasies, and straight into a place the demon guarded. It was a place holding a relic, something that was once a heart, a soul, a compass.

Now a shrivelled and neglected thing, it twitched.

A tear slowly rolled down the child's face. "I trust you. I want you to trust me … " He sniffled.

The centigrade rose back to normal. The white noise began to lower. The demon, repulsed by the boy, disintegrated into the shadows.

The boy wouldn't disappoint him.

The demon was gone. Debbie and Arnold were at the school. For the first time since his mother's apartment, he had his headspace back. It was only him in there, and now he had time.

What was ahead of him was an overwhelming endeavour. He started to panic, prioritizing his tasks. Beads of sweat started to form on his brow as he took the stairs, two at a time, back up to the kitchen. He came back with a cold glass of Gatorade for his sister and a piece of bread with butter. Ultimately, he would only be able to move as fast as she did. He needed to finish cleaning her, get her dressed, and make sure she ate …

"Ya need to sit up now … drink." Scooping his hand behind her head, he lifted it off the mattress and put the cup to her thin, dry lips. Her eyes flashed with gratitude and then went blank again. But she drank.

"I need your help. You have to help me. I need to clean your … unda side … " She understood him. They both knew it wasn't going to be pretty. The poor girl had been coming into puberty for the last six months. She didn't have much, but it was enough for any preteen girl to be embarrassed about. With her help, the boy pushed her onto her side and began to wash the back of her neck. The once clear, soapy, hot water was now warm and dirty. He would need to change the water or it would be a waste of time; she had taught him that …

Before he got up to refresh the bowl, he wrapped his arms around his sister's bony back. Grabbing her wrists in front of her and holding them gently, he pressed his lips onto her shoulder and left a kiss. He held her, making sure she felt him, pushing all the love and compassion he had down his arms and into her heart. He held her until he felt the physical moment she had received it and let him in. Then he let her go, grabbed the bowl, and raced back up the stairs.

Leaving the bowl to fill in the sink, he flew through the house to Debbie and Arnold's room. He rummaged through the dresser drawers one by one, and it was immediately apparent he would need some pins to be able to use any of Debbie's clothes on his sister. Standing in the sunlit room, he held Debbie's massive panties over his head, his eyes wide with amazement.

"Woah!" He let out a boyish giggle and threw the underwear onto the bed.

He had forgotten!

Arnold liked to keep things … did Debbie, too? Making a mental note to ask them both about that, he moved to the closet. He opened the door; a few white shirts and blouses hung droopily off their hangers. He pushed them to the side. On the floor there was a metal rack and shoes the dog got.

Shit. Nothing?

He peeked his head around the frame. There was a little more to the closet than what you initially saw through the door, but not much. Beside the shoe rack was a beat-up cardboard box.

"Ha! Bingo!"

Weaseling around the doorway, he wedged his fingers under the box to lift it out. It was heavier than he thought it would be; his muscles strained as he tugged with all of his might to get the box up and over the rack. He dropped it onto the bed, relieved not to be holding it anymore. Pulling at the flaps, he opened it. His fingers wiggled with anticipation. It wasn't just that he had found exactly what he had been looking for — there were, indeed, clothes to fit his sister in the box (mostly panties) — but it was insight.

It was a glimpse of what Arnold, his dad, was before him. It felt like finding treasure.

Time. Time! They would be back soon.

He pulled through the locks of hair, jerky-like skin, jewellery and various mementos to get to the fabric that promised to be some sort of outfit at the bottom. He couldn't have gotten luckier. Wrapped in a pair of denim overall shorts were a pair of slightly blood stained powder blue panties and a worn, rose coloured shirt with a *My Little Pony* character on it.

Clothes in hand, he raced back to the sink. He threw the clothes over his shoulder and lifted the bowl out. He was careful going down the stairs, making sure not to spill, and not to let the clothes slide off his shoulder. When he reached the bottom, he heard the rattle of chains coming from the back. His sister was moving. Good.

"Wh- wh- what are you doing? Where is the- that woman, and Arnold? ... Do- Do they know what you're doing?" She had sat up on the mattress, the glass of Gatorade in her hand. Her eyes stayed fixed on the boy as she took a sip from the glass. He could tell the half empty cup was hard to manage. Getting her out of the house would take some work.

Although her eyes were still dark, they were no longer blank. They were hard, and untrusting. He would have to fix that. He needed to give her back her hope; it contained her drive, her will.

Stepping closer, he placed the bowl on the ground and the clothes at the edge of the mattress. "I don't have so much time. I'm sorry but I need to finish washing you, and then you need to get dressed ... and then we need to go ... OK?"

He watched her face as she studied him. She didn't know if she could trust him, but what were her other options? She had none. It was written all over her face; she was going against her gut — for now.

Inching closer to her, he slowly reached for the leather dog collar around her neck. Her face bowed in embarrassment as he undid it and gently removed it from her, tossing it on the floor away from them. Ringing the water out of the cloth, he moved back to her side and told her to lie back down. She winced and tightened as he pulled apart her butt cheeks. The crack wasn't just raw with neglect and filth; it puckered out of her, turned inside out permanently from the frequent sodomy.

Working quickly, but gently as possible, he cleaned the build-up of dirt, expired cum, and smegma emitting the smell of rot from her vagina. Whispering to reassure her she was going to be OK, they were going to be ok, he wiped down her legs, and then her feet. He took care to wash in between her toes and the bottoms of her feet, doing as good of a job as what she had done for him once.

"Do you want to brush your teeth?"

She nodded, in pain and humiliated.

"Mmk, I'll go find you a tooth brush. Do you need me to help you get dressed?"

No longer able to hold her brother's stare, no matter how kind the gesture, she stared down at the cold dirt floor. She slowly shook her head. It pained him to see her this way; if only she was that resilient little girl she was only a handful of years ago. Deep, angry scars riddled her body; she was so much more damaged than he had thought. Was he responsible for that? Would it matter now?

He bolted the few steps towards her. She flinched, shielding herself from the blow she expected him to deliver. Instead, he put his hand on her arm and ever-so-lightly pushed it down. Getting onto one knee, he was eye to eye with her.

"I'm sorry. I'm so sorry," he pleaded.

Her arm came around to his back.

"I know. I know … it wasn't you. What could you do?"

He brought his tear-filled eyes up to meet hers and hugged her. They stayed that way for a moment before she whispered, "It'll be OK now. Go. I'll get dressed."

"You have to hurry. They'll be back soon."

She nodded, and he turned to go back up the stairs.

By the time he found his toothbrush and started back towards the basement, it had only been a couple of minutes, but he was panicking. He had seen things being much more expedited than they were. If things weren't timed perfectly …

There was a noise by the back door, near the stairs. Arnold and Debbie couldn't be back yet. There was a twinge of doubt in him; maybe he shouldn't have so readily pushed his companion out. The demon could have given him a heads up. Putting the toothbrush behind his back, he carefully approached the noises.

His sister stood at the entrance to the kitchen, propping herself up on the wall. The clothes he had brought down for would have been the right size had she not been so underweight. They wouldn't have hung off her the way they did.

She followed the hallway to the washroom. She was only gone a minute, but when she came back she was ready for him to lead her by the hand out the back door and down the stairs. They were out.

Brother and sister took in the silence of the valley, appreciating how neither one of them could hear the sound of Arnold's approaching truck. The sun was just beginning to go behind the walls of the valley. The first signs of twilight showed across the gravel road. The road leading up to the highway slowly sunk into shade. An orange glow outlined the trees lining the path. As they moved away from the house, the cool air made his sister shudder. He should have brought her a jacket.

"I'm sorry. It's cold. I'm cold, too."

"It's OK. It's all gonna be OK." She hugged him closer. She was hopeful again.

Walking in stride with each other, they watched as the small rocks tumbled in front of them with each step. The boy pursed his lips to contain his delight. Yes, it would be alright.

The boy had grown considerably since he had arrived at the farmhouse. With a good appetite, he had grown taller and stronger than the boys in his grade. It was no wonder he had the upper hand so quickly with Mikey, or why he was able to support his paper-thin sister as they walked up the valley road.

As they got nearer to the top of the road, the boy's senses pricked. His thoughts were drowned out by the sound of his breath; the taste of blood filled his mouth. The road in front of him became as blurred as his thoughts. And then, immediate clarity.

The demon was back.

"Are you OK?" His sister held onto his arm tightly. She stopped walking, waiting for him to reassure her.

Goosebumps formed at the tops of his shoulders and crept down to the tips of his fingers. He surged with energy; from the expression on his sister's face, she could feel it, too.

"Mmhmm, I'm OK. C'mon, let's go." He urged her forward. It was nothing he was going to stand around and talk about. Not with her, anyway.

The boy opened his mind, let his thoughts be free for the taking, just as he had years ago. But the voice whispering into his ear was not the same voice that had befriended and guided him years before. It was smooth. It was everywhere and nowhere all at once. It was not frantic or menacing. It was the clear voice of a man.

"Make me proud, boy."

He bit down on his molars to hide how the normalcy of it had startled him. Just for second, the boy glanced over his shoulder, searching for the source.

There was nothing to see. No one standing amongst the trees, or eyes staring back at him through the flourish of yellow and orange.

He tried to contain his anxiousness, slowing his breathing as much as he could. It was no use; his heart thudded with panic. He needed to get her into the woods. He had run out of time.

"What's wrong? Why are we going into the bush?"

"C'mon, we have to hide. I have a bad feeling."

"OK, OK."

It had already been asking too much for her to make it up the hill, even with her brother's support, but to walk through overgrowth and forest … She had to, this was the only way. Leading her by the hand, he stomped the grass and branches down. If it scratched at his legs, it would scratch at hers, too, slowing her down. He moved quickly, but chose every step carefully. Timing would be everything.

She was so weak, so beaten down physically and mentally. He saw now what he needed to do. He was not Arnold.

His sister followed him lackadaisically, as lost in her own thoughts as he was in his. When he stopped abruptly, she walked into him and knocked him off balance. He couldn't control the eruption of rage that swept over him before he turned to her. The expression on his face became dark and hard, his nose crinkled. She gasped in surprise at the aggression, but, hopefully before she had a chance to form a clear thought about it, he relaxed his face.

He brought his finger to his lips. "Shh."

Shifting her eyes to the left and to the right, she searched the brush, and through the trees surrounding them. She appeased him by nodding, to show him she took him seriously, But he knew she couldn't hear anything.

Turning his back on her, he listened. He could hear the leaves rustling in the trees, the sound of the wind plucking an individual leaf off of a branch above, and then its descent to earth, finally landing on the forest floor as if it were a bowling ball. He listened to the web scraping out of a spider's abdomen like a violin as it frantically wrapped a screaming moth in its tomb. He listened to his sister's weak heartbeat, thump-thump-thumping behind the cage of bones that rose and fell. He heard the low rumble of an engine and the rocks underneath the tread of each tire. He heard the hairs on the back of his neck, and up his arms, spike up out of their follicles.

"We should stay by the road. It's easier to walk through, c'mon."

𝕷𝖁𝕴𝕴𝕴.

THE GIRL

North Battleford Outskirts, Saskatchewan
March 6th 1991

She didn't think twice. He was right; her mind was in a whirlwind. She was in a state of reflection while physically in a state of escape. It had been hard to walk with him, side by side, with him wedged under her armpit. Walking a step behind him, she stared hard at the boy's back. Silently reaching out, looking for warmth, compassion, any connection at all. She took a deep breath in and had a hard time letting it go — she felt the consistency of her life, cold dis-connection.

She turned into herself, her thoughts racing. The scars, the pain, the isolation, she was groomed for it all. She was happy to no longer have the responsibility of her brother's fate on her shoulders. She was happy to give motherhood to Debbie; she seemed to provide for her brother in a way a young girl couldn't. The moments summarizing her life had been sad, unfair, painful, and repetitious, but she knew she could endure them until her death. Scrounging through her memories, she searched for any sign her brother had endured with her. They were in this together.

The messy, dirty child that never cried, sat so quietly, was on her side of things, wasn't he? Had he ever been so caring before today? The boy was only eight but there was something about the way he moved. The look in his eyes as he stared at her, as if he meant to watch her destruction and violation from the side-lines, was not a child's. Those eyes were not bright and innocent eyes being forced to watch, they were studious and cold. Weren't they?

What itched at the girl's brain was a faint notion she might not know this boy who walked in front of her, this boy who had spent time, real time, in the shadows of monsters.

He had done absolutely nothing until the moment he walked down those stairs … to save her …

Her thoughts were whirling when her brother stopped short of the road. It was as if he had read her mind, the way his shoulders tightened, the way he inspected her face with squinted eyes. Her jaw clenched under the sudden scrutiny.

"I think we can walk beside da road now … What's wrong, why are you lookin' at me like that?"

In an eruption of thought and emotion, she decided they were in this together and it was no longer all on her. She was frantic. "Where are we gonna go? I'm scared. I don't wanna go back! I don't want us to ever go back to that place. Those people, they're evil." Exhausted and sobbing, the tears welled into overflowing pools.

Her brother stepped towards her, wrapping his arms around her. "You're strong. Don't give up, don't be scared. You survived. Don't ask what for … I'm not gonna go with you — you have to go. I have to go back."

She pushed him to arm's length.

"Don't look at me like that. You can go for help an' come

back … or don't. I'll be OK."

The small, frail boy she had taken care of had filled out and grown up. His eyes don't quite meet hers as he delivered his message.

"No! You have to come with me! What do you mean you're going to stay? You can't!" Wrapping her hand around his wrist, she prepared herself to drag him the distance with her if it was the last thing she did.

One foot neared the road. They had swapped positions; he had put himself closer to the direction of the house.

He shook his head. "No." He pulled his wrist out of her grasp. He was strong. "Why didn't you ever ask me about what I did to Mom?"

"Mom? What?" She couldn't answer; the answer was as complicated as the question. The memory was as horrific as the truth. Why was he asking? Why weren't they running away?

"You know, I don't even think it matters … But maybe that's why you could keep going, 'cause you thought I had saved you. No matter how badly you were hurt here, it would be OK 'cause you thought I loved you … "

"What are you talking about? You did save me. You saved us. Mom was sick! You didn't know what was going to happen to me here." She tried her best to believe what she said.

"And you think it's gonna get better?"

"It is! We're so close! Let's go!" She grabbed for his hand again. He didn't flinch when her hand landed around his.

"Do you think I love you?" His question came out slowly. Each word landed with a malignant force.

She didn't respond. She tried to catch up as fast as her mind would let her. Hope and denial fought the fact he had spent two years letting her rot, and yet, here she was, tugging at his arm, pulling him to safety.

"You're so dumb! After what you saw me do? After what I watched happen to you? Still? You think I love you?"

Her breath caught in her throat, her heart raced. She could swear the clouds had rolled in directly behind him like a great shadow threatening to swallow her. She felt tiny, her little brother towered over her.

A faint rumble in the distance became louder.

Time was up.

Somehow she knew it, but still needed to hear more; she needed the pain to keep going … he was right …

"No one loves you. No one will ever love you."

This couldn't be happening.

She loved him so much! As she shook her head frantically, his blurry silhouette stood still and strong, withstanding her pulls.

They could run away together. They could get help. She could show him what normal was, what real love was.

"Why would I have saved you?"

She heard his words as they were intended. She was able to hear through the illusion of her kid brother. He might have resembled that baby she fed and bathed, and protected, but her instinct had been right; he was no child. A wolf in sheep's clothing.

"Why didn't you just let them KILL ME?" Her scream was desperate.

Pouncing towards her, he clasped her wrists with a strength beyond hers. His grasp threatened to snap her twig-like bones. There was no way to escape him. Her knees began to shake, threatening to give out. She was losing clarity of her environment. It was impossible to see anything but her brother's eyes. The coldness. The playfulness. It was petrifying.

As the trees were lost to the black storm hanging over her brother, his face came closer to hers. Digging her feet into the ground, she summoned all of her strength to pull away. If she could get onto the road, she'd be out in the open, and somehow that would make her safe. Free.

Nose to nose, he whispered,

"Because it wouldn't be as fun to kill you when you wanted to die … "

The earth quaked softly. She felt her death rushing towards her.

The energy emanating through her brother's touch was violent and frenzied, and yet he stood, seemingly calm. As she frantically tried to pull herself free from his grip, her feet slid through the leaves. She craned her head towards the road. If she could just run … Break free and run …

Before freeing her of his hold, he jerked her closer, so close that as he whispered his final words to her, their lips brushed. " … say hello to Mom."

She saw the truck. For a second, she was even able to make eye contact with Arnold. Had she not been struggling and pulling so hard to get away, she wouldn't have been catapulted the way she was when he finally let go.

As she fell back out of the brush and onto the road, she was free for only a moment, before the speeding '72 GM pickup ploughed into her.

In that moment, she saw her brother was not alone standing just behind the brush. It was not a great storm looming behind him.

The red eyes of the demon and the blackness of her brother's soul were the last things she saw and felt. They burned into her in such a way she finally welcomed the death that had chased her for so long. His last words lingered as the truck made impact, imbedding what little skin she had into the truck's heated front grill.

LVIIII.

THE BOY

North Battleford Outskirts, Saskatchewan
March 6th 1991

Smirking from where he stood with his companion at his side, the boy broke down the scene to the millisecond.

He would chase this high. The high one can only accomplish by destroying someone beautiful, strong, full of faith. Crushing their hope, raping them of their security, draining every ounce of self-worth, so even they knew they were better off dead.

The moment she recognized him, the moment she saw the evil supporting him — the realization of betrayal in her eyes, that infection in her heart — would stay with him for his lifetime.

He watched, satisfied and content, as she slid up the hood of the truck. Her head smashed into the windshield, cracking both her skull and the glass.

Her body rag-dolled into the air, slapping onto the roof like a deflating bag. Blood spurted out from her nose and mouth. She would have thought death's angel was coming to kiss her, softly embracing her in cold finality, but instead, giggles bubbled from the boy's lips as he watched the demon sodomize her with his barbed and scorching talons. Dragging her to that special hell, where she'd relive this death, with them, time after time, forever.

As her blood spilled down the windshield, sliding through the strands of hairs and jagged pieces of pink scalp, her body flew the opposite direction. It pin-wheeled through the air. The boy didn't need to see it hit the ground in a malformed sack of blood and bone, because her soul was with him now.

As he hiked down the hill, pushing the brush away from his legs, he heard the muffled, "Gat dammit! Sonofabitch!"

LIX.

DEBBIE & ARNOLD

North Battleford Outskirts, Saskatchewan
March 6th 1991

C an you believe that pin-headed prick? Who does he think he is? Sitting behind his desk all high and mighty. I had a good thought to jam a pencil right into that little fucker's eye!"

"Oh, Debbie. You read ma mind."

Arnold took his eyes off the road to look at Debbie in such a way that showed his deep appreciation for their bond. It was a bond so intense he didn't have to speak a word of it. She gave him a flirty grin and knew exactly what he felt. Debbie clutched her purse tightly in her lap, blushed and turned away in a little fit of giggles.

"Arnie, we have to talk about that boy."

"Mikey?"

"No! Our boy! What the fuck would I need to talk about that lil prig of a child Mikey for?"

Turning his attention back to the road, Arnie bobbed his

head up and down in agreement. "Brought us some trouble today. I don't think it's nuthin' ta worry 'bout though. Boys'll be boys, Deb."

"Boys'll be boys? Is that what this is? 'Cause here I was thinking he meant to kill that Port boy. He got caught, and that's the only thing that stopped him. It's a good thing he got caught before he killed him, 'cause it's pretty sure as shit he would have been caught after, too!"

"Think so?"

"Arnie! Know so! I know you've seen his shit trail 'round the property, too. I have never seen such a filthy little boy in all my days — leaving innards and cat's parts in the shed. I found a whole box of rottin' birds under his bed. Stunk like something wretched, Arnie. It's a whole other problem that this kid doesn't clean up after himself. Thinks I'm his god damn slave, here to fuckin' wipe up after him, cleanin' up his shit trail wherever he goes. He's gonna kill someone, Arnie. I can feel it. I can see it. A mother knows."

"A mother knows, hey?" Arnold asked with a half-smile.

Her body gave a slow wriggle in her seat, as if to make herself more comfortable with the statement. "That's right. That's what I said. No matter what kind a pig shit this boy is, he's my — he's our pig shit. And I love you both. And we need to help him."

Arnold gave her a nod in agreement. "Well, whataya wanna do there, love? I have been tryin' to turn him on his sister, but that boy will do what he wants.. Won't touch 'er much. I don't know what the fuck he's doin' down there in the dark wit' her, but it's not what I'd hoped. Think if that girl's gonna die, it'll be by us. He's made it clear. Should I go scoop up a couple of dogs from the shelter?"

"I know. She's a quiet subject for him. The way he goes after them animals, or the rage he put down on lil Mikey there … it don't make no sense to me. He's a complicated little man … quiet … reminds me a lot of you, Arnie." Love glazed over her eyes as she smiled with her crooked yellow teeth at her husband. "Dogs won't do … Oh, Arnie! Let's go downtown! Let's go pick us up a throw away!"

"Deb — "

"Just like we used to, Arnie! C'mon!" She scootched closer to Arnold, interlocking her arm in his and rested her head on his shoulder. "We could bring some sort'a nothing back to the house, have our fun … like we used to … you remember when we used to do things together, Arnie? Before we had the kids? We could even let the boy finish 'em off. That'd get it outta his system. We could pick one up every month! Family night!"

"No, Deb."

Releasing Arnold's arm, Debbie sulked back to her seat.

"It'd bring trouble. Same kinda trouble that Port boy and now that boy's parents are gonna bring us. It's gotta be something else."

"LIKE WHAT THEN?"

In an act obstinacy, Arnold had passed Battleford, and was now making the turn down the first dirt road that would bring them home. Debbie saw there was no chance of her getting her way. Like a child, she crossed her arms in a huff.

"I think he should come on a haul wit me, Deb."

"A haul? No! The boy needs to stay in school. He needs to stay here, and be a kid and — "

"Kill the students? Maybe a teacher. Someone's pet? If we keep him here to do what we know he's gonna do, it's gonna be hard to hide, babe. At least if he comes with me — "

"Arnold, I said NO. N — O. NO. Nope. Not gonna happen. I understand what yer gettin at, and I'm saying no. The road ain't no place for a child."

"That boy ain't no child!"

"Arnie!"

"No, Deb. You know I'm right. I don't know why you gotta be so fucking stubborn and thick headed 'bout it either … You on your lady time or something?"

"You're a piece of shit!"

"Deb, c'mon now. All I meant to say was maybe that's why you're not seein' things clearly."

"'Cause of my lady time? Fuck you!"

"Fuck you!"

The truck slid over the gravel road towards the couple's home. As the argument escalated Arnold's foot got heavier. Debbie noticed, but instead of saying anything, she let it ride on her nerves, which in turn made her voice grow louder.

"I could show the boy how to properly manage this stage of his life. If we don't set him up properly, he's gonna be reckless and stupid. He's gonna bring us all down!" explained Arnold.

"Stage of his life? … And what are the teachers gonna say when he misses all that — "

If the girl's eyes hadn't been so wide, they might have missed her standing beside the road. But she had been looking at them. She saw them coming. There were two little hands sticking out of the bush, which were only momentarily attached to her.

Arnold hadn't lifted his foot from the pedal. Even if he had, there would have been no time to stop the truck from hitting her head on. Arnold had the distinct idea there was no way for him to have avoided this collision. The word "timing" whispered over and over in his head.

The smack on the hood, followed by the spider-web crack in the shield, made his eyes go wide with interest. Arnold slammed on the brakes. Beside him, Debbie let out a startled yelp as she was jerked forwards. Both sets of eyes shot up to the roof as the metal warped under the body slamming on top of it. Arnold's eyes shot to his rear-view mirror to see a mess of pink, denim, and black hair land behind his tailgate and out of sight. The dust settled around the truck.

"Hunny, you OK?" Reaching over, Arnold put his hand out to Debbie as she pushed herself back onto the seat.

"Gat Dammit! Sonofabitch!" Arnold slammed his palms down onto the steering wheel.

Debbie reached for the door handle. "The boy goes with you. Get the girl in the truck. We need to get home … NOW!"

"The girl?"

"Who the fuck you think we just hit?"

LX.

LILI

Calgary, Alberta
August 10th 2003
3:20 a.m.

I stand inside the shed, savouring the silence and the moment to rest. I have this vague inclination the night is nowhere near over for me.

I study the back walls and the roof carefully. There is no telling where the chest came from, or where Ephryium is. We clearly need to work on our communication skills.

The shed is spooky as fuck. So is the backyard, all blanketed with a thick fog. I figure if I can't see out then no one can see in, either. The thought doesn't help me shake off the feeling of being an intruder, like I don't belong, like I am invading the quiet spaces of night. This little world Ephryium has led me to isn't a shed in my parents' backyard. It's a far-off place where time has stopped, allowing me to catch up. The fog hides more than just the façade of the house; it hides the future, it hides what would be next for me, and that depends on what exactly is in this box.

I don't recognize it at all, but lately, it's the one thing I can rely on — just not knowing what the fuck in general. It's becoming almost comforting. *Almost.*

Old, worn iron runs along the sides and top. The wood is covered in small markings along the bottom and top edges. Interesting, but not as curious as the latch for a lock being broken. Recently or not, I can't tell. Getting down on my knees, I flip the lid open. The inside of the box is lined with dark blue velvet. Underneath the lid, the initials *D.M.* have been embroidered on the fabric. Pressing my lips together, I think, *Who the fuck is D.M.?*

The chest is filled with an overwhelming amount of papers. *Well, Ephryium, bring on the demons in my brain, because I would rather go another round with that other motherfucker than read documents.* I look to the ceiling, expecting to see him standing over me, but instead I see rafters covered in cobwebs. Very disappointing.

Seriously? Nothing?

I sit and stare at the floor for a bit, hating my life, before I let out a sigh. I need to trust I am right where I need to be, no matter how terrible or tedious. I am right here for a reason.

I need to begin.

First on the pile is a stack of envelopes bound together with a light blue ribbon. The address on the top envelope reads:

1 Rand St N
Ignace, ON
P0T 6Y7
Canada

The *To:* is printed and easy to read but the *From:* is written in calligraphy. It is impossible to read. I make out a *7* and *Paris* and give up. I open the aged envelope, being careful not to tear the thin paper. The calligraphy on the envelope matches the message written inside, and except for the symbols at the top and bottom of the page, it seems to be written in French. The name at the top reads *Antoinette*. At the bottom, it is signed *Mon Ami, Mon Amour, Josephine*. I put it on the floor beside the chest and move on.

There are a couple of photos from the 80s. Everyone is rockin' some serious hair, especially my mom.

"Nice outfit, Ma." I smile and laugh. My brain stutters to a complete stop as it forces the registration of what, of who, I am looking at. "MOM?"

You don't have photos any photos of you, Mom? Oh, they're all lost? Really? Why hide them? Your hair isn't that bad!

I start flicking through the photos faster, focused with new motivation. Mom is in a bunch of them with people I don't know. In one, she is so young. She has to have been a teenager. She is standing in front of a black car with a guy … who isn't my dad. So who is this guy?

"You slut!" I joke.

The guy is good looking. His arm is around Mom's hip. They are comfortable with each other. This guy loved Mom … and she loved him, too.

In another, Mom is even younger and standing next to someone who, given my mom's resemblance to her, I think is my grandma. I wouldn't know for sure, though; all my grandparents died before I was a twitch in my dad's dick.

The next photo is Mom hugging another girl who looks a lot like her. Shit, *exactly* like her. *Hmm, highly suspicious.* Is 'D.M.' my aunt? Does mom have a sister? Does she still? Where is she?

The next is another of mom, but in this one she is holding Vinny.

How does a baby look like a criminal? His dirty blonde hair is slicked back. His little mouth is in a tiny frown. All he needs is a little fedora and a thin moustache above his lip! I have never really seen a picture of Vinny this young before. He came out of the vagina looking like he wanted to sell you a couple grams of coke. A goombah! He hasn't changed!

As soon as my eyes fall on the last photo, I become uneasy.

The people in the photo are all wearing long black cloaks, with hoods covering their eyes. Class photo day for the cult in the woods. *Or Hogwarts … please let it be Hogwarts.* The edges have been singed. Flipping the small stack of photos over, I check for dates and names. It's blank, except for a small character, parts of which are lost in the singe.

This is it. These people are it. Call it intuition, but I know. My skin tingles. This is where it started. I am holding my beginning. I am staring at the people who have the answers.

In all my years worshipping nature and drawing pentacles on things, I have never seen this emblem before. It is a six-pointed star within a circle, not at all resembling the six points of the Star of David. If the pentagram is a symbol for protection — what would this be? And what is this photo doing in a stack of photos of my mom?

Biting into my lip, I think hard. I make up a thousand stories in my head that give me some explanation, but still leave me in the dark.

Hidden against the wall of the chest is a folded piece of paper holding a thin stack of newspaper clippings within it. I pick one out at a time, reading each one of the headlines.

"OPP Investigate Man's Death"

"Gruesome Discovery Leads To Suspect — *child believed to be missing*"

"Shaken Town Lose Three More"

"Tragedy in North Ontarian Town"

"OPP Officer commits Suicide in Wake of Family's Death"

"Merlo Family Presumed Dead —
Search Called Off"

All are from '86, in Ignace, Ontario. Shivers run down my arms. I pick up the clipping entitled 'Gruesome Discovery' and read:

November 3rd 1986.

Kenora County. Ignace, Ontario. 4 dead, 3 missing, 1 injured and in custody.

The grizzly quadruple homicide was discovered on October 31 by Ignace residents … with their children. A parent heard a man's moaning … Local RCMP were called … The murder, took place on Rand St North …

I continue to read uneasily about Maria and Daniel. *What happened?* I am more than relieved there had been a suspect. *At least they got the piece of shit.* My hopes are quickly dashed in reading Maria's baby, her mom, and her sister Daniella, were missing. *Probably dead, too. A whole family — just like that — destroyed. So sad. Why?*

I lean over, scooping up the envelopes I had put to the side and reread the address mentioned in the article. *Holy fuck, I am having a detective moment here.* I read the article again; the addresses were the same.

D.M.

Daniella Merlo … So my mom knew this family? Why would she have Daniella's trunk? I finish reading the other articles. So much death all at once. How come I have never heard about all of this? Shit like this isn't typical for Canada. The news reads like *Helter Skelter.* Whole families just wiped out?

Daniella, Antoinette, and Marco were never found then? At

least if they were, it wasn't here. My heart broke a little for Marco, only two years old … *Vinny would have been two in '86.* I wondered if Marco had been there — witnessing it all happen. Did he run or was he taken? Seeing all of that would fuck up a kid up for sure. I held a little hope in my heart for Daniella and Marco, and a little sorrow for all those people who knew a pain that was so similar to mine.

Putting the clippings back where I found them, I push my arm down through the papers until I hit the bottom of the chest. I wiggle my fingers underneath the heap and then began to pull my arm slowly out, letting the papers slide over my fingers as I do.

I close my eyes and let my intuition do what I know it does best. At about the middle of the stack, I touch it: the thing not like the others.

I grasp it and pull out two small books.

"What in the mother of fuck?"

I know a spell book when I see one. There are bits of moss and feathers hanging off the spine and the cover. It is covered in little protection runes. There were a couple symbols I don't recognize, but then there is one I have just seen recently. It is the same six-point star on the photo.

The spell book is just like mine. I open the ornate leather-bound book and find everything a nature child would hoard: flowers and grasses, pages filled with pretty, loopy designs, poems, and incantations. But then the pages become darker, angrier. The little loopy flowers are gone, replaced with symbols, scratched over and over into the paper.

The scribbles on the page morphed from *Invoking Elemental Spirits*, *Blessings*, and *Banishments*, to *Astral Projection*, *Dark Divination*, *Spirit Sacrifice*, and *Mutilation Ritual.* There is a dark line that was crossed here. Whoever had studied witchcraft had studied thousands of years of different practices, torn between Wiccan and

Christian influences and something much older, much darker.

The mood, not just in the book, becomes darker. My ears ring. As the hairs on the back of my neck rise, the room starts closing in on me. The book takes on a dangerous persona. The last pages are splashed with blood and dirt. My heart beats faster; the ringing in my ears gets louder.

No, thank you.

I drop the book like a ton of bricks onto the ground. The ringing stops. The room seems suddenly lighter.

Some serious shit for sure.

Boy, oh boy. I just can't wait to read the other book.

As I flip through the pages, it is clearly a journal. 'D.M.' had etched their initials into the cover. This is what I was meant to find. I know it. This has to have the answers! I am so fucking tired of being in the dark.

Taking a deep breath, sucking in all the air I can, I open the book to the first page.

March 14, 1984

My Life is over!!!! Maria is pregnant! Her and Danny came over to tell mom n dad tonight, they both freaked out. Everyone was yelling. Maria and Danny want to keep the baby! What is she thinking?!?!

Mom and dad came to tell me we are going to move to a bigger house in some town so ma can help Maria, and dad can work up there too.

Everyone is looked after but me. I'm so hurt.

I just want to die.

Fuck Maria — why should I have to uproot my life because of her stupidity? I'll never forgive her.

D

Well, something tells me Maria and Danny don't make it ...

Every page is filled with scribbly writing. Daniella was a devout journal writer; each line is filled with every emotion, every laugh, and every tear. I can see the evolution of her life as a teenager taking place on the pages. It is a lot of reading. I skip through chunks at a time, not that 'Julie; the bitch at school' isn't superduper important, but if I want to pull any answers from Daniella's journal, I will have to get to the important parts.

June 16, 1984

The House is HUGE! There are NINE bedrooms!

There is a week or two left of school here. Mom said I didn't have to go, but I want to see what it's all about, it'll be good. Maybe I'll meet some people too.

I am really grateful Mom and Dad waited to move us so I could finish out the year with my girls. Cory was so hurt that I was leaving, I shouldn't have promised him I would come back ... I think I am going to be happy here, in Ignace.

Speaking of things that are huge — Maria!

I am never having babies!

Dad is going to work in a mine. It's not too far from us, I think it's called Matabi?

Mom moved in really quickly. A group of women even came to the house today, I was only half around — but I think mom knew them. It would be great if she had friends here too ... maybe they have sons ...

Not as bad as I thought it was going to be.

D

November 22, 84

Marco Daniel Merlo was born today.
8lbs2oz
He is so beautiful, I'm so blessed to be his aunt. He is so perfect.

Maria and Danny are going to be great parents. I am so happy we are all under one roof.

Gods please protect this sweet baby boy.

Proud aunt right here!

Livia and Ev came by today, they brought some gifts for Marco. Some normal baby stuff, but they also brought cedar (?!?) wrapped in ribbon, they hung it over the door of his room.

Mom's friends came over too. Mom seems to get tense when they come, I don't know, it's like she's trying to be friendly ... they were in the living room talking really low, I think they might have been fighting and not wanting us to hear ... They def came to see Marco — the whole thing made Maria really uncomfortable — so she left.

Small towns ...

D

Frustrated, I flip ahead again, stopping at a thin piece of newspaper sticking out of the pages by just a hair. I try to unfold it and pull it out, but it is coming apart. The part of the headline that I could read said: "**Matabi Miner Found in Accidental Death**." The opposite page is smudged and messy.

They found dad.

He's dead.

Life will never be the same.

Mom won't come out of her room. She hasn't spoken to me or Maria for almost a week.

I feel like she knows what happened to dad

— It was like she was expecting it —

I should be slapped for thinking that ... but I can't shake the feeling I could have done something.

And I didn't.

D

Tears well up in my eyes. I can't help it; it is impossible for me not to empathize with Daniella. I can't imagine losing my dad. That would kill me. Holding the tears back, I tell myself I can't fall to pieces now. I still have more to read.

I flip through a couple more pages.

March 85

Last week I was brought into the circle. Everything is different. I can see everything, FEEL everything.

There is an abandoned cabin behind the work yard. The girls said if I was going to be a part of their circle I would need a place to practice too. Yesterday after school I couldn't find them, thought they might have gone to the cabin. Rebecca was there. She hasn't been a bitch to me but she hasn't been nice, it's weird — I don't get a good feeling when she's around, I feel like she's sneaky ...

She told me the cabin was a stupid place for Livia and Ev to have picked — it's practically in the open, everyone knows about it.

I felt stupid being there.

Before she left, she told me everyone knows I committed myself to a coven now — maybe I shouldn't have been so quick to do that ...

I swear to God, while she walked passed me, she never looked at me, but I felt as if everyone else was ... when she left ... I thought I heard her say it was good to have some "real power" back in this town ... but I don't know — I felt so embarrassed, I can't be sure she said anything.

But after the invocation last week — what the girls had said ... said they were happy they had got me ... I hadn't thought about it as anything ...

I decided — creepy as she is — Rebecca might be right, I brought everything I had at the cabin home. My shadow should be with me at all times. Not lying around where anyone could get it, right?

D

Witchcraft in the sticks?

The back of the book has gone through some shit, probably the same dastardly shit the other book had gone through. This is the only evidence of what Daniella had gone through. The pages have been dried out after being very wet. They have old blood smeared across the paper, under the ink. Daniella was knee-deep in something serious. With each page, I can see she was drowning in whatever was going on around her.

I have no more patience for this. The dates become sporadic, the messages on the pages more desperate.

March 21, 86

What have we done? Did I ever have a choice in this?

Enzo is going to the congregation tonight to see if he can appeal to Persephone and Mom.

There's still time to save my baby from all of this. From everything I've done

D

July 86

I don't know how she found me.

I didn't mean for any of this to happen. I am not going to be able to fight much longer. I'm getting big.

The baby will be here soon. If I can't save myself I might as well put my baby in the hands of the beast myself.

If I prayed would God hear?

I wish Maria and Danny and Marco were still here. I wish I had somebody.

Even if it was to tell them — I did this to myself.

I want no pity.

Just mercy on Lili, I can't believe she is meant for this.

D

My breath catches in my throat.

October, 86

It's done.
There are no words.

November 7, 86

I am so alone.

I have to be strong. I should have never asked Maria to come back, this wasn't her fight.

Their deaths are because of me.

The gods I pray to have been very clear as to what they have to offer.

What do I do? Where do I go?

Marco asks me questions. He saw. He doesn't say he saw it all, but I know he did. His spirit, my spirit, is forever changed.

My gut tightens.

December 1, 86

In one way or another Sergeant MacDonald has gone through this with me. He has lost just as much as me. I can trust Bruce. We would be lost, maybe dead without his help. There is just no way I can ever truly show him my gratitude.

The apartment isn't great, it's small and old, but it's perfect. It's a hole, one of many in obscurity. I know that he is risking his life to help bury us in this small world.

If I perform one last task in the name of the spirit, it will be to protect him, and us.

He came today, brought us food. He was able to get a new birth certificate for Marco and myself. He knows that Persephone — if she is still alive — and my mother will stop at nothing to get me back into the circle. He said I would need to change our last name. Plan to leave Thunder Bay. Leave Ontario.

Don't repeat my mother's mistakes.

Never come back.

He told me I had to pick new names, it seemed so silly compared to the pain that's rotting my heart.

I have lost everything I have ever loved in the last two years. Everything that was a part of me, that I cherished, is gone. I won't make the same reality for my babes, and they will never know about the pit of evil we escaped.

Bruce took me to a doctor here in Thunder Bay.

Marco and I listened to my growing daughter's heartbeat — it's so strong. She will be so strong.

I wish Enzo could have been there, to hear her heart beat, to hold my hand. To be here with us.

I cry so much thinking about him. I don't know if I will be able to repair myself from this.

My baby will never know this pain. I need to be strong. I need to make sure I can put us as far away from this as possible.

There will be no escaping how special or how nefarious our daughter will be. No matter, she will have my heart, my soul and I will bless her every day she breathes.

I cling to this hope.

I renamed Marco after the men in my life that lost their lives loving and protecting me. My daughter's father and my father.

Vincenzo James.

He's already getting used to the new name "Vinny" — he thinks he's a spy and this is all just a game … I hope childhood will have a part in erasing the memories. I hope I can be as good to him as Maria would have been.

Renaming myself was a crisis! — I truly had to disconnect myself from everything that ever mattered to me.

I couldn't rely on my grandmother's last name — especially not my mother's — every name that would connect me to the life I'm fleeing would expose me. Every other name seemed hollow and contrived, made up and meaningless.

If Mom and the others hadn't been so persistent with naming Lilith, I would have named her Carmella.

This life will bring more happiness than the last. Won't it?

Đ C

Looking up from the book to digest all of the information, this whole new fucked reality that is my life, I think I'm going to puke, but instead I blubber like a baby. I fall away from the chest, still holding onto the book, and I cry. Sobbing into the pages, I mourn Maria and Danny, my aunt and uncle. They died, and we lived. I regret being an ass, being insensitive. I realize I was robbed of so much before I had even been born.

I sob harder when I try to picture myself in my mother's shoes: losing her dad and then her sister, becoming a mother in such an abrupt and violent way.

My dad.

Oh my God.

My heart breaks for her, then again for me. The pain pounds in my chest and hurts so much my hand instinctively comes up to hold it, to shield it from any more harm. My dad, isn't my ... no, I can't accept that! My dad is my dad, always will be, but the love of another man had created me ... and Vin — Marco? Jesus fuck, does he even know? Holy shit ... we're not even brother and sister! Mom and Dad aren't even ... his truth is even more depressing than mine.

Panic takes over. I want to leave. What am I supposed to do? Bring this up at the breakfast table? Maybe wait till the next Bible study, when mom has her hand up to answer a question pertaining to Jesus and his disciples? I could jump out of my seat and accuse her of holding our family together with glue made from LIES!

"LIES!"

All of it. How did that woman wake up each morning starting each day with a lie bigger than yesterday's? What happened to her matters. It's the foundation on which my life is built, and guess what? It is all fucking bullshit! What makes me even madder: these major life-changing bombs that have just dropped all over my life disintegrate what little normalcy I have left.

The journal took away my balance. I need that part — the 'Vinny' part of me and the 'Rocco' part of me and the 'Mom and Dad' part of me — to stay normal. I'm a freak with a façade. I was just like everyone else. More or less. Now? There is nothing left to hide behind.

Everybody my mom lost, I lost, too. Aunts and uncles and grandmas. *Did they all die because of me?* The thought has the ability to crush me. *Everybody dies because of me.* We had a family. A past. Was she ever going to show this to me? She took me out of one hell, and threw me down into another. I want to pick the chest up, break the door down, and throw it down on her. I want to hurt her, make her endure the same shock of pain I do. I want to destroy her façade and expose her.

My face is caked with blood, dirt, sweat, tears, and snot. I smell rotten. I re-evaluate my priorities; I need to wash myself. I need to pack a bag, and I need to go somewhere to figure all of this — and myself — out. Everything starts with taking a deep breath.

I have discovered this festering wound but still haven't gotten to the bone. I have no explanation as to why Ephryium is here, or why I am able to see the things I see, know the things I know. And I hate him for that, too.

As I push myself up off the floor, I get lightheaded and stagger forward. I catch myself on the wall, not surprised to see the tall, shadowy figure standing just outside the door. I can't stay focused. My thoughts have all slowed down. I feel like I am devolving into a drooling monkey when my phone starts to ring.

My phone? No, I lost my phone. Whose phone was

r i n g i n g i n m y p o c k e t?

Every tone of the ring is slowed down and comes out singularly. The sound of my heartbeat fills my ears.

Lethargically, I reach around and pull the phone out of my back pocket.

What the fuck? PRIVATE?

My thoughts — and time — come rushing at me all at once. It hits me like a bullet to the brain:

This is Justyne's phone.

I'll never see Justyne again.

I love her so much.

I killed her.

Her blood is on my face and down my neck.

The man I grew up thinking is my dad is not the man responsible for me being alive.

A man my mom met when she was a teenager living in Ignace, Ontario, where she was part of a group who worshipped a dark power, is my dad.

I had an aunt and uncle named Maria and Daniel who had a son.

Marco, my brother Vinny, was their son.

They died helping my mom and I escape.

My mom has buried us in a shroud of lies in order to keep me from ever knowing "why."

Earlier tonight, I was a conduit to what I can only describe as a demon.

Along with the power to take it on and see it,
I can see everything else in the shades of spiritual grey,
in-between the lines of the living, the dead, and the omnipotent.

There will be no escaping how special or how nefarious I will be.

My name is Lili, and I am a disaster. My dead best friend's phone is in my hand ringing, and I am going to answer it.

LXI.

3:20 a.m.

"Hello?"

"Hey, Just! I hope you don't mind, I got your number from Alex. I'm glad you're awake, it's — " It was a guy's voice.

I cut him off. To be honest, I don't want to talk to any of Justyne's fools. "No, no, Justyne isn't here." *Why did I answer?*

"Oh, oh shit, my bad. Where's she at?"

"She's out." *She's dead.*

"Huh, OK. Well, who's this?"

"Uh, no. Who's this?"

He laughs softly. In spite of myself, the laugh softens my defenses. "This is Delano. I'm a friend of Justyne's. If she's not there, maybe you can help me?"

I start to get nervous. I haven't had time to think up a story. *What if he asks questions? I am going to get caught in a lie. Why did I answer? I answered her phone? Holy fuck! I can't believe myself sometimes. I am such a dumbass!*

Delano? Delano? Delano? Holy shit. The hug.

I don't know, Lili? Where IS Justyne? Why do you have her phone?

Did you KILL her? Hmm?

> *I'm going to jail.*
>
> *Hang up hang up hang up!*

"Yea, sure, maybe. What do you need?"

What had Justyne told me about him?

"Were you out with her tonight? We saw each other at after hours. She was there with another girl."

Ah Fack!

I can't seem to control the verbal diarrhea exploding from my lips. "It was me." *Lili, you're on your own. You obviously don't care what I think.* [Brain exits premises.] "She was with me."

I can hear him smile. It makes me smile.

"Oh, no way. I was wondering if you were OK. You seemed pretty high earlier. I got worried when I didn't see you around after you bolted."

A wave of euphoric memories sweep over me: him holding me, wrapped in the security of his arms. The fact that he said he had been 'worried' made me suspicious. *Why? Why are you worried about me? Hmm? Huh? Why?* But without any real rationalization, the thoughts were put to the side, and I became a giant bowl of Jell-O, happy he had been worried, happy he had cared about me.

"It wasn't a great night, Delano, but I wanted to thank you; it could have gone a lot worse. Thanks for, I don't know, being there." *Really? If I hadn't gotten a hug, the night would have been worse ... than it was? What the fuck is happening to me?* "Well, is that it? You wanted to know if I was OK?"

"Uhh, yea, and I dunno, maybe get your name?"

I laugh into the phone. Mostly at myself and the fact I haven't even told him my name. "Lili."

"Hey, Lili."

"Hey." *I am doomed! I should have nothing to do to with him. I should just be alone.*

"Listen, I know it's late as shit, but you don't sound like I woke you up, and I'm not in bed yet … "

"Yea?"

"Well, do you wanna meet up? Smoke a joint or sumthin?"

Smoke a joint? That and a bullet to the brain.

I swallow my guilt. Actually, a toke would be pretty amazing right at the moment.

"I don't, Delano. You're right. It *is* late. The busses aren't running, and I'm not paying for a cab." I throw every excuse I can think of short of the truth: *I smell like shit, and am covered in blood — murder is tiring and being bastardized is emotionally draining. Call it a night?*

"Well, where you at? I'll come grab you."

This is all just too much, but I can't say no. *He saved me once from myself, maybe I should let him save me again?*

"My parents live in the hills. I'm in the backyard. How long till you're here, you think?"

"Where in the hills? Wait, you're in the backyard?" He laughed. "What are you doing?"

"Prowling around like a cat in the night."

He snickers. "Lili? Are you still high?"

"Ugh, stiflingly sober, actually. We're up in the ridge. I'll text you the address, all right? I'll be out front."

Am I sure about this? I can just go inside my house, pretend like I live a very different life than I do, have a shower, grab a book, and read till I fall asleep. That sounds a thousand times better than guessing if Delano wants to fuck me all night. I am so much better at keeping people out rather than letting them in, but right now? Lonely does not even begin to describe how alone I feel. I need someone. And I don't think finding refuge in fictional characters is going to cut it. Not tonight.

"OK, it might take me a minute. I'm coming from the

southeast. What do you want to go do?"

You asked me out, man. Get it together. "I could use some quiet, you know? This has been the never-ending night from hell. I just want to die." *Subtle.*

"I know that feeling. I have a place. It's quiet. I think you'll like it."

"I hope you don't think you're about to get your dick sucked. I don't want you to think I don't mean exactly what I'm saying. I am not going with you to fuck you, OK? I really need a friend right now, and I don't have any of those to call so … "

"Woah woah," he interrupts. "I understand. Shit, Lili that was really honest."

"Sorry, I just — "

"No, no. Don't be sorry. That's good. You said exactly what was on your mind. You gotta know though, I can't stop thinking about you. As soon as you walked away, I wanted to follow you. Do you ever feel like sometimes you were just meant to meet someone?"

I don't know how to answer. I can't help but wonder if he's being genuine.

"Lili, if all you need is someone to chill with, that's fine with me. That's more than fine. Whatever you want. Just give me a chance to be there."

I feel uncomfortable, embarrassed. I can't find the words.

He gently breaks the silence. "So, I promise — no surprise fucking. Can I come?"

"Yea, come grab me. What's your number?"

I shakily punch each digit into the phone.

"'K, I'll text you. See you in a bit."

"'K, see you."

As I hang up the phone, I turn around to face the open chest on the floor. Something underneath the stack of papers shifts. I stare intently, and the papers shift slightly but quickly again. My eyes start to dry out, but fuck if I am blinking; that's when the monster will lunge out of the box and attach itself to my face. *I'm not new here. I am going to wait it out.*

Something slowly descends from the ceiling of the shack. The boards underneath my feet creak and moan. The noises work their way up the walls. With the lightest touch, something comes to rest on my shoulder.

Going against my intuition of what will happen if I take my eyes away from the chest, I look. I know what it is before I see it, but I look anyways. I could have just brushed it off and kept the box monster at bay with my penetrating and ultra-intimidating stare (that's what I am doing, right?) But no, I look just in time for the demon spider that is on my shoulder to dart onto my face. No matter how scary a blood-covered, skinned demon is, spiders are still fucking scary.

So, naturally, I scream like a little bitch, slapping and clawing at my face until there was no doubt in my mind that I got it!

Glowing in victory, I stand up straight with pride. Until my attention is brought to the unnaturally large egg sac bursting inside the wooden chest. As it overflows with a frenzy of spiders, black masses descend from the beams in the ceiling.

The blood drains from my face.

I need to take the journal and the spell book with me. I want to take the whole chest, but it's too big, and I don't want to touch the spider-infested volcano, let alone lug the thing around with me.

I'll have to though. Oh, the feet! The little feet scramble over my face. Nests of spiders in my hair, scurrying down my arms and rappelling off of my fingers. Like a mad woman, I give my body a vigorous and violent wipe-down before getting on my knees, grabbing the books and papers that are left on the floor, and throwing them out into the fog.

"Oh, fuck fuck fuck!"

Grabbing either side of the chest, I dump the contents out. Myriads of spiders spill in front of me, scattering up the walls, out the door, and towards me. Using the bottom of the chest, I start to squish little armies of them.

"I don't have time for your shit. I have a date, mother-fuckers!"

Once my blood lust is satisfied, I gather everything that has been dumped out of the chest and shovel it back in.

Some stragglers are still dropping down by my feet. I stand in silence, waiting to see what will happen next.

Nothing.

I shove the phone back into my pocket and grab the chest. I step out of the shed. Out of Wonderland. The books and letters are still scattered on the lawn. Quietly as possible, I put everything back into the chest and make for the backdoor. Every move I make is so fucking loud. The noise of putting the chest down so I can flip the mat up and grab a key is offensive to my ears. Every couple of movements, I freeze in place and listen to the house.

I tiptoe á la Pink Panther down the pitch-black hallway, suck-ing my breath in each time the floor creaks under my foot. When I get to my room, I place the chest on my bed, strip, grab my house coat and proceed to have the hottest, most luxurious shower any-one on the face of the planet ever had in their life — ever.

I only pull the curtain back once when I feel eyes on me. After that, I refuse to give in. So what if something is there? For the first time in my life, I am able to differentiate the entities that have forced their way into my body. For the first time, I realize Ephryium has always been with me, and tonight is the first and only time I have been attacked by something else. Maybe he is responsible for that?

Recalling the conversation between Ephryium and the demon I had eavesdropped on, it seemed as if they knew each other. The demon had been so convincing, so enticing. I almost wanted to give in to the carnage, I can't imagine how Ephryium felt. The demon had said Ephryium could have done that to me. Taken control of me. Made me kill. Made me a monster.

After all this time with me though, all of the sudden, out of nowhere, he decides to be present? Show up like an old friend … outside my shower? As the events of the night run through my head, I appreciate Ephryium immensely. I wince at the thought of an entire life spent like tonight. That's within Ephryium's power. Up until tonight, he has never forced his way in like the demon. He has never locked me away into a dark hole within my mind to watch as he took over. But he could.

Was he just as dangerous as that demon? Capable of … would I be able to defend myself?

I come back to the thought: would the demon still have attacked me if I didn't have Ephryium, and these "gifts"? If Ephryium wasn't here — would Justyne still be alive? So I see shadows, dead people, and have killer intuition … what had this ever done for me besides riddle me with anxiety, and isolate me?

The water runs cold. Time's up.

Happy to no longer smell like the devil's asshole, I creep back to my room. I go straight to my closet to grab a travel bag. *What do I need? How long am I going to be gone for? I'd need the essentials. Travel light, Lili.*

Jeans, shirts, hoodies, makeup —*yes, make up. It's bad enough in a couple of minutes I'll be homeless, do I need to look it, too?*

I start stuffing books by the handful into the bag, along with jewellery and heels. It is apparent not only has my practical mind left, but the bag has no chance in hell of closing. Letting out a huge sigh of exasperation, I realize the entire contents of my room will not fit into one bag, no matter how hard I try.

Chucks will work; the heels come out. Most likely, I'll lose the jewellery anyways, so it comes out. I grab my journal out from under my mattress and stuff it into the bag as well. My mind is spinning. I know I have to leave but am still desperate to bring it all with me.

Do I want to bring my mom's journal? Yea, and the spell book, too. No matter how resentful I am right now, I know I have to go through them.

Does Vinny know, too? All this time, does he know he isn't really "Vincenzo"?

The anger wells in my chest.

Did he lie to me too?

Delano will be here soon. I stuff as many papers from the chest into my bag as I can, pull on a slouchy toque, and my black Chucks. Everything starts and ends on a deep breath. I inhale as deeply as I can and rid myself of my attachment to my room, to this house, to all the sleeping people inside of it. As I slowly blow the air out, my heart strains to stay intact. A storm of emotions sits just below the surface. My breath wavers. I swallow painfully. This goodbye is only superficial; I know this place and these people are always going to be a part of me. It's time to make sure I'm in control of the terms in which they would be in my life.

I need to take control of so many things, and I'll never be able to do that here.

The chest still sits on my bed; at least she will know why I am gone. I give her more than she deserves. More than she gave me.

I slip out the front door, back into the night. It shuts behind me with a soft click. Without thinking, I stop, put my bag down, and draw in the condensation on the front door window. Jaw clenched, eyes focused, I draw the six-point star, circling it twice, with an unknown but definite purpose. It's one last 'fuck you' and 'good bye.'

I write the letters of my name in between the spaces of the star points. The glass vibrates under my finger. I can hear all of the windows, not just on my house, but all of the houses on our street, come under the same pressure. The sensation is so intense my face tingles, like the front of my entire body has fallen asleep. As I slide my finger down, finishing the *H*, the window seizes. With an abrupt *snap*, the pane fractures with cracks.

Quickly grabbing my bag, I step back, away from the house. All of the windows on the houses as far as I can see wear the same shattered panes. Only one has my name on it though.

I make my decision. "I bind you here, Ephryium. I need to feel safe. I need to be free from you. I don't want your gifts. Stay here. Keep them safe. Haunt my mom. Not too bad, just enough for her to know that I know … I bind you here, Ephryium. I am going on … without you." I whisper my spell to Ephryium and on my house. I open my eyes, knowing it is done.

Behind me, the sound of a low, purring engine approaches. I turn around to see a shiny, black Mustang pulling up to the curb. A dark figure emerges from the driver's seat, coming up to rest his arms on the roof.

It's Delano.

"Whoa! What happened to the windows?"

I gawk at him, doing my best *'genuinely confused.'* "I don't know. Weird … We should probably go."

His dark eyes drift from me, to the windows, and then back again before squinting suspiciously. "OK … "

Rushing around the car, he beats me to the passenger door. I blush at his chivalry as he offers to take my bag and opens the door for me to get in.

Sign of a keeper right here.

He glances at my bag curiously. "We runnin' away?"

"Mmhmm yes, maybe a little bit." I blush again as I sit down. "This car is insane! Seventy-three? No! Sixty-nine?" *Yes, Lili, change the subject.* I await his answer eagerly.

"Yea! How do you know that?"

"Brothers." I shrug. "Did you restore it yourself?"

"No, my bro- my bro, he's a mechanic. It was a candy store for him."

"Well, it's perfect."

He is about to say something. Instead, I can see him make the quick decision not to. Smiling, he shakes his head and closes the door.

As soon as he gets back into the car, I turn to face him. "What? What were you going to say?"

He smiles. "Nuthin."

The way his eyes flash, bright and warm, the way he looks at me … My face goes hot again.

"You're pretty sexy, Lili."

Sinking as low as I can into the leather seat, I tear my eyes off him and stare down at my hands. "You don't even know me."

"I don't need to. You're overflowing with sexy. Just sitting there, all sexy. It's crazy. I can't believe you're sitting here — with me! And then! And then! When I think it isn't possible for you to be any sexier, you go and do that."

"Do what?"

He has my eyes locked into his again, only for a moment, before he peers out the windshield and answers. "Talk."

I burst out laughing. "Shut up."

"No, Lili. You said you want a friend, and if this is going to work out, you're gonna have to cut that out. And that, too! Stop smiling and blushing and looking all gorgeous while you do it. You're gonna have to *ugly* it up, Lili!"

Just like that, in my lowest moments as a human being, Delano steals my heart.

Scraping my teeth along my bottom lip, I try as hard as I can to stop smiling. I bite down into my lip and meet his eyes. He is struggling just as hard not to smile, too. We both laugh again.

"'K," I say through giggles. "Let's go?"

"Let's go."

LXIII.

THE BOY

North Battleford Outskirts, Saskatchewan
July 13th 1999

"'mon, Ma, it's a quick one. A day. What's a day? We'll be back in no time. I bet you're not even gonna miss us." The boy heaved the cooler into the open door of the semi-truck.

Debbie stood off to the side with her arms folded across her massive chest, disapproval on her face. She couldn't help but survey the growth of the boy. He had grown so much, filled out, a truly handsome young man. He was a typical teenage boy, always on the phone with girls, getting into minor mischief with friends. The boy was charming, witty, and popular, especially with all of the little girls at his junior high school. It was the only reason Debbie didn't put her foot down against the trip; it would get him outta town, keep him outta trouble — or at least keep the trouble off her door step — and maybe he would go a little longer before giving his heart to some town floozy.

"You've been gone more than you've been here. You gonna

spend the whole summer co-piloting your daddy then?"

"Maaa, c'mon, don't be like that. I miss you as much as you miss me. Besides, like I said, this one is a short one. Two days tops. Next one I'll skip. Me an' you can hang out here instead."

"Hang out?"

She really didn't know what the term meant, which caused the boy to stop in his tracks and smirk endearingly at his mom. He put his duffle bag down at his feet and walked over to the aging woman. His chin was at her nose now. He wrapped his arm around her and pulled her in to land a peck on her cheek.

"You do this every time, Mom … I love you … be back soon."

The morning sun crested over the valley hills, marking the day's arrival. It was time for the boys to go if they wanted to be in Okotoks for lunch. The truth was: it was a day trip. Debbie knew it, too. It was sometimes entertaining to watch the boy bull-shit. If they left now, they could do the loop and be back by ten pm. But it didn't matter. Most boys didn't want to spend any time with their parents at his age. She was grateful. Even if he was a little bull-shitter, he was a bull-shitter who wanted to spend time with his dad.

The screen door closed with a bang, and a few subsequent smaller bangs as the door bounced off the frame. "We all packed up an' ready to go, boy? Mornin' shit has come an' gone. It's time to hit the road!"

Debbie's cheeks flushed red as Arnold grabbed two hand-fuls of her ass. He said sorry for the mess he left, gave her a kiss on the cheek, smacked her ass hard enough to make her yelp, and yelled his farewells as he jogged to the ready and waiting rig.

Hours into the trip, they were approaching Edmonton. They were making good time. The boy sat in the passenger side of the truck, listening to Arnold explain how he and Debbie had used the insurance money they had gotten from their house in

Battleford to bribe a First Nations adoption agency handler for his birth documents and for a legitimate adoption record. Arnold thought it was all so brilliant, he smiled and slapped at the steering wheel with excitement. No matter how many times he told the story to the boy, and he told it a lot, it always ended with "You know we didn't do the same for yer sister there, but I tell ya, I knew you was mine from the moment I laid eyes on ya."

He unwrapped two breakfast burritos Debbie had packed for them. The boy really did love sitting passenger, listening to Arnold yammer on about stuff an' things. The two had been hauling together for more than a couple of years now.

A brief memory skirted through the boy's mind. An autumn forest, a boy named "Mikey"? Blood on a rock — and then of punishment. He was forbade to ever "shit where he ate" ever again.

That's when he had started making trips with Arnold. Since then, since his sister, and with help, he had developed into a finely-tuned killer. Some trips, he let Arnold take the lead. On short trips. Not that Arnold's tastes were completely singular, but they didn't need time. Only quiet and space. Arnold showed the boy making a mess of things could be just as enjoyable as breaking them down slowly.

This trip, the boy knew, Arnold would already have it in his head they would be doing it "nice in quick. In an' out." It was important to the boy things be done differently this time. This time would be a first for both of them.

"The Loop" was Battleford to Edmonton, to Red Deer, to Calgary, then Lethbridge, and back home. About eighteen hours' worth of driving. Arnold could do it without stopping, but he liked to take his time when the boy tagged along. They had done a cross-country trip in early June. It was hard on the boy; the hours were long. Arnold had made sure to stop on the other side of Banff, and they'd grabbed a hitchhiker.

The boy had taken Arnold outside of his comfort zone and had asked if they could keep the young hitchhiker alive for longer than Arnold would have liked. Arnold had found the way in which his boy handled himself poetic, and even though the boy hadn't meant to, he had revealed to Arnold the difference between them. The two boys had sat in the back of the truck's cab, talking and laughing for hours before Arnold turned off the highway so he could join in on the … fun.

Taking the boy along on hauls had accomplished what he sought out to do: help the boy hone in on blending in, doing what he needed to get done without it being a spectacle. Arnold showed the boy how to pick people who wouldn't be missed. Taught him the darkness was and always would be his friend. No killing was ever to be done out in the open. Always find somewhere off the beaten path. To destroy every remnant of any event ever taking place at all.

In the time in between, Arnold and his boy bonded. Long nights were spent driving, eating, and talking. Arnold would never forget in the boy's younger years, through his long-forgotten lisp, he told a story of the moment Arnold had passed him his "friend." Arnold only ever made half sense of it all.

By the time they hit Calgary, it was lunch. They made a plan to stop in Okotoks and hit up a burger joint. There couldn't have been a better time, father and son, sitting down to eat together, to reveal something to Arnold that shook the very fibres of his world. Nothing could have ever prepared him for the ensuing conversation, or how to deal with it.

"Dad? I want to have sex."

Arnold's jaw slacked, hanging open as his eyes widened in shock. The only response that came from him was in the form of a dollop of mayonnaise; it had been hanging from his burger and landed on the tray with a *plop*, causing the boy to break eye contact and glance at it.

"Uh … hmm … OK."

The boy pushed through his dad's inability to communicate properly. "I have been dating Bobby for a while, and I … I dunno, I think it's time. But I … I don't, well, fuck, Dad! I don't know what the hell ta do!"

Calmly resting his burger down on the tray, Arnold leaned in closer. Resting his elbow on the table, he looked the boy square in the eyes and lowered his voice. "You wanna fuck a boy?"

"Dad!"

Arnold quickly put his hands up to stop the boy, even closing his eyes as if that would deafen him to what was coming. "No, no. You wanna fuck a lil boy, you know, that's OK. Better a boy than nuthin', I suppose." He gave out a little chuckle. "Makes this conversation even easier. The boy's only got one hole down there. Less confusion on where ta put it."

"Oh my god, Dad. What the fuck? I'm not gay. Bobby's a girl!"

"Oh! My bad, my bad. Well, what the hell kinda parents name a girl Bobby?"

The boy laughed hysterically at his father. Through his laughs, he thanked him for being so supportive, but he'd need more help than that to ensure Bobby didn't wind up with an asshole full of dick … and on that topic, what was the etiquette on that?

"So, that's why your Ma was telling me she'd see us tomorrow. You wanna give the old practice run before you have a go with Bobby?"

"Exactly."

"And how do you think Bobby will feel about you getting your dick wet with someone else?"

The boy raised his eyebrows, leaned in, and stated matter-of-factly, "I don't think it's Bobby's business what I get up to when she's not around. To be honest, I hadn't even thought of it."

"Okie dokie, then. It's settled," he said as his hands smacked the table. "There's a little not-so-butt-fuck town near Lethbridge I can drop you in. It's not gonna give you much time, maybe two hours or so? You're a good lookin' kid, though. If you can't pick up a girl — even one that looks like a potato — in that time, I don't think there's hope for the rest of us." Leaning back in his seat, Arnold picked up his burger with a great deal of satisfaction written on his face. Parenting for the win. Debbie would be proud. However, the boy didn't seem satisfied with the conversation.

"No, Dad. I'm gonna need a bit more time. I was thinkin' we would spend the night somewhere … "

"Oh, boy. Now I think you got something in your head about this bein' an overnight deal cause of the movies an' what not. But your first time? You're gonna need an alley and three minutes — IF that!"

The boy wasn't impressed. "Dad, I was thinking something a little more … creative than that … know what I mean?"

Arnold got it. He sat up at attention. Just when he thought he was in control, the boy rose to the occasion to show him otherwise. It had been a weird decade getting used to this. He could fully assume the boy knew exactly what his night was going to look like. After the twinges of jealously and inferiority passed, he was happy the boy wanted to include him.

He was proud.

Fort MacLeod came quick. The town was a well-maintained antique. The original architecture of the eighteen- and nineteen hundreds was covered in polished red brick and untarnished limestone. Kitschy coffee shops and restaurants littered the downtown area; even a movie theatre, which was exactly where the boy headed when he jumped out of his dad's truck. He told his dad to keep hold of his cell phone; any girl he was going to pick up would have her own. He'd call when he was ready to meet up.

The theatre was quaint, with a marquee board on either side of the green double doors. In such a small town, the boy was surprised to see both movies were current. It took a couple of seconds before his eyes adjusted to the dimly lit interior, a stark contrast from the summer day he left outside. The air conditioning hit him like a brick wall. He lingered under the cool vent for a second, and when he spotted the washroom, he decided to go and give himself a once-over.

Theatre two

She's waiting for you

Back row

Pink   green

the lord be thy   saviour   and thy noose

The fluorescent lights overhead cast deep shadows down the boy's face, but even then, as dangerous as he appeared, he was still inviting as ever. Making sure the joint in his pocket had survived the ride, he glanced once more in the mirror. His long-time friend was standing in the reflection. A memory of the seething, blood-lusting nightmare who hissed in his ears as a child — who still used Arnold as an outlet — darted through his memories. It had been a long time since he saw the monstrosity that haunted the basement and held a permanent residency in Arnold's head. Since the moment he took control, the entity stopped being a monster, had taken down its façade to reveal something resembling a man. An all-powerful, all-knowing, immortal man. They looked as if they could be father and son, with their dark features, and the ability to be threatening and disarming at the same time. The boy gave him a wink and received a respectful nod in return.

He paid for a ticket. Got a jumbo bag of Nibs and a Coke.

His heart raced: performance anxiety.

The boy had appreciation for the town, for the theatre, for the ornate, golden door that opened to the corridor leading to theatre two. The previews had already begun; blue light from the screen washed over the theatre. And there, in the back row, sat an exquisite bird, a virginal beauty, an angel. Nothing in this world had ever come close to tainting even a strand of undyed hair on her head. Every sun-kissed freckle was perfection. She wore pink cut-offs longer than any other girl her age, a testament to her parents' conservative nature. There was a sparkle on her neck, a gleam of gold, small and feminine, like herself. Her cross.

Containing his smile, he glanced up and thanked God. *I'm going to enjoy every bit of her*, he thought.

He was answered with, "Stop mocking him. He's not here." A dark laugh followed and faded into nothing.

The boy fell hard into the seat next to hers. Managing to startle her.

Leaning over the armrest, he whispered "Sorry." And waited for the girl to look at him.

"It's OK."

He held her eyes for a moment longer than was appropriate for strangers. He blinked slowly and smiled. The way her head dipped as she blushed was enough for his dick to twitch with that twang of arousal.

She wouldn't have a chance.

As the teen romance played out in front of them, he let his hand slide over hers. Ever so subtly, but-never-the-less, he caught her eye, moving her to smile, again and again. It was like catching a baby bunny in a snare. He was going to be her summer romance, that whirlwind that every teenage girl wishes silently for.

When the lights came back on as the credits rolled, both were awkward smiles and sweaty palms.

It was inevitable.

There was no turning back.

"Hey."

"Hi."

"What's your name?"

Closing her eyes, she shook her head slowly. "No, what's your name? You're not from here are you?" The smile lit up her face was never interrupted.

"No, I'm not. I'm from Saskatchewan. My friends call me Chico. I showed you mine … your turn. What's your name?"

"Chico?"

"No way! You're Chico, too? What kind of parents name their daughter Chico? That's weird!" His eyes were open wide; he knew they were being misinterpreted for being genuine and revealing. He smiled charmingly as she burst into a giggle.

"No, no! I'm Ashley." Her hand thrust out to shake his.

"Nice to meet you, Ashley."

"Thanks. Did you like the movie?"

"Well, I would have." He glanced down to the bag of candy in his hands. "But this weird girl kept on distracting me, making me smile and touchin' me an' shit. I mean seriously, the nerve!" He read her eyes, watching her face change into an amused and shocked expression.

Letting out a gasp of disbelief, her jaw fell. "Me?"

"So then you admit it. You were playin' with me the whole movie … I'm going to complain, ask for my money back."

"Me? Ugh! No! You!"

"ME?"

"Mmhmm." Her head bobbed side to side, as if her inner Latina chose to defend herself.

"OK, OK. Maybe the girl wasn't so bad? Maybe? Only maybe though, 'cause these things are truly subjective."

"Oh yea?"

"Yes, very. Maybe the girl was the most beautiful girl I had ever seen in my life, and the two clowns on screen had nothing on what I was feelin' for this girl at this very moment?"

Ashley took a quick breath in, nervously grabbing her cross. She rubbed it slowly between her fingers as if to will away the urges flooding through her.

Touchdown!

"I gotta leave in a couple of hours. My dad's gonna come pick me up. You wanna hang out till then?"

Nodding slowly, she whispered, "Yea," once and then said it again, louder. "Yea, I think that'd be good."

For the first time since they had engaged, Ashley turned to her friends. They sat behind her, watching her conversation take place with this 'out of towner.' She quickly tried to dismiss them while the boy eavesdropped.

"His name is Chico. We're just gonna go for a walk or sumthin'."

"Chico? What kind of name is Chico? Ash, you don't even know this guy."

"That's the whole point, you guys. I'm going to get to know him. Can you cover for me?"

"I dunno, Ash. This doesn't seem like a great idea. Let's go for a coffee like we planned, c'mon."

"Yea, Ash, what if your dad finds out? He's gonna kill you."

"He is not gonna kill me. 'Cause he's not gonna know! You guys go for coffee. If my parents call, I'm gonna say I'm with you. I won't be gone long — his dad has to come pick him up anyways.

I'll meet you after."

There was a concerned silence between the friends.

Finally, to the relief of the boy, one of her friends gave her the go. "'K. Just be careful. And if he turns out to be a douche, call us!"

"'K! Will do! Love ya. See you in a bit!"

LXIII.

THE BOY & ASHLEY

July 13th 1999
Fort Macleod, Saskatchewan

shley and the boy had wandered to the paths running along Old Man River. The sun had been setting for the last two hours, adding to the ambiance of the teenagers' deep and honest conversations.

Ashley's little sister had died when she was six. It left her family devastated. They turned to God for hope and strength. She pointed out the church where she had been baptized when she was thirteen as they walked past it. She had been a youth minister since then. Her eyes filled with tears of empathy when the boy related to her; his sister died when he was eight as well. It had changed him.

"But not for the better. It was like I lost my way. If I had ever had it. I dunno."

He had feigned modesty when he asked to hold her hand, showing her he would be open to her rejection, if that was her choice. But she put his hand in hers and squeezed her fingers around his.

He pounced.

She was in the mouth of the beast, wearing a smile.

No alarms seemed to go off. He watched for signs; there was no panic or distrust in her eyes, no tremor in her voice when he suggested they go under the bridge. She followed like a lamb to slaughter, laughing at his jokes, reaching up to hold onto his bicep so she "wouldn't fall on the rocks."

It was curiosity that filled her eyes when he first put the joint to his lips and lit it. She reluctantly let him put the joint to her lips, while telling her to inhale as deeply as she could.

As far as she could tell, he inhaled, too. They had partaken together; they were connecting. She wouldn't forget these fond memories. He might even come back to visit her.

He hadn't inhaled.

The GHB was meant for her only.

He let her take another hit. She blushed when he told her how cute she looked. He'd miss her. He would have to get her number, come back soon.

She's almost there

Callllllll Arnold

Across the   bridge

"Hey — you got a cell phone I can use? It'll be quick. Mine's dead. I should call to check in with my dad."

Reaching slowly into her purse, she pulled out a grenade-sized phone and tossed it to him. Her eyes drooped when she blinked. As she staggered closer to the river, she dragged each foot behind her.

"Dad? You wanna meet me by the bridge by the water? Third to Water Street then take a — yea? Awesome. Be right there." He hung up the phone and turned back to Ashley. "Hey.

Hey, you don't look so good. My dad is gonna meet me across the bridge. I'll ask him to give you a ride home. It's late."

The life had drained from her face. She stood, swaying from side to side, falling asleep standing up. Fuck. He needed to get her to the truck fast. It was going to be suspicious as fuck if he was seen dragging a pretty, young, blonde girl across the bridge and stuffing her into the cab of a rig. She needed to walk. He needed to wake her up. Thinking quickly he walked to the water's edge, where she stood drowsily, and grabbed her hand. He tugged her towards him.

"Where are we going?" The words came out slowly. Pretty soon, she would be slurring. The roofie had hit her hard. He thought he would have had fifteen, twenty minutes? No, he had maybe five.

"We gotta go, babe. Come with me. I'll take you home."

She tried to pull her hand out of his. "Noo, my daaad, he can't see. Chico? I feel funny."

"It's OK. That's normal. You're gonna be OK. I promise."

As he stood at the top of the bank, he held onto her hands tightly and pulled her up. It was a struggle; her eyes were half closed. She was losing control. Holding her by the waist, he moved as quickly as he could across the bridge. Sometimes, he just lifted her off the ground and carried her for a few steps, until a small moan came out of her mouth to put her down and "let her walk."

In a small, dusty parking lot on the other side of the river, Arnold's rig lights shone dimly: the boy's finish line. Arnold was waiting outside by the passenger door, ready to grab the girl from him and put her in the back of the rig. A thick roll of duct tape waited on the stained mattress, but as Arnold quickly saw, the girl wouldn't need to be restrained.

"It's G and weed. She's gone for the night, trust me."

Arnold couldn't help but be impressed by the boy's initiative.

Although, he wondered if he would miss the cold stiffness around his dick … *no, no* — he shook off the thoughts — this one wasn't for him. This one was special, for the boy. He should take them someplace … special.

They drove for over an hour on the main highway. The first minutes after pulling onto Crowsnest Pass were filled with tension. They always were. The moments determining whether someone had seen them, reported them, or were following them. The moments that determined if they were caught. Chances were, if no one had noticed Ashley was gone after an hour of her leaving with the boy, it wouldn't be until midday tomorrow she was officially reported missing. No one, besides family and immediate friends, would be looking for her. And they certainly wouldn't be looking for her in Buttfuck Nowhere, Alberta; Taber.

By the time the local RCMP would put out an AMBER Alert for Ashley, with no lead other than the appearance of an unknown boy, her charred, bony remains would be in pieces floating down Old Man River.

Silence hung in the air between Arnold and the boy. Even the demon, who kept the girl company in the back, stayed quiet but present, filling the girl's head with gore.

The red, neon letters of VACANCY ripped through the darkness. It was perfect — a dingy motel that attracted the type of people who didn't want to see you, and didn't want you to see them.

The boy crawled into the cab with Ashley while Arnold walked over to the small house of a front office. From the outside, he could see the top of a balding head behind the front desk, illuminated by a TV screen somewhere in close proximity. The top of the balding head was attached to a preoccupied and uninterested Italian man. As soon as the bell above the door jingled, he swivelled around on his chair to face a wall of keys, selected one, and whirled back around to face the TV.

"Seventy for the night. Thirty for the hour. Room Ten. Second house." He flicked his cigarette into a nearby ashtray and dropped the key onto the countertop. Arnold handed him the cash, snatched the key, and jogged back to the truck.

They moved the unconscious girl as quickly and quietly as they could. Arnold dropped her heavily onto the bed while the boy shut the door and blinds.

"You can go for a while." Standing at the foot of the bed, the boy peered down at Ashley. His eyes stayed fixed on her for a moment after he spoke. Then he peeled them away to glance at Arnold, then the door, then back at Arnold.

"Are yuh sure, now? Don't need no help figurin' the ins an' outs?"

LEavE

"I think I got it, Dad. Gimmie an hour or two? Then she's all yours!"

Arnold closed the door behind him, looking somewhat disappointed his son hadn't wanted him to be there for this critical moment in his life. But the gangly, yellow-toothed smile smeared across his face was the anticipation he just couldn't hide.

The boy listened to the silence. The rev of the engine he had expected never came; wherever Arnold was going, he was going by foot. He had packed a token of appreciation for his dad, not that his leftovers of Ashley wouldn't have been sufficient. He had brought an expensive bottle of scotch he had stolen from a liquor store while they were on a run to Vancouver in June — when the idea of picking up a girl had first crossed his mind. He wanted something to commemorate the occasion.

He would have to go to the truck and get it, but he didn't want to leave the girl alone in the room either. He eyed her suspiciously; what if she was faking? Waiting for her moment to run? He had never given anyone drugs before; he had only been told what to expect. But there was a huge difference in study and application.

Biting into his bottom lip, he squinted as he watched the slow rise and fall of her chest. The gold cross hanging loosely on her neck reflected the dim light of the lamp. His energy came to a roaring boil as he leapt on the bed. Ripping the pink shorts open, he jumped back to pull them down her legs, tossing them over his shoulder and into the corner. He tore off one Converse at a time, with a palpable rage in each movement.

He felt as if his limbs were possessed. He barely had any control of his fingers as they tore into the lavender lace thong, pulling at it until the fabric ripped under the strain, leaving long, red marks down her thighs.

He watched her for a reaction, any stir at all. She lay lifeless. He ripped her shirt from the neck down to her bellybutton, hoping to see a set of perfectly sculpted tits, but instead a black bra covered her chest. His hormonal rage dulled into exasperation as he realized how many fucking layers he had to tear through before this bitch was naked. God damn!

Flipping the girl over onto her stomach, with her bare ass exposed and pointing towards him, he spread her ass cheeks wide and spat as much saliva as he could muster onto the puckered eye of her asshole. His dick throbbed with a want that vibrated through his entire body. He was so startled by the sensation he reflexively grabbed at the growing boner as if it might escape.

Bringing his thighs closer to the sun-kissed ass, he slid his thumb down the crease, pushing the coarse hair to the sides as he did. He sunk his finger into her asshole. She was warm and snug around his it, never flinching at the invasiveness. Yanking his thumb out of her, he dragged his tongue from the small of her back to the top of her shoulder. Reaching around, he stuck the wet thumb into her mouth, prying her teeth open to slide it down her tongue.

Yea, she's out.

Giving a nod of security, he slapped her ass with the palm of his hand. He was delighted to reach into his pants and pull his semi-hard dick into the band of his underwear. Satisfied she was dead to the world, he left to get the bottle of Macellan from Arnold's rig.

The motel parking lot hung heavy with stale, damp air. A fog had settled in. Arnold was nowhere to be seen. The boy wondered if he had gone far. The moon cowered behind a veil of cloud. Even the neons gave off a fuzzy aura as their light choked under the mist. It was like the whole world had gone quiet, darker. No one was present but the boy and the demon.

With the bottle of scotch in hand, he walked through the haze of shadow, noting not one car had passed since he first stepped out onto the cracked concrete. As he approached the green weathered door, he felt a buzz, a vibration, coming from the building. He thought the parking lot, the fog, his head, this whole situation felt full, overflowing, everything was about to burst. It sent panic to his chest, causing him to fumble with the key.

The boy had a sense of foreboding, of something else waiting for him. Something bad. Finally, shoving the key through its slot and turning it to hear the click, he burst through the door to see Ashley on the bed. Just as he had left her. Sitting in the corner, closer to human than ever before, sat his damned angel or angelic demon. It was so hard to tell the difference.

But there he sat, waiting listlessly in the chair with his head resting in his hand. He stared, seemingly idle, at the naked girl laying still on the bed. A smile sprung to his face to see his friend with him. He didn't give another thought to his faulty intuition. Kicking the door closed with his foot, the boy walked across the room to where the angel sat and placed the bottle beside him.

"Not for you. For Arnold."

"How sweet. Father-son bonding?"

"He wanted to be here for this. It's my way of showing him he was, ya know?"

"We won't have a lot of time before your body starts to deteriorate, but with my help, my strength, you work faster and feel more."

"Not that I'd want it — but why not? Why can't you possess me without slowly killing me? I mean, I've already seen you just completely annihilate that girl at day-care — just by whispering a word to her. I'm different, aren't I? Why can't — ?"

Tipping the bottle to read the label, the demon casually examined the scotch. "Short answer? — call it genetics. Your blood, your soul, it just isn't made to take the weight of mine. But you're right: you are different. We think more and more humans are becoming susceptible to our suggestions just by being thousands of years' worth of inbred evil. Seriously, kid? You always pick the most fucked up times to have these conversations with me. We have been in a truck together for seventy-two hours at a time and nothing. Are you still not ready?"

Staring at the girl on the bed, the boy didn't reply, didn't move.

"You've deprived yourself of this brand of power for so long. But once you know it — especially you — you'll see there is a different type of submission, a unique way of manipulating and ruining the body and mind that is ... addictive. I'm excited and honoured to be here with you for this ... "

The boy descended onto the bed, straddled Ashley, and started working to unclasp the hooks on her bra.

Across the room the demon sat, watching the boy with an excited anticipation. Their eyes met and locked. A vision of pent up rage, fuelled by lust and depravity, surged through the room. His voice filled every corner of the room as a whisper. His human-like form decayed. The flesh eroded away to reveal the pitch black monstrosity underneath. The demon, like plaster being poured into a mould, took shelter in the boy.

"Let's begin."

She lay there, lifeless on the bed. His palms were sweaty. His blood surged. The energy inside him was overwhelming; he had no room for second thoughts.

Had it been a mistake to drug her? Would it have helped calm his anxiety to have her taped-up mouth moan in terror? Pangs of regret swept his mind; it would have been fun to have her awake, to terrorize her. He made a mental note for next time. And there would be so many next times.

He was the only thing in his own way. The thoughts whirled through his mind separating themselves from each other like oil and vinegar, psychopathic and just your average teenage boy. Thoughts of how it could have been had he not drugged her, of how it was going to be with his girlfriend, then about drugging his girlfriend's friends came to a halt.

The calm came suddenly. A whisper behind his ear pushed him forward.

"You have nothing to live up to. Covered in blood, or in a wedding dress. Ten or forty-two. She doesn't matter.

Put your thoughts to rest.

It's easier to feel the transfer of power once inside. You will feel her life, her emotion, even her mental state hug around you.

Ease in."

The boy kept his thoughts focused and calm. As soon as he got them under control, he felt the tip of his head, so hard that the skin was tight, touch the opening of Ashley's disengaged vagina. At first it felt like a wall, such a tiny opening. The boy hesitated to push forward. He felt the soft, skin around her pussy give to his erection, a small trickle of blood slid down the crack of her ass onto the yellowing sheets of the motel bed. Taking a deep breath in through his nose, he thrust into her as hard as he could.

"Holy fucking shit. Oh fuck!"

As he pushed into her, his eyelids immediately felt heavy. Finally, the front of his balls made contact with her taint. The heat, the tightness enveloping his dick threatened his focus on not exploding inside of her. He couldn't pull out. It was too dangerous. It was *too* good.

"Oh fuck! Ohh fuuuck."

Pleasure was measured in the millimetres of movement. He sucked in his breath and held it, as if that would stop the cum that was ready to go, waiting in his balls. The shaft throbbed once, then twice inside of its new, snug home.

"No, come on, come on."

He slowed his breathing. He needed to distract from how good it felt if it was going to go on any longer. Once the throbbing had subsided, the tip of his tongue poked out of the corner of his mouth, curling ever so slightly onto his lip. Even while he readjusted the girl, grabbing both of her thighs under his forearms, bringing her off the bed and closer to him, the feeling around his dick was so good. It was enough to make him wince.

As his climax approached, the boy thrust faster and faster. He reached down, clenching his hands around the girl's neck. Her face stayed calm and unmoving as her golden complexion flushed to a deep cherry red. Her body began to tense involuntarily in an attempt to breathe. The walls inside of her tightened around the boy's dick, throwing him over the edge of sensation. Releasing her neck, he collapsed as he gushed into her.

Closing his eyes, he caught his breath.

Sleepy time.

LXIV.

LILI

Calgary, Alberta
August 10th 2003
4:36 a.m.

I stare through my reflection, focusing on the houses and then the buildings, as we pass them. With my head leaning on the window, I try my best to not seem so damaged, so tired, but I am. I can't be anything else at this moment. My head is loud — questions about my mom and her journals, her past, my dad, what happened? Why? I know it resulted in me being the way I am, but why not Vinny? The more I think about it, I wonder what my dad's role is in it all. And then I remember — he isn't actually my dad. Someone else is.

The one person I could sound this all off on is gone, and that's my fault. My heart breaks for Justyne in such a way the pain in my chest brings tears to my eyes.

"What happened?"

The sound of Delano's voice crashes through my thoughts, shattering them into pieces. "Hmm?" is all I can manage.

"You look so sad. What are you thinking about?"

The words spill out. "So many bad things happened tonight. I dunno. It's everything, everyone." I surge with guilt and confusion, not ready to admit my part in things I haven't made sense of.

"Where's Justyne? Wasn't she with you tonight?"

I have nothing left. My mind tenses, but my body doesn't have the energy to be nervous about it. I just shake my head slowly. "She's gone. She's not comin' back."

"Fuck. Sounds like a big one."

"A big one?"

"Yea. The fight, it must have been pretty big. What did you guys get into it over?"

A lump forms in my throat. I try to choke it back, but it pushes itself up. I don't have to talk about it, but if I don't, he is going to wonder why I am crying like my best friend just died.

As soon as I open my mouth, the tears spring forth. My voice is high and desperate. I speak as fast as I can to get it out of the way — the half truths.

"I thought I found someone who I could be myself around, someone I didn't have to hide anything from." I swallow back the tears, but am left with no choice but to talk through them. "I did! I loved her so much!"

Delano, deeply concerned, slows the car down. Taking one hand from the wheel, he grabs my hand and looks at me momentarily before turning his eyes back to the road in front of us. "What happened? You can tell me."

He wouldn't understand why I shook my head so hard at the proposition.

"No, I just … I shouldn't have. I just thought it would bring us closer, you know? And it didn't? It took her from me — it destroyed her." I sob, crying so loudly my face turns red with embarrassment. I struggle to breathe, and my short gasps just make it worse. I am spiralling into heartbreak. The dam I have spent years — my whole life — building up, to guard against being scared and getting attached to transitory things, comes crashing down.

"Aww, I'm sure she'll come around."

I wipe the tears from my cheeks. "No, I am sure she won't. What's done is done. I have myself to thank for it. This is on me." Ashamed, I stare at my lap again.

He gives my hand a squeeze, letting the silence build as he thinks about what to say. I appreciate the moment to recover.

"Just let it out then, Lili. Let it all out."

So I do.

I watch the lights go past us, one after the other, until they become one long, burning line, blurred together by my tears. Delano doesn't say another word. His fingers lace with mine. He just holds my hand and lets me cry. There is nothing to work out. This is my life. These are the facts.

I am a victim and a monster.

I'm lost to the dark.

And finally, I have no more tears. I'm sure I have cried every ounce of fluid out of my body. The silence I have appreciated is now overwhelming; it leaves me to sit there in my embarrassment. I can only think

Well, this is good. First date — last date. No one wants to be with a crazy cry baby. Shit, nobody wants to date a girl and her demon. Or the girl who hallucinates spiders coming out of her face. No one is ever going to be like, "You know who's really cool? That girl who likes to kill her friends! Yea! She's awesome!"

To be alone as I am is a strange experience, not having the shadows or the whispers, in background. Ephryium isn't here; he really did stay away ...

We take an off-ramp to downtown when I ask, "Where are we going?"

Delano smiles at me mischievously. It makes me smile and blush.

"Well, I was going to take you back to my place and try to have sex with you, but I don't know. You don't seem like a lot of fun right now, so I'm going to take you somewhere else. Somewhere quiet. I think you'll like it."

"But where exactly?"

"You'll see. We're almost there."

Downtown is deserted. Driving on the empty streets that are usually so busy is weird. I imagine we're the last two people left on earth. As we pass Central Memorial Park, I let out a groan.

"Central Park? Are we stopping? This place is filled with bums. I'm not going here. Try again."

Delano gives me a challenging stare. "Yes, don't you like it? Isn't it romantic? You don't like the smell of pee and homeless people sucking dick for money in the dark? Well! Aren't you classy! *Tsk tsk*, Lili. Ye of little faith."

He makes me laugh again. I can't help it. Even though I feel like shit, he makes me forget it, like I can laugh, and it will be OK.

We park. Before I can reach over to open my door, he is already outside and opening it for me.

"Thank you."

"Gotta treat a classy lady with class right?"

I blush and smile at him, biting my bottom lip as he grabs my hand and leads me to the side walk. The Memorial Library stands like a beacon, wrapped in old-world limestone, bathed in cool, white lights. It's one of my favourite buildings. I wish it was open.

As we cross over the grass, I am surprised to see we are headed for the back doors to the library. I follow him up concrete steps leading to two ornate wooden doors. I turn to him, still interested to know what we are going to do here.

Putting his hands on my shoulders, he gently pushes me backwards until my back touches one of the Roman pillars that make up a larger doorway. I am in the shadows of the building.

"Stay here, 'k?" Before I can object to him leaving me, he adds, "I'll be right back. Don't move."

I nod as he turns and bolts back down the stairs, then to the side of the building and out of my sight. Chills run up my arms. I grow paranoid as I survey the park, past the trees at the silhouettes moving in the dark. Are they shadows of people? Or the vengeful spirits of Krish and his friend? Is Justyne going to haunt me now? She is never going to be as nice as the ghosts from my childhood. I would never be able to push her back into the shadows like the others; she'll be wanting a different kind of justice from me ... I can't stand to be alone anymore.

The faraway flicker of a burning cigarette calms me down. I won't die by demon tonight, but maybe I shouldn't have been so quick to dismiss the one advantage I had over all the fucked up shit that seems to be drawn to me ... or maybe evil shit is drawn to me because of Ephryium?

Fuck! Where's Delano?

No sooner have I lost my patience with being left alone than one of the wooden doors opens with a soft click.

"What the fuck? How did you get inside?" I don't hide my astonishment to see Delano behind the door, quietly waving me in. I am more than quick about it. If this is the name of the game, I don't want to get caught, but I'm not about to turn down going inside a building I have always meant to explore.

Through the lobby is a large, wooden checkout desk illuminated by two flickering candles. Delano grabs one and hands it to me before grabbing the other. Without saying a word, he walks past the desk through another set of double doors. I watch him walk a couple of meters before he stops, turns around, and whispers, "Come on."

The double doors lead into a deep, crimson room filled with towering wooden bookshelves. Delano stands, candle lit, in this back drop — waiting for me to react, to say something. If there ever was a place I could feel safe, it would be a place surrounding me in books and candlelight.

"This is incredible, Delano." Shaking my head in wonder, I walk to him. "How did you break in? If we get caught — "

He shushes me. "We're not going to get caught, trust me. Come through here, there's couches and a table. It's blocked from the windows."

Following him through the maze of books, we come to a small nest of an opening with two velvet couches and a wooden coffee table between them. After he sets his candle down, he casually falls onto the couch furthest from us. Carefully, I take a seat on the couch across from him and set my candle on the table beside his.

I have found my happy place.

"Thanks for bringing me here. This is … this is … " I take in the room, not able to find the words. The way the flames make the rich wood shine, the smell of old books, the tufts in the couches …

"When shit gets to be too much, and I don't want to see anyone, phone goes off and I come here. You seem like you could use a place like this. Helps me get all my shit in order."

"So … you can tell I have lots of … 'shit'?"

Laughing, he responds, "Oh yea."

Great. Rolling my eyes, I lay back into the couch, immediately appreciating how comfy it is. I ward off the sleep.

Rolling onto his side to face me, his eyes flicker up at the ceiling and then back to mine. "You don't have to talk about it, but if you want to you can."

"What do you wanna know?"

"About you? Everything."

"Never!"

"'K. I'll settle with what happened tonight — why you have such a huge bag of stuff in my car and why you didn't want to stay at home."

I don't know where to begin. Pressing my lips together, I mull over what version of events he would get.

"So after Justyne and I — " I hit a wall with my first lie. Why is it so hard to lie to him?

Come on, Lili, get it together.

" — fought, I went back home. I don't know what I was thinking. Maybe I just thought I would feel better there? But I didn't. Instead, shit just got even worse."

"What do you mean? Did you tell your mom and dad about it all?"

"Uh, no. No, I didn't do that. I wouldn't. I couldn't talk to my mom or my dad about anything that happened tonight, anything that goes on in my life ever. And that's it. Right there. I thought it was *me* keeping my life a secret from *them*. Tonight, I found out I had it all fucking wrong."

"They hid stuff from you? Like what?"

More tears are at the ready. As I speak, I almost snarl I am so upset.

"Delano! Everything! Everything I thought was — isn't! My whole fucking life! They knew! I didn't have to be so alone, you know? But instead they just fed me bullshit, and made me feel like I was crazy. Fucking hypocrites!"

"Oh. I see." He gives me a sideways look, as if not to make eye contact with a gorilla.

Yea, I sound like a crazy person. There is just no real way to say what I mean without … saying what I mean. I laugh at him and at me as I sniffle. I let out an emotionally exhausted sigh.

"Lili? I know you're upset and feeling a bit … intense? But I actually know what you're trying to say. At least, I think I do. It sounds like there wasn't any trust. Your parents should have clued you in. It's their job to help you, to see you don't feel alone. It sounds as if they put their needs in front of yours. Whatever they hid from you was essentially more important than you?"

This. Exactly!

"Well, now you know why I have a big bag of my shit in your car. How am I supposed to live with that? With them?"

"Do you know where you're gonna go?"

I shake my head slowly. "No, not right now. It's kind of fresh. I haven't had a chance to just stop and think about it … but I have this feeling I'm going to be OK."

"No doubt. You seem like a really strong chick."

"Thanks." My eyelids are monumentally heavy. My body is about to do a forced shut down. "Hey, Delano?"

"Mmhmm?"

"You mind if I rest a second?"

"Go for it."

As my eyes close, I see Delano lying on the couch, putting a cigarette into his mouth. My eyes are already closed when I hear the flick of the lighter then smell the tobacco smoke and then —

I am gone.

LXV.

Arnold

July 14th 1999
Taber, Alberta

The darkest hour of the night had passed. It had been hours since Arnold had found the shithole of a bar a couple of blocks up from the motel. He had sat quietly at the bar, nursing drink after drink.

Two rough-looking women sat in a booth at the back. Rough not because they were tough, but because life had been. Judging by the shade of their lipstick and the hems of their python-skinned skirts, they would have accepted a good time if Arnold had approached. It took all of his willpower to just keep on sipping his beer and keep his eyes on the back of the bar.

TAkE ThEmmm

                     MAKe   Her WATCH

          WhOreS!

              TasTe Her BlOOd iN your Mouth

BoDyPaRtSinTHE DumpSter

            killthemboth

Always hungry for more, for violence, for the rush. But not this time. This time was for the boy. Arnold felt sorry for himself as he thought on the boy's dismissive words. He had wanted to be there more than the boy knew. Shit, Debbie would have loved to have been there to help the boy along as well. It was only right; they were family. And family was there for each other.

But Arnold didn't regret the decision to leave the boy. He knew he would have all the help and direction he needed — if he needed it at all.

Sip your beer, stay put.

He didn't move from his seat until the bartender came and told him, "That's it. Night over, bud. Closin' time."

The neon-lit Budweiser clock hanging by the bathroom door read 3 a.m. Time to go see what the boy had made with his prize …

The stroll through the deserted street was a quiet one as Arnold staggered back to the motel. He was a little heavy of heart but still proud the boy had come to him to get the job done. He knew their trips would be good for the boy, he just didn't know how much it would mean to him, having someone to share them with. He felt infinitely closer to his son.

He knocked lightly on the door. As he did, it fell open slowly, releasing a sliver of light from inside the room. It troubled Arnold to know the door was open. What if it hadn't been him to come knocking?

We   kNEW

WElComE To ThE   ShoW,   PopS

Making sure there was only enough room for himself to squeeze through, Arnold stepped inside and closed the door quickly behind him.

The boy stood with his hands behind his back in the centre

of the room, waiting to greet Arnold. The smell of iron and feces lingered. He surveyed the scene. The bed had been stripped of all the pillows and blankets, leaving the mattress bare. Behind the boy, there was something a shade darker than the shadows, something watery; something that, for less than a blink of an eye, hung sinuously in the air. Then it was gone, quick enough to make Arnold wonder if he had seen anything at all.

In the corner of the room, a figure sat in the chair, draped under a yellowing sheet, prompting Arnold to ask what he already knew the answer to. "Where's the little girl?"

The boy motioned to the sheet and calmly replied, "I have a surprise for you. I wanted to say thank you."

"Is that right? Well, it looks mighty clean in here. You have yourself a good time then?"

"Oh, yea. Dad, it was fucking awesome! Not the anal though … Shit. Everywhere. Not cool. She was a champ though. Stuck it out until the end."

Arnold's head bobbed up and down as he smiled at the boy's excitement. He remembered the first time with Debbie fondly. "Alright, well let's see'er. Witchin' hour's come and gone. We're gonna need to head'er soon."

Clutching two handfuls of the sheet covering Ashley, the boy beamed up at Arnold and said, "Well, I hope we have time for a drink." He pulled the sheet off as he spoke and let it fall to the floor.

Arnold's jaw dropped in curious excitement. Naked and covered in blood, the girl's ankles were tied together with a cord. It had been placed behind her neck so her feet were held up to either side of her head. The cute, little Christian girl who just wanted to kiss a boy and talk on the phone was long gone. The boy left violent red marks around her neck. Arnold couldn't help but wonder if that's how he killed her. The red bags under her eyes suggested so, but he could only fantasize at this point.

He had to get closer to see the boy had cut a portion of her head off on one side. The top of a plastic bag hung out of the hole. It seemed her head had been hollowed and the bag was filled to the brim with … ice?

Arnolds face was filled with curiosity, wonder, and joy.

"I borrowed some stuff from the truck. I hope you don't mind. But you overlooked the best part!" the boy said with a smirk.

"Best part 'a what? What is this?"

"Look!" The boy pointed at the girl's vagina. Arnold could hardly believe he had missed the tip of a bottle spout poking out of the girl.

With an idea of what this meant, Arnold was entirely impressed by the effort and creativity.

"Watch!" The boy bolted across the room to grab two short glasses off the dresser. Coming back just as quickly, he scooped the ice out of Ashley's hollowed head and into both of the glasses, making sure not to push too hard so her body wouldn't lean to the side.

Handing Arnold one of the glasses, he told his dad to place his cup under the spout protruding from her vagina. The boy gripped the cord that was fastened to her ankles and brought it up and over her head. Her pelvis came down onto the chair and the amber liquor poured into the cup. Arnold let out an astonished laugh and slapped his leg.

"Well, wouldja look at that!"

When the glass was half-filled, the boy lifted the cord, which lifted her pelvis back up and stopped the stream of scotch. Arnold handed him the other glass, which he proceeded to fill in the same manner, much to Arnold's delight.

After securing the cord back behind her neck, the boy raised his glass towards his dad.

"For this. For everything, Dad. For everything you've shared with me, I wanted to say thanks."

Tears welled around the brim of Arnold's eyes as he brought his glass to his son's. Keeping his gaze on the boy, he took a gulp. He immediately appreciated the boy had gone out of his way to get his hands on some good booze for the two of them, but it was too good for the boy yet; he had closed his eyes tightly. His face gave a little shake as he forced the burning liquid down.

"Fack, that's awful!"

Arnold let out a laugh and slapped the boy on the back. "At'll put lead on yer pencil, for sure!"

"Better than shit … By the way, I know we usually get rid of 'em and all … but I was thinkin' … how about we just leave this one here?"

Arnold's first instinct was to say no, but after a moment the proposal began to grow on him.

"I dunno if that's such a great idea. I thought we could dump 'er somewhere along the river? Besides, we was seen. Guy at the front desk I'm sure knows there's two of us here … maybe even enough to come up with a description … " He finished off the rest of his glass in one gulp.

Even though the words hadn't been spoken, the boy took the gesture as Arnold's way of closing the conversation. He stared down into his glass, still filled with the red, shit-tasting booze, and hesitated for one more moment before he tossed it back. He watched Arnold watch him, making sure to hold back the shudder this time.

As casually as he could, with a mischievous grin smeared across his face, the boy made a suggestion.

"We could invite him in for a drink."

LXVI.

LILI

Calgary, Alberta
August 10th 2003
5:08 a.m.

I wake with a start. The couch across from me is empty.

Where's Delano?

Our candles sit on the table, still burning, at the end of their wicks.

"Delano?"

I am answered with silence. And shadows. As I strain my ears to hear more, there is a faint click somewhere far away in another part of the building.

"Hello?"

Holding the anxiety back, I wait for a response. When none comes, I jump out of my chair, convincing myself this is going to be OK. Delano is here somewhere, and to stop being such a pussy.

I pick up one of the candles and make my way down a dark path towering with books. I am sure this was the way we'd come, but even if it isn't, I am capable of finding the front door.

Why would Delano have left? Fuck, this is my luck; there is no running from it. Turn after turn, I walk through the rows and rows of books, no exit sign in sight. My frustration builds, of not being able to find my way out mixed with my anger about the state of my life. Every time a little light comes into my life, it is blotted out. Delano just fell into the trend.

And then so does the candle. The little light I have in my hand, snuffed.

The extinguished flame's smoke fills my nostrils as I inhale stiffly.

"Delano? Please! Delano! Say something! Please!"

The hairs on the back of my neck slowly stand up as something brushes my arm. My heart beats at a speed that makes me aware of the blood pulsing through my veins. I will never be familiar with terror. My mind races to why?

What?

Run!

My hands slam into the shelves as I awkwardly try to make my way out of this nightmare. I need to listen! Holding onto a wall, I try to hear over my own panting. I hold my breath. The sound of my heartbeat fills my ears.

Breathe, Lili, breathe. Calm calm calm.

I hear a crackle, then a pop. It's wood. It's burning wood. Why isn't there smoke? It's a building full of books!

I need to get out of here now! The shelf under my hand trembles. My stomach drops as I hear a low rumble, again and then again. The floor under my feet, the shelf under my hand, vibrate with each distant boom.

I navigate down the row of shelves I'm holding onto. There is a dull light emanating from somewhere. The choices are: face the fire or face the dark — the dark that brushes up against my arm, the dark that makes the ground tremble under my feet. My eyes strain into the deep shadows of where I came. Glowing scarlet eyes stare back at me from a space so distant it can't exist.

They rush towards me.

I run to the fire.

The way it warms my face is familiar. I see the door on the other side of the blaze. I know this place … from a dream.

The rumble that had been so distant comes towards me, faster and faster with a thunderous roar. The building shakes, making the books drop off their shelves around me.

Don't look back. Don't Look Back. I can make it!

I can see the door. I commit to the burns. I commit to the consequences.

I look back.

The darkness is gone. The terror is upon me. It reaches into me, freezing my blood in my arteries. My heart takes the plunge into my stomach. My breath is ripped out of my lungs as I am slammed onto the floor. The piece of shit that took me once has his talons in me again. I'm being crushed into the floor as its weight, its heat, its energy pushes into me. My screams ring in my ears. The way it echoes, again and again, it's all too familiar.

With the intensity in which it came, it's gone so suddenly. The heaviness, gone. My eyes are closed tightly, as if to protect my soul. I think I am safe enough to open them. I see the demon face to face with *Ephryium*.

As the flames around them grow, I draw back towards the darkness. I watch as Ephryium's huge claws dig into the frame of the demon's wretched face. Tearing the rotting flesh away from the bone, releasing a deluge of tiny black and red spiders. Panic consumes me as I watch the flames spread along the walls and ceiling. As the spiders pour from the demon's face, the demon seizes Ephryium's arms and legs in its tendrils. The gaping wound seems to grow larger, pushing forth more of the parasitic arachnids. In waves, they crawl over Ephryium's chest, down his torso, encasing him in a restless shell of their bodies. The shrill screams of the tiny demons ring in my ears, going off like a fire alarm. It is happening faster than he can control.

She wAs AlwYS   MEANt For

uSSssss

She Is YouR StAr Crossed OrPHaN No MORe

Don'T YOU   SEE?

FATe   HaS   INterVenEd

SHe Has CASt You ASIde

Find AnothER For REdempTion

She Has been Delivered   TO US WITHOUT YOU!

IF

YOU have Her

YOU Have Her   WITh USsss

The hissing voice. That voice. That voice that had walked side by side with Justyne. That horrible voice. It came as a whisper behind the spiders, under the flames.

The familiar pulsating veins reach around Ephryium's now perfect, angelic frame. His golden skin is slowly being scorched. His sapphire eyes glow with a deep love and ancient wisdom. They stay calm as I watch the precious colour being sucked from them, leaving them empty and as grey as stone.

Am I staring at my damnation or my salvation?

I run towards him. I don't want him to die; he is mine. I run for the flames. The demon releases his python grip to welcome me into his reaching tentacles.

I am arm's length away from Ephryium and being snatched

by the mammoth shadow when Ephryium rushes towards me. Blood gushes from his wounds. His flesh is exposed and bloody. His crown of bone is once again mounted atop his head. His arms break through the cocoon of spiders just as the first slippery vein brushes my shoulder.

"See!" his voice roars as he pushes me back.

I fall further and further away from him, from the flames. The spiders engulf Ephryium again, as the dark evil that towers over his body stares directly into my eyes, an instant away from pouncing on me.

Like a bullet train, the demon charges through the darkness I'm falling through. Its red eyes growing bigger, more intense as it speeds closer.

I never hit the ground.

I wake with a start.

LXVII.

LILI AND DELANO

Calgary, Alberta
August 10th 2003
6:02 a.m.

"Lili! Whoa, whoa! You're dreamin'. It's cool, you're OK."

What do I need to see? Delano's here. He didn't leave me. I let out a sigh of relief. *It was a dream.*

"I dreamt you left."

"No, why would I do that? I was here ... who's Ephryium?"

"Uh ... My dog — my parents' dog." I push the hair off my forehead. I'm sweating. *Really attractive.* My head pounds.

"Oh, you screamed his name pretty loud. Shit, Lili." He laughed. "You are SUPER intense."

"I'm sorry. Sorry, you got me at a really bad place, I — "

"So I got you then?"

I press my lips together. I don't answer, but my eyes can't hide the stars.

"Morning's comin'. We should go. I wanna show you something first though, 'k?"

"'K'"

Grabbing my hand, he pulls me off the couch and proceeds to lead me down a dark row of books. We go up a flight of stairs tucked away in a corner. He leads to a funny-looking wooden door. Glancing over his shoulder, he smiles before opening it, pulling me through.

"It used to be an old elevator shaft, but they don't use it anymore."

We climb the narrow, metal stairs until we reach a steel door. As he pushes it open, he reveals the morning sky, still on the cusp of night while the sun has yet to rise. He takes off one of his shoes and wedges it in the door as he closes it behind us. He holds my hand tightly, watching me mindfully. I realize we are on the roof.

"Wanna watch the sun come up?" Taking a seat on the maintenance stairs, he gestures for me to sit with him. "It's insane watching it from right here, 'cause when the sun comes up, the light hits all of the building's windows, and it's sunshine times a thousand. It bounces off in every direction, it's ... crazy!"

I can't help but smile at his sincere enthusiasm. "You bring all the ladies up here then?"

"Oh yea, it's a huge hit!" He smirks as he pulls a small joint from his pocket. "You smoke?"

"Yea."

"All right."

He was right. It is like sunshine times a thousand. As the sun comes up in the sky, it makes the clouds creamy and warm. *Vanilla skies.*

Inhaling deeply as I can, letting myself feel the burn in the back of my throat, I let the calm serene colours of the sky take me in.

"We should go, hey?" He stubs out what is left of the joint

and flicks it into the gravel.

We both stand at the same time. Our heads whirl around to the sound of the man's voice coming from below.

"WHAT THE FUCK ARE YOU DOING UP THERE? THIS IS PRIVATE PROPERTY! I'M CALLING THE COPS!"

"Shit!" A little bit more than concerned — but not much more — Delano puts his hands on my shoulders and asks, "Have you ever heard the term 'book 'er like a hooker'?"

"Yep."

"We're gonna do that now, OK?"

"OK."

A fat security guard, drenched in his own sweat, waits for us outside the double doors. I know he didn't even bother to see if they were open. We smash through them — really, it's just me following behind Delano. Despite the round man being pushed off balance, he manages to grab Delano. I raise my fist to come to Delano's defence but halt in my tracks as he shouts for me to run. I don't know what the security guard's end game is. He and Delano go on struggling with each other when I reach the car. The sweat circles under the guard's armpits are massive; his whole face shines under the street lamp. He can no longer hold Delano in place, he struggles to hold himself up as his knees buckle.

"Delano, Run!"

Both of the men glance at me. Even from here, I can see they're both over it. Delano rears back to punch the guard in the face. Together, me and the exhausted guard wince. He closes his eyes and puts his arm up as a shield to block the impending blow. But it never comes. Delano drops the guard and sprints towards me.

It all happens so quickly. It's exciting — a different type of excitement. Different from the usual the-devil's-underneath-your-bed-and-is-going-to-chase-you-out-of-your-house excitement I'm used to. The car comes to life with a mean purr, and I'm thrown against the back of my seat as we peel away from the curb.

Both of us, high off the adrenaline, laughing in acknowledgment of how fucking close we were to being caught, and gratefulness we weren't. My eyelids grow heavy again. I try my hardest, but I can't push the sleep away.

"Hey, Lili? Where do you want me to take you? I know you don't want to go home … "

My head sinks to the side as my eyelids come to a crashing close. I manage to mumble, "Mm, somewhere safe … "

The dark is heavy and inviting. I am warm and secure. I welcome the sleep.

LXVIII.

LILI & DELANO

August 10th 2003
Just Outside North Battleford, Saskatchewan
12:03 p.m.

My seat vibrates. I shake with little jiggles until my eyes open. I'm refreshed, a little cramped, but revived and awake. Stretching my arms and legs, I look out my window to see trees, lots of trees, on either side of us. Delano drives, eyes straight ahead. The car descends down a large hill, on a curve, making it impossible to see where we came from or where the road leads. A flutter of panic goes through me.

"Where are we?"

We come out of the corner. I check out the valley of Buttfuck Nowhere. It gives no indication as to where Delano has brought me.

"Hey, you're up! You were passed the fuck out for hours. Dead to the world. You feelin' better?"

I look back and forth, out the window, and at Delano for answers.

"Yea, yea I am, but seriously, where are we?"

"You said you wanted to go someplace safe. Don't be mad. I took you to the safest place I know."

The car rolls over the dirt road to an old, white farmhouse. A man and woman come out from a rickety screen door on the side of the house and approach the car. They are two characters from *The Hills Have Eyes*. I'm unable to hide my obvious reservations about the situation.

"Delano. Where am I?"

"You're near Battleford."

The car coasts to a slow stop.

Battleford? Where in the fuck?

"Lili, this is my parents' house. Come meet them. You'll really like them."

Without another word, he hops out of the car. The door falls shut heavily behind him. I sit for a moment and watch him hug the taller-than-average, overweight man whose plaid shirt lay open, exposing a severely stained wife beater. The woman is the most oddly shaped woman I have ever seen in my life. Delano is fucking adopted. He *has* to be!

They all turn to face me, which is obviously my cue to get out of the car.

I can't move less urgently as I push the huge door open. Trying my hardest not to grimace at the yellow and black-toothed smiles, I hold my hand out as Delano introduces me.

"Lili, this is my mom, Debbie, and my dad, Arnold."

LXIX.

PERSEPHONE

Ignace, Ontario
August 9th 2003

"I'm sorry, Sarah. I really I am. The baby will not live through the ritual." The woman caressed the new mother's sweat-covered forehead as she lay helpless, holding her new baby on the table. The fire blazed in the hearth. The other women stood ready for Persephone's direction. They had all been so hopeful. Sarah's long, hard delivery had ended in haem-orrhaging: two years of ceremonies, bleeding out onto the table. They watched Persephone practice her patience with Sarah. Her touch was gentle; her words were soft.

Sarah held the new born closer to her chest, overwhelmed by an instinct to protect her child. "Please don't take him! He can be one of us. Let me raise him, Persephone."

"Sarah."

"Please!" she sobbed. "Please don't take him." Beads of sweat ran down her face with her tears. "He doesn't have to die."

Time was of the essence. Sarah's skin paled. If they could save her, she could be bred again. They could try again. With a heartbeat in hand, they could use the failed baby as an offering for help.

"What would you have, Sarah? That he be raised in the stables with the slaves? As a creature, there is no place for him here!"

"But your son — "

Persephone's hand was quick and sharp against the new mother's cheek. Her patience had ran out.

The baby wailed as Sarah begged for Persephone to let them

go, let them leave this place. She wouldn't tell anyone. Persephone took the operating knife from the table, gently guiding her hand beneath the woman's chin. She stared into her eyes for a moment. She considered Sarah's life behind the girl's scared blue eyes. She had helped raise Sarah. She had been there since the moment of conception. She respected this moment; she would be here at her death. As she carved into her neck, she told Sarah a gentle, "No."

Blood poured from the mother onto the child. Persephone let Sarah's head drop onto the table and grabbed the baby.

The baby's wails wavered as all new born babies did. Holding the baby above her head, she readied him for the fire at the hearth.

"I am humble before you. Not as your servant but as your equal, I ask for your help. Help me! Please! What am I doing wrong? I ask for your wisdom. I ask for strength. I have exhausted all forms of worship for her. I ask for your guidance and direction. Take one of mine. My blood, for yours. Accept this gift." She released the baby. He fell into the blaze, and she stepped back as embers overflowed from the pit.

As the other women watched Sarah's child burn, Persephone's focus moved from the baby to his mother's blood. It flowed out of her vagina, onto the table, spilling onto the floor. It began to bubble and stir. The room became darker as the flames waned.

"PersEPhone."

The voice came from atop the table. Persephone and the other women followed the hoarse voice back to the unmoving corpse's mouth. Persephone rushed to Sarah's side. A perverse silence settled over them. Even the embers ceased to pop. The winds outside no longer knocked pine branches into the windows. Persephone was ready, even eager for every word as Sarah's hand fell off the table and snatched her wrist. Her dull lifeless eyes bore into Persephone's.

"She LiVes. ThE SpELL Is BrOkEN. The Guardian iS BouND."

The blood drained from Persephone's face. She repeated the information as she understood it. "Lilith? Lilith is alive? Does she know?"

"ShE KNowS ... ShE IS WiTh Us NoWw ... " The demon sank back to lifelessness. Persephone's hand fell to her side.

Tears filled her eyes. The only sound in the room was the gentle roar of the fire and Persephone's sharp intake of breath.

"The daughter lives."

ABOUT THE AUTHOR

After a decade of wandering the United States and the greater part of Canada, M has amassed a house full of curiosities, a head full of stories, and a unique perspective of the world.

Although M has settled — for the moment — in a small northern Albertan town, some truths will always remain the same of the author: Rocks in pockets, drink in hand, laughter at the ready, and a story on the mind.

This is M. M. Dos Santos's debut novel.

www.mmdossantos.com
www.facebook.com/m.m.dossantosauthor
www.instagram.com/m.m.dossantos_NotWriting
www.twitter.com/MMDSNotWriting

CPSIA information can be obtained
at www.ICGtesting.com
Printed in the USA
LVOW11s1841091116

512299LV00002B/431/P